G000060014

TO KILL A PRIEST

BY

WESTON KINCADE

The Priors, Part 1

Visit Weston Kincade and enjoy more fantastic stories at KincadeFiction.com

For information about special discounts for bulk purchases, please contact Weston Kincade at weston@kincadefiction.com or at http://kincadefiction.com.

Book Design and Editing by Weston Kincade and K. Sozaeva
Cover Art copyright ©2019 by RockingBookCovers.com
The text for this book is set in Calibri.
Manufactured in the United States of America

Summary: In a universe with infinite realities, could you settle for just one? Humankind is evolving. Madelin has special shifting abilities, and a government black-op agency knows it. To free herself, she will have to trust an unknown godfather and men with questionable pasts to test the limits of this world and break them... but will the next be any better?For those who love books with complex, tortured characters and action-packed adventure, Weston Kincade's first book in The Priors series is the thrill ride for you. Join the rebellion. Read To Kill a Priest today.

ASIN B00RIIHUPU (eBook)
ISBN 9798606273904 (Print)

ACKNOWLEDGEMENTS

I would like to give thanks to my editors: David Chrisley, Tavis Potter, Jeremy Carter, Stephen Marshall, Scott Rhine, and Katy Sozaeva. I also could not have written the series without the support of my wife, friends, and family. Thank you for everything.

NOTE FROM THE AUTHOR:

Dear Reader,

The Priors is a thrilling story of one young woman's attempt to overcome a black-ops agency set on using her abilities for their own devious means. The nonstop adventures begin with her assisted escape from a government-run institution, only to find that the first trained assassin of her kind is after them.

This was the first book I ever wrote. I originally released it under the title *Invisible Dawn*. As an author it has always held a special place in my heart. However, initially there were things that needed to be changed and reworked. Now, years later, I spent a great deal of time revising the story so readers can get as much entertainment out of it as I did writing it.

I hope you enjoy.

Weston Kincade

TABLE OF CONTENTS

Prologue

Questionable Sanity

For the first few seconds of consciousness, Daniel Robertson sat on the edge of his bed, staring at a ghastly image in the full-length mirror. A child stared back through eyeless sockets, its skin seared to a charred remnant of its former self. Even in his waking moments, he saw the same nightmarish memory. It was as though sleep hadn't found him.

His digital clock glowed red, 5:04 a.m. The nightmares never let him sleep through the night. He groped for the most recent bottle he'd haphazardly tossed aside the night before, but gave up when he spotted it on the floor.

His eyes returned to the wooden stand, but the phantom child was nowhere to be seen. Instead, his own depressed reflection peered back through eyes that spoke of more pain than his age should have allowed. Years spent serving in the Middle East had dried him out, so deep his bones even felt parched. A large X marred his cheek, long-ago healed, but it was a reminder of his inescapable past. Sweat swelled from nowhere and grudgingly streamed down his forty-three-year-old, leathered face. At each wrinkle there was a split-second hesitation.

Fragments of his past flickered through his mind in a jumbled mess. Piecing them together while semi-conscious was like constructing a jigsaw puzzle, but suddenly the sequence of horrific events snapped into place like snapshots from someone else's travels. Glimpses of unwanted memories returned that even alcohol couldn't drive away.

"As though I could ever forget," he muttered, thinking back to the horrifying visage.

The dim glow of a streetlamp streamed through the window and cast tall shadows across the room. His yellow complexion melded with the aged bedsheets like a sickly chameleon. Even in El Paso, a heat wave like this was unusual.

A slight breeze startled the curtains to life, and newspaper clippings fluttered on the wall before resigning to the push pins' insistence. The sound drew his attention, and he flicked on the nearest table lamp. It did little to illuminate the room but was enough to see by. The victims stared out at him, their lives amounting to a small blurb. Above their heads, the articles announced, 'Man Found Dead in Car Explosion,' and 'Woman Killed in Foiled Carjacking,' among others.

He knew them by heart. Each represented a failed attempt to save his ex-employer's targets. They were all that remained of his recent pursuit for salvation. He sniffed at the stale tobacco odor that permeated the apartment. It was as though the small space could never get clean—a feeling he was quite familiar with.

Lifting himself from the bed, Daniel straightened and listened to the crack of his joints. He stretched his arms and crept over to the open window, his skin masking the muscular build beneath. With each footstep, the floor announced to his neighbors that he was awake. It was a reminder of the innocent lives he put in jeopardy by staying here for two months. Black Force was after him, and they were just as well trained as he. His old mercenary friends wouldn't take hostages, and they had no qualms with eliminating witnesses.

He needed to move on before he was found, but it was difficult to give up such an ideal location. One reason he chose this dilapidated part of the city was the unfriendliness of the people. His weathered complexion helped him to blend in, and the fact that he spoke not a word of Spanish afforded him his solitude.

Daniel smiled as another faint breeze drifted through the window. Seeing an oncoming car, he stepped out of the moonlight and alongside the curtains. There was no need to broadcast his presence. Watching the sidewalk below, his attention was drawn to an interesting individual.

The man was different from other street inhabitants headed to work. He casually strode under the streetlamps holding an AK-47, but no one took notice. It was like the armed man was invisible. He passed the taco vendor Daniel frequented, and even Marco failed to greet him. The old food salesman hailed everyone while grilling his morning breakfast burritos, but somehow overlooked this man.

The oddity was barely visible at this distance, but the early risers on the streets should have spotted the gun. His clothes made him stand out like a leopard at a zebra party. Through the sporadic flow of traffic, Daniel watched the man's russet coat and fedora bob behind passing cars. His checkered golf pants shone under the streetlamps, and he walked with a slight spring in his step. He was like an armed ostrich bobbing down the city street, ready to go hunting.

Could he be with Black Force?

He doubted it, but what if his old employer had hired someone new? It was odd for a mercenary group to hire out to a competitor, but Daniel might have eluded them too many times. Either way he needed answers to his questions, and this guy might be his key. They were questions that had plagued him for years, like, *What could he do to stop Black Force or at least get them off his back?* He just wanted a chance at redemption before he died. The pain he had caused was unforgettable, especially in his dreams.

His hand unconsciously went to the three scars crisscrossing his large bicep. He ran calloused fingers along the smooth skin. It wasn't until the last few years that he came to care about others. Up to then, he did what he wanted and what he was told without question. The scars were just a reminder of one of his father's early lessons on obedience—something his old boss and good-old dad had in common. They didn't take "no" for an answer.

Losing sight of the man behind a group of chatting women, Daniel was startled into action. He needed answers, and this guy was his best chance. He searched the sidewalk for the bounding pedestrian. Seconds later, the man appeared without having lost a step. Anticipating another disappearance, Daniel gave the street a cursory glance.

Satisfied, he threw a blue button-up over his sweat-stained undershirt. It trailed behind him like a cape as he crossed the room. His hand automatically grabbed his 9 mm off the end table and tucked it into his pants before bringing the door to a close.

Taking the stairs two at a time, he swept through the first-floor foyer and onto the sidewalk. He searched the opposing walkway for the brown fedora. The hat materialized over a taxicab, and the yellow lamplight overhead illuminated its creases like the golden eyes of an animal peering through the shadows.

Daniel bolted across the busy road and narrowly avoided a rusted-out farm truck. The only warning of its approach was a deep, male voice crooning through its open windows "Oh, *mi amor,*" while a salsa melody plucked along in the background.

At least I won't be the latest obituary in the Sun Herald, he thought as the guitar melody faded.

He leapt over the last car length of asphalt and rushed up the sidewalk. Sidestepping the barrage of pedestrians, he weaved through more oncoming groups and attempted to gain on the odd man. Daniel pumped his muscled legs harder. He threaded his way through the sporadic traffic while keeping the man in sight. It still surprised him how many people walked to work on this side of town. He felt like a running back for the local Panthers football team, dodging moving targets. Unfortunately, he couldn't remember a game they had won, and his progress was worthy of the same praise. Somehow, the bobbing fedora was still drifting further away. Daniel broke into a run. Passing men and women gave him sidelong glances. A few locals cursed as he shoved them aside, attempting to close the gap with his prey.

The loud shouts didn't bother the man in the fedora. He never turned or glanced back. He just continued down the packed street, his dark hat bobbing overtop the crowd. As Daniel closed the distance, the unusual man walked directly into a father and daughter walking hand in hand. The stranger faded into a misty existence and phased through them. Without anyone realizing, the anomaly solidified on the other side and continued as though nothing had happened.

Daniel halted mid-step as his heart skipped a beat. "Whoa, this guy can't be Black Force," he muttered. "He's like their hopped-up, crooked cousin."

The possibilities tumbled through his mind. *Either way, this guy's looking for trouble.*

He was tired of waiting for them to find him. He had to act. "There's no such thing as coincidence," he whispered with renewed confidence.

The retired mercenary redoubled his pace and began gaining on the fedora. The old courthouse was around the next bend, and the sidewalk grew more congested. His broad shoulders cowed some people, but others he cast aside like scattered chess pieces. Faces whizzed by in a blur, man... man... woman... man ... child, but his attention remained on the armed stranger.

Daniel made his way to the corner, but was unable to reach his prey before the man entered the busy street. Stepping out of the packed sidewalk, the ex-mercenary stopped at the curb edge to watch the man cross. The armed apparition passed through cars undetected, heading for the municipal building. The muzzle of his rapid-fire gun came up as he approached the building front, but still no one reacted.

The veteran's gaze followed the apparition across as the sun peeked over the mountainous horizon, but his eyes stopped abruptly when the courthouse came into view. Around it was a dimly outlined building, much larger than the courthouse of his reality. It stood overtop the historic building like a spectral shadow. He tilted his head, attempting to find the pinnacle, but its towering peak disappeared into the dawn sky. The building was enormous, like those in larger cities. It was a phantom skyscraper attempting to exist in an already occupied space. Its edges stood out against the stone structure of the courthouse, glistening blue like the threads of shimmering spiderwebs.

He stood motionless, in awe of the sight. Much like the man he had followed, it gave no one else reason for pause. He looked around, but even the fedora in the distance didn't break its casual stride. A moment later, the man disappeared into the miasmic building.

"How could such a thing exist?"

At the base of one luminescent thread appeared a woman dressed in an outlandish, white-belted kimono. She finished thumbing the wall before turning around. Daniel peered at the block wall, searching for what she had been holding, but nothing was there. He could have sworn something had moved under her hand, but it was gone. Unlike the man in the fedora and the spectral building, her presence didn't go unnoticed. She stood out in her tattered, oriental gown. The shredded kimono swirled about her with every intention of hiding her graceful curves, but failed utterly.

Her auburn hair shone in the sun's morning rays, framing a pale face and wild eyes. Over the years, Daniel had come to know the look of fear in others. Judging by her face and the way people avoided her, she was in full flight. His brain went into overdrive as he remembered that people were looking for him. He had made a huge display and left disgruntled pedestrians in his wake. They would have no problem identifying him now.

"Dammit!" he spat. He had to do something… He had to move. And right now, this woman needed his help.

Entering the road, Daniel allowed morality to guide his search for redemption.

Chapter One

Keeping Promises

Two days earlier, Jedd Altran slid an ID badge over the petroleum tank at a local gas station. The words, "Thank you for your patronage, Bradley Thomas," scrolled by on the monitor, and he selected premium fuel for his new Kamota Speedster. It wasn't like he was paying for the gas. Besides, insurance would cover the cost.

His friend Koiyo had put together the ID badge, and so far, it had proven invaluable. The new technology accessed the records of previous customers and then randomly selected a new identity and account to charge. He would have to thank the tech-savvy guru the next time he saw him. For years they had been an inseparable team, but recent circumstances had made his visits dangerous; today's would be the last. He couldn't bear for something to happen to his old college friend.

After the bike was fueled, Jedd slid his helmet's reflective face shield down and rode into traffic. He had become an expert at hiding from his pursuers and found a casual, inconspicuous attitude to be essential when in the midst of the city's denizens.

Under a desert sky, Jedd parked his bike in one of many vacant spots at the shabby hotel. He passed the outdoor pool and hot tub. The children splashed and played but avoided the drained hot tub. A glance told him why. A layer of sludge sat in the bottom, littered with dead rats. Jedd walked up the stairs to the room he had occupied for the last week. The tan stucco peeled and cracked as he passed, as it had been doing for years. He attempted to maintain a casual stride, but it was difficult to stifle his anticipation at Koiyo's new program.

Stepping into the room, he shut the door and seated himself in front of his laptop. Jedd typed in his password, and the computer loaded his programs. Then, Jedd pulled out the new, portable hard drive and plugged it into the computer. After a few keystrokes, it *whirred* to life. As the computer processed the hardware, Altran took the few minutes necessary to pick up the remnants of his stay. What he was about to attempt could require a quick escape.

Throwing the last sock into his bag, Jedd reseated himself in the uncomfortable desk chair. The computer's completion bar finished its march to the edge of the window, and its flashing cursor prompted Jedd for his next command. He hoped this would finally allow him to keep his decade-old promise.

Before cuing the new software, he brought up a program of his own creation, then ran his IP redirection protocols, bypassing and looping through various locations worldwide. With his security measures intact, Altran started the new equipment. Pages flew onto the screen and disappeared as his hands fluttered over the small keyboard. Within a few minutes, the flurry of activity stopped, leaving a solitary window on the computer display. It said 'Access granted, Phillip Darling.' The next few windows came up, and he was gratified to see 'PASTOR Department' heading the top of each screen. The acronym stood for Phantom Assassin Shifting Technology & Organized Reconnaissance, but the nature of the government-funded department was so secret that few knew of its existence.

After years of searching, he'd found what he was looking for thanks to an incompetent corporate adviser. Looking at the list, Altran searched through files labeled by numbers and names. Each one was accompanied by a picture. At the top of the list was one titled 'Shifter 1.' He perused the file that opened with the press of the mouse pad. A young man was pictured with an elongated face and icy, blue eyes. One reference named him as 'Leodenin.' It seemed that the man was the first successfully trained shifter from the department. He was entered into the program when he was eight. There was no reference to the whereabouts of his parents. Toward the bottom of the file, a list tracked his assignments. A few assassinations were outlined; leaders of small countries, but it seemed he had recently been incorporated into the training of future shifters. The final line listed future goals: 'Integration into plane shifting, subterfuge, and control of ruling governments.'

That's gotta be a joke, thought Jedd, but his instincts and past research told him otherwise. This covert department was hidden from the public's view for a reason. If their existence ever became common knowledge, it would be easy for the US Government to deny any association or knowledge of the PASTOR Department's surreal intentions.

Moving on, the hacker found a link labeled 'Trainees.' A list of files opened to him. He glossed over pictures of young boys, other victims of the department's ongoing pursuit of trainable shifters. He paused on a few girls with similar features to who he was looking for. After a few seconds of thought, he returned to the previous page. Before long, certain files became inaccessible. He tried others and received the same error message, 'Access Denied!'

Someone's shutting down the connection. They must be onto me...

Chapter Two

New Revelations

With his time limited, Jedd jumped to the bottom of the list. If the administrator was operating sequentially, he might gain access to a few more before he lost the connection. Luck was with him. Scanning the files of young abductees, one picture stopped his fingers. The facial-recognition program gave her an 89 percent match, but he could see her mother's features reflected in the image. Her oval face and petite nose told him it was his goddaughter. Jedd could barely contain himself. He felt like shouting to the world, hoping for an echo that might repeat his success back to him.

He prodded the keyboard with urgency, saving the file to his computer and portable hard drive. Unplugging the drive from the computer, he slipped it into his jean pocket and disabled the connection. Jed slid the mobile computer into a duffle bag and set it next to the door.

"Better safe than sorry," he had always said.

Jedd grabbed the appropriate cash from the dresser and slid it into the payment terminal on the wall. There were too many ways for hotel owners to track you down, so the key was to never give them a reason. He had enough people looking for him already, and they needed no help. He cautiously peered out the peephole and slipped on his hat, a random purchase made at a local gas stop. Along the brim it advertised for McCartey Racing, a common favorite in the local circuit.

Opening the hotel door, Jedd hefted his bag over his shoulder and stepped into the dry, El Paso air. After that close call, he wasn't about to take chances. His eyes were plastered on the area around him. He didn't want a gun-toting PASTOR agent to suddenly appear from around a corner. Seeing no one lurking about, Jedd stepped across the parking lot. He paused to glance at the kids shouting and splashing in their bright bathing suits.

Altran continued past the sport bike without a glance, surveying the occupied spots for a new mode of transport. Rule number one: Never be predictable. Keeping the same vehicle would be asking to get pulled over.

He spotted a sleek but modest car and pulled out another of Koiyo's inventions. Slipping what looked like a penknife into the sedan's lock, Jedd slipped a pair of black, leather gloves on while waiting as the blade cycled through digital combinations. Within seconds, it found the right sequence. He smiled as the door opened beneath his hand. This was the invention he prized most.

The owner won't be happy to find the vehicle missing, but considering the reputation of the hotel and its temporary occupants, they probably won't report the theft. At the least, any report they file will be pure lies, thought Jedd. This was why he chose these locations. The people that used them normally desired discretion.

After placing his bags in the trunk, Jedd slipped into the front seat and started the engine. It was time to find another place to lay low. The best location that came to mind was a local coffee shop with free Internet. He had grown quite fond of the cafés, but had to limit his visits. He didn't wish to become predictable. Predictability would lead to disastrous consequences, most of which included his death, and this time there would be a real body in the casket... his. Over the years, he had discovered a lot about the PASTOR program. Most politicians would deny any knowledge or association with it, but he knew better.

Altran pulled out of the decrepit hotel and left the stuttering vacancy light behind. From the car dashboard, the fuel gauge flashed at him expectantly. He would have to fill up on his way. He coasted down the road, meandering through traffic.

Jedd pulled out the computer hard drive and synchronized it with his cell phone. He could have used the car monitor, but didn't want to leave a trail. He began scanning the screen as he drove, sifting through the file using voice commands. To take the next step, he needed more than his gut feeling and 89 percent; he needed proof.

After scanning the file for a few minutes, he found what he needed. There was a reference to the trauma she suffered before her capture and the subsequent memory wipes... more than one. The vicious nature of her parents' murder had become a recurring nightmare. Reading further into the document, he noticed that other than her patient number, 914, there was only one mention of a name, Madelin.

How would someone deal with the loss of all childhood memories? he wondered. *Is she still the same beautiful child I remember?* Jedd dismissed the question the instant it came to mind. If she were different, pained, hardened to reality, then it was because of PASTOR. They kidnapped her and wiped her memory. There was nothing she could do.

His hatred grew, infusing him with adrenaline as a flash of memory took over his senses. Before she disappeared, he last saw her huddled alone in the driveway, watching her house burn with her parents inside. She wavered back and forth as Jedd watched through the flames, out of sight of the PASTOR operatives milling around the front lawn. That day, they looked like flies in their black, Kevlar outfits, hovering around the fire and Madelin, but never coming close enough to touch her.

The dingy, white nightgown clung to her sweaty body. She clutched her ash-covered teddy bear to her stomach as though it were her last link to sanity; she had named him Deedee. Jedd hadn't seen her since, but vividly recalled tears streaming down her face as the flames danced across her soot-blotched skin. They left dirty rivers of carnage streaking from innocent, green eyes. It was as if the sight was trying to singe itself into her memory forever, like it had his... and her green, tear-filled eyes; he always felt as if they were nearby, peering over his shoulder, but she was always just out of sight.

Jedd again felt the emotional uselessness he had known that day. Perched atop the hill overlooking the riverfront house, he watched Madelin through his binoculars. It pained him that he couldn't aid her in the presence of so many armed men.

"There's never been a more heartbreaking sight," he muttered just as oncoming headlights drifted in front of his eyes. Startled, he caught the wheel of the car and swerved back into his lane. His heart rate tripled, but as he sped down the asphalt road, the organ resumed its normal pace.

Punching the door's control pad at random, he smiled as the window lowered to admit a comforting breeze. He had to stay focused, but as the car motored on, his thoughts again drifted to Patient 914. This was his Madelin, and it seemed that the same memory was also haunting her.

What have they done to you? Even after the wipe, if the memories are persisting, what PASTOR is doing should be reversible. But how can such a thing be done...? First thing's first, though... There has to be a way to find you.

Pulling into the gas station, he wiped a few tears from his face, then stepped out of the car and slipped his new badge over the payment reader. The monitor responded, "Thank you, Vanessa Carlisle."

So far so good, was all that came to mind as he pocketed the handy ID with the reflective bar code. Setting the pump to auto-fill, Jedd leaned against the car and massaged his bloodshot eyes. *How do I reach her?*

Another memory came to him, one of Madelin sitting on his lap at the age of three. *This is a more pleasant one,* he thought before his mind began searching for clues to his next step.

The memory reappeared, and questions came to mind. *How, at such an early age, did she speak so clearly? She said a lot, but barely moved her lips.*

He was sitting in the worn, brown sofa chair that had always been Lane's favorite. He remembered watching football and soccer in that living room, with its rustic, western feel. Throughout the years of friendship he and the Boatweit family had cherished, they enjoyed numerous conversations and parties in that room. On game nights, the chair was always reserved for Lane, a tall lanky man with a jovial smile and wit that would put a professional comic to shame. Earlier in their friendship, he wouldn't have imagined that smile leaving Lane's face, but over the last few months Lane had adopted a more somber demeanor.

Her father wasn't there at the moment, though, and the television was silent. Jedd had been asked to watch Madelin while her parents were out. It was only later, after Lane's drastic change, that Jedd had been told about PASTOR and the threat looming over his goddaughter's life. Eventually, Lane told him of Madelin's extraordinary gift. Thinking back on it and reliving a pleasant memory of Madelin's early childhood, it seemed to *click.* He hadn't made the connection until now, but as he remembered sitting in that old, worn chair, it became clear how she said so much with so little effort.

As the memory played through his thoughts, he watched Madelin's lips. Nothing was said other than "Uncah," her endearing name for him. He had always assumed she said more, but as he played back the scene like an old DVD, he wondered if his subconscious were imagining things.

It would explain a lot, but seems unlikely, he concluded.

In the memory he knew what she wanted, which book she wanted him to read, and automatically knew when to refill her sippi-cup. Thinking back to other memories, it became more and more likely that her abilities that manifested later weren't the first. If telepathy were another one of her talents, maybe it worked both ways. He might be able to speak with her.

But if this works, what do I say? Will she even know who I am anymore or what she can do?

Based on his investigations of abducted children, they rarely knew who they were or anything about their pasts. Knowing what he would find, he suppressed the likely outcome. He preferred to bet everything on the solitary hope that she would retain one memory of her loving godfather.

The pump retracted, and Jedd jolted from his wistful thoughts as a prerecorded voice spoke up from the pump. "Thank you for visiting. Have a nice day."

He pulled into the street and continued to the coffee shop. At this time of day, it would be busy, with a host of customers filling the lounge chairs and tables. Most people would be glued to their laptops, accessing the café's server. This would help to hide his electronic footprints. A small smile crept onto his face as he considered the next step, assuming his vain hope worked at all.

At the café, 'Cup o' Jo' was barely visible on the sign above the storefront. Jedd ordered a hot mocha and desert to calm his nerves, swiping his ID as payment at the automated teller. The earthy tones of the café were relaxing and pleasant, and the uninterrupted expanse of tinted windows left him with a great view of the parking lot. He smiled inwardly as the machine thanked yet another generous philanthropist for shopping at the establishment. He could feel the PASTOR agents' noose loosening as his trail became more difficult to follow.

Gathering his meal, he found an uninhabited corner with a leather, lounge chair, seated himself, and peered out the window. The coast was still clear. It would be morning before a report was made about the car, assuming the authorities were called at all.

Pulling his phone out, Jedd started his rerouting software and synchronized it with the portable hard drive. Then, he logged onto the public server. After an hour, he found what he was looking for. The first obstacle was to break the encryption on the F&M Architecture and Contracting Firm's server. The company was hired to build the research facility where she was being held... another tidbit he'd discovered earlier.

In an astute decision, PASTOR had chosen a less than desirable location. Building on top of the abandoned site where the original atomic bomb was tested would certainly deter any curious visitors. White Sands, New Mexico, was known for its albino sand dunes, and few would question the selection of such a site for a government-run mental-health facility. Everyone knew the government was thrifty when it came to health-care expenditures.

Once he knew where to look, discovering the exact location became easy. From then on, the majority of his time was spent obtaining data files on current employees at the institute and the various security systems the facility had in place. Surprisingly, the system server was easier to crack. *Thanks, you damned overconfident dandees...* Having obtained the digital layout of the complex and an assortment of employee files, he was certain he could free Madelin from her prison.

Jedd took a generous bite of his cooling Danish, logged out, and finished his coffee before grabbing a refill from a young waitress. Then, he accessed earlier files he had obtained on other test subjects. He scanned them for references to strange abilities. If Madelin turned out to be unaware of what she was capable of, then he would have to teach her whatever he could. The waitress returned a moment later, and he slid the card over the edge of the tray. Holding her eyes in his, a coy smile on his lips, he muttered an affectionate, "Thank you," while waiting for the payment to process and the screen to clear. When it had, he dismissed her with a wave and turned back to his research.

She stalked off, flustered.

Time passed quickly. His steaming coffee turned cold as the sun crept below the barren mountains outside. Its light cast a pale hue upon sparse clouds, illuminating the horizon in pink and orange. The shadow of night loomed over the city and its rocky guardians. Jedd massaged his chin, smoothing the edges of his goatee as he stared at the screen. Consumed by the task, he was oblivious to the fading light around him. However, as the hours wound on, the fading pastels tempted his eyelids to droop and lured his chin to his chest. Soon, a subtle snore was all that escaped his corner of the world.

Chapter Three

Undiscovered Talents

Many of the customers had left or been replaced by new clientele. The traffic along the sidewalk outside slowed as other stores closed for the evening. While Jedd's unconscious mind wondered, he dreamed about Madelin and where she might be. His thoughts went to the facility imprisoning his beloved goddaughter. Though he had never seen it before, an aerial image solidified in his thoughts. He had seen the blueprints, and the layout looked right.

Gazing down upon the research facility, he sought her out with a wistful sigh. A moment later he felt himself moving downward, through the meager clouds and into the confines of the building itself. He gained momentum as his mind focused on Madelin. He knew she waited inside. Within seconds he passed through the brick-and-mortar outer layer, into the crawlspace and vents. Unable to stop, Jedd slid through the ceiling and into a hallway.

A young nurse in a white, fitted uniform meandered through the sterile hall, and he again tried to stop, but only managed to slow himself down. After gathering his bearings, Jedd looked at the oncoming woman. It was odd. After so many years of researching the agency's heinous crimes, he was astonished that a PASTOR employee could look so… normal. Instead of a sinister smile, this woman walked with a composed, professional manner, as though she were about to diagnose a child with a runny nose. The white lab coat and her cordial smile gave her the look of a family doctor. Perusing her notes, she strolled further down the hallway without noticing him. It was as though she were oblivious, even with Jedd less than an arm's length away. She smiled to someone in an open doorway and nodded her head before continuing around the corner. Her shoes almost left tread marks on his forehead, yet she hadn't seen him. The thought baffled Jedd.

The limitless opportunities of the dream brought a crooked smile to his face while he drifted through the multistory structure. He floated along corridors and into rooms, at times even drifting through the building's various occupants.

After consideration, it occurred that the details of these people and the building itself were too real to be his subconscious at work. Their faces were perfectly flawed and too well defined.

If this isn't just a passing dream, he thought, *then it's probably the best reconnaissance ever discovered.* He was positive he would recognize the people upon waking. Passing through a multitude of sterile passages, he slowed to a stop in one of the rooms. *The whole place looks like a modern-day hospital, from the outside in.*

Once he had emerged from the room's ceiling, Jedd peered down and found the eyes of a bedridden patient staring up at him. The young man was strapped to the railings of his bed, his eyes fixated on the retired computer programmer. The look stunned him and stopped his progress. It took a moment for the shock to wear off. The boy looked familiar.

Jedd's memory served him well, pulling up a file he had once come across in his search. Although they had never met, he remembered the boy's picture. There were a few marked differences, though, the most obvious being that the patient's head was clean-shaven, with fresh razor burns along his skin. His time at the facility had allowed the dark tan in his picture to fade, leaving him pale as a ghost. He also had a sunken complexion, as though he just stepped out of Auschwitz. The sheets covering his thin arms and legs moved up and down, but the patient's icy, blue stare seemed uninhabited, vacant, which disturbed Jedd most of all.

What the hell did they do to you?

The earlier photograph was of a young man in his late teens, whose eyes danced with exuberance. The unblinking gaze supported his suspicion; the very tests they used to develop these children into competent agents, also sapped their souls.

Tears welled in Jedd's eyes. He wiped them away, but found nothing present. Looking down, he could see his hand, but as he attempted to touch his cheek, it unnervingly passed through his face.

No matter how vivid this is, he reminded himself, *it's nothing more than a dream.*

His thoughts turned to his goddaughter with growing concern. Without warning, his form angled southward, building momentum as it went. The boy's lifeless gaze drifted from view, and Jedd felt a weight lift from his shoulders, only to be replaced by something ten times larger.

An uneasy feeling grew in his stomach, and he frantically scanned the rooms for his goddaughter. Sinking further into the tall building, he came to a stop in a room like the rest. Much like the other patient, this one was pale, but fared better. She seemed healthy, but something about the sight tugged at him. Her wrists were tied to the bed railings with short straps, a more common sight than he liked. Even with her eyes closed, Jedd knew his goddaughter within seconds. Relief found him, and the angst that accumulated during his thirteen-year search began to ease. He had given up his life for her over a dozen years ago.

An instant after the thought crossed his mind, a picture of his loving, yet distraught wife appeared. Leaving her was a decision he hadn't made lightly. He had chanced to follow her once after his feigned death and found her bowed low in the heat of the noon-day sun. She had fallen to the ground in a city parking lot. Her legs protruded from under her disheveled skirt like a small child, unaware of social graces and expectations. But unlike an eager and curious, little girl, her fragile hold on reality had fractured. She sobbed uncontrollably, screaming his name. Onlookers gawked from the entrance to the big-box retail store, but no one rushed to her side. It was as though her guttural shrieks could be heard the world over. Driving away and leaving her on the blistering asphalt was the hardest thing he had ever done.

At least her screams didn't escape the deepest recesses of my mind.

Jedd tried to reassure himself with the thought, but paranoia threw his gaze at the door before returning to Madelin's prone body. Seeing his goddaughter's eyes still lidded, Jedd let out a sigh. With great difficulty he suppressed the memory, pushing it aside until another time. As usual, Madelin's safety was of greater concern.

Something about her still tickled the back of his mind. Jedd pinpointed what was aggravating him. She wasn't coping well. Her nails had been chewed down to the quick, and a drug-filled needle sat beside a vial on the tray next to the bed. Taking a closer look, he noted the name, 'Piroxiten.' He was vaguely familiar with the sedative, but the thought of using such a potent drug on Madelin was revolting. It sat waiting for the mad doctors in case the patient needed to be put under.

Jedd watched Madelin's medically induced sleep for a few minutes. Even now her lidded eyes shifted as her brain acted of its own volition, breaking through the chemical haze and immersing her in a disturbing dream.

It must appear more real than anything in this place, he concluded.

Her head and hands quivered while Jedd stood over the bed. His heart went out to her. As his emotions took hold, his desire to help pulled him toward the girl. He became aware of his reality altering. Madelin and the building around him shifted, becoming a bad imitation of life. The hospital scene faded from sight, leaving him peering through tear-filled eyes at a scene he knew all too well.

The heat from the flames of Madelin's family home singed the hair on her arms and around her face, but she couldn't look away, and neither could her godfather. The voices around her were no more than murmurs, like the buzz of bees, and the people in black treated her as though she were infected with the plague.

Madelin's hands grasped tighter to Deedee, her favorite friend and the only other thing to make it out of the house alive. She clutched him close. Her fingers dug through the ash and singed fur, finding the fluffy stuffing underneath. A course crosswind blew, causing her to shiver in her sweat-soaked nightgown. She watched the flames devour her past and future.

Does she even know what the dream's about? Jedd wondered.

Madelin gave him no answer. She just stared into the fire with the infinite patience of a statue. Jedd watched the flames dance amongst the gentle, red curls hanging tousled about her head. Knowing time was of the essence, Jedd pulled himself away from the scene that still haunted him and concentrated on the young, heartbroken girl. Her emotions vibrated through her mental synapse, and he sensed what she felt, as though sheltered within the recesses of her mind.

Chapter Four

First Contact

He opened his mouth to speak, but a raspy, smoke-filled cough was all that crossed the void before disappearing in a field of static. Trying a second time, he croaked, "Hello," but still an invisible curtain blocked his words.

Watching the suffering young girl standing in the driveway, he started a third time with more force. "Hello, Madelin!"

The young child's head whipped around, and a haunting, remorseful stare drilled into Jedd's heart. It pierced through every curtain that could ever separate two people. The look wounded him, forcing him to retreat from the memory and her thoughts, back into the stark hospital room. Madelin's eyes fluttered open but he continued to withdraw, only stopping when he sensed the wall approaching from behind. Standing opposite her, he watched with longing as she looked around the room. He didn't wish to leave the woman who had unknowingly controlled each decision he had made for more than a decade.

Awake, Madelin sat up and glanced around the room. Seeing no one present, she muttered through tortured lips, "How horrid."

Her shoulders slumped as tears threatened to flood her jade eyes. She tried to restrain the onslaught, but her emotions won out. Tears emerged and masked her eyes like a translucent film, clouding their inner light. Salty rivers streamed down her sunlight-deprived cheeks. The flow intensified, and sobs wracked her body. She tried to stifle the noise in the sterile, white sheets, but her bonds didn't allow them to reach her face.

As she wept, Jedd heard her questions. "What does it mean? What's wrong with me?"

She clutched large fistfuls of hospital linens, much like she'd held Deedee minutes before, tensing under the restraints. After the bout of confusion and self-pity, her white kimono was drenched.

Unable to stand the heartbreaking image any longer, Jedd stepped forward. The static distortion crackled before parting to his will. "Madelin, little one, don't cry. I'm here to help."

The interruption startled Madelin, and she sank into the bed further than seemed possible. The fear that infused her glazed eyes left Jedd feeling worse than before.

But what else can I do?

The flood gates closed at the sound of Jedd's strange voice. Peering over the wrinkled mass of bedsheets, she replied with a stutter, "Who-o-o are you?"

Seeing her fear turn to curiosity, Jedd took heart. He was aware that she was unlikely to believe him, but summoned the courage to answer. "A friend from a long time ago, but we don't have much time. Are you okay? Do you know where you are?"

"No, but how do I know I'm not still dreaming? I can't see you. Where're you hiding?"

Jedd's voice responded, accompanied yet again by the static, "I'm not hiding, and you're not dreaming. We're speaking like we used to, back when you were a child. You remember?" The question was tinged with the last ounce of hope he could manage. Jedd listened for the door to announce any newcomers, but the room's quiet was only disturbed by Madelin's sniffles.

"No," came the reply. She shook her head.

His heart dropped like a stone, but he noticed that her searching eyes had now focused on his location. She squinted at him as he spoke.

"We'll have to work on that, but first we've gotta get you out of here. Can you walk?"

She interrupted him with an excited shriek. "I can see you, when you talk! You're standing by the window, where the moonlight hits the floor. But then you disappear—why is that?"

Jedd thought for a second. Seeing no way of explaining what he really didn't understand, he replied, "I can't tell you now. We don't have time. Can you walk?"

Madelin squinted as he talked, waiting for another glimpse. Then, she answered with hesitation, "Yes... but I don't know where to go. I can't even get out of bed without someone following me around with a handful of keys and a loaded needle. What do they want from *me* anyways?" The last question almost grew to a shout.

"I'll answer your questions later. Right now we've got to find a way out," Jedd whispered insistently to break through the static. He forced his voice to remain calm in the hopes that it would be contagious. "I can show you the way, but I can't do anything about the straps."

Before the static had dissolved, her eyes lit up. An opportunity at freedom had come her way. "I can get the nurse's attention..." As she finished the thought, her words dwindled. "But she won't take them off."

Seeing an opportunity, he replied, "She will if you don't give her a choice. Can you reach the large needle on the table?"

Comprehension dawned on her, and mischief illuminated her face as she glanced at the nightstand. "Maybe."

Her courage hasn't diminished, thought Jedd with a smile.

She reached toward the tray holding the sedative. The restraints held fast, leaving her fingers straining inches away. "Maybe if I..." and without another word she thrust her body at the nightstand.

He shuddered at the sound as inch by inch, the locked wheels of the bed squealed. They resisted, but Madelin's forceful jerks brought the bed closer to the small table.

The static flared as Jedd abandoned his calm. "Hurry! Before the nurse hears you...," but his words trailed off as the door swung open to admit a short, broad-shouldered woman in her forties.

'Helga,' as her name tag read, swept into the room and toward the half-pulled curtain with the confidence of a no-nonsense mother with wide hips that looked to have cradled many suckling children. Having inched close enough to grasp the needle, Madelin stuffed it under the bedsheets. In her rush, she caught the edge of the tray and knocked its contents to the floor with a metallic crash. Helga came into sight a moment later and looked curiously at Madelin, who was feigning sleep. His goddaughter quivered under the wrinkled mass of sheets.

Seeing this, the nurse whispered, "Poor baby... poor... poor... baby."

With a shake of her head, she began to sing a soft lullaby. It was a nursery rhyme Jedd remembered from his own childhood. Approaching the side of the bed, the nurse bent down to pick up the tray of medicine, unaware of her silent observer.

"Oh poor gal, have ya had a bad start from those awful dreams again? Well ol' Helga'll make it all better," she whispered after finishing the first verse.

A smile spread across Jedd's face. He could see Madelin shaking under the covers. *The situation couldn't have played out better,* he thought. *She thinks Madelin's suffering from nightmares.*

Jedd knew the adrenaline rush coursing through his goddaughter's veins, and he watched anxiously as the nurse searched the floor beside the bed. Helga stood partway up with a perplexed look, but it was short lived as Madelin thrust the needle up to the nurse's neck—only just able to reach against the restraints. A look of pure terror engulfed the broad woman as Patient 914 threatened to pierce her esophagus.

"Take these things off me, *now!*" Madelin demanded in the face of the startled woman. She spoke with such viciousness that Jedd wondered if he had found the right person.

Glancing out the window, the grounds loomed up at him.

Whew... I did drift a long ways, he thought, seeing one level separating them from the ground floor.

Below them were decorative bushes flowering in the moonlight and a landscaped, grass lawn. Gauging the distance to the ground, he realized that it was still too far for her to jump. His first idea thwarted, Jedd turned his attention back to the white hospital room.

"I c-c-can't," the nurse stammered back. "Y-y-you just a-a-aren't feeling well. L-l-lie d-d-down, darlin'. H-H-Helga will help—"

Before she could finish, Jedd's eyes widened in shock as Madelin plunged the needle into the nurse's neck. With half its length visible, the nurse's eyes bulged.

Madelin snarled, "Do it *now!*"

Helga stared into Madelin's unwavering, green glare, attempting to maintain control. Seeing few options, her demeanor turned to submission. She released the closest wrist restraint. Her head resembled still life in its lack of expression, as though it were a trophy stag mounted upon a wall of thin air. Her hands worked without vision and sought the last strap across the bed.

Seconds felt like minutes as Jedd peered from the nurse, to the door, and back again. He could see excitement creeping into Madelin's eyes, but Jedd was afraid of what hurdles they might still have to overcome.

How long have I been here?

Glancing out the window again, he noticed that the moon was still high in the sky. He hoped time passed the same in this state.

What'll happen if someone finds me in the café? It's a twenty-four-hour joint, but how do I look to people? If I'm out too long, will the employees call the authorities? The questions built up in his mind as he stared at the large, waxing moon.

He looked back at Madelin's situation, helpless to assist. She struggled free of the horizontal jail cell while holding the woman at arm's length. Helga carefully stepped back as Madelin slipped out of the bed. The kimono-like hospital gown clung to her in wrinkled clumps, revealing her stomach's sunlight-deprived skin. Standing upright, the top of her forehead reached the large nurses chin, but she glared at the older woman with the cold hatred of an abused slave, finally given her chance at retribution. Her tenacity was more than Jedd had bargained for, but it gave her an edge she would need. She still had the same courage she possessed as an overzealous child, but the tests and captivity had twisted her perception.

What will she do? he asked himself. *Does she know when to stop? Does she still have a conscience? What have they done to her?* The questions flew through his mind unhindered. Madelin was more vicious than a lioness protecting her cubs. He knew she would never forget what they had done to her. *If only she knew the true extent of their meddling,* he thought morosely.

He watched Madelin's eyes blaze like green fire and noticed a change as a question came to her. She looked where he had been, but his silence left him invisible. Fear took hold, and the needle quivered.

"What do I do now?" she screamed, her nerve slipping.

Chapter Five

A World Apart

"Sir," a young woman with dark, shoulder-length hair repeated as she shook his shoulder. "Are you all right? You were yelling in your sleep."

Jedd's eyesight cleared, and he looked over at the woman. An apron displaying the café's crest was strapped around her neck and waist.

Clearing his throat, Jedd replied, "Oh, I must have dozed off."

He glanced around. Other customers in the restaurant watched him with dismay. Some whispered like mice hiding in the corner, then snickered and glanced away. It was apparent that he had overstayed his welcome at this particular venue.

"Sir, if you don't mind, we'd like to offer this seat to a paying customer. I can recommend a local hotel if you wish," the waitress prompted.

"No, no, that won't be necessary. Sorry for the inconvenience. I'll be leaving," he replied, packing up his electronics in a hurry. Then, Jedd steered toward the back door.

How could I have dozed off in such a public place? Those rules are there for a reason, he chided. *They've saved my ass time and again, and here I go doing something so incredibly dumb. If there's a bomb strapped to the bottom of my car, I deserve it.*

Ashamed, he tried to avoid the stares, but everyone else was at a standstill. It was as though he had stepped into a mannequin factory. Flipping up the collar of his jacket, he winced as a moist spot slapped his cheek.

I must have been drooling, too, he thought in disgust.

He could never return here, but that wasn't his primary concern. He had to get somewhere safe and find Madelin. She needed him.

Jedd glanced down the aisle of cars, searching for anyone suspicious. He saw no one and walked to the car. He scanned it for newly acquired technology but found nothing. He unlocked the vehicle, started the car, and took a mental note of the time, 2:28 a.m. It seemed that time passed at the same rate in his dream as it did in the real world.

Shifting into gear, he sped out of the parking lot and into traffic. He had to find a quiet hotel before the agency caught up to Madelin. Without any memories or knowledge of the area, she was a sitting duck. It was too much for him to bear!

I put her in this position. I should've been more careful, he thought, promising never to forget his mistake. *But what if it really was a dream… a vivid, life-like dream?* He dismissed the question. Wasting no time, he stomped on the gas and weaved through traffic.

He found a shoddy motel some time later, slowed, and pulled into a spot under the awning. It was another hole in the wall, ideal for staying off the radar. He shut off the car and checked the time again, 2:45 a.m. Grabbing a ticket from the teller machine, he picked up his key and shot up to his assigned room.

Madelin may already be out of time.

He thrust the door open, stepped inside, and locked all five padlocks. It would slow them down and give him a second longer to live. Falling onto the bed, he sent his mind searching, mentally shouting, "Madelin!" After an unusual ride through a host of spiraling colors, he emerged in the sky above the phony hospital. He was pulled toward her, over the dessert. His momentum increased, faster and faster, until he was speeding over white waves. The terrain coursed by with urgency, leaving him nauseous.

I'll never adjust to this, he thought pessimistically. Focusing on his objective, he clung to the hope that nothing happened in his absence. Jedd found himself drifting toward an abandoned replica of a small town, built deep in the albino desert. *Maybe she discovered a place to lay low.*

As his concern percolated to the surface, Jedd moved toward a small, concrete hut. It stood solitary and decrepit, but somehow regal amidst the ruins surrounding it. It was one of the few to survive the atomic blast that decimated this survival-town replica. Much of the neighborhood had been reduced to wood and concrete rubble. It was now covered by layers of sand and vegetation. Jedd scanned the dim ruins for life, but nothing moved, even from his vantage high overhead. Maybe there was still time. Drifting downward, small corners and concrete framing peered over the white dunes. The moonlight cast sad, distended shadows across the bleached landscape.

He drifted into the midst of the pale devastation and was drawn to the small home that remained. Through a glassless window, he saw the huddled form of his goddaughter. The sand in front of her was stained with blood as she picked large shards of glass from her palms, souvenirs of her recent escape. He passed into the small house.

Madelin grimaced as one sharp end disappeared into the backside of her hand, emerging seconds later from her palm. She worked diligently, taking short, ragged breaths. The pain of the procedure clouded her eyes, and blood pooled below, mixing with her salty tears.

Before he said a word, Madelin looked up and asked, "Where've you been?"

"Can you see me?" asked Jedd, his shock evident.

"Not unless you say something, but I can tell when you're around."

"Something happened," he answered. "I'll explain later."

Madelin glanced back at her injured hand. After a few minutes of searching for more hidden fragments, Jedd forced down his emotions and broke the awkward silence. "Are you ready to keep moving?" It came out vacant through the static distortion. His goddaughter noticed the change in tone.

Glancing up, she replied calmly, "Sure. Are we out of time?"

"Just about."

It's incredible how well she's coping, thought Jedd. *She's distant… but I can't blame her. No matter what I've been through, it doesn't compare to what they've done to her for years straight.*

Jedd returned to the situation at hand. "We need to get moving before the military finds you. There aren't many places for them to look before they check here. Bury the shards and any evidence that you've been here."

Madelin did as instructed and covered the crimson sand, but it proved impossible to hide as rivulets of blood seeped from her hands. The effort was difficult, and he could see the pain each particle inflicted as it dove into her open wounds. Every vicious speck struck at his heart like a dagger, but he watched her struggle through with pride. When she finished, she tore strips from her kimono-like gown and wrapped them around her hands. Rising up within the concrete home, Madelin stepped over the covered glass with renewed confidence.

A nearby explosion had renovated the place long ago, leaving an open doorway through the back wall. Peering out, she saw no movement across the bleak landscape. The white dunes shone in the moonlight, and sparse cacti stood out against the rolling mounds of white.

While searching the outlying hills, Madelin whispered, "Where do I go from here?"

"Northwest of us is a gate, and there's a small New Mexico town beyond that. There're guards, but I'll take care of them. I'll tell you what to do once we're there. Let's get going."

As soon as the words left his lips, Madelin shot out of the ruined house like a racehorse leaping from the starting gates. Hitting her stride, within seconds she left him behind. Jedd sprang forward, attempting to catch up as his thoughts went with her. But after keeping pace for a while, he felt drained. It was difficult to part the curtain that hid him from Madelin, and he began to slow. He had spent hours in this state. Unable to continue on his own, he stepped into her mind and breathed a sigh of relief.

"You sound better," said Madelin as she plodded through the desert, the irradiated sand slipping between her toes with each step.

"I feel better," came the voice, "but I'm astonished by how well you're doing."

"It's hard... but I have to run... a lot in the hospital... too," she said between short breaths, "but with the added... benefit of probes... my insides displayed... on every monitor." Although broken, her words were filled with satirical hatred. Nothing more was said for much of the run as Altran attempted to maintain the last of his energy, but Madelin's silent determination became clear.

Before long, the glow of a bright light bobbed above the dunes ahead. "Slow down and keep out of sight. That's the streetlamp over the gatehouse," commented Jedd. "Creep up to it, but keep a dune between you and them. You've come too far to fail now. I'll be back in a minute. Stay out of sight." He need not have added the last. Her persistence proved all too well that she had no intention of going back.

After his final warning, Jedd disconnected himself from Madelin. It was as though he were being sucked backwards through a small tunnel before entering his own body with a jolt.

This isn't something I'll ever get used to, he thought.

Opening his eyes, the television's digital display shouted, 4:52 AM. He had to work fast. The sun would be up in no time, exposing Madelin to all within view. First, she needed transportation. Jedd pulled out his cell phone and connected to the hotel's wireless server. Finding the nearest rental agency to White Sands, he booked a car under 'Gloria Ramirez' and scheduled it to be dropped off. The car would be waiting by 6:00 p.m. He smiled as another wonderful philanthropist unknowingly rented the vehicle for their cause.

With a glance at the television, he saw that twelve minutes had passed. Time was running out. Next, Jedd hacked into the Communications Regulatory Authority monitoring all wireless communications. He first searched the server frequencies of area radios. Discovering some listed as unavailable, Jedd delved deeper and cracked into the classified military channels used by the departments on base. As the television display approached 5:20 a.m. and the sun peered over the mountainous horizon, Jedd took control of each individual radio terminal. Blocking the access point of the doctor in charge, he input his own instructions to the I-70 east gatehouse.

Jedd watched his screen as the two soldiers in the shelter awaited their orders. A digital voice relayed his instructions. "All stationary guardsmen, proceed to District 5 research facility immediately for emergency orders."

"Please let it be enough," Jedd muttered at the screen. He hoped they would disobey their previous instructions and leave the gatehouse unattended, but his luck had never been that good.

Without waiting to see their response, Jedd disconnected from the regulating site and pocketed his cell. The television flashed 5:26 a.m. as he leaned back onto the bed, slipping effortlessly into the trance-like state.

I think I'm getting the hang of these transitions, he thought, *surprisingly,* as he slid into the slick tunnel. *With a little more practice, I'll be a pro.*

After a stomach-churning slurpy ride, Jedd found himself in Madelin's thoughts. Although nauseous, he was thankful of the direct connection.

What would happen if I got sick in this form? While curious, he had no intention of finding out. Settling his nerves, he turned his attention to the gatehouse.

"The sun's coming out, and one of the two soldiers jumped into the patrol car," whispered Madelin.

"Good. That just leaves us one to deal with. Wait here while I check him out. When I tell you, make a run for the edge of the road and hide behind the nearest rise."

"Okay." Breathing deeply, she prepared for the upcoming sprint.

Jedd gathered himself before stepping into Madelin's shadow. Without her support, his flimsy form was uncooperative. The pressure of keeping his figure together and willing it to move slowed his progress to a sluggish crawl. It was like an elephant had tagged along for the ride.

The gate drew closer at a snail's pace. Minutes passed before he arrived at the gatehouse window, but eventually he got a look at the soldier. The man wore a camouflage uniform but looked like he still belonged in high school. In a failed attempt to appear older, the young soldier had grown a sparse mustache. Each hair stuck out like the quills of a porcupine. The boy sat casually in his army fatigues, watching a show on his cell phone, a booted foot propped against the counter. Although the soldier didn't move from his seat, he occasionally glanced at the road and the surrounding desert.

He's facing traffic from outside the base, thought Jedd, *so sneaking up on him shouldn't prove too difficult, but I can't pit Madelin against a trained soldier, no matter how young he looks.*

Jedd watched him from a scant few inches away, counting the seconds that passed between each glance out the window. The albino vista outside was becoming a shining beacon of blinding sunlight.

Summoning a forceful whisper, Jedd seized the opportunity. "Come up to this side of the gate and hide behind the down-hill slope of the road."

His words came across distant and strained, but it was enough for Madelin to hear. She moved with swift determination, following his instructions to the letter. Upon reaching the gate, she flopped down in the sand and sighed thankfully as it muffled her landing.

While he looked in on the uniformed soldier, Jedd peered back to make sure he had no shadow. There was nothing there. It was as if he didn't exist. Content, he turned back to the gatehouse. As the sunlight streamed into the building, the soldier threw up his hand and shaded his eyes.

Then, Jedd gave his final instructions, a disembodied whisper that sapped the last of his energy. "Slip around the fence and sneak off a ways, but stay parallel to the road. About ten miles away you'll find a gas station and a car. Take it to El Paso and find a place to hide. I'll be with you again soon... Gloria..." The last of Jedd's words trailed off in static as he lost consciousness. His form dissipated in the bright sunlight like drying morning dew.

Madelin moved through the open gate as soon as Jedd began doling out the instructions. Sinking down ten feet beyond the fence, she sought him out in the morning light. His final words were like the death of a lighthouse beacon on a stormy night. Seeing nothing except an unaware guard peering into his lap, she slowed her breathing and reassured herself that everything would be all right. The next step was to carry on as he had directed. She gathered her bearings and slipped through the waves of sand, keeping hidden. Once the gatehouse fell out of sight, she pulled herself up and loped into a comfortable run.

How long will it take to reach the old gas station? she wondered.

* * * *

Madelin emerged from the bleached dunes of White Sands, New Mexico with a dust storm whipping around her. Holding her arm over her eyes, she avoided some of the oncoming sand, but the wind whipped the shredded edges of her hospital kimono in all directions. The gas station came into view far ahead, but appeared ghostlike in the chaos of the storm. Its obscure facade faded in and out with each wave of sand. She forced her legs onward, demanding that her feet keep moving. The hours of travel had seemed never-ending, but this last leg of the journey was almost too much.

She ignored the screams of her ravaged feet and the sand-filled cloud clogging her nostrils, instead focusing on the gas station ahead. Its form solidified as she closed the distance.

Chapter Six

Demons

A few people stood motionless under the store's awning, watching her struggle through the piercing wind. To them, it was a sight to behold.

They would later tell the military investigation team that it was as though a supernatural being (demon and angel alike were attested to) had stepped out of the last rays of the setting sun, consumed in a white fire that withstood the steady barrage of desert winds. The one thing both witnesses agreed on was the unwavering green eyes that stared out from the white shroud as it drew nearer. Both men stood stunned by the sight as the wind consumed their hats and fought to steal the clothes off their backs. Unmoving, they watched its approach onto the broken asphalt. Their tale went on unusually, reporting that the creature entered a waiting sedan and drove away.

The onlookers stepped up to where the sedan had been and noticed a trail of wet, sand-filled footprints. The gas station owner dipped his finger into one of the petite prints. It occurred to him what the sticky, red residue was, the blood of the angel. Before long there was consensus among the witnesses. The pale, fiery angel had been cast out and forced to endure the savage elements. The bloody footprints were the final proof.

Chapter Seven

Escape

Once Madelin got into the car, she sighed, grateful to be off her feet and out of the storm. Her bandaged hands had stopped bleeding as she ran, but her feet had blistered in the heat, and their soles were shredded. It was as though she walked the distance over sandpaper. Sinking into the seat, she took a few minutes to rest before looking over the car's interior. The voice had said for her to take the car to El Paso, but how was she to turn it on? Looking around the steering wheel, Madelin noticed a button with the words 'On/Off.' She pushed it and was surprised as the car came to life with a steady hum. Lights appeared on small monitors, scrolling from side to side.

A feminine voice then spoke up. "Hello, Gloria. Thank you for using Farasat Rentals. Where would you like to go today?"

Remembering the last word her invisible friend had said, "Gloria," Madelin now understood what he meant. In a very short time, she had grown used to disembodied voices and responded with her new destination, "El Paso."

"Thank you. Sit back, relax, and enjoy the ride. The commute will take approximately one hour and ten minutes." An automatic buckle slid across Madelin's lap before the car pulled out onto the vacant interstate. The vehicle got up to speed in no time, and Madelin watched the dunes whip by her window with childlike intrigue.

Wow, she thought. *The hospital officials can't catch me now.*

As she watched the world pass by, her eyelids grew heavy and her head came to rest against the driver side window. Exhausted from her travels, she was cast into a sleep so deep that even dreams eluded her, a welcome change.

An hour later, the feminine voice spoke up again and drew Madelin from her long-needed nap. "Gloria, we are approaching your destination. Where would you like to go in the city?"

It took a few minutes for the mist clouding her brain to clear, but as it did Madelin thought back over the last night. She couldn't recall her new friend giving a specific location, but after a few moments replied, "Take me to the town center."

"Yes, ma'am," replied the car as it continued down the highway.

The expanse of desert and barren mountains dwindled as signs of human habitation dotted the landscape. Old gas stations and mini-marts became more prevalent the closer she got. Madelin watched as digital billboards advertising everything from shampoo to soft drinks, gave way to metal buildings that pierced the dark, night sky. They loomed larger with each passing second.

The traffic grew as the car approached the city limits, and Madelin was intrigued by the sites around her, like a child seeing a city for the first time. Making her way through the town proper, she noticed painted, fluorescent artwork on store walls. People sat on street corners listening to loud, blaring music. She could understand some of it, but most just left her bewildered and curious.

Upon entering the business district, the huddled groups of friends disappeared, as did most of the artwork. There were more people walking along the sidewalks in suits, business skirts, and other professional attire. After fifteen minutes of meandering through crowded streets, the car pulled up next to a towering, reflective building and said, "Welcome to the town center, Gloria. Thank you for using Farasat Rentals." With that, the woman's voice faded, and the hum of the car disappeared.

The door opened without effort, leaving Madelin to stare into a world she never knew. Her curiosity got the best of her, and she stepped onto the pavement without a notion of where to go. Fatigue settled on her shoulders the moment she stepped from the car. An hour of sleep was just not enough. She chose a direction at random and headed down the street. After a short time her body and shredded feet shouted in pain, overwhelming the novelty of seeing the huge buildings around her, so she searched for a place to hide. Spotting the crook of a building's inset corner, she sank to the pavement. She was unconscious the instant she felt the ground beneath her.

Sometime later, something prodded Madelin's shoulder over and over, pulling her from a peaceful slumber. It was still dark, but the air seemed to have been imbued with a slight chill now. An unkempt woman stood over her in a dirt-encrusted dress that might once have been red. White, floral petals danced across its creases, somewhat visible beneath layers of grime. The woman extended her hand again and poked Madelin with a pudgy finger.

"Hey! Hey, you! You're in my spot," the woman blurted. She adjusted the cardboard box she'd modified to wear as a jacket while she waited for an answer. "Get up. Move it! I ain't got all day."

"Oh, sorry," mumbled Madelin as she rose to her feet. They ached with the strain, but she forced them onward, down the city street. The ragged woman stared after her, muttering a string of curses. Then she began pacing the sidewalk, skipping over the lines and cracks.

Madelin shook the cloud of fogginess from her eyes. Lamps lit the street periodically. She fought off a morning yawn while gazing at her surroundings.

There has to be something around here I know, something that stands out.

Lights and advertisements were everywhere. Passing strangers gave her odd stares, but she took no notice. Her eyes were drawn to the buildings around her once again, each one competing with the next in an attempt to reach the dark heavens. The area was unfamiliar, like the music-loving groups she saw the night before. Seeing nothing of interest, she continued past the storefronts and stepped onto a busy street corner. A few yards away stood a corn-dog vendor just setting up for the morning commuters.

Chapter Eight

Phantom Friends

While watching the morning traffic in front of her, the first few rays of morning began streaming down. Buildings became distorted with static before returning to normal. Madelin questioned her own sight, but as the sensations continued, she noticed a connected sequence. With each instance, life became a television show with bad reception.

Out of nowhere Madelin heard her name, or number by which she was more often referred to, echo through the static. "Please be on the lookout for Patient 914. Patient 914 has been convicted of crimes against the PUS, Parliamentary Utopia of States."

The words defined themselves unbidden as the automated alert ran through her mind. Everyone around her hesitated a second, simultaneously listening to the DME Announcement, (Digital Mind Enhancement). The nearby corn-dog vendor faltered while handing a customer his change, and even the traffic lights skipped a second before flashing green. Her head throbbed with the pulsing, electronic waves. The flow synchronized itself with the blood seeping through her veins. Each rhythmic thump was in line with her heartbeat and sent droplets of red blood out onto her hands.

A small stream trickled through her fingers and onto the pavement below. Subtle pinpricks of pain broke through her consciousness. She lifted her shredded hands, hardly aware of the blood congealing around them. Looking closer, Madelin watched as the static altered her surroundings, but not her. Through splayed fingers, she watched the brief interference of the announcement warp the world. Someone was standing in front of her.

The dark-legged pants of the slender man she knew became visible but disappeared at the end of each static occurrence. Through the distortions, Madelin heard a voice again, but not clearly. "Please be on the lookout for Patient 914. Patient 914 has been convicted of crimes against the PUS," repeated the announcement. She tried to focus, ignoring the reality of the street around her and pushing aside the robotic voice inside her head. Her friend had found her, but why were there two conflicting voices? As though attempting to gain better cell-phone reception, she wandered around the street and sidewalk, eyes closed, and tried to focus on the man's urgent voice.

He called her name, the real name she heard the attendants at the facility use. "Madelin..." Beyond that, his words faded into the message. She missed him, even knowing so little about him. He was her link to a past she knew nothing about. Thinking back, she succeeded in finding only darkness, an absence of life and memories. Her life had been stolen. She was an empty shell.

Just then, hands clenched around her waist and arms. She fought through the layered realities, wishing to call out, to wail under the forces descending on her. A scream rose in her throat. Her trachea felt as though it would burst under the pressure.

"We've got her," muttered a man from behind her head. The announcements stopped, and her friend's distorted words became clear too late.

"Madelin, run, *now!*"

With her arms clasped tightly to her sides, an agent lifted her from the ground and removed any chance at escape. The door to her cell clanged shut in her mind, and she stared through the bars at her brief stint of freedom, now out of reach. The scream died in her throat as a sharp blow to her head engulfed the mental prison in momentary flames. Then, as quickly as it began, her senses faded to nothing.

A short time later Madelin awoke and opened her sea-green eyes. Pain pierced her skull. The limited light that filtered in was unbearable. She shut her eyes to find relief, but instead discovered invisible imps playing snare drums on her skull. Pain still pulsed through her palms, but was reduced to a dull throb—the only positive thing she could identify considering her new situation.

I didn't escape these vile people to be blindsided in the middle of the street, she swore to herself. *I'm never going back there.*

After the pain subsided, the words she deciphered through the static reverberated in her mind, "Madelin, run, *now!*" The statement reeked of urgency. And, who was that shadowy figure in the dark pants anyway? He helped her get this far, but she still didn't know his name. This wasn't the place to find answers, though, not while she was stuck in the hands of her captors.

She focused on what she could hear and feel. Traffic noise filtered in around her, and the gentle hum of an automobile vibrated through her prone body. The fluctuating momentum of stop-and-go traffic shifted her over and back on the seat.

'Here' could be anywhere.

She had little knowledge of the facility she escaped from and knew even less about El Paso. Her headache began to fade, but she feigned sleep for a bit longer. Her past was a blank canvas, but her gut told her to keep quiet. Again, the mysterious figure's words flashed across her eyelids, as though advertised on a digital billboard.

At least the warnings of my escape have stopped.

The force of the driver applying the brakes brought her thoughts back to the car. She lay on her side, covering the width of the vehicle. With her knees pulled up, the car's momentum almost forced her into the floorboard. A set of feet slammed down in the seat behind her, and a man yelled, "Jesus, Johnny, what you think you're doin'? Remember, we can't damage the goods or there'll be hell to pay."

"I know, dammit, but the roads full of nuts this early in the mornin'," the driver shouted back. "Feel free to use 'em for target practice, Rick."

Johnny's complaints went on with enthusiasm. Rick chuckled and allowed his partner to continue his whining rant. Over the next few minutes, the diatribe became a collection of mumbled, incoherent sentences.

Madelin fluttered her eyelids, testing the light, and found it bearable. A few rays of sunlight made their way through the car window, but the lamps lining the street were still on. She glanced over and located the door handle before returning to her sightless observation.

This is my chance.

She flexed her muscles to test for restraints. Something bound her wrists behind her back, but her feet were loose. She wriggled a slender hand free. The wrappings caught on the plastic zip tie, but eventually came undone.

Remaining still and taking measured breaths, she waited for the perfect opportunity. Her adrenaline grew in anticipation. So far, the driver had encountered no further opposition. Cars whizzed past, and horns blared.

Then, before she could act, Rick whispered, "Hey, Johnny, I don't think the baggage is still sleepin'."

As soon as the words left Rick's lips, Johnny slammed on the brakes. Madelin silently thanked him as she fell into the floorboard and out of her captor's reach.

"Drug her again, Rick!" Johnny exclaimed. The car's tires squealed on asphalt.

She scrambled for the door handle and pulled. As the sounds of a busy street greeted her, she glanced back at Rick's awkward face. He reached over the back seat and clutched for her head. Instinctively, she swung her right foot up into his nose. His eyes bulged as though competing with his inflated nostrils. Rick flew back into his seat with a muffled roar while Madelin propelled herself out the door on a coiled leg.

The car was still skidding forward, and Madelin tumbled onto the pavement, narrowly missing oncoming traffic. She stood up in the street and tested her legs. Bruised muscles tensed, but nothing seemed broken. As the car shuddered to a stop, she looked for an avenue of escape.

Her captors jumped out and searched the road for her. Johnny was more alert at this point and spotted her within seconds. He leapt the front end of the car. His footsteps clapped onto the pavement, and he sprinted forward. He would be on her in moments.

Panic set in. Seizing her chance, Madelin ran in the opposite direction.

I've got to lose them, but where?

No answer came, but she had to keep moving. As the storefronts flew by, she was oblivious to the tall buildings plowing through the clouds above. Some seemed to be constructed of mirrors, and she raced her reflection down the street.

Running through the crowds of people along the sidewalks, she made her way into a different portion of the city. Her breathing was labored, and her heart hammered in her ears. Looking around, Madelin tried to summon a semblance of safety.

Where are they? Did I lose them?

Time had lost all meaning, her legs ached for a moment's reprieve, and her lungs burned as though inhaling fire. She turned onto random streets and alleyways in the hope of losing her would-be captors.

After passing numerous city blocks, she contemplated finding a place to rest when a familiar voice broke a static barrier and said, "Madelin." She stopped mid-stride, teetering to maintain her balance.

She listened as the voice repeated its pleading search. "Madelin…
Madelin where are you?"

Although wary, she found herself trusting him once again. He hadn't
let her down so far, unless she counted bringing her endless pain and then
leaving at the most dire of times. But, what other option did she have?

Madelin panted, "I'm here… I ran… and now I'm here… on a street
corner… Those guys from earlier are following me." After a hesitation,
another thought occurred to her. "Who are you?" The alerts were still
silent. Maybe she had time.

Pedestrians passed by and gave her sidelong looks as the
conversation continued.

I must look like a deranged lunatic, she thought with a chuckle.
Pushing the thought aside, she turned her attention back to the ghostly
assistant.

"You'll have to trust me," he said, his words tinged with concern.
There was silence as the speaker waited for her response. She second-
guessed her decision, but her gut said he was her way out. Besides, she
had already followed him this far. A moment later, the man continued,
"Find an alley to hide in as we work."

Work?

Still, she did as he asked. Stepping down the street, she disappeared
into the morning shadows between two red, brick buildings. Madelin
glanced back the way she had come. Seeing no one, she leaned against the
brick wall and let out a deep sigh. Her body shivered and then relaxed.

"Okay, I'm here," she whispered.

A moment later, the man's voice spoke up with urgency. "We'll have
to hurry. They have your position and are heading your way."

"How do you know, and who are you?" she asked, annoyed.

He spoke over her, as though he hadn't heard. "Focus on one place
that's solid. Concentrate and watch for it to happen."

Confusion spread over her face. "Watch for what?"

She stared at the wall across from her, unsure what more to do. Her
fingers pried at the bricks, but found nothing unusual.

"I can't find what you're talking about. What is it?"

"Stop talking and focus. Concentrate and you'll see it. It's the whole
reason they're after you. Focus!"

She did as he asked and searched each brick for something that might
stand out. What was he talking about? How did he know so much about

her, even more than she knew about herself? She almost screamed in frustration, but instead fought for calm.

The voice came back to her again as if reading her mind. "I'll tell you so long as you stay focused. Just listen and concentrate." There was a pause before he continued, "You can travel through worlds similar to our own. They differ based on the choices people made throughout history. Few people can do this, and it could tip the scales of power on our plane. There's a government agency created to deal with people like you. It's called PASTOR. They'll do whatever it takes to get you back. They're the ones who killed your parents. I was a close friend of your father's. I've been looking for you since that day, researching this PASTOR agency and trying to discover their plans."

Madelin listened to his words. As the sympathetic tone of his voice sank in, her hatred for the men in pursuit reached a new level.

"You can't remember because they messed with your head, stifling your memories. They were trying to mold you into a unique operative with talents like no one has ever seen… one that wouldn't ask questions."

Madelin considered the plausibility of his story as she fumbled at the wall. Though far-fetched, it rang true. Her anger ran rampant, and she felt the budding flower of a dark rose grow in her heart. With the mentioned horrors this PASTOR group inflicted on her family, the petals began forming, harvesting her hatred.

These people are horrid, she thought, *but I'll be the one with the last word.*

"Madelin, Madelin, *Madelin*!" his voice repeated. The name became a shout and broke through her thoughts. "Hurry and focus! I can see them. They're turning down your street, now. You have to find a way out."

Madelin looked away, searching for some place to run.

"No, the wall. *Look* at the wall!"

Again, she focused her attention on the bricks in front of her, searching repeatedly for something out of place. She felt the surface of the aged bricks, picking and prodding with her fingers. The rough edges chafed her delicate skin.

Before she could find anything more than dust and deteriorating brick, the voice said, "Dammit! Forget it. Run! Take the alley."

She paused, still attempting to find what she wished she could grasp.

"Time to go, *now!*" he screamed. His voice was firm and solid. Without looking back, she sprinted down the alley, away from her pursuers.

Within seconds, she was up to speed. She took the alleyway corner without slowing and narrowly missed an open dumpster that had seen better days. She continued, looking ahead and wondering if there was another turn. It was hard to tell in the dimly lit alleyway. Suddenly, a brick wall loomed in front of her. It spanned the length of the alley, blocking her path.

She sought an escape route and found two doors to local establishments. She frantically tried them, but they thudded against their metal locks and refused to open. Peering back, Madelin was distantly confronted by two more PASTOR officers. They were dressed in dark military uniforms that threatened to disappear in the shadows. As they approached, their faces passed through limited rays of morning sunlight that made it into this narrow location. They were the same two she had encountered earlier.

Rick's nose was swollen and inflamed. His glaring eyes flashed with hatred. Johnny spoke to someone, listened for a response, and muttered something back. Rick hadn't said anything, so it had to be some form of communication. Rick leveled her with his gaze. Seeing his prey trapped, he hurtled headlong down the alleyway like an infuriated steam engine.

My God, panicked Madelin. *There's nowhere to go. How do I get out? I need to get out. He won't fall for the same move twice.* From the look on his enraged face, she knew it didn't matter. A kick wouldn't faze him.

Slinking back into the shadows, something caught her eye. Painted on the wall was a graffiti image of a black rose tinged with red from the dust of the bricks. It spoke to her like nothing ever had, latching onto her very heart. The petals opened, and a dark liquid caressed their edges. The detail was exquisite and unlike anything she had ever seen. The flower grew from the wall as the petals unfolded and the substance pulled each one southward.

The flower reached for Madelin as she backed away from the oncoming train. His coal-black eyes carried death. Madelin felt the edges of the closest petal...

A growl gurgled from the depths of the large agent's stomach, rising as he charged forward...

The growl rose to a deep snarl and reverberated off the walls around them...

She plucked the petal, and a lip of the bricks came away with it, slicing through the air...

His heavy boots stomped along the pavement, accompanying his guttural scream. The steaming freight train loomed over her shoulder... the distance between them dwindling... disappearing...

A liquid partition glistened with an eerie, blue hue, drawing her eyes where the flower once stood... Her friend's voice spoke up through the tumult, whispering, "Yes, that's it. Slip through—" but he was cut off as she stepped into the morning light of another world. The sound of rampaging footsteps vanished.

Standing in a rock-strewn yard, a large building stood in front of her with regal appeal. She released the graffiti flower's petal, and it drifted to the ground on unseen currents. Madelin peered back through the portal and winced in anticipation. Rick was almost on her. Clutching the planar lips like curtains, she pulled them closed before the large operative came barreling through. The rift sealed at her touch, forming a thick scar. As a sudden sense of safety settled on her shoulders, she exhaled the breath she'd held.

Looking around, people gawked at Madelin and gave her a wide birth as they walked along the sidewalk.

The agents are gone now, but what have I gotten myself into? She felt more lost than ever before, an outcast from her own world. She was truly alone. *Where's my friend, and where am I?*

The honking of passing cars and the stiff smell of exhaust were all that replied.

Chapter Nine

Red-Headed Beauty

D aniel glanced at the web-like lines glistening around him as he stepped onto the sidewalk. The El Paso Courthouse stood out like a majestic piece of history, overshadowed by the thin, blue lines. It was as though they were outlining a building that was a figment of his imagination. He pushed aside the notion that his own sanity might be to blame and the urge to find another bottle of whiskey. Then, the terror-stricken woman saw him.

People gawked at her disheveled appearance as they unknowingly strode under the sparkling, blue lines. Her wild attire looked more appropriate for an Asian whorehouse than outside a judicial building. Her bandaged hands and bloody feet concerned Daniel, but he knew to approach with caution.

Stepping closer, he said, "Hey there. My name's Daniel… Daniel Robertson. What's yours?" His words sounded patronizing, as though he were attempting to calm a spooked horse. He winced as soon as they left his lips.

Madelin acknowledged the weathered gentleman with a wary eye. His accent was strange, even compared to those she had heard in the streets of this unfamiliar city… or at least the one she was in moments before. The words were slow but clear, like the woman's voice in the car.

"Gloria," she replied, unsure if she could trust this strange man. "Can I help you?"

"You look like you might be the one in need, Gloria." Daniel glanced at her wounds and pointed to her hands. "Did you run into a little trouble? Do you have a place to go and wash up?"

Reminded of her injuries, her hands began to throb. While fleeing she had set aside her discomfort, but now she grimaced. Struggling for a response, she replied, "No I don't, but I… I… I'm sure I can find a place."

"Well, my apartment is just a couple blocks away, or I could arrange for a trip to the hospital," he offered.

The mention of a hospital prompted Madelin to panic. "No, no, that won't be necessary," she replied. "I'm sure I can make it till my friend joins me."

"Well, why don't you come with me to wash up and get out of the sun," Daniel prompted, noticing the bright sunburn along her arms and face. "I'll help you find your friend, too," he added, seeing her hesitate. "Please, you can trust me."

Madelin could feel the sun sapping her energy and was reassured by the similarity to the words her mysterious friend had spoken the night before.

How long will it take him to find me? she wondered. *What if he can't? What if he gets caught up or can't get through to this place?* The questions built up in her mind, and she shook her head to rid herself of the pessimism. *I can't think that way. He said he'd find me. He did it before, so he can do it again. Until then this man's right, I need to find a place to hide. It's what... what was his name?* she wondered again. *Well, it's what he said to do, but can I trust this guy? He doesn't look like an agent, but until today the only people I ever saw wore white lab coats.*

Preferring the cautious path, she replied, "Thanks, but I'll be okay."

Madelin took a few steps across the rock-strewn yard, ignoring the pain as porous objects dug into her feet. She circled him and stepped into the crowd to find a place to lay low. She attempted to turn into the oncoming traffic, but the flow of pedestrians forced her the other way. Giving in, she fell into step with the businessmen and women. Some of them glared, but the looks only lasted a second as they went about their business. She caught a glimpse of the scarred man in the open shirt before he disappeared into the crowded street behind her. As the courthouse fell from view, she watched to see if he was following, but the crowded sidewalk made it impossible to tell.

The buildings in this world were different. While some resembled the tall skyscrapers she had seen less than an hour before, most were brick like the courthouse. Then there were others covered in a tan coat of something seamless and coarse. A while later her limbs began to ache. The sidewalk was harder on her than the sand had been.

Seeing a cloth awning stretched over a brick storefront, she sought refuge from the sun. She leaned against the wall and closed her eyes. Fatigued, she slumped down to the cement and clutched her knees to her chest while waves of people continued to pass by. She reminded herself to keep her eyes open, in case the time came to run again. Frustrated, but not wishing to wind up back in the hospital, she opened her eyes to the world around her.

A few minutes passed before she saw a recent face staring from across the sidewalk. It vanished in the multitude of travelers, but reappeared the instant the flow broke. The muscular man from before stared down with pitying eyes. The wind blew open his shirt, revealing a sweat-stained undershirt that might have once been white. Now it resembled his tan cargo pants in stiffness and color.

What does this guy want? It looks like he's got enough to keep him busy. And he doesn't look like the suited people walking around. Matching his gaze, she considered her options.

Seeing that she wasn't about to run, Daniel brushed through the oncoming traffic and lowered himself next to her. "Mind if I join you then?"

Madelin considered the question. After glancing up both avenues, she shook her head. He seated himself less than a foot away. Leaning back against the wall, he let out a strained sigh.

After a few minutes of silence, he stated matter-of-factly, "Don't trust anyone?"

The observation startled Madelin, and she sent him a sidelong glance. He didn't mince words. She shook her head again. Daniel nodded, understanding the sentiment.

"I don't blame you. I don't either." There was a pause before he continued, his eyes staring into the busy milieu of people. "Honestly, I don't know why I offered, or even why I followed you here, but I can tell you need help. We all do at times. God knows there've been times when I could have used some. Maybe if I'd had it, I wouldn't be in the position I'm in today."

Madelin tried to block the man out, but his words invaded her thoughts until they piqued her interest. Unable to help herself, she asked, "And what's bothering you today?"

Daniel let out a chuckle. "A lot... the same things that've been on my mind for years. We've all got a past, things we regret. I wish I could stop running from them, but no matter what you do, your past always catches up. The question is, will you be ready when it does?"

Madelin thought about his assessment of life for a few minutes. Without much experience to draw on, she couldn't dispute the statement. "Why can't you outrun it?"

"Well, you might be able to, but it'll always be there... up here," he said, tapping his temple with a crooked finger. "You can't outrun what you carry around with you."

Madelin laughed. *If only he had a PASTOR doc around. They could take care of things. I can't remember a thing before a few weeks ago.*

Giving up, he interrupted her thoughts with a shrug. "Well, at least I tried. Hope you find your friend."

Getting up, he stretched for a moment and gave her time to reconsider his offer. He took a step toward the crowded sidewalk, but stopped as a hand grasped the bottom of his shirt. Looking back at her shadowed form, her green eyes pleaded with him.

"Do you have a place I could hide?" she muttered.

He smiled, nodded, and handed her an open palm. "You can try, but you can't run from the memories."

Well you can't run from what you don't have, thought Madelin with a silent chuckle. She wished to be away from prying eyes and accepted his offer.

He carefully pulled her to her feet and motioned back the way they came. "This way."

Daniel escorted Madelin along the right side of the walkway, away from oncoming traffic. She watched the buildings come and go, astonished at the differences in the two cities. There were more people clumped together in the streets here, and trash had collected in the corners of the storefronts.

The grueling pace he set along the sidewalk pained her shredded feet, but she pushed on. Daniel noticed with a glance that her suffering, while stifled, was leaving its mark on the sidewalk with each painful step.

"My God, woman!" he exclaimed. "At least let me carry you."

"No thanks. It's fine," she replied through clenched teeth, thankful that he had stopped.

Daniel searched the street for the shoe store he saw earlier. He found it just three doors down. Slipping one arm under hers and the other around her waist, he said, "Sorry, but we just need to go up here."

At first Madelin tried to push him away, tensing as he lifted her, but his grip was like steel. It was something he had always prided himself on.

Carrying her was no more difficult than hefting a bag of groceries, and as his words sank in, she began to relax in his arms. "Will you at least take a pair of shoes? There're still a couple blocks before we reach my apartment, and I can't watch you rip your feet up."

Before she could even consider the question, they reached the storefront of a small, brick building and he lowered her to the ground. Assorted shoes were propped up in the window for sidewalk traffic to see.

"Do they give them to you?" she asked, looking up at Daniel with childish hope.

He peered down at Madelin, one eyebrow raised, before replying, "They'll give 'em to *you*. Wait here." Then he strode up the steps and into the small store.

Minutes later, he returned with a moist rag, socks, and a pair of white, canvas shoes. Motioning for her to sit on the stair, he overturned one foot and washed the bloody bottom. With her foot cradled in his hand, the tenseness fled from his touch. Her calf relaxed as he massaged the dirt away from her swollen heel, and a long, cooling breath escaped her lips.

Daniel assessed the damage and frowned. Unable to do more, he slipped the ankle-high sock and shoe over her toes and tied it. Then he set her foot down and did the same for her other. Flipping the towel over, he mopped around her bloody fingers and rewrapped her hands with strips from her kimono.

He hoped this would be enough for her to make it to his apartment, and wherever else she was headed. Standing up, she tested her new footwear. Although her feet were clean, he could see that they ached with the pressure.

At least the shoes will shelter them from the heated pavement, he thought. It was the best he could do if she wouldn't see a doctor.

As he stood up, Madelin looked into his towering eyes and muttered, "Thank you."

"You're welcome," he replied. "Think you can walk?"

"Sure," she said. A large smile brightened her face. As they set out, he noticed her eyes searching the street like a feral cat. Seeing nothing, she stepped into the sunshine and matched Daniel's steps.

Chapter Ten

Trust?

Madelin maintained her wary search as they walked. Her smile returned each time Daniel looked at her, but was gone a moment later.

"Are you running from someone?" He knew the words were abrupt, but there was no easy way to broach the topic. If she was, he would do what he could to protect her. It was obvious that she had been through a lot. *Who would attack such an innocent, young woman?* he questioned.

Madelin hesitated before mumbling, "Yes, but I don't know if they've found me. I don't know what they're really capable of."

The answer was vague, but enough to satisfy Daniel's curiosity... for the moment. "How long've you been here?"

"Not long. I just got to town. My friend is supposed to find me."

"Where'd he tell you to meet him?" Daniel asked.

After a brief hesitation, she answered, "Well, he'll find me. So, just in the city, somewhere..."

She knew this was vague, but didn't know what else to tell him. This world wasn't as advanced as the one she came from. There were fewer billboards, and none were digital. Everything she saw was archaic; although, there was no denying that it was the same city. Even the buildings looked older.

How much would he believe, coming from this simpler place? she wondered.

Daniel looked at her in askance. "I don't understand. How is it that he'll find you... anywhere?"

After a few deep breaths and a prolonged silence, Madelin gave in. This man seemed pleasant... caring even. "My name's actually Madelin. I wasn't sure if I could trust you before, but... I think I can now."

She elaborated on the events of her story, laying them out as simply as she could. It wasn't too difficult since she knew so little about the world she came from.

Daniel listened with a dedicated ear, but couldn't help the skepticism that crept into his thoughts. They walked past various musical groups socializing on paint buckets and were approaching his block when her story wound to a close. The most unbelievable part came at the very end, when she described the dark, tainted rose budding out of the brick wall and her unrealistic escape.

He considered what she said in the lengthening silence that followed. So much of it seemed unbelievable, defying everything Daniel had come to know over the last forty-three years. However, her curious appearance told him there was much more to her story than one would think. He didn't know if it was true, but in the end time would tell. What plagued him was that something about her story seemed right. He weighed his options, but stopped when he looked back at her fragile body. It didn't matter if he believed her. He was still going to help. Looking up, he noticed that they were standing across the street from his apartment, the same spot he had first seen the bobbing man. For a second he was reminded of the odd building superimposed on the courthouse and wondered if it would still be there the next time he made his way to that part of town. Glancing at Madelin, he concluded that there were some mysteries that might be best left unknown.

Madeline peered at the building and asked, "Is that your place?"

"Yes," he responded, "for now."

She gave him a quizzical look before following him into the street. The blinking ghost of a man was threatening to disappear from the stop light overhead. They walked through the propped door and past the hotel attendant without a word. The man's eyes flicked up before returning to the El Paso Times spread wide in front of him. Daniel proceeded up the stairs with a glance back to ensure she had kept up.

Madelin understood and followed with downcast eyes, counting the aged flowers embedded in the carpet. As they wound up the flight of steps, a slight breeze penetrated the building, drifting through the window at the end of the hallway on the next floor.

Most of the lights were off, which left the building a degree cooler. *Every little bit helps,* thought Daniel as he tiptoed down the creaking hall. He reached apartment 309 a moment later and motioned for Madelin to step back and stay against the wall. He unlocked the door and opened it a crack to peer inside.

Madelin did as he asked, but questions were forming in her mind. *Who is this man? What's he running from? Whatever it is, he'd better explain himself, and soon,* she concluded. *What the hell have I gotten myself into now?* The shadowed hallway hid her expression well.

Daniel stepped inside, and after a brief survey of the room, he opened the door for her. She refused to take her eyes from him as she glided past and into the stale room.

Grabbing a towel from the bedside table, he reached up and broke the hallway lightbulb, crushing it in the towel. He scattered the remains in front of the door and along both sides of the wall. Then he stepped back into the room, tossed the rag into the trash bin, and reached for the door. As soon as it shut, Madelin began checking off the questions that popped into her mind.

"Now, I've been completely honest with you, but you haven't done the same for me. Why are you prowling around your own home? Why the hell are you tossing glass in the hallway? And what do you mean, this is your apartment, *for now?*"

Her tone was harsh, and a hiss inflected the ends of some words, but at least she knew not to raise her voice and jeopardize either of them, he thought.

Daniel sat down in the faded, corner chair and stared at the outraged woman, astonished at the venom this innocent flower could create. The willpower it must have taken to keep that emotion from spilling over was impressive. Daniel braced himself as the tongue lashing went on.

"In fact, who the hell are you really, Mr. Robertson?" she finished with a whispered shout.

Her blood boiled. She reminded him of automatic artillery, still smoking and spinning after depleting its rounds of ammunition. Heat radiated from her like the agitated weapon, but he chalked it up to the sauna he lived in.

Giving her a moment to collect herself, Daniel watched her breathing slow and the fire in her green eyes dwindle to embers. Her tattered kimono fluttered around her as a small breeze drifted through the open window. The sunlight streaming in around her added a majestic flare in the dim apartment. The room was too small to hold the presence of such a woman.

After an agonizing minute, he whispered, "Dangerous people are after me, too. You think these scars are from cooking?" A hint of a smile lingered on his lips as he pointed at the healed slashes crisscrossing his lower cheek.

"No, but I—"

"Let me finish," he interrupted. The embers within her eyes glowed with renewed intensity. Her features seemed too fragile to contain such rage. The fire within her incited thoughts of passion—especially when she was half his age—but he dismissed them just as quickly and for the very same reason. Her porcelain cheeks paled again as he continued, "I offered to help you with the best of intentions, but my reasons for doing it were a bit selfish."

Madelin slid into the wooden chair by the window, never taking her eyes off Daniel.

"I've done things in the past that I regret," he continued, "and recently I tried to fix them, to... make amends. Some people aren't too happy about my decisions of late, though, and they've placed eliminating me at the top of their to-do list this year."

He paused in thought, but Madelin knew better than to speak up. She wanted—no, needed to hear him out.

"Now, I don't mind dying—that ain't the case. God knows I pray for it, but I need to correct a few wrongs before I kick it. These people aren't pushovers, and I've tried to stay out of their crosshairs. I didn't want to bring you into it, but I couldn't leave you at the steps to that courthouse in the shape you were in. It wouldn't have been right. I just hope I didn't drag you into their sights, too."

His eyes were downcast as his voice trailed off but glanced up at her bloodstained hands and feet. *Will they ever stop bleeding?* he wondered. *Could it be stigmata?* His recent pursuit for salvation had brought him to consider religion as a solution, but blind faith was still a troubling obstacle. He let the thought die without a voice.

The worry showed in his eyes. "I see," she replied with a wavering voice.

They sat across from one another, pondering their newfound situation, while the wind whipped through the window. It seemed to have kept pace with the increasing intensity of the room.

Chapter Eleven

A Fight for Power

Caesar Leodenin stood in the same shadowed alleyway Madelin used to slip away less than an hour earlier. A slight breeze caught the edge of his classic, black duster, twisting it behind him and revealing the Roman collar encircling his neck. It stood out in stark contrast with the rest of his black attire. His eyes were locked on the brick wall where they said she shifted from.

It looked to the men standing around him like the rest of the brick building, but Leodenin was searching for something quite different. He could see the shimmering spiderwebs outlining buildings on other planes. Everywhere he looked, alternate planes superimposed themselves on his reality. The difficulty lay in finding which of the fluorescent lines Madelin had chosen. Each color represented another reality, and whenever a rip was made, it left an indelible glimmer of memory under layers of thin scar tissue. But which was hers?

Lifting his hand, his fingers marched across the bare, brick wall, caressing each line under the indiscernible scar. His forefinger tasted the connection to the world and the people close to it. Father Leodenin, as he was known to the soldiers around him, was searching for a familiar aura print. Eventually his calloused finger settled on a deep-crimson line. He felt the familiar taint of the woman he had been studying, along with something else.

What is this? he wondered. *It's odd, like nothing I've encountered.*

The men around him stood poised for action. When his movement stopped, a gruff voice spoke up. "Did you find her, Father?"

Dismissing the feeling, Leodenin subdued his rising anger at the man's interruption. Without glancing at the mission commander also tasked with finding Madelin, he replied in a soft but patronizing voice, one a father might use with an unruly child, "I've supervised a large part of Madelin's training over the last eight years and at various stages of retraining. She's been difficult to educate, but the recent wipe, and those we administered previously, can't change her fingerprint."

Marlin hated this tone with a passion, especially when directed at him—a man twenty years his senior. He saw the fake father as a long-haired know-it-all and expected him to get them killed on this mission. He had spent more than a decade working in the PASTOR government division, but that didn't matter. The ranking officials who decided to incorporate Leodenin into their retrieval team didn't give a damn for his opinion. Even though Marlin was a veteran who had time and again proven his loyalty to the department, his vote was far outweighed by those wearing white lab coats.

Dismissing the condescending tone, Marlin Liyolla replied, "So, can you get us to her?"

Father Leodenin's crystal-blue eyes peered out from under thin, black eyebrows, their hard stare shifting to Marlin. "Of course I can. If I couldn't, then why the hell would I have come?"

The stress of the mission was getting to Leodenin. Marlin stared back at the slender, pale-faced man without reaction. "So, what do you want us to do?" he asked, peering around at the men fiddling with their holstered pistols. Watching something they could neither see nor understand was unnerving. They were probably wondering whether Leodenin could accomplish the task. It was a question that had also sprung up in his mind.

Leodenin replied vacantly, "Just wait."

The mission commander voiced further concern, but Leodenin heard none of it. Turning back to the crimson thread of choice, he laughed at the thought of going to a more primitive reality and the reactions they would get. This thread led to a mirror world—one that felt as though it had accumulated a layer of dust.

Did Madelin consider the implications of her choice? he wondered. *I doubt her skill has advanced to that point, but how's she gotten this far?*

The questions were piling up. Pushing them aside, he turned his attention back to the glistening string. Focusing on it and the surrounding brick wall, he searched for what he knew would appear. Time lost its meaning, and an image grew out of the wall. It was one he had come to know well over the last dozen years. Leodenin stopped scanning the bricks and watched the approaching figure.

The head of a black stallion soon pulled away from the wall, its legs running through red-brick depths. It stood glistening black as night, but miniature at four inches tall. A regal white diamond blessed its forehead.

Defying gravity, it stood erect on the wall and stomped an impatient foot. Its eyes watched Father Leodenin's finger, awaiting his next order.

The sides of Leodenin's mouth climbed upward in a smile at the sight of the elegant steed. Placing his finger at the top of the threaded scar, he traced along its center. The horse's eyes followed, its head moving in tandem as his hand drew out the desired path. After the father's intentions became clear, the miniature stallion broke into a long-striding dash up the brick wall. It went to the very point the priest had indicated and followed the path he traced down. With each step, the galloping steed lifted the lip of a newly formed tear, allowing it to flutter in the wind from both worlds. Once the miniature horse reached the end, its solid, black eyes found Leodenin's. Then it reared back in acknowledgement of the completed task and dove into the walled reality of this world, speeding into obscurity.

Leodenin held in his laughter. It was like this every time. The stallion had never failed to show when called... not since his early attempts when learning to hone his craft. The skeptical soldiers around him chuckled at the comical look that now consumed his face, but their laughter soon changed to astonishment as he stepped back. The operatives gawked at the rift.

The tear quivered with the wind currents, and as it grew, a vague world appeared in front of them. A dusty, sun-worn building stood behind Roman columns and a long flight of stairs. Watching Father Leodenin create the portal left Commander Marlin questioning the courage of his men... and himself.

Tapping the small microphone at his ear, Leodenin announced their success. "Captain, we've made contact with the plane the patient escaped to."

A small voice spoke back as the others stood in wait. "Good. Father, you have a green light to shift." Leodenin turned to the others and nodded at the window, signaling them to move in.

Marlin had watched Leodenin do this before, but never had he been ordered to step into another plane. He swallowed his fear and barked orders to his operatives. They responded according to their training. He smiled, thankful for the time he spent assembling the most capable operatives the department had to offer. Now it was time to put their training to the test.

They formed two single-file lines, and the eight men followed Marlin over the lower lip of the tear. They were careful not to touch it for fear of suspected dangers. Rumors had circulated—speculation that the edges would sever whatever they touched. No one wished to test the accuracy of the rumors.

Father Leodenin watched with a chuckle. He had heard the rumors, too. *People always fear what they don't understand. The chances of someone getting cut by a portal are practically nonexistent. Besides, the only thing these windows can hurt is organic life unlucky enough to be standing where one's made.* Leodenin shook his head then followed the last man.

Marlin crossed into the sunlit yard, and the columned building loomed over him like a force of nature. Stepping aside, he allowed his men to pass by. He scanned their surroundings and found that the people of this world weren't too dissimilar from his own, but dressed in suits and styles reminiscent of twenty years past. The residents gave Marlin and his men a wide birth. Seeing the remaining agents peering through the floating window, some took off running. After Father Leodenin stepped through, he turned and ran what Marlin liked to think of as his *magic finger* along the rip, sealing it like it had never been. Only someone with Leodenin's capabilities would see the temporary scar left by the gateway.

Tapping the microphone again, Leodenin waited. A minute passed with no response. He tried again, but static was all that replied. He plucked the device from his ear and disposed of it in a pocket. Then he turned to the others, a hint of a smile playing across his lips. "Looks like we're on our own, boys."

Now, I'll be the one calling the shots, he thought with pleasure.

While the group huddled in the yard, sirens blared in the distance. Commander Marlin looked at the tall man, who nodded in silent agreement. It was time to leave, but where would they go? Leodenin scanned the ground for some clue to where the escaped patient had gone.

It didn't take long to spot the congealed blood of her small footprints. They led across the rock-lined yard and onto the paved sidewalk. In no time, the group began following their commander's lead. As they proceeded, Marlin pulled out an electronic, handheld device, and a look of confusion creased his brow.

The long-haired father stopped mid-step. The flow of traffic avoided them, detouring across the street and around the group. His eyes were locked on the vacant sidewalk. Two bloody prints were visible below, barely a foot apart. One continued in the direction they were heading, while the other passed opposite it. Marlin tapped his screen when he saw the prints.

"That's what I thought," he commented. "I told ya we needed the GPS. She's back the other way."

Glancing over, Leodenin replied with irritation, "Yes, I realize. Why the hell do you think I stopped?"

The youthful shifter turned around and doubled his pace, following the new set of prints. The repetitive police sirens were growing louder.

We've got to get out of sight before the authorities arrive, thought Leodenin.

Marlin and his men followed on his heels but said nothing. The commander kept his eyes on the handheld device in case their prey fled.

"What? Nothing left to say?" asked Father Leodenin with a grin. As they advanced down the sidewalk, the pedestrians ahead leapt out of their way.

Marlin snorted. "Like I said, it's this way. You're goin' the right way now, so there ain't no need to say nothin' more."

His men knew he lacked the patience to deal with someone so egotistical, but fearing his wrath, they hid their smiles.

The father ignored the angry tone, replying, "See, you just gotta trust me. No need for the electronics. How do we even know the scanner's working properly?"

Pushing aside his anger, Marlin's voice drifted. "It ain't a matter of trust, only a guarantee that we'll find her ASAP."

"Not if it isn't working," concluded the white-collared man, a slight quirk lifting his lips. He loved being right.

Glances followed them as they kept to Leodenin's stiff pace. Leaving sight of the courthouse, they found their way to a group of men seated on buckets and dressed as though showers were a luxury. Their jovial conversation died at the operatives' appearance, and they watched as the odd agents jogged past. Once out of sight, the unintelligible conversation picked back up.

Sirens sounded behind them as the police arrived at the scene, but none followed. It wouldn't help to get caught up in the legal system of an alternate world. Just to be safe, Leodenin picked up the pace once again. Their hunt came to an abrupt end upon reaching the entrance to a small, brick building. An assortment of shoes stared back at him from the storefront.

This must have been her first stop, thought Leodenin as he put the puzzle pieces together.

He signaled for Commander Marlin to wait outside with the men and stepped into the store, the tail of his coat trailing after him. The sweltering heat had drenched the men in sweat, and the choice of black clothes over their bullet-proof vests was becoming more than the normal hindrance. However, Marlin gave no order to disrobe. He stood staring through the window at Father Leodenin, watching the interaction.

A small bell chimed, announcing the arrival of the pale, crystal-eyed father. Stepping into the shoe store, he searched the floor for signs of her passing. Although the carpet inside was dark, blood would still have shown in the well-lit room. To his disappointment, he saw none. Instead, a dark-skinned man looked up from the counter where he stood lacing a canvas shoe.

The older gentleman sized the tall stranger up in a glance and said in an aging, Spanish accent, "Hello, may I help you, Padre?" His eyes were still considering the dark-haired man when, with a wave of his hand, he said, "We have whatever you want." He pointed at dozens of shoe boxes stacked along the wall.

There was a pause for consideration, his tanned lips pressed tight in thought. "A man in need of boots… yes, good solid boots. I have just what you need. Come in, come in." He stepped down the narrow aisle and · found what he was looking for. Pointing at a section of wall, he said, "There! Right there you are."

Father Leodenin stepped further inside and let the door shut on its own. Then, in a phony attempt at kindness, he interrupted the old man's sales pitch. "Excuse me, but I'm looking for a young foreigner. She was wearing a white gown. Have you seen her?" His artificial attempt at sincerity was almost passable.

The store clerk furrowed his bushy brows in thought. "Oh, I'm sorry. I thought you be in need of shoes. Those duds you're wearing look a bit worn," he replied, nodding at the matching black hiking boots on Leodenin's feet. "Where'd you get those? They don't look like any I sell."

"Sir, please," Leodenin tried again. "Have you seen her?" He continued his feigned attempt at concern, but the strain on his patience was evident in his voice.

The shopkeeper glanced down at his own shoes and tapped his head in thought. "My memory isn't what it once was…" Giving up, he countered, "What you need her for anyway?" This side of the city wasn't known for its hospitality, especially to strangers. Even here, while respected, a strange priest was still an outsider, especially one dressed such as Leodenin.

Leodenin's voice grew in volume as his composure cracked. "I believe you know who I'm talking about. Her bloody footprints lead right to your doorstep." His hands flexed into fists as he spoke. His knuckles popped as his eyes drilled into the salesman with a look that would make mountains quake.

To Leodenin's annoyance, the stubborn shopkeeper stared back as though he hadn't heard. One hand scratched at his short, rugged beard while the other drifted under the counter, finding his personal pump-action line of defense. His eyes drifted to the left and right, delving deeper in thought, and his voice was firm in its response. "I don't know of this woman you speak, but you should go before I call *de policia.*"

Adrenalin pumped through Leodenin's veins like a geyser, and his eyes held the dreams of a demon, promising every torturous notion known to man. Thoughts of various planes he had opened in practice sessions raced through his mind with relish—places of utter horror where bloodshed and suffering were daily occurrences. Leodenin had familiarized himself with a few that piqued his interest.

Leodenin picked a particularly gruesome one and thought to himself, *Yes, that's just where he deserves. It'd be a wonderful place to send this joker.*

"To hell with the police, old man!" he spat. "Spare me the attitude and tell me what I want to know."

To his astonishment, the old man held his resolve and stared back, unperturbed, until the bell announced Marlin's entrance. Stepping up to PASTOR's prized bull, Marlin placed a firm hand on Leodenin's arm. He could fill the adrenaline trekking through the father's veins as he stood, hands clenched, like a child who hadn't gotten his way.

The department'll have to update their training to include social aptitude and communication, Marlin thought with a mental chuckle. Then, his past experience selling cars on his brother's lot kicked in. He threw a smile at the wizened store clerk, one that would gain the trust of the most frugal customer.

"Don't mind him. He's just a little distraught over his missing sister." The tension eased from Leodenin's arm as Marlin attempted a more subtle tact.

"Oh," said the bearded man, "so that's how it is. Come to think it, they do look a lot alike." The man's newfound smile didn't fool Marlin. He could see the speck of distrust lingering in the shop owner's dark eyes.

"Did you see where she went?" Marlin asked.

The old storekeep shook his head. "Sorry, no. I wasn't paying attention. Is a shame she went and got lost, but feel free to stop by another time if you find that you be needing some shoes."

With that, the Latino clerk dismissed them and turned his attention back to the countertop. He lifted the unlaced shoe with his free hand and admired it. Marlin guessed the location of the other. The man was quite believable, but instinct told him otherwise. He had known people like this throughout his life—men and women that seemed as meek as kittens, but were always ready to strike like a viper.

He turned to Father Leodenin and guided him to the door. Marlin could feel the old man's eyes on them until he escorted Leodenin out of the building. This was a man of experience and courage, one to be respected in his own right. Leaving the unyielding man's view, their entourage fell in step behind them.

Marlin chimed in, a breath louder than before, "Give it a rest, Leo. We know where she is." He pulled the small gadget out of his shirt pocket and continued down the walk.

Father Leodenin walked alongside, hands shoved deep in his pockets as though searching for something hidden for ages. He hated being called Leo, especially by the man who just got him out of a jam.

This's proving more difficult than I expected. Damn electronics!

Marlin remained glued to the machine as they distanced themselves from the sirens. He was so focused that he almost took out three light poles. Leodenin held his tongue, preferring to watch, but his ploy was foiled as one of the operatives steered Marlin clear.

"Thanks, Shanahan," muttered the commander after the first close call. The shifter didn't try to hide his smirk as he watched Marlin's eyes return to the small screen, determined not to show his frustration.

Chapter Twelve

Discovered

In the second hour of the search, the small contingent of agents crept closer to the red dot on Marlin's screen. Leodenin kept his eyes peeled, ignoring the sweat streaming down his back and underarms. He refused to take off his duster and admit that the wardrobe had been a bad choice. Instead, he comforted himself with the knowledge that the sun would be down in another few hours… eventually. Setting comfort aside, he looked for signs of Madelin, but found very little.

They crossed streets with Spanish names plastered on blue road signs, not unlike his home. He glanced at the different structures along the way, and shadow buildings appeared outlined in vibrant, colored webs. Some were smaller than those in this world, while others were bigger. A few times he spotted buildings he recognized from home, superimposed on this one. They were all carryovers from closely linked planes. Phantom people crossed his path regularly, oblivious to the mirrored realities.

This was something Leodenin had grown accustomed to throughout his training. He only needed to reach out with a knowledgeable finger to make each of the worlds accessible, but according to the researchers, the more he shifted, the more difficult it would be to find his way home. This was why he had never crossed over. The agency put too much money into its patients to risk them before they were ready. Glancing at what had to be the fourth fruit vendor they passed, Marlin brought the group to a halt. The abrupt stop pulled Leodenin out of his layers of thoughts and memories.

"This is it," said Marlin, staring at the rundown apartment building in front of them. He wiped the sweat from his forehead with his shirtsleeve before glancing down at the device to double-check their location. "They haven't moved." His voice was calm and measured in its certainty.

Confidence and training had made stoic readiness second nature, and it took over as they approached the apartment building. He wiped the sweat-covered screen on his pant leg before returning it to his pocket. The streetlight on the corner turned red, stopping traffic, and the men crossed the wavering pavement as it cooked in the El Paso heat. Leodenin fell back behind them.

They're bodyguards. It's their job to stop the bullets, thought Leodenin.

Marlin took the lead, sidestepping the metal fan rattling against the entryway door. None of the men made a noise on the worn carpet as they stepped into the lobby, guns drawn. A slim clerk sat at the front desk, his dim lamp casting shadows on the wall behind him. The top of his balding head was visible over the cheap countertop.

Father Leodenin caught a glimpse of the man's tired eyes before fear lit his chair on fire. He leapt to his feet, stammering, but the words were lost as Marlin leveled his 9 mm inches from his quivering nose. The commander placed his finger across his lips, and the man responded with a series of quick nods. Without a word, the finger directed the man back into his seat, which he obeyed. Then in one fluid motion, Marlin reached over the counter and ripped the phone cord from the wall.

In a quiet but firm voice, Marlin asked, "What room is the woman in the white gown in?"

"Th-th-three-o-nine," stuttered the aging desk clerk.

With a wave of his hand, Marlin directed his second in command. Shanahan circled the desk and emerged behind the frightened man with a roll of wide, cloth tape. Within seconds the man was bound to the chair and knocked unconscious by the butt of Shanahan's gun. The agent propped the clerk's head on the desk, clicked off the lamp, and slipped back into the main group. Then Marlin signaled for the other half to separate and find another route up.

The commander led his group up the rickety stairs. They followed, single file, backs to the wall and eyes peeled for any sign of an ambush. Very little of their procession could be heard, even from the defunct floorboards. However, Leodenin was having difficulty avoiding them. He gritted his teeth with each creak of his footsteps.

Why do I even have to be here? he wondered. A nagging voice in the back of his head reminded him that he had asked for this assignment.

Some agents cast condescending looks at him with each noise, but most kept their eyes on the rooms and hallways above and below. They were in their element now. With each sound of aging wood, Leodenin's breath stalled. He expected something to pounce, their stealthy approach having been given away by his ineptitude, but each time the ambush was postponed. The air in the building was stifling, and his nerves were wearing thin.

The group stalked up the two flights of stairs and stopped at the third. The stairway opened to a hall lined with apartment doors. Waiting with the others, Leodenin controlled his breathing and watched Marlin check the scanner. Then he nodded to Shanahan, who stepped around the corner and down the darkened hallway. The light from the window at the end of the hall revealed little.

The place is like a ghost town, thought Leodenin, half expecting a tumbleweed to roll by.

Marlin turned to Shanahan and motioned for him to head further down. The men streamed by like a school of fish. He followed, with Leodenin bringing up the rear. As they came into position, a shudder ran down each man's spine. This was what they lived for, but also what they feared.

With their backs to the wall, the other agents slid their feet, avoiding the glass shards on the floor, but Leodenin's booted foot came down on one with a loud crunch. The others froze.

Aware that their ambush was compromised, Shanahan took advantage of the second of surprise that remained. He lifted his muscled leg and kicked the rotten door in. The flaking paint and plastic room number disintegrated as the door splintered and shot into the room. Large slivers of the wooden frame flew through the air like sharpened stakes.

Chapter Thirteen

Stretching Boundaries

Jedd awoke groggy and more tired than the night before. After a cursory glance around the room, it seemed that all was as he left it. The television advertised the time as 5:13 p.m. He moaned at having left Madelin for this long. Perturbed, he buried his face in the pillow and shouted muffled insults until his stomach growled, interrupting the self-deprecating barrage.

He was still exhausted enough to sleep the week away, but Madelin needed him. He didn't question whether the night's events were real. In fact, he was certain he had found her. Setting aside his feelings, Jedd forced himself off the rumpled bedcover. His tensed muscles ached after hours of hibernation. His cellular peeked out from under his leg on the edge of the bed. He stuffed it into a jean pocket before heading to the restroom.

Jedd was stunned to find a gaunt man with sunken eyes staring back in the mirror. He ran his hands along the sides of the mirror in disbelief. Finding nothing, he peered at the haggard face staring back and finally concluded that it was his reflection. He looked like death warmed over. His stomach gurgled, reminding him of the need for sustenance.

This kind of hunger isn't normal, thought Jedd. *The dream must've taken more out of me than I realized. Gotta get some food before I try it again, and quick. Madelin's out there all alone.*

Jedd grabbed his jacket and key and slipped out the door. A neon sign announced a twenty-four-hour breakfast joint next door. He leapt across the parking lot and filled up on all-you-can-eat pancakes, courtesy of another generous patron. As he ate, his mind whirled with the possibilities of what Madelin might encounter in his absence. Concluding that Madelin was at least lost and scared by this point, Jedd folded a handful of pancakes into a burrito, dipped them in the dwindling dish of syrup, and sped back to the room.

His concern grew when he caught sight of the television display— 5:46 p.m. The time haunted him from the middle of the darkened room.

Rejuvenated, Altran flicked on the lights, locked the door, and downed the last of his soft drink before flopping onto the wrinkled bedspread. He exchanged glances with the man in the mirror as he leaned against the headboard. His dark, olive color had returned with the influx of a syrup-drenched breakfast.

"At least PASTOR'll have a hard time recognizing me," he muttered to the man across from him, a slight quirk drifting to his lips. Without another word, he closed his eyes and searched for Madelin.

Another stomach-churning ride of loops and swirls greeted him before Jedd found himself in a dim room. The wallpaper glistened as though the very walls were sweating. A rough-skinned man sat slouched in the corner of the dark room with his head held in his hands. A stream of light slipped through the blinds, illuminating his short military cut. His graying widow's peak gleamed under the scant rays.

Standing across from him was the woman that had consumed Jedd's thoughts for the last decade. The window lit her from behind majestically. The sight of the bloodstained bandages reminded him of the consequences of the previous night's journey. While he'd drained every ounce of energy he had left, Madelin had suffered far worse. The tattered remnants of her kimono allowed her a shred of decency, and her short-cut hair blazed in the sunlight.

She stared down at the older man with jade eyes that glowed ferociously, but the longer he looked, the more emotions he saw hidden beneath her gaze. The scene stalled, and the fire in her eyes dwindled as she slumped into a wooden chair.

A prolonged silence settled on the room, and Jedd forced her name over the static gap. Madelin's head whipped around, and shock flooded over her, but soon the look was replaced by a familiar smile.

She wasn't able to see him, but the voice had become a comfort in this unfamiliar world.

Sensing that something had changed, Daniel's head drifted up. "Madelin, is something wrong?" he asked, his whisper carrying across the sweltering room.

With a glance, she replied, "No, everything's fine."

And then, as though speaking to an unseen presence, a stream of jubilant conversation flowed from her lips. "You found me. Are you okay?"

Daniel watched from the darkened corner as she prattled on in a one-sided conversation. Insanity was all that came to mind, and if that were the case, there was little he could do to help her. It was heartrending to think this beautiful woman might be inflicted with such a thing, but the explanation solidified in his mind with each utterance to the faded wallpaper. In the hope of discovering a more accurate rationalization, he leaned forward and pulled out and old WWII ammo box from beneath the bed, keeping his ears tuned into her conversation. Madelin's face betrayed nothing. Her reactions to the conversation were genuine. Daniel flipped open the bolt and began filling the pockets of his cargo pants with spare magazines. He was dismayed by this new revelation. He'd hoped her story would somehow check out, but whatever happened, his gut told him trouble was coming. He allowed the odd monologue to continue without interruption, finished, and slid the now empty ammo box back beneath the bed, resuming his earlier position.

While pondering Madelin's sanity, the recent memory of her mysterious appearance interrupted his thoughts. Her tale was so far-fetched, he doubted even a lunatic could create such a story. Searching for an inkling of reassurance, Daniel's gaze rose to meet Madelin's as she shifted her attention back to him. He delved into her bottomless, green eyes, and it seemed that time stood still. At that moment, he knew that no matter how unusual her story was, he couldn't give up on this enchanting woman.

No mystery remained in Daniel's gaze, and Madelin stood stunned by the openness with which she saw him. His strength lay hidden beneath his dignity and pride, but trickled around the edge unimpeded. In that moment she learned more about her newfound friend than she knew about herself. She saw who Daniel Robertson truly was and knew he saw the same. The pain and loss he had endured were clear, but under the folds of memories clenched in a fist of sorrow stemmed the strength that kept him going. After what felt like hours of soul-searching, the voice of her familiar friend chimed in.

"Madelin, I don't know how close they are to finding you, but it'll be better if you wait for me. I can help. Where are you?"

Madelin broke her profound gaze and turned from her seated companion. She relayed a description of the surrounding area and their hotel to her mysterious godfather.

Buying into her story, Daniel's concern grew.

What the hell's she doing? If there really is someone there, she can't tell them where we are. Who is it she's talking to? What if they give us up? Shit! he almost shouted. "Who in the world are you talking to?"

Madelin turned back to the darkened corner and replied, "The friend I told you about. He's coming to help."

Unable to argue with an invisible man, but finding it impossible to discredit her odd behavior, Daniel shut his mouth. He watched the one-sided conversation continue and stifled his anger.

He reached over to the worn nightstand and gripped the neck of a tequila bottle he left open days before. He considered finishing the last third, but instead spun the bottle an inch over the wooden tabletop, let it dangle from his fingertips. The sound of alcohol sloshing was strangely soothing. While staring at the waves within the opaque glass, he considered his options.

I got myself into this, for better or worse. I'll see it through, he concluded. *I just hope destiny'll give me enough time to make amends.*

"Can you trust this man?" asked Jedd.

"Without a doubt. How will you find me? I ran through some kind of rip in the wall."

Silence answered back. Time stretched, but eventually a whisper carried through. "I'll try crossing where you did. I might be able to find it. Then you can reopen the portal. Can you meet me there?"

"Sure," she said, brightening at the thought of seeing her illusory protector. It occurred to her that she still didn't know his name. Shaking her head at the absurdity of the situation, she asked, "And can you finally tell me your name, or should I keep calling you my imaginary friend?"

A chuckle carried to her ears before he replied. "Jedd Altran. I was a close friend of your father's, but we'll get into that more later. Do you remember anything about the area you shifted from?"

"Shift? What do you mean?" she asked quizzically.

"The place you escaped from, where you walked through the wall. It's called shifting."

Madelin shook her head, and a frown creased her face. "No I don't. It all looked the same."

"Okay," he replied, "Stay where you are. I'll find it and meet you there as soon as I can. Wait for me."

Seeing Madelin perk up gave Daniel hope, but always the pessimist, he wondered what problems might lurk in the near future. His hand drifted from the bottle to the Glock 19 on his bedside and caressed the pistol grip. The gun had been with him for longer than he cared to acknowledge, and he felt naked without it.

At that second, Daniel heard the soft crunch of breaking glass outside the apartment door. Gun in hand, he leapt across the room and shoved Madelin toward the window.

Fear sprang to her eyes as he whispered, "Out the window, *now*! Someone's here."

Without a second thought she did as ordered, stepping out the open window and onto the emergency fire escape. Daniel followed on her heels, but just as he leapt out the curtained window, all hell broke loose.

Black-clad agents kicked the door in, shattering the frame and showering the room with wooden projectiles. The PASTOR operatives flooded the room like a swarm of ants. Weapons readied, they drew down on Daniel. The ancient windowpanes shattered as the first few agents riddled them with bullets. The rest of their silenced shots peppered the wall and windowsill.

Altran watched in horror as four black-clad soldiers filed into the ancient hotel room. Powerless, he roared, "Run, run, Madelin!" He slid through the wall and into the air at the top of the fire escape.

Madelin climbed the stairs like an Olympian, but with each step, the decrepit staircase threatened to detach from the brick wall.

Unable to do anything but watch, Jedd drifted to the roof and searched for an escape. It didn't take long to come to a horrifying conclusion: There was no escape.

Daniel topped the foot-high wall encircling the roof and came to the same realization. Positioning Madelin behind him, he hid behind a brick smokestack and peered around the corner, waiting with his weapon readied.

As fear took hold, Jedd floated back over the stairwell and peered down at the well-trained men in pursuit of his goddaughter. There was no way out. Panic set in, and he let out a vicious battle cry that pierced the void in which he stood, erupting over the discordant static of this world.

The bloodcurdling scream that escaped Jedd's lips chilled Madelin to the bone. For an instant she saw him over Daniel's shoulder, sparkling in the sunlit sky. A man of average height, he wore a leather jacket with jet-black hair. He stood over the stairway, held up by nothing but air. Arms outstretched, he glared at the climbing operatives. She watched as Jedd summoned his remaining energy, his muscles contracting into quivering knots of rage. Even the air around him seemed to contract. Random gunfire lanced through his incorporeal body harmlessly. Then, with a flip of his legs, he hurled himself down at the agents. His war cry echoed back to Madelin as he hurtled toward the ground before breaking off a few moments later.

A tear escaped her eye as a fearful assumption came to mind. "Is he dead?" she asked, but before she could give it further thought, the first of their pursuers peered over the roof's ledge.

Chapter Fourteen

A Father's Sacrifice

Emotion, passion, and writhing hatred were all Jedd felt as he flew down at the black-clad operatives storming the fire escape. The suddenness of his appearance had startled the agents. Bullets soared through him but did nothing.

After all I've gone through to find her, you aren't about to take her away, he swore to himself.

Adrenaline flowed through his veins like the fiercest of rivers. He passed through the first, second, and third agent without effect. His helplessness further fueled his fury. Picking up speed, he swept through a multitude of stairs and the last remaining agent. Then a man he knew from his research stepped out from Daniel's apartment window. Standing tall and ominous in his long, foreboding trench coat was the PASTOR operative known as Father Leodenin.

If anyone deserves a torturous death, it's this man, thought Jedd as he sped toward Leodenin. *His name keeps popping up in everything I find.*

The thought was fleeting, but passionate. Stretching out his arms, he reached for the devil below and bellowed to the gods. As the bloodcurdling scream reached its peak, his hands clenched into fists of iron and crashed into the false Father's chest.

Jedd smiled at the sound of snapping bones. His momentum carried them both into the corroded railing and sheared the bolts. As it gave way, they tumbled toward the cement alley below. Seconds passed like minutes as Jedd struggled to break every bone in the slender man's body. His blood surpassed its boiling point, and with each strike his hatred became an inferno. He thrust a clenched fist at the long-haired man, striking his ribcage and face. He landed blow after blow.

Leodenin fought back against the unforeseen foe. Grasping at anything he could, he pounded him with knees and fists in an attempt to break free. As the twisted mass of appendages fell to the earth, Jedd's screams echoed from building to building. Flipping through the air, the long coat engulfed them both in a suffocating grip. It was as though it had a life of its own. The wind roared past, drowning out his war cry, but it didn't matter.

I'll kill you! kill... kill... kill... Jedd swore. The words swept through his mind amidst the turmoil of his hatred. He wasn't sure whether he said or thought them, but he didn't care. This man had to die.

With each blow he landed on an icy eye or pale cheek, his bloodlust grew. He was awash in a shower of the father's blood, but his ardent attack was curtailed at the last moment. The paved alleyway loomed over the dark shifter's shoulder, and a split second of fear pierced Jedd's focused hatred. It wasn't a fear of dying, but dread that PASTOR's prized pupil would escape the punishment he so justly deserved.

Before diving into the pavement below, Altran pressed his feet into Leodenin's chest. He smiled maniacally and cherished the thought of the false father dying at his hands. Then he propelled the man into the shadowed pavement below.

Chapter Fifteen

A Show of Loyalty

Marlin and his men cursed as they ran up the fire escape. The burst bulb wasn't a coincidence, and the tip-off had been just enough for their prey to escape. Whoever she was in league with was trained for just such a situation. He vaulted up the last few steps, reaching the small palisade encircling the rooftop. He peered over the ledge with his silenced 9 mm at the ready.

He spotted the battle veteran's worn boot peeking from behind a sunbaked chimney protruding from the tarred rooftop. Then it disappeared. Marlin fired a warning shot into the exposed bricks before leaping the low wall in a catlike motion. Without a second thought, Shanahan followed his lead, propelling himself over the ledge and onto the black tar.

With nowhere to hide, they spread out and surrounded the chimney. The sun had heated the black roof, melting the tar, and their shoes were soon mired. They were forced to break free of the gooey muck with each step. A sickening sound followed them, like pulling apart liquid Velcro.

Shanahan wasn't deterred, but Marlin reconsidered their current approach. A rooftop restricted the fugitive's movement, but it was like trapping a wild animal. With no place to go and nothing to lose, they would fight back to their last breath. Inches away, the ledge was an ominous reminder that he was locked in a cage with Madelin and her friend.

This isn't the best way to recover the patient, thought Marlin, a little too late. *Considering the consequences, it might be better not to return at all, especially if we kill the woman.*

* * * *

Daniel ducked further into the aged chimney's shadow. Reaching behind him, he reassured himself that Madelin still remained hidden.

"If I can take care of these two, we might have a chance. When I say so, make a break for the roof over there," Daniel whispered, nodded to the building across from them.

The details of his plan became clear when Madelin looked at the five-foot gap between buildings. Her cool composure fractured at the thought of leaping from one rooftop to the next. The demise of her one tie to a family she no longer remembered flashed before her eyes. Echoes of her godfather's hate-filled screams ricocheted through her mind. She quivered at the thought. Fear took hold, and her new shoes shuffled backward as though capable of depositing her into the very pores of the bricked chimney. Daniel seized her wrist, and she froze in place. Teetering at the edge of the shadow, his solid hold helped to subdue her panic.

"It's okay. I'll help you," he said, but her reaction made the futility of the plan quite clear. Her head shook back and forth while her eyes remained locked on the small chasm. For a moment Daniel contemplated throwing her across himself but dismissed the idea after considering the consequence of a simple mistake. His plan crumbled at the thought.

If she isn't willing, I'll have to find another way. There has to be something I can do—God, I need a drink.

Driving the thought away, he focused on the problem and searched the rooftop for an answer. Another gunshot reminded him of the immediate threat encroaching on their position. With nothing coming to mind, he shifted his back to the edge of the brick wall. Holding his Glock 19 poised, he chanced a look around the corner. The light-haired agent unloaded another shot at his exposed face, sending flakes of brick and mortar into his eyes. Daniel ducked back behind the brick wall and shook away the remnants, clearing his vision. The sounds of their approaching boots squishing through the tar and the clatter of more on the metal fire escape prompted him to action.

"Well if you want me, then you got me," Daniel muttered under his breath. Keeping the jutting chimney between him and the two men, he sidestepped a few more inches, still holding Madelin away from the visible sides. "They're trying to surround us, and more are coming up the stairs. It'll be checkmate if we don't act now," he told Madelin. After a slight pause and a deep, calming breath, he continued. "You stay here." All of his emotions fled with his decision to act, leaving his voice stern and vacant.

Before the last words left his lips, Daniel released the magazine into his hand, checked the bullets, and hammered it back in with his palm. The clip clicked metallically, signaling the weapon's thirst for blood. Madelin looked back at him in astonishment as his plan dawned on her.

Daniel ignored the look. Resting his forehead on the cold, metal barrel, he took a few measured breaths then strode around the shattered brick corner. His gun's muzzle sighted the two men on instinct.

The beast Marlin feared emerged from the shadows with eyes of stone. Rays of sunlight glinted off the barrel. The gun spat once... twice... three times at Shanahan. The agent spun under the gunfire. As a bullet caught his shoulder, he was tossed off the rooftop. Daniel continued his march toward Marlin, shifting targets, leveling the Glock on the commander as his pistol hungered for more. A bullet tore across his shoulder, and Daniel smiled as Marlin grimaced, his foot lodged in the tar. *Must have thrown his aim off.*

Daniel pulled the trigger but was blindsided by an agent surging across the rooftop. The impact knocked him off-balance, and the shot went wide.

The man tried to grapple him to the ground. Daniel resisted the onslaught and twisted out of the man's fingers, forcing his arm behind him. Daniel's shirt trailed in the wind as he landed on one knee. His metallic friend settled on the older agent's midsection, ready for another chance at blood.

Marlin's unwavering black pistol held another death stare from a few yards away. "Let 'im go."

A calm serenity settled on Daniel's shoulders, and he pulled the hair trigger before rolling out of reach.

The split-second response of Marlin's firearm missed Daniel, instead eating through his shirt as it trailed after him. The pistol swept over the rooftop, carrying out the commander's wishes. The bullets dove into the apartment building, inches away from Daniel's tumbling figure. Flipping back onto a knee, Daniel's finger tensed to unleash another lethal shot when a fourth man leapt over the parapet and bulldozed him from behind. The collision hurled him face-first into the tarred roof. Marlin seized the chance, kicked the gun away, and stomped on Daniel's hand with a boot heel.

Madelin's sole protector fought back with an elbow to his new assailant's chin. Breaking loose from the man's iron grip, Daniel surged into Marlin. The commander's black pistol quenched its blood thirst, licking at the veteran's side. Unaware of the pain, his momentum carried him upward. His clenched fist smashed into the commander's chin with the force of a charging bull. Marlin flew backward, and his knees buckled. Daniel turned to confront the two new aggressors as they regained their footing on the windy rooftop.

His adrenaline soared through the clouds, and he neglected the blood lapping at his soaked undershirt and shoulder. His loose button-up billowed around him as though straining to reach the other men.

Standing unarmed, Daniel tensed and braced for the charge. The soles of his combat boots sank into the inch-thick tar beneath him. He shifted his weight and dug the ball of his foot into the ground as he prepared to pounce. The air was charged as the three men glared at one another. Each waited for a signal, an opportunity to gain the upper hand.

"You ready to die?" asked Daniel viciously.

"You're the one's gonna die today," shouted the larger of the two agents. "Ready to meet your maker?"

"I've been ready," Daniel growled back. "Here's to spilled blood."

* * * *

Madelin's fear flared back to life. Curbing the growing uneasiness in her stomach, she braced herself against the wall. Gunfire buffeted her ears, but it was over before she could summon the courage to emerge from her hiding spot. Fearing the worst, she edged over to the corner and peered out at the isolated rooftop.

The chaos that had erupted milliseconds before slowed to a crawl. The agent that followed them was on the ground, almost attempting to mold itself to the torrid rooftop. Three men stood stock still, perched at the edge of tumultuous air currents.

The calm before the storm ended as swiftly as it began. Daniel bolted toward one man, flecks of tar flying from his shoes. He lowered his head and tore over the rooftop faster than she thought possible in the circumstances. The two PASTOR agents appeared out of their element. One reached for his gun but wasn't quick enough. Surprise blossomed on his face as Daniel bounded toward him. The other operative attempted his own charge but was slow to leave the gate. Each step was delayed by the tar's insufferable grip. Seeing his error, he reached for his gun as an afterthought.

Daniel's target was a trim operative without an ounce of fat on him. He had no sooner caressed the handle of his pistol before Daniel tackled him low, pinning the man's arms to his side. Rising up, Daniel lifted the sandy haired man from the roof. The wounded veteran's arms slipped lower, encircling the agent's knees like a wrestler. He grinned at what was to come.

The agent struck at Daniel's face with a freed hand, but the veteran's grin was immovable. Shifting his weight, he spun in place like a top. Gravity pulled the agent's torso away, and his knees bent under the centrifugal pressure, lowering him into the wind like an airplane propeller.

As Madelin watched in anticipation, the hulking man standing between them leveled his gun on Daniel's head. Without thinking, she launched herself out of the shadows. After crossing half the distance, she leapt into the air, and her feet slammed into the man's back just as he pulled the trigger. The impact hurled him forward, arms flailing and face exposed as the shot flew wide.

Seeing his chance, Daniel sent his captive into horizontal flight, propelling him into the unsteady operative like a trebuchet hurling a boulder. The momentum of the collision powered both agents over the ledge. A series of metallic crashes echoed from the alleyway as the more fortunate of the two landed on the shaky stairwell. The sudden shock forced the top flights to collapse and trap him in place. The one unlucky enough to have missed the jutting stairwell screamed in horror, flailing his arms as though he might find salvation. Seconds later, a heavy *thump* granted him eternal silence.

Daniel flipped back around, ready for more, but found Marlin still lying unconscious. Seeing no further threat, the throbbing pulse of adrenaline drained from his ears. Madelin stood up from the scorching, black tar and wiped her hands free of clinging globs. Daniel turned to her with an air of compassion, thankful that she had come away unharmed.

"Thank you, Daniel." Her voice was sincere, and she spoke with a kindness he had never known.

He was about to reply when a shooting pain rippled through his stomach. Daniel fell to his knees and clutched his side. A wet substance oozed through his fingers. Memory of the viper bite from the commander's gun flashed through his mind. His hand came away coated in red. A dull ache in his shoulder also pained him, but it wasn't his primary concern.

There's too much blood, thought the veteran. He placed his hand back over the wound. *How much time do I have?*

Madelin watched in dismay, helpless as a baby lamb. A whispered, "My God!" escaped her lips as she knelt next to him. She placed a hand over his in an attempt to stall the bleeding. "We'll get help. I promise."

Her words were like a soothing balm, but the peace was short lived. Voices echoed across the rooftop from the main stairwell. Pounding blows rang out as they discovered the locked door. Summoning his courage, Daniel pushed aside the pain and rose to his feet. He waved Madelin away and prepared himself for another onslaught.

I can't believe I made it through that last meeting, he thought. *But it ain't over. There's more to do and still time enough to salvage something of my life.*

"It's okay… I'll be okay." Daniel lied, taking a few ragged breaths. "Hurry. We've gotta get out of here."

Glancing down the fire escape, they watched the PASTOR agent attempting to extricate himself from the crumpled mass of metal. His efforts looked futile. The other agent lay sprawled at the bottom of the alleyway, unmoving.

Daniel ran through a list of escape plans, counting each one with a finger as circumstances ruled them out one after another. Within seconds, each finger on his free hand was extended, and he could think of nothing else. Accepting the final verdict and the sentence that had been passed, he pointed a blood-soaked hand at the shadowed chimney.

"Get over there. I'll take care of this." His voice was firm and distant.

She obeyed without complaint, which Daniel appreciated, but he couldn't shut out the worry welling up in her eyes. He knew the disappointment and fear she would feel after this was over.

I wish I could stop it, keep her from feeling abandoned. It isn't her fault. She didn't choose for this to happen. Those bastards just keep coming, and they ain't after me. I know Black Force ops when I see them. What the hell is with these guys? he wondered. *Why do they want her so bad?*

Silence answered his questions.

I hope I can last long enough to take some of them with me, he thought, grinding his teeth. *Maybe she'll have a chance if I whittle down their numbers.*

He could feel his blood draining onto his shirt. He applied more pressure and felt the flow diminish. His mind whirled with fatigue... but something plagued him. *I shouldn't even be standin'. Thank God for small miracles. I wasn't able to do as much as I'd hoped, but maybe this'll be enough.*

As the world around him changed, the memory forced him back into one of many nighttime horrors. The doorway to a small mud hut was blockaded with clothes and wood scavenged by mercenaries.

Did I help pile those against the door? The answer that echoed through his mind shamed him further.

He tried to stop his hand from pushing the torch into the thatch roof, but the past couldn't be altered. He shoved the flaming branch deeper, and it illuminated the children within. They stared at him from the dancing shadows, the whites of their eyes pleading for him to stop. The smell of dust and sewage interwove itself with the burning stench of the house, flooding his nostrils as the flames grew. The voices of children, mothers, the elderly, and all that were left in the village, cried out in terror. Their sounds mingled with the now roaring flames.

How many did they stuff into that small cottage?

He had no idea. He hadn't counted at the time, but with each memory it seemed that more eyes stared out at him. He felt as though all the innocents of the world were burning for the sins of those like him. The nauseating odor of cooking flesh swept through Daniel, cutting off his air and threatening to strangle him.

Opening his eyes, the rooftop reeled around Daniel's waterlogged gaze. The sights and sounds of the PASTOR agents breaking down the door reminded him of the job he had to do. Taking a few deep breaths, Daniel urged his legs to work and forced himself over to the unconscious commander. Once there, his knees thudded to the ground. Daniel leaned down and picked up his metallic 9 mm, the closest thing he ever had to a friend, and stashed it under his belt. He ignored the warmth from the smoking barrel that seeped through his clothes. Sliding closer to the grey-haired operative he'd knocked unconscious, he pried the black pistol from his hand and contemplated ending the man's tyranny that very moment. The gun wavered, its barrel mere inches from the man's tar-splotched hair.

I can't do that. He's defenseless. If anything would condemn me this late in the game, it's outright murder. He'll be out long enough for Madelin to get away anyhow, he reassured himself. Conscience urged him to store the gun next to his own. His hand grudgingly followed its orders.

He pushed himself up off his knees. A wave of nausea and dizziness attempted to submerge his consciousness. Fighting the onslaught, the soldier attained his balance just in time. The door across the rooftop buckled as Daniel steadied himself, assuming the calm and composed focus of battle.

* * * *

Madelin paced over to the chimney once again. Watching Daniel waver in the wind like a fragile antenna while the other operatives battered down the door was heartrending. There had to be something she could do, but only one thing came to mind. It was something she had very little control over.

What if I can't do it again? The self-doubt ate at her as she watched Daniel prepare to confront the devils. *I have to try. If I don't, he'll die.*

Madelin stepped up to the brick chimney and summoned the memory of her lost friend. Altran's words echoed through the distortion once again. "Focus… Concentrate and you'll see it. You can do what most can't." His words whispered through her thoughts, so real that Madelin had to remind herself that he was gone. A tear welled up at the thought of him before streaking down her tar-stained face.

Madelin did as he instructed as she stared at the darkened wall, whispering the words time and again as she searched for the dark rosebud. Each crack called to her, but she sought a place far from here. Rough edges appeared as she scanned the rows of bricks.

Eventually, a fine line emerged, curving up into the dagger-like tip of a petal. Centering her attention, the mysterious blossom took shape and began to peel itself from the wall. As it rose from the silent bricks, a tainted life infused it with glossy blackness. The few rays of light pouring around the smokestack reflected off the delicate petals.

Madelin concentrated harder, and other petals took shape, the bud opening itself to her. She was entranced by its dark beauty. As the lustrous, black stem stretched out from the brick partition, needle-sharp thorns surfaced. Looking closer, she noticed that the stem was composed of numerous fine lines. Each stripe glistened wetly in its own separate color, but was overshadowed by the dark nature of the rose. Madelin followed individual lines up the stem, intrigued and horrified by the visible pulse within each one. They were like veins, and the worlds held within their boundaries were the life's blood of the rose.

Madelin's desire spoke from within, and one vein began pulsing more than the others. Its crimson essence oozed from one petal's tip. The vein throbbed faster, matching the rhythm of her heart, and the thick droplets fell to mix with the black tar below.

Madelin grasped the delicate petal and peeled it away from the flower. The blossom didn't resist, but separated from the stem like ripping paper. The tear continued beyond the stem, slicing the bricks apart like a knife through butter. Once the opening was large enough, she let go of the rose petal. It fluttered to the ground and disappeared. The blossom glinted once more in the shadowed light before dying and falling to the floor itself. It too disappeared.

Madelin's gaze shifted back to the rift as a slight breeze caught the edge. It rippled in the wind, and through the movement, she saw a murky, red film separating the two worlds. Beyond that, a dwindling sun highlighted the treetops of a large forest.

Then the rooftop door burst open, bringing this world back into startling focus. A barrage of gunfire lit up her world from the other side of the brick wall. Madelin leaped around the chimney in time to see bullets whiz past her protector, some thudding into the roof at his feet. Spurts of tar flew around him as he returned fire. It was as though his guardian angel had chosen this time to step into the fray. He stood tall in the dimming light, unmoving.

This won't last, she thought as he drew the other weapon and unleashed the fury of both hand cannons. *At least the size of the doorway is holding some at bay.*

His legs were planted for support, but she knew his time was limited. The stain on his shirt grew to encompass his pant leg, and his head drooped with the exertion.

"Daniel," she called out to him, but was drowned out by the roar of gunfire. "Daniel!" she screamed. Her voice cracked with the strain.

Daniel turned his head and spied Madelin waving him over. He continued the rapid fire, but forced his legs into motion. With each footfall, excruciating pain broke through his isolated calm. With the final step, two more pistols boomed in tandem. The first dug into Daniel's muscled calf, and he stumbled into Madelin's arms. The second missed his forehead by a hair.

Madelin caught the brute of a man as he stumbled into her. His tense, muscled body landed in her hands, and his feet tried to hold himself up out of stubborn futility. He clutched his guns in a death grip, and his fingers continued working the triggers, firing the last shots into the rooftop below. The click of hammers finding empty chambers accompanied her words as he gave in and slumped into her arms.

"I've got you, Daniel. I've got you," she whispered.

The petite woman folded her arms around her protector and hefted him to the portal. His shallow breaths caressed her neck.

Thank goodness for small favors, she thought.

Clutching Daniel to her, she lifted him awkwardly over the rift's threshold and through the crimson haze.

Chapter Sixteen

Makeshift Remedies

Madelin's first steps into the new world left her feet submerged in a moss-covered marsh. Looking around, Madelin ignored the strangeness of the environment. She searched for somewhere to lay Daniel and free her hands. A large tree stood a few yards away, its roots elbowing above the marshy surface.

Lugging the well-muscled veteran over, she propped him in its arms and raced back to the portal. Madelin pinched the edges of the tear together, similar to what she'd done before, and watched them merge into a thin scar, sealing out the operatives as soon as they stepped around the chimney. With the rift closed, she turned back to Daniel. His broken body sat slumped over the crooked roots like a fallen king.

He did this to protect me, and he expected to die, she concluded. She was certain of it, but wouldn't allow it to happen.

Madelin sloshed back through the muck and quickly inspected his wounds. She had no medical training that she knew of, but expected the damage to be more severe. The skin around his wounds even appeared to have what looked like new scar tissue forming at its edges, but it was hard to tell with all the blood. *What do I know?* she asked herself.

Ripping small sections from the less stained portions of her kimono, she used them to clean his wounds. Then she folded other strips into squares and covered the bullet holes to stop the bleeding. By the time she was finished, her kimono came to her knees and covered very little of her stomach and arms.

Pulling his button-up off, she tore it into long strips and wrapped them around his torso, shoulder, and leg. Then she pulled his stained undershirt back over his head to hold the bandage in place. Afterwards, she admired her rudimentary medical skills with pride.

It's far from the care he'd receive at a hospital, even the one I left, she thought, *but maybe it will do for now.*

Cupping some water from the marsh, Madelin tipped her hand over his face. The revitalizing water awoke Daniel, wrenching him from the horrid memory he was reliving yet again. He opened his eyes, and a pleasant sight greeted him with a smile.

She looks familiar, but where do I know her from? His memory lapsed from fatigue.

The cool sensation running over him soothed the pain that inflamed his leg and side. Looking up, he lost himself in her emerald eyes. Insects muttered in chorus-like conversation while the last rays of daylight dwindled. Stars were even starting to show overhead.

"Hello there," she said, the words fluttering off her lips like butterflies.

He replied flippantly, "And hello to you, too. This is a hell of a dream, the best I've had in years."

"Dream?" she asked. Her tipped hand stopped midair.

"Yes, course I know it's a dream, but that don't mean you have to stop." His words slurred as though intoxicated.

Madelin cupped another handful of water and poured it over his head. "And why do you think this is a dream?"

"Because if it weren't I wouldn't do this," Daniel replied, his intentions clear to all but the most naïve.

With a time-hardened hand, Daniel pulled her face down to his and caressed her lips. She tried to pull away, but within seconds a sweet affection she had never known delved past her defenses and sought refuge in her emotions. The suddenness of the kiss pushed all logic aside. Her attempts to break the embrace dwindled and then stopped as passion took over. Minutes later, their faces parted. His hand caressed her cheek, and he gazed into her eyes.

She mumbled breathily, "As much fun as that was... I have to say, this isn't a dream."

Daniel's smile disappeared as he jumpstarted his mind, searching his memories for a connection. "What do you mean? I remember getting shot, the nightmares, and then this. It's gotta be heaven or a dream. It ain't what I expected, but I'll take it."

To allay his fears, she said, "Daniel, I shifted us into a different place while you were fighting the agents at your apartment. Remember me waving you over?"

There was little for him to remember outside of the firefight, but he thought he recalled seeing her before passing out. "Yeah... I think I do," he said, somewhat unsure of himself.

"I carried you here and then closed the window." After a moment she continued, "You were bleeding a lot, so I did my best to bandage the wounds. It looks like the one in your calf went all the way through, but the one in your side was deep. I wasn't able to find the bullet. There was a lot of blood, but..." She hesitated, unsure whether it was a good idea to give him hope where there might be none. "But they seem to be healing," she finished. "We should find someone to look at it as soon as we can, though, to be sure. I don't know much about anything, but I tried."

"I'd say you know a mite more than you think," he commended. "I feel much better, so good I coulda swore I'd died and gone to heaven." The reminder of what he had done came to him, and he dropped his head, unable to meet her gaze. "My God, Madelin. I'm so sorry. I ain't got an excuse, 'specially after what you did for me." He would have cursed himself had he not thought it would offend her. "I'm so sorry."

She spoke up with self-assured vigor and tilted his grizzled face up to hers. "It's okay. I understand. It felt great, but my life's sort of confusing right now. I don't know what's going on, or even what's coming around the next corner. As much as I enjoyed it, I think it would be best... simpler, if we just forgot about it for now." Daniel nodded, but his eyes shouted his disappointment. Seeing this, she tried to comfort him. "Maybe we can try it when our lives are figured out. I hardly know who I am right now. Besides, they'll be onto us soon. Maybe we can get a head start before they figure out where we went."

"Okay," came his reluctant reply. After a minute's thought, he probed a bit deeper. "Are you sure you're okay with things the way they are?" An ember of hope seemed to rise from within him at the question.

"For now, yes." Her answer ate at her as she watched the last flaming ember of his passion simmer and die. It was as though she doused his hopes in an endless cascade of water. Pushing his feelings aside, she tried to move on. "Do you think you can walk?"

"For now, yes," he mimicked quietly, the words unconsciously barbed. His thoughts again turned to his accustomed solution, but there wasn't a bottle to be had.

Will I ever find anything stronger than water in this God-forsaken place? His hands shook at the thought.

Suppressing her emotions, Madelin ducked under his arm and helped him to his feet. Once they were situated, she scanned the world around them. Three different moons now stood above in the approaching night, and their colored moonbeams intermingled to cast shadows in odd directions. The moonlight reflected off the marsh water all around in a dazzling ballet of lights. A trail through the forest was lit like twilight runway lights of blue, red, and gold. The path curved in the distance, but something else caught her attention. In that same direction, faint lights glimmered past the trees, drifting through the night. Thinking it might be a village, she set off down the waterlogged, twilight path with her savior in tow.

Daniel tried to bear as much of his own weight as possible and even found a branch to use as a crutch, but his body was still somewhat weak. After a time, he gave in and allowed her to support him over their long march. The pace she set was grueling, but he kept his complaints to himself.

It was rare that she would stop, but the few times she did were blessings. The first time, he leaned against a nearby tree trunk, breathing in the night air and resting his limbs. It was then he wondered how they got here. It had taken a while for her words to sink in, but hours of traveling had given him time to think.

Is it possible she did what she said? Is she insane, or is there more to this?

As his thoughts progressed, exhaustion took hold and he drifted off to sleep. Each break Madelin would interrupt his long sought-after sleep, praise him on his surprising strength, and announce that she hoped to put enough distance between them and Leodenin's men. He was amazed, too. He'd seen people kill over from less strain, but the reminder was enough to bring him back and get them moving again. Fear was a useful motivator.

Chapter Seventeen

Irreparable Mistakes

The sudden thrust of his legs forced Jedd into the adjacent building, but at the moment of impact he vanished.

Sitting on the cheap hotel bed, Altran's eyes jumped open, but he could still see his surroundings from seconds before. The black mane of hair that hung over the dark father's shoulders framed a pale face of hot fury. Smeared blood coated his arms.

How'd I get back here, he wondered, *and how'd I manage to touch Father Leodenin? I remember the fight, but I couldn't touch anything else.* The stack of questions was growing like a pile of his son's dirty laundry.

Unable to focus through the rush of adrenaline, his attention shifted. His thoughts turned to the family he hadn't seen in twelve years.

When did I last see Edwin? he whispered. *He was two. I remember that much. He'd be in high school now.*

He scolded himself for leaving, as he always did, but then reassured himself that it was for the best. If he had stayed, Edwin might not have made it to kindergarten.

And what about Faith? How is she? What kind of life has she led over the last dozen years? Being a single mother must have been difficult... What did I do to my family? The torturous questions ran through his mind. *But Madelin suffered more... much more. How could I leave her alone in the world, at the hands of the agency that killed Lane and Waverly? I had to!* he screamed through his thoughts. *Her parents couldn't do anything for her.*

As the memory of the dream came back, Jedd relished the instant his fists met Father Leodenin's muscled chest. A tainted smile played across his face as he remembered. The shock and pain on the shifter's face brought Jedd pure ecstasy.

As consciousness returned, Jedd's adrenaline level lowered and his muscles slackened. His mind numbed while the memories played through it, eventually returning to the orphaned girl and the knowledge that one broken man was her only defense. His scars proved he had survived vicious opponents and lived to tell the tale.

But how could he have protected her from the agents swarming up the stairwell? I have to go back.

Closing his eyes for yet another journey, he tried to focus on Madelin and where he had been minutes before. Each time, the furious face of Father Leodenin appeared, enraged and in pain. His leg was twisted amidst an assortment of black garbage bags. The PASTOR shifter screamed at him, spittle flying all around. Jedd looked up at the broken stairway and away from the man, but his eyes were drawn back to the crystal-blue gaze. It was as though he had lost control. Letting go of the connection, he drew back into his body, infuriated that he hadn't killed the man.

This isn't good, he thought. *If he's still alive, what happened to Maddy?*

His eyes fluttered open in the cheap hotel room. Bringing himself out of the groggy sleep, a fog of lethargy took hold of his mind. Staring into the room, he could make out vague shapes and colors. This had happened before, but not to this extent. His body felt like churned pudding, and his arms were impossible to lift. Determination set in as his thoughts returned to Madelin.

How can I help her if I can't reach her? he asked, infuriated by his own limitations. *I've gotta find her in person, like I originally planned.*

Summoning the willpower to overcome his body's fatigued state, he pushed away the fog of exhaustion. The world came into focus. With a glance across the room, he scanned the mirror image of himself sitting against the faux-wood headboard. Some of the gauntness had come back.

Feeling seeped into his extremities, and there was a sensation of something congealing to his skin. Jedd looked closer. Something dark had splattered over his clothes and arms. Glancing at his hands, he discovered pints of the dark shifter's blood, remnants of the fight.

Nothing's ever carried over before, but there's still a lot to learn, he reminded himself.

Slipping off the bed, he hobbled over to the hotel sink. He slid his hands and arms through the hot faucet water, ridding himself of the devilish man's blood. Underneath the blood he discovered a host of bruises. His hands were tender and swollen. Aches and pains rippled through them. Running the hot water over his bruised knuckles felt like hell, but began to loosen his muscles. It took effort to unclench his fists.

After a survey of the rest of his body, he grimaced at the multitude of tender brown spots.

Looks like it goes both ways.

Before long his mind drifted back to his goddaughter, caught at the top of that decrepit building. Concerned, he finished and threw on another set of clothes. Jedd gathered the bloodstained clothes and threw them into the trash bin. Tying up the plastic bag, he hefted it and his duffle bag in one hand, while pocketing his cell phone with the other. Jedd slipped a few bills into the rent collector and slipped out of the room.

He headed down the stairs and over to his waiting sedan. Throwing his bags in the trunk, he leapt into the driver's seat. Seconds later, the car was speeding out of the parking lot. The north-eastern side of town was no more than twenty minutes away. If he was going to find her, he had to find her transference point. Jedd pulled out his phone and checked the records he had discovered years before.

Yep, thought so. There's always a transference point. The report called it a 'temporary fingerprint.' He growled when he saw the name scrawled at the bottom of the digital file... 'Father Leodenin.'

The car rocketed over small hills of roadway and past a variety of digital billboards. Passing under the many stoplights, Jedd's thoughts returned to his search. *I hope no one's patrolling these streets. The last thing I need is to get pulled over by a rooky cop, let alone have to explain the stolen car and lack of ID.*

As luck would have it, the patrolmen must have been busy elsewhere. Jedd rolled to a stop at a graffitied stop sign, not far from where he last saw Madelin in this world. Each road was as good as the next. This section of town housed one dilapidated building after another.

"Dammit!" Jedd shouted, slamming his palm down on the steering wheel. *I should have paid attention to where she went. I hope that friend of hers found some way out 'cause this could take a while.*

Choosing the road straight ahead, Jedd stepped on the gas and motored forward.

An hour later, he was still searching. He passed store signs that seemed familiar, but by this point he might have passed the same stores four times or more. Every place looked familiar and his frustration was growing. Glancing down each alleyway, he allowed the car to coast along the road. His nerves were frayed. There had to be a better way to find where she crossed.

Then something unexpected caught his attention down a darkened alley. Jedd slammed on the brakes and stared into the shadowed passage. A dark shape lay huddled on the ground. Questions flew through his head, attempting to make a connection to Madelin.

Could she have attacked someone before slipping through the rip? He couldn't shake the possibility. As he sat there, the car idling in the street, a collection of vehicles honked from behind. Some were accompanied by verbal pleasantries of a more undesirable nature. Spinning the wheel, he pulled to the side and jumped out of the car. Maybe this person could provide some clue. He flew across the street as fast as his feet could take him, ignoring the vulgar insults.

As he approached, subtle differences stood out between the prone man and the agents that had been here before. This man wore blue jeans and a brown, leather jacket. He shivered uncontrollably, but Jedd stood transfixed, hesitant to waste time on a stranger.

What if Madelin's portal is around the next corner? He almost chuckled out of aggravation. He had been saying that for the last hour. It was already too late. He would have to find another way.

Peering down at the man lying before him, his thoughts turned to the crumpled form. Although the sun had dropped behind the mountains, the cool desert winds hadn't picked up yet. He was sweating, yet in the blessed shade of the alley, this man was quivering.

It certainly isn't an agent.

Jedd stepped around him and took a good look at the man's blood-coated face. He had a bulbous, crooked nose, and his eyes were swollen shut. His hands were bloated from countless broken bones. Jedd couldn't tell how bad the man's injuries were, but they were gruesome enough to distort his features. It was hard to gauge through the dried blood and swelling, but he guessed mid-thirties. Jedd glanced down at his watch and grimaced at the reminder. It was almost eight o'clock.

"Dammit!" he cursed under his breath, the reality of the situation setting in.

"H-hello," came a muffled voice from the mound of flesh lying at his feet. In a thick Cajun drawl, he asked, "Is someone there?"

After a few silent minutes, Jedd cursed his luck and answered the man. "Yeah, yeah, I'm here, but I don't have a lot of time. Can I do anything for you?" The flat, uncaring tone of his voice scared him.

What have I become?

Leaving it up to fate, he gave in and committed himself to the welfare of this injured soul.

"Look, man, you seem to be in a bit of a fix. Is there anything I can do?" Jedd asked, actual concern showing through his words.

Sniffling a bit, the bloodied man tried to speak louder, as though making a joke. "Well, if you've got a grand or two you could spare, it would go a long way."

The hearty chuckle that escaped his lips turned into a cough that wracked his whole body. Then the shivers returned. The prone man let out a slow, pain-filled sigh.

"C-could you help me up?"

The man held a swollen hand up to Jedd. One inflamed eyelid opened a slit. It revealed a soul tormented by pain and suffering. Jedd knew that life, the one he saw in the man before him... knew it all too well. Kneeling down, he placed a gentle arm around the man's bruised body and lifted him from the ground.

The limp man anchored his arm around Jedd's shoulders and whispered through a quiet grimace, "Thank you."

The words were sincere, and the stench of sweat and dried blood permeated the man's damp jacket. It occurred to Jedd that this was probably the only help he'd received in a long time.

After hoisting him upright, Jedd propped him against an aluminum trashcan. He turned to face the unsteady man, leaving a hand on his shoulder for support. Jedd knew it was wrong, but it occurred to him that the man was wavering like a drunken monkey he saw on a comedy clip long ago. The memory brought a brief smile to his face, but disappeared as he chided himself for thinking such things. The man had undergone enough abuse to last a lifetime.

"Look, I'm no doctor, but you've gotta be in some serious pain. Let me help you to my car, and we can go see a friend of mine." As he tried to assist the unbalanced man, he was surprised to be pushed away.

"No... no doctors. They ask too many questions." The words came out slurred as he attempted to maintain his balance. Somehow, he managed to stay upright.

"Not this one. She's a friend of mine—no worries." Jedd let the words sink in before asking, "What's your name anyways?"

"Roger."

"And how'd you get in this mess?"

Jedd had a pretty good idea that Roger had a gambling problem and paid the price for it. Jedd was never much of a risk taker, but he'd been through his share of close scrapes. Some good friends had gone down a disturbing path because of the addiction. Flashes of old friends, long gone due to unfortunate circumstances and a few badly thrown snake eyes, crossed his vision.

Roger mumbled, "Lady Luck left me high and dry last night."

Coaxing Roger with an arm over his shoulders, he eventually leaned into Jedd for support and shuffled across the street to the waiting sedan. After getting the unlucky man situated in the back seat, he started the car and hit the speed dial for Maria. She picked up after the third ring.

"Hello," echoed a feminine, Spanish accent.

"Hey, Maria! Long time no hear. It's Crux," he replied, as though speaking with a long-lost friend.

He had never liked the nickname, but after the patch-up job she did for him, he couldn't bring himself to dissuade her from using it. There had been nowhere else for him to turn. Besides, it afforded him some anonymity. To this day, she hadn't asked for his real name.

"Well hello, stranger," came the melodious voice with more familiarity.

"I thought I might stop by. I've got something that needs looking at. You got the time?"

"Now, don't tell me you went and fell down the stairs again. That bullet was hard to find." The absurdity of his earlier excuse hadn't been forgotten.

"No, not at all. I have a friend I'd like you to meet. He's anxious to see you." Earlier in his life, the vagueness of such conversations would have seemed impossible to keep track of, but he had learned.

"Okay, I get off in a half hour. Meet me there."

Hanging up the phone, Jedd turned at the light and sped up the I10 ramp. He would have to push it to get to Maria's in time. The sedan roared as he floored the pedal. Switching into gear, it settled back into a mechanical rhythm. Glancing in the rearview mirror, Jedd smiled as Roger slid across the back seat, as content as a baby with the engine crooning its soothing lullaby.

At least he isn't shivering like before.

The half-hour drive across town gave Jedd time to consider his options and what the next step would be. The panic and frustration he felt before had passed and been replaced with hope and determination. If the rugged man she was with was unable to protect her, he was certain the PASTOR agents had been ordered not to harm her. She's of no use to them dead. He wanted to contact her again, but the fact that Leodenin had controlled his focus was troubling and something that would have to be dealt with.

Besides, driving while asleep probably wouldn't be the best idea, thought Jedd with a laugh. *I'll deal with it later, when I've got the time.* He hated to put her off, but now wasn't the time.

His thoughts went to the man she befriended. *Why's he helping her? What does he stand to gain?*

Before he came up with an answer, they entered the warehouse district. The sedan came to an open gate of rusted, chain-link fence topped with barbed wire. A faded sign hung off the fence. 'No Trespassing.'

Passing beyond the old gate and into the large expanse of overgrown parking lots, Jedd angled the car toward a small cluster of buildings on the far end of the lot. As they drew closer to a small, white building, he saw Maria's extended SUV parked alongside. Jedd pulled up next to the building, behind her vehicle, and rounded the car to help Roger out of the back seat. The disheveled man stumbled over the warehouse's threshold and into the building with Jedd's assistance. Stepping into the unlit room felt eerie, and the stale air greeted him like a meat locker. A light illuminated an opaque curtain in the corner opposite him. Without a word, Altran cradled the hurt man around the waist and pulled him to the enclosed area. Jedd stepped through the plastic curtains and found a dark-haired Maria laying out her instruments on a metal stand.

Chapter Eighteen

Cash Only

"W"ow, Maria, you look great. What've you been up to?" The small talk had become normal on the few visits Jedd made to this warehouse, even while she was stitching him up. It helped distract him since she only used mild anesthetics.

"Thanks," Maria replied with a grin, but her mind was on the necessity for her services. Business first. "So where's this friend of yours?" Looking up from her instruments, she found the answer to her question sliding off Jedd's shoulder.

The sight of Roger changed her demeanor in an instant. She grabbed his other arm and helped him onto the medical bed. After getting him situated, she reached into a metal bowl and drew out a damp, white hand towel. She rinsed his face and arms, careful not to apply too much pressure. Roger winced a couple times, but otherwise looked as though he had drifted off to sleep.

Jedd almost continued the banter, but then thought better of it as he watched her hands and face. They moved with a diligent and firm certainty. Roger was the patient this time, and Jedd noticed a few things he hadn't before. Maria stood straight and thin, a lab coat housing her slender body. Her black hair was pulled into a ponytail that revealed high cheekbones and dark eyelashes. They complimented her dark skin tone. She wore very little make up, but glowed with a natural, Mexican beauty. She had been out in the sun recently, and the deep tan helped to enhance her good looks.

Before his thoughts could continue, he was interrupted by Maria's firm, professional voice. "So what's his name?"

With reality setting in, Jedd suppressed his desires and focused on the question. "Oh… uhh… Roger."

Maria's dark eyes sought him out with a questioning, sidelong glance. "Roger… What about a last name?"

The one, solitary, probing question was more than she'd asked anytime before, but he'd put her reputation on the line by asking her to help someone new. Her motivation occurred to him. He knew what was about to come, but answered honestly, "I don't know."

She had no reaction, just continued to poke and prod various spots on Roger's arms and face.

"What happened to him? Did you push him down the stairs?"

"He got beaten to a pulp, I guess," Jedd replied, trying to infuse the statement with a bit of uncaring laughter, but it faded at the look she shot him. "From the little he said, I figure he has a gambling debt and couldn't pay up. He's a very recent acquaintance."

Maria's anger flared. Her accent made the words almost indistinguishable. "You haven't known him long enough to figure out more than his first name, yet you felt it was okay to put my neck on the line! Do you even know if it's his real name? If he owes somebody money, how long do you think it'll be before my name comes up? I don't need calls from bookies or other crooks..." In anger, her rapid words transitioned into harsh, inflected Spanish before trailing off.

Jedd stared at her blankly. Turning away, she glared at the metallic ceiling high above them and searched for some logical explanation for why he'd enlisted her help. After a few minutes, she assumed her professional demeanor and turned back to the patient, unbuttoning his shirt for a closer look.

Jedd interrupted her thoughts with apologetic words. "I trust him."

Her fingers paused at one of Roger's shirt buttons before she mumbled, "How could you? You've known him for how long?" All pretenses had disappeared with her outburst, but at least her calm demeanor had returned.

"I know his kind...," he began, but trailed off to a whisper.

He wanted to say more, to tell her that he was just like him, a man suffering through life, unable to get a grip on anything—a tide of unfulfilled expectations and inevitable death buffeting him from all sides, threatening to throw him over the waterfall of mortality at any minute. But that was too much. His secrets were his own, now, as they had been for more years than he could count.

He left off with downcast eyes and the final word on Roger. "I trust him as I do myself."

No more was said. Jedd turned and walked through the fold in the curtain and headed for a dark corner. Now was the time to think about more important matters. *Where's Madeline?* Finding a spot on the concrete floor, he sat down and propped his back against a steel column. With legs outstretched, he watched Maria's shadow work through the drawn curtain before sleep overtook him.

Jedd found the search for Madelin to be much more difficult than he expected. The most recent attempts had placed him in her vicinity, but this time Jedd appeared in the sky far above the city. Looking down, he watched a multitude of people heading to and from work. The echo of cars honking and people shouting carried on the winds. Concentrating on Madelin didn't help. Considering the worst possible outcome, he was left heartbroken.

If she wasn't able to escape, will I at least be able to find her body?

Unwilling to accept the possibility, Jedd flew closer to the city for a better look. He began what might prove to be an endless and futile search by skimming overtop. His thoughts combed through the crevices. The more rundown areas of town were closest, so he went to the north-east side first. Searching the crowded streets was tedious, but if they'd somehow cloaked her signal or something had been done to her, he would never forgive himself for not checking every possibility. She could have changed clothes, so basing the search on her attire wasn't enough. Willing himself down to the streets below, he searched face after face.

After hours of thorough investigation, and having covered only a fraction of the city, he found himself drained and depressed. Unable to focus, he lifted himself higher, to the tops of the buildings, and scanned the rooftops and windows. He now knew this section of town well enough to draw out each block and building in minute detail. However, the effort seemed to have been in vain.

Jedd gave up and let himself be drawn back into his body. Having adjusted to the trip, he felt nothing of the queasiness that plagued him days before. He awoke on the cold, concrete floor, his limbs numbed by the moist, refrigerated air filtering into the building. He wished the deadness could spread, encapsulating his heart and freeing him from the decisions that had tormented him for so long. Now he felt nothing but sadness—complete and utter futility. His failure weighed on him, as though he were the Greek God Atlas, holding the world on his shoulders.

As his eyes adjusted to the darkness, Jedd glanced at the backlit corner of the building. Maria was nowhere to be seen, but Roger was stirring on the medical bed. He had no wish to move, just to die where he lay, but his curiosity tugged at him. Pulling himself off the floor, Jedd attempted to work out the kinks and stiffness that had invaded his back and made his way toward the makeshift operating room.

Once he stepped into the light, Roger drowsily looked his way, attempting to focus on what Jedd concluded must be three different versions of him.

Evidently the drugs are in full swing.

Much of the swelling had abated, and the stranger's face was clear of blood, but a few cuts and a lot of bruises were now visible. The patient's shirt hung over his shoulder while he lay sprawled on the bed, one foot dangling off the side. Looking Roger over, Jedd noticed that his nose was still bent and crooked. This wasn't the first time it had been broken. There were a few scars on his arms that the bandages failed to cover, but what stood out most was the navy tattoo on his bicep.

Potius Mori Quam Foedar, he read to himself. The Latin phrase seemed familiar, but outside of computers, languages had never been his forte.

Shifting his head to see the newcomer better, Roger opened his eyes and swallowed deeply before speaking. "Hey, I remember you."

"Good to hear. Has your head cleared a bit?"

"Yeah it has." Roger's hands roamed over the various bandages Maria had applied. "Your lady friend knows what she's doing."

"She's good at what she does," Jedd replied, his thoughts turning to her earlier rampage. He was ashamed of his reasons for trusting this man, but the familiarity was too much. He couldn't bring himself to leave the man lying in the alleyway. Clearing his throat, he asked, "How's everything else feeling?"

"A mite better than before. That's for sure. The Latino gal gave me some pills to dull the pain." The potent drugs allowed his natural Cajun accent to distort his speech, slurring his words like a drunken sailor, but it was still an improvement from before. Raising himself onto a wavering elbow, he shook the bottle. It was almost overflowing.

"That should last you a while."

"Hopefully I won't have to go through them too fast. Some of these might be good for later. Ya never know when ya might get in a scrape. That's my motto."

Jedd pulled a solitary chair out of the corner and seated himself next to Roger's bed. With the mention of mottos, he had to ask. "How about that one on your arm? What's it mean?"

The reminder of the past shook Roger, and anguish flowed into his eyes. He slid back onto the mobile hospital bed and shut his eyes to the world before speaking. "It's a motto I adopted long ago, but have a hard time livin' up to." Pointing at the tattoo, he translated the Latin phrase, "That means, Death Before Dishonor."

Jedd had heard it before, many years ago. It was yet another fragile connection in a small, disturbed world. Lane Boatweit, a dear friend, had had the same tattoo emblazoned on his shoulder—a remnant from his stint in the navy.

"Military?" he asked.

Roger's voice became distant as though speaking to Jedd from another time, but he was still listening. "Yeah, I did some time in the navy—probably the best years of my life. As soon as I took the helm though, things spiraled out of control."

Jedd considered his own mishaps and bad luck before commenting, "I know what you mean. Life can sometimes be brutal."

"In the service I didn't have to worry about anything other than where a little spare cash might come from." Roger narrated the story, reliving a dozen years under curtained eyelids. "I didn't have to worry about betting so much that I couldn't eat, or pay the rent. I won my fair share on the ship. Enough that I could buy a carton of smokes here and there on someone else's dime. I was on easy street."

A subtle smile appeared as the lone man's story spoke of better times, but flipped the next moment. "Then I got out, and my luck went down the crapper. Everything changed... I got discharged for medical. They said I couldn't keep up with the other seamen. I was even up for my next rate, but as soon as we hit port, they tossed me out on my ass so quick, I nearly took out the beam." The last statement came out with a drunken laugh, as though the end of his happiness, even narrated, should be told with a smile.

"I don't blame them, though. It was my own damn fault. I got caught up in the cards. We even played when we was on watch. I was supposed to be trainin', and all I'd be thinking about was Aces, Kings, and Flushes. Hell, I'd even dream about them damn cards. And it wasn't no better when I got out. It just got worse." As Roger's discourse continued, the meds faded, but his Cajun drawl persisted.

There were few interruptions as Jedd agreed or commented on his experiences, but Roger's decisions tormented him. No matter what he did, he always suffered in the end. By the time Roger finished, Jedd felt a kinship to this man, something he lost when Lane was killed.

"And what do you have to show for it now?" he asked, referring to his choices.

"Not a damn thing," Roger replied. "How about yourself? Ya got any vices ya can't seem to throw overboard?"

After reflecting on his own life, Jedd considered divulging a bit of his past to his new acquaintance. Normally alarms would sound when he got this close to letting someone in, but this time all he heard was silence. "More than we've got time for, but one in particular has me doubled over and screaming for mercy right now." He sighed before explaining further, as though the telling gave him release. "I lost my family years ago. What's worse is... it was my choice. They're still livin' and all, but my presence put them in danger."

"Man, that's harsh," said Roger, meaning every word. Taking an interest, he hoisted himself up on one elbow.

Jedd's head was bowed as he spoke to the floor, as though it would help keep his secret. The words flowed from him, allowing him to feel relief after so many years of isolation. So engrossed were they that neither heard the slight shuffle of Maria's footsteps as she made her way out of the darkened office and up to the backlit curtain. Hearing the soft baritone and tenor voices, she stopped and listened.

"I got responsibilities that I have to take on, because no one else can do them."

Roger interjected, "But ya got family responsibilities too, man, don't you?"

"Yeah, but there's no one that can do this other thing, and I made a promise." After a short pause, Jedd pleaded, "A little girl's life depends on it. My son... as much as I love him... he has his mother. This little girl's got no one. I'm damned if I do, damned if I don't."

Roger watched the top of Jedd's dark head bob, but said nothing as his grief audibly ate through the inner cage of turmoil that had held it silent, now revealing itself to the world like a mischievous, birthday-cake leprechaun. The shame and betrayal was mirrored on Roger's face as he watched with heartfelt pity.

Maria listened behind the opaque curtain, the starless sky of the building showering her in darkness. Tears created rivers that no dam could stop and hung from the base of her chin like stumps of shattered icicles.

Echoing Jedd's logical mind, Roger broke the silence. "Then ya had to, man. We're all dealt a shitty hand at times, and yours seems worse than most, but ya had to."

Jedd's muffled voice echoed off the floor. "I know. I keep telling myself that... but did I really? She isn't my real daughter, but my family doesn't know the truth. They can't know. No one can..."

"Look, man, I know it's hard. I had a wife... no kids, but I had a wife. She left me and took everything left from our marriage—and with her went the little pride I had left. I've been tossed a bum rap, but most of it was my own doin'." The admittance was difficult for Roger to say, but he pushed on. "The one thing I can say is that at least those were my choices, no one else's, and I've got to live with them. And so do you." He grimaced as a cramp swept through the bandages and up his side. The bruises were giving him a bit more trouble as the meds wore off. Popping the cap on the bottle, Roger threw two pills down his gullet and swallowed.

Jedd couldn't deny the logic of Roger's argument. *I'm feeling sorry for myself while Madelin's still out there,* he thought. *I haven't found her yet, but she's got to be there.*

Taking hold, the programmer met the concerned face atop the medical bed. "You're right. I can't feel sorry for myself, especially while she's out there." Sitting back in the chair, he let the cool air fill his lungs, in control once again.

A sniffle announced the presence of Maria as she swept aside the curtain. Stepping in, she said, "Good to see you both awake."

A sorrowful glance told him how long she'd been listening. He couldn't blame her, considering the pack of lies he told the last few times they met, but he was sure she understood why they were necessary.

Maria split the sandwich she made for Roger in two and handed half to each of them. "Is it just me, or do the two of you look like you've been through a meat grinder?"

The memory of the gauntness he'd seen in the mirror haunted him. He was so caught up in his search for Madelin and his own self-pity that he hadn't considered how he must look.

"Uhhh... it's been a long day," he replied.

"Not long enough to do that, *mi amor.*" Her voice was flecked with some of its previous lightheartedness. "Eat. It should help. Unfortunately, I only have the bread and meat."

Roger accepted his graciously, his eye brightening with her appearance and the gift of food. "Ya certainly know the way to a man's heart, don't ya, beautiful?"

With an appreciative smile and a light pat on his cheek, she turned and disappeared the way she came.

A rueful smile played across Roger's lips as he admired the sandwich. Without another thought he dove into it, devouring the crumbs and licking his fingers afterwards. Jedd ate his slower, his concentration focused on Madelin.

Chapter Nineteen

A Consequence to Every Choice

A faint image of the man he grappled seconds before hovered in front of Father Leodenin, glimmering in the fading sunlight. He unleashed every vulgar word that came to mind. But, while preparing for the next verbal onslaught, Jedd vanished. Leodenin scanned the alley from his prone position amongst the garbage, but didn't find him.

There must be more to this world than I thought, he concluded. *Judging from how closely linked the worlds are, I expected things to be different, but not like this. Each world seems full of unforeseen developments.*

Once the distraction was gone, a sharp pain coursed up his leg. He cursed, but searched for the source amongst the black, plastic bags. His foot poked out from under one, moist and sticky to the touch. The pant leg clung to him like a leech. The false father clenched his jaw against the rotting stench and lifted the bag with a grimace, then threw it across the pavement, into the wall opposite him.

"That'll be impossible to get out," he growled.

Leodenin willed the leg to move, but it failed to respond. Instead, his side twinged. The feeling was excruciating. Teeth clenched, he grasped his thigh and calf in trembling hands, twisting them back into place. A roar of pain clenched his stomach in an iron fist, tightening with each second. He gasped and fought to contain the scream that rose inside. The facility's doctors had forced him into test after grueling test, but this was agonizing beyond belief.

Leodenin pulled a wallet-sized container from his belt and removed a syringe of liquid Satia—an experimental cocktail combining anesthetic, painkillers, and growth hormones. He popped the top, plunged it into his leg, and injected the contents. The man's face defied logic and paled further. He gnawed at the air as the chemicals forced his body into overdrive. He held the limb still until the bones fused together. A short time later, the anesthetic kicked in and the ragged breaths came easier. He stowed the medical package and crawled off the large pile. Testing the leg, he found that normal mobility had returned.

One thing those docs do well is fix a good cocktail. If they could just figure out which chemicals should kick in first.

Leodenin shook off the remnants of nausea and looked up the alley. A bodyguard lay in a pool of blood just yards away. Above, the stairway fought to submerge another man in a heap of rusting metal. As he ground his teeth, something caught his attention. He shifted it with his tongue and spat onto the concrete. A tooth peered out from the glob of bloody spittle. Dismissing the sight with a snort, he turned toward the doorway he'd entered minutes before.

How many of my men survived? I hope that annoying commander made it. I was just getting to like him. It would be a shame to lose him before the task was done.

Father Leodenin rounded the corner to find another body face-up on the sidewalk. Bullet holes riddled the man's vest and shoulder. It wouldn't have been fatal, but the fall finished the job. Blood caked the man's sandy hair and seeped out from beneath him.

I knew this one—Shanahan, I believe Marlin called him. This was his second in command. How many men does it take to capture a simple girl, unless the same thing that attacked me went after the others? I'll find the man who did this.

Just then, some of his operatives stepped out the front door. Five disheveled men smiled when they saw him up and about, but the grins faded as their eyes found Shanahan at his feet.

"Where the hell is Marlin?" barked Leodenin, jolting their gaze.

The closest one responded. "Sir, he's on the roof with Frank."

"Are these the only two we lost?" he demanded in a tone that would sever stone.

"Y-y-yes, sir."

"Did we get her?"

The men standing behind the vocal operative cast their eyes to the ground. Hesitant, the agent answered, "No, sir."

Leodenin's previous frustration flared, illuminating his eyes. "And then there were six," he muttered with a frustrated shake of his head.

The operative rattled off, "Sir, she made another portal, and they disappeared before we could reach them."

The man's firm voice amazed him. It revealed none of the fear Leodenin saw in his brown eyes. "Then, how the hell did these men die if they ran away?" Each word was flecked with outrage.

"Sir, the fire escape buckled when Gabe fell off the roof. He's okay, though, just a little bruised—nothing we aren't used to." A look in Leodenin's eyes brought him back to the father's question. "We found the stairway from inside and went to the top, but it was locked..."

Leodenin ignored the rest and marched through the group, into the building. The agents followed at a distance.

"Where the hell is this stairway?" the long-haired father shouted.

"Down there," answered the young man, leading him through the lengthy hallway and up the shadowed stairs.

Upon reaching the top, they arrived at a passage that almost resembled a doorway. Bullets pockmarked the shattered door frame and the wall behind it. The setting sun outlined Marlin, who stood on the rooftop, leaning over one remaining agent. Frank sat against the parapet, pulling off his body armor and bloody shirt. Once free of the encumbrance, Marlin handed him a container of salve and patted his back.

"Clean it up, soldier. You did well."

Frank nodded and did as he was told.

Leodenin strode over to Marlin, his relief at seeing the man alive lost in the fury of his eyes. "How the hell did you fail to capture a simple, little girl with amnesia?"

"Dammit, Leo! Shut your trap."

Marlin's retort further fueled Leodenin's fire, but before he could react, the commander grabbed his jacket collar and flung him into the smokestack.

From an inch away, Marlin rasped, "Now listen here, you sniveling brat. You may be in charge of this mission, but these men are my responsibility, and you can't do a damn thing without us. I don't need you throwing failure in their faces when they did their damnedest. They saved my life at the expense of two of their own—and all for a simple little girl! If you and the docs had done your jobs, we wouldn't be on this ridiculous crusade in the first place." Marlin held tight, allowing his words to sink in. "If you need to say something to me, do it in private. Now, I'm gonna take care of my men and deal with those we lost at the hands of... What did you call her? Oh, right, a 'simple, little girl.'"

Leodenin stared back through eyes of ice as the commander released his jacket. He even surprised Marlin by stepping so close that he could smell the trash adorning his clothes. In a voice of steel, Leodenin said, "I hear you. Now, you listen to me. This is my mission, and your failure is my failure. The longer we have to follow this girl, the more difficult it'll be to get us back. So if you want any chance at returning to that shit hole you call home, you better hope you picked the right men for the job and take care of business. As for time, there isn't any. Remember those flashing lights and autos that came rushing up as soon as we appeared? How long do you think it'll take them to get here after all the gunfire you let loose?"

Turning away, Leodenin shifted his arctic gaze to the agent who led him up the stairs. "You, what's your name?"

The operative hesitated and would have shied away had he not been singled out. "Samson, sir."

Leodenin suppressed the coals burning inside and attempted to sound more personable, almost conversational. "Okay, Samson, where's this portal?" A puzzled look appeared on the young man's face, but he led the shifter to chimney.

Maybe Marlin was right, a little kindness will go far... at times, thought Leodenin, although he would never say as much aloud.

"It isn't there now but it was, I swear," admitted the young operative, an edge of panic underlying his words.

To Leodenin, the scarred reality stood out in stark contrast to the fading light. "I believe you. Go see to your comrade."

Once he was out from under the father's gaze, Samson allowed an audible sigh of relief.

Good, thought Leodenin, *they still fear me.* He knelt next to the scar and traced it with a magic finger. Each line hid just beneath the surface. Separate stripes attempted to rise at his touch, allowing him a brief sense of the world it led to. He thumbed through the alternate realities, his fingers working as though searching files in a cabinet. Each one, while different from the last, failed to give him the familiar sense he knew to be Madelin's.

The tall man lowered himself to one knee and peered closer at the planar webs. His lengthy bangs fell into his face, but he didn't notice. His fingers delved further into the depths, leaving behind all worlds with any semblance to this reality. Seconds passed like days before his forefinger caressed a blood-red string hidden amongst the others.

Astonishing! How did she go so far?

The distinct touch and smell of Madelin clouded his senses and pushed the question aside. Again, there was something dark in its touch, a lingering taint from Madelin's rift. The first time he suspected it was specific to the plane, a remnant separate from the shifter, but this wasn't coincidence. Running his thumb and forefinger along the scarred tissue, the muted, red filament rose to his touch, enhancing the taint reminiscent of Madelin.

This has to be part of her ability, but it's so peculiar. How could an innocent girl have such a presence, and what does it mean? Her essence feels stronger, more developed than before. She's learning fast, but how? He added yet another question to his broadening list as the sound of sirens grew in the distance.

Without removing his eyes from the pulsating string, he shouted, "Marlin. Get over here."

Minutes passed before the commander trudged around the chimney. "What is it, Leo?"

The stooped man forced down his annoyance, then asked, "Are we ready to go?"

"Well, from the sound of things, we better be. More importantly, are you?"

"Yeah. She chose a very different one, so be ready for some surprises."

"Great! That's just what we needed, more surprises," Marlin barked with a sadistic laugh. "Line up. We're leaving." Within seconds the remaining operatives were organized behind him, including a half-dressed Frank.

One thing I have to give the old man, thought Leodenin, *his guys respond at a moment's notice. Not once have I heard a complaint from them, at least none about their commander. There've been a few regarding me, but that's nothing. What does it matter what a few stiffs say anyway? So long as they do their job, that's enough for me. Machiavelli once said, "It is far safer to be feared than loved."*

He returned his attention to the bricks and searched for his diamond-blessed steed. It didn't take long for the stallion to appear. Sensing his impatience, the horse bounded up to the edge and leapt out onto the wall. Leodenin traced the scar, highlighting the chosen thread as it pulsed under his finger. The miniature animal followed his directions without fail, running along the indicated path, its hooves slicing through the scar before retreating into the depths of the wall.

Leodenin stepped back to gaze through the hazy partition. A forest stood beyond the window. He nodded to the rift and lifted one side. This time, the men didn't hesitate. After each had passed through, Leodenin lifted the tail of his duster and followed, leaving the authorities to deal with the bodies below.

The sudden sensation of water filtering into his boot was a revelation. His injured leg was still numb, but the other spoke volumes about the differences between worlds. He knew it would be unlike his world, but he hadn't expected this. Turning around, he sealed the rift and watched the scar form over the opening. Then, he looked to his surroundings. Each man appeared as a ghost of a different shade depending on where he faced, and not one, but three moons stood tall in the night sky. One was an all too familiar yellow, while the others were new.

The first was blood red and matched the cord that led him here. The other stood tall but shadowed and cast a mottled, blue hue upon the world. The three moon's rays intermingled across the waters. A rainbow of cascading colors rippled across silent waves. Even the insects shone under the moonlight, shifting colors with each turn they made.

This is more than I expected. The foliage looks the same, but it's hard to believe that once this world and mine were one. What happened to change it? Marlin's voice brought him back to reality.

"Dammit!" the older operative muttered, smacking the device in his hand. The screen flared back to life but refused to acknowledge Madelin's signal. He slapped it again. "Son of an illegitimate whore," he swore, as though the mother's legitimacy mattered. This process repeated itself before Marlin realized he had an audience.

He froze and Leodenin guffawed, as did most of the men. Those not caught up in the scene were new recruits, Samson and another man with a youthful complexion. They stared at the others, uncertain how to react.

Marlin slipped the mobile tracking unit into his pocket and wiped his sweaty palms on his jacket. "It isn't funny, Leo. This damn thing's broken. It can't pick up on that girl of yours at all."

"It's okay," Leodenin replied, attempting to subdue his own laughter. "I can find her." The words came out self-assured, as though he knew something no one else did. After a few minutes, the laughter was reduced to sporadic chuckles, and Leodenin assumed his businesslike temperament.

Two auras drifted through the forest ahead. One, a vibrant green, somehow reminded him of Madelin, while the other, a muted gray, remained unidentified. *Maybe this world has some unforeseen advantages*, thought Leodenin with a smile. He pointed at her aura and led the march through the six-inch-high water. "There, she's that way."

Seeing nothing but dim forest and swaying shadows, Marlin quirked an eye and cracked his lips, but thought better of questioning the father in front of the men. Marlin motioned the men to follow and joined the shifter as he high stepped through the muck. "How do you know?" he murmured. "You didn't even check the area."

"I just know. A quirk of this world is that I can see her, even at this distance."

Marlin sloshed through the murky swamp with skepticism creasing his face, but it hid in the varied lights of the moons.

A couple of hours into the trip, the father muttered, "She's noticed us. They picked up the pace and are veering off."

"How the hell can she see us?" Marlin hissed.

"I told you. I see her, so I'm sure she sees me, too."

Leodenin could tell the commander wished to say something more, but Marlin kept his opinion to himself. The silence of the swamp was only disturbed by their footfalls and the nightlife fluttering around them. The shifter quickened his pace, and the others matched it. If they moved fast enough, they could intercept the fugitives.

The marshy terrain sloshed around them and threatened to consume their boots with each step, but the men plodded on. Startled insects leapt away as they jogged past. Each hour they altered course, veering with their prey. The long-haired father's thighs burned with the grueling pace, but he tried not to show it. None of the agents were visibly fatigued, so Leodenin gritted his teeth. Somehow, they were gaining on the two runners, even through the torrential rainstorm that sprung up in the night. The men were astounded by the multicolored droplets illuminated in the moonbeams, and the bone-shattering thunder that accompanied the deluge.

It's a test of wills, thought Leodenin, reveling at the challenge. Gusting wind and sheets of rain enveloped him. Dense fog rose from the waters.

Chapter Twenty

Truth or Lies?

With his mouth still full, Roger commented, "Hey, buddy, I never got your name. Ya got mine, while I'm left wonderin'."

Caught up in the conversation, Jedd had forgotten about the formalities. "Sorry, Roger." He lowered the volume to a whisper. "It's Jedd... Jedd Altran."

The change clued Roger into something he hadn't realized. "Wait up. Ya mean to tell me, Maria don't even know that name?"

"Something like that. We know each other on a more professional level that requires a necessary vagueness." Jedd peered deep into Roger's eyes as he said this, reinforcing the significance of the statement.

Buying into the story, Roger lowered his own voice. "How do I know this is your real name? How do I know ya aren't just playing me like the guys who juiced me up last night?"

Jedd's face adopted every facet of seriousness before he answered with a pointed finger, "Roger, do you think I would've introduced you to Maria, a friend who should not be discussed outside of our little circle," he reminded him, "if I'd meant you any harm? Let alone picked your swollen ass up off the sidewalk?"

With a chuckle, Roger held up a hand as though waving a white flag and pleaded through his laughter, "Okay, okay... I give. Ya got me there. My head must still be swimmin' a bit. Besides, those guys have it out for me. I'm supposed to have a grand to them by the end of the day."

Reminded of the more immediate threat looming over Roger's head, Jedd asked with concern, "So, what are you going to do?"

"No idea, Jedd." The name rolled off his tongue without hesitation. "I know I don't have the money."

"Well, I could get the money, but if I did it would come from somebody else's pocket." After a moment's pause for thought, Jedd mumbled as though someone might be listening around a curtained corner, "Do they deserve the money? How'd you lose it?"

Roger considered his answer. It was an odd thing to ask. "Well, there's a lot of people who've got money and don't deserve it, but I did lose the money legit like in a game of cards." He allowed his answer to sink in before adding a moment later, "I don't think the real question has to do with who deserves what... The real question's one I've had a hard time dealin' with for years: What's the honorable thing to do?"

The question forced Jedd to a shuddering stop and threw all thoughts out of orbit. The words echoed through his memories, but the voice was different. How long had it been since his old friend Lane had said those words to him? He was certain Madelin couldn't remember her father, but Jedd's memory of him was vibrant and alive, which made reality that much more unbearable.

"Honor's something I don't have much time to think about, but I do understand."

Jedd considered the reaction of the unfortunate person who would find their bank account coming up short and knew it wouldn't be right to float Roger the money. *It's not mine to give,* he thought. *Besides, I could never pay it back. Food and other necessities are one thing, but paying off Roger's debt is another entirely.*

As the answer became clear, Jedd spoke up with finality, "If it's a question of honor, then I can't get you the money."

Roger shook his head, having come to the same conclusion. "And I couldn't take it, even if ya were willin'. Like I said, we all have to live with our decisions. I bet what I didn't have. Unfortunately, it looks like your lady friend may have gone to all this trouble for nothin'. These guys ain't forgivin', but it's what I deserve."

Thinking fast, Jedd couldn't help but contradict the last statement. Roger's immediate willingness to give up was irritating. "Well, if it's what you deserve, a higher power will decide it. Don't give up. Take your life back, and let fate decide. You can't live in fear."

How can he get out of this? Jedd considered. *If he's limited to doing things honorably, there isn't much he can do. But what if he comes with me?*

"Roger, what if I can show you an option that'll give you time?"

"What do ya mean?"

"I think I know how to find my little girl, and it might also be a solution to your problem."

With his interest piqued, Roger leaned in. "How so?"

"Well, that's where it gets a little complicated. You'll just have to trust me when I say, I can take you where they'll never find you."

"Wait a second," interrupted Roger. "I know how I've lived, but if I'm to make some changes, I can't run away. Besides, these guys'll find me wherever I go."

"No, no, no," Jedd reassured him. "Look... the responsible thing would be to pay them back. If you can't do that right now, and they're not gonna give you the time, then you have to find a safe place until you have the money. Then you can pay them back later, with interest. That would be the most honorable way to take care of things."Roger leaned back on the bed in thought as Jedd added, "Besides, you'd be helping to save the life of an innocent, young girl."

Roger interlaced his fingers behind his head and weighed his options. This was a chance to repay Jedd's kindness and trust while also doing the responsible thing, in a roundabout way. Speaking up from his prone position, Roger said, "Okay, I'm in. I owe ya big for what ya done for me. What do I have to do, and where can we go?"

Jedd pondered the question for a minute. *Roger's doing this to pay me back, but how far will that loyalty go? I've seen these debts forgotten too often when times get tough. For the last thirteen years, people've been trying to kill me and my family. The road ahead's gonna be rough.*

Unwilling to allow Roger to walk into the same situation his family had been in, he added, "Look, Roger, I don't want you to do this out of some feeling of obligation. My life is full of people trying to kill me. I've even had to kill myself to stay under the radar." The shock and realization of what he had said stunned Jedd into a moment of silent reflection. "According to the real world, I'm dead," he clarified with a nod.

Gathering his bearings, he continued, "This is a solution, and it'll allow you some safety from those guys who're looking for you, but don't think it'll be a cake walk. With me you'll have to deal with my problems, too. It might be like jumping out of the frying pan and into the fire." Jedd let that sink in a moment. "Don't get me wrong, I could use your help and so could Madelin, but I don't want you to walk into something without knowing what you're up against."

Roger chewed on this new information. "Jedd, listen. I get what you're saying... I do. It ain't a problem. I deal with things when they come up, and I can't leave here the same man I was when I stumbled in." Indicating the tattoo on his own shoulder, he continued, "This is what I've got to get back to. This is who I really am. Ya saved my life, whether ya believe it or not, and ya ain't gettin' rid of me with a few stories about bogeymen. I'm a man who pays back his debts."

The last statement was said with finality, and Jedd could see the determination in Roger's face. There was no hope of dissuading this man if he wanted to. A smile crept up on him as he watched the loyal nature of his friend. Offering a hand, Roger took it, but winced at the pressure.

Then the gambler asked, "So, what do we do now?"

"That's a little complicated."

The vague answer caused Roger's brows to furrow.

Jedd explained further, "I wasn't able to find Madelin before, but I can't just give up."

"I know that," Roger replied, appalled that Jedd would even consider the idea. "Look, there has to be a way to find her."

Jedd took a moment to decide how to approach the next step. "I know, and I think I know where to look now. Let me rest here a few minutes and sort things out. Then I'm sure I'll know what to do."

Puzzled, Roger stopped himself from asking anything more. He just watched as Jedd sat back in the chair, closed his eyes, and drifted off into a quiet sleep. The one indication that he was even alive was his deep, repetitive breathing—more reliable than a navy band metronome.

Leaving Jedd to rest, Roger slid off the bed with a chuckle. When his feet hit the floor, the smile vanished. He attempted to ignore the firing squad that began pulling the trigger, hitting every bruise on his body. Taking a deep breath, he shuffled out of the curtained room in search of Maria.

* * * *

Jedd returned to his position floating over the city. He knew what to look for now and where to look. Heading toward the last place he saw Madelin, Jedd spotted the scarred veteran's old apartment building and rushed to the top. He walked the perimeter, looking for something that might show where Madelin exited, but nothing stood out. The other buildings, while close, offered little in the way of escape. Rounding the edge adjacent to a small, retail building, Jedd found that it was close enough and shorter than the others.

It's the best route of escape, and Madelin was capable of making the jump, he concluded, remembering her flight from the institution.

Drifting over to the retail-store rooftop, he scouted for any sign of a shifting rift like she made before, but again nothing stood out. Jedd aimed a stiff kick at the brick chimney out of frustration. The momentum sent his foot straight through the smokestack and reminded him of his current limitations.

Staring down at the chimney, Jedd's gaze shifted to the black tar. It had dried as the sun disappeared, but a variety of prints had been left by birds and other animals. Jedd looked down at his own feet and noticed that they never touched the roof.

However, with all the people that were up here, there should be some sign.

Jedd searched the building for footprints, but found nothing human. He glided over to Madelin's friend's apartment and scanned it for prints, but still came up empty. Racking his brain for clues, a thought percolated to the forefront of his mind. Altran leaped through the building and sped to the fire escape where he had surprised Father Leodenin. Seeing the intact stairwell, a thought struck him. *I must be on the wrong plane. Before I was always taken to Madelin's world, but where is she now?* The question had become more elusive than ever.

Unable to give up, Jedd soared toward the city center. Minutes later, he gazed at the skyscrapers reflecting the dark heavens above in wonder. She could be anywhere, on any world. He glanced back at the streets far below and followed his sedan's path, noting where he found Roger. A glint of light caught his attention from a couple streets away.

He chuckled, realizing the irony of his earlier statement—that it could be around the next corner. *And here it is.*

The object flashed in the starlight as though beckoning him forward. As Jedd drifted closer, it appeared that the light was glinting off a wall, a small space extending southward to the ground. Once he reached the alleyway, he knew what he was looking at.

The remnant of a recent scar was unique. It was reality itself bending and reflecting the light as it struggled to heal the rip a shifter had made through its very fabric. Looking closer, he spied not one healed scar, but two. The second rip was made along the same lines of the previous. Father Leodenin and his men had been standing on this spot not a day before. Jedd followed the scar to each end and watched as this world's reality repaired itself, the edges of the scar disappearing from sight like they never existed. It was at a snail's pace, like watching grass grow, but again he was reminded that time was running out.

After so many years of searching, why's everything now on a rushed schedule? It's enough to make a guy pull out his hair. And how do I open it?

The answer eluded him, but with no other options, he had to get back here fast. Noting his location, Jedd stepped back into his own reality. His eyes fluttered open and adjusted to the spot-lit room that rushed to meet him.

Roger had disappeared from his bed, but whispered voices echoed across the empty warehouse. He stood up and stretched his stiff legs while his stomach let out a hollow complaint. Jedd followed the voices to the small, dim office. It was sparsely furnished with a small refrigerator and a wooden desk. A miniature lamp perched on top threw shadows onto the walls. Roger was seated in the far corner, while Maria was perched in an office chair behind the desk.

She was laughing at something Roger had said when Jedd walked in. His footsteps announced him to the others, and both heads turned in tandem. A look of concern contorted Maria's face as he stepped into the doorway.

She shot out of her chair and exclaimed, "What the hell happened to you?"

"My God!" grunted Roger from the corner.

"What…? What's the deal?" asked Jedd, startled.

"Look at your face," Maria screeched with concern.

At least she didn't slip back into Spanish, he thought.

Rushing toward him, she pulled out a pocket compact and flashed it in front of his face. Staring back at him was the same gaunt, holocaust victim he saw after his first venture into the astral plane. Glancing back at Maria, her eyes brimmed with worry. By this time Roger had shuffled over and was staring at him, too, as though Jedd were a museum exhibit.

"What happened to ya, bro?"

"Well…" His mind sought an answer, some way to leave Maria out of his dangerous world, but nothing plausible came to mind. "Okay… look, you two, it's okay. I just need something to eat. Could I get another sandwich?"

Maria turned and slapped two slices of bread around a handful of meat, shaking her head in disbelief. "What caused this?"

"Yeah," chimed in Roger. "What in the world happened? You've been sacked out for the last hour. I watched you fall right off."

Finishing the sandwich, Maria turned back around and handed it to Jedd. Her face refused to admit his condition was nothing to worry about.

Jedd accepted the sandwich and motioned for each of them to return to their seats. Maria did so with slow, grudging steps, while Roger was more animated. The time spent up and around seemed to have done him good. After retrieving another chair from a back room, he plopped down in his chair and waited for Jedd to explain.

"Thank you," Jedd said, accepting it. He took a few bites as the others stared in rapt attention.

"Look, this has to be quick," he started, his mouth still full of ham. "Roger and I are running out of time, but I think I owe both of you an explanation." They nodded. Giving up his attempts at obscurity, Jedd started from the beginning. "Maria, you can't tell anyone what I'm about to tell you, okay?"

Maria nodded again, her eyes never wavering from him.

"My name's Jedd Altran, and so far as anyone knows, I'm dead." The explanation continued, to some of which Roger nodded, having heard it hours before, but as Jedd went on, looks of incredulity passed over both faces. By the end, both of them sat in stunned disbelief.

"How?" Roger asked first.

"I don't know how, but I've just found Madelin and discovered what I'm capable of."

"It looks dangerous," added Maria, "judging from what we've seen today."

"Well, this happened once before, the first time I used it." Getting up, Jedd fixed himself another sandwich and then continued, "If I eat and replenish my energy, I'll be fine in less than an hour."

"Are you sure?" she asked.

"So far, yes," he replied, "but we need to head out. I came across the portal they used to follow her a few minutes ago." Looking down at his watch, he noted that another precious half-hour had already passed. "Roger, are you still with me?"

Roger considered his options before answering. "Sure, bud, whatever ya say."

The answer wasn't as reassuring as Jedd would have hoped, but he understood after the unbelievable story he'd just laid out. *At least he's still willing to go along. That's something.*

As they both rose from their chairs, Maria interjected, "Wait. Are you sure you don't need to see someone about this?"

The question was asked in all seriousness, but Jedd couldn't help the laughter bubbling inside him. Suppressing it, he said, "I wish the whole thing were just inside my head."

Stepping out of the office, he walked out of the building, hesitating long enough to check each direction. Opening the trunk, he rummaged in his bag. He pulled out a banded wad of bills, stuffed a small clump in his pocket, and returned to the office where he found Maria preparing two more sandwiches. Spying him, she handed them over.

Jedd's voice drifted across the shadows. "Thank you, Maria. Thank you so much, for everything."

"You're welcome, but I still don't know what to make of your story, Jedd."

"I understand, and you don't have to believe me, but please just keep it to yourself. If you don't, the consequences could be dire." He handed over the folded wad of bills. "Just to show my thanks. Like always, you never fail to live up to my expectations."

Their eyes locked as she accepted the money, her fingers gliding over his. "Look, Jedd. If it's real, please take care of yourself. Try not to fall down anymore stairs, okay?" As she spoke, her hands caressed his battered knuckles. She reached into a pocket and withdrew a small vial. "Put this on your hands. It'll help." She smiled as she opened it and dabbed some of the gelatin-like ointment into her hands. Then she massaged it into the top of his with the touch of a lover. "Good luck, Crux."

The reminder of her pet name brought a smile to Jedd's face. He didn't want to let go. He leaned in, touched his lips to hers, and whispered, "Thank you."

Letting go of the money, his hand drifted away and they parted. Turning, Jedd headed for the curtained room.

Roger was buttoning his plaid shirt when Jedd pulled aside the curtain. He looked better than he had earlier.

Jedd handed him one of the bland sandwiches as he munched on his own. "About ready?"

"Yeah, just about." Roger tugged at the bottom to straighten out the creases.

"That a new shirt?" Jedd asked, spying the blood-encrusted one in an aluminum trash bin.

"Yeah, your lady bird has something for all occasions…," but after a thought, he corrected himself, saying with a chuckle, "Well, almost any situation. If only she had one for us."

Jedd sighed. "Yeah, if only."

Roger looked for Maria as they made their way out the door, but it was as though she'd vanished. Their solitary footsteps echoed through the spacious building behind them. Wasting no time, they stepped through the moonlit night, deposited Roger's new bag in the back seat, and jumped into the sedan. Pulling around Maria's SUV, they began the next step of their journey in silence. Jedd watched as Roger pulled a worn deck of playing cards out of his pocket. He gripped each half in curled fingers, shuffling and reshuffling them in midair.

Chapter Twenty-One

Forming a Partnership

The alley looked just like it had in Jedd's dream, and the scar glinted in the sedan's headlights.

Roger's lilting Cajun broke the silence. "What are we doin' here?"

Jedd nodded down the alley. "Can you see the reflection, over on the wall?"

Roger squinted where Jedd indicated, but nothing appeared out of place. "You mean the trash cans?"

"No, not the cans," Jedd spat. He opened the door and stepped into the arid night. "Come with me."

Before Roger could act, Jedd strode into the headlights and toward the far wall. Roger hesitated, but his curiosity got the best of him. "What do ya see?" he shouted, unsure if this was the product of a disturbed mind. "I don't see it."

Jedd squatted in front of the foot-high scar in the wall and admired it from end to end. In his dream, the rip had healed six inches on either end, but it had progressed further over the last couple hours. While the web of lines shone deep blue in the headlights, the seam of the tear had two edges. Each one was imbued with a different color: one deep purple, while the other shimmered emerald.

One must be Father Leodenin's and the other Madelin's. It's kind of like a fingerprint.

The discovery surprised him. He could tell they had both accessed the same world; the same string lay beneath both seams. He poked the blurred scar. The surface was slick as ice, but colder, and froze his finger at a touch. He jumped back and examined the wound.

Roger approached from behind and leaned over his shoulder. The end of Jedd's longest finger was black, as though dead. "What the hell? How'd that happen? Ya barely touched the damned wall," commented the Cajun, his accent thickening. Unconsciously, he took a few steps back.

Jedd couldn't take his eyes from the blackened skin, but was amazed when the splotch began to shrink. In seconds only a speck anointed his finger. Jedd waited for the last bit to disappear, but it never did. *It happened so fast. As soon as I pulled my hand from the scar, the pain vanished.*

He rubbed a thumb over the spot and noted the absence of sensation. Jedd glanced at Roger and muttered, "Roj, look here."

He held up the finger, and Roger's brow furrowed. "I could've sworn that thing was a hell of a lot bigger a minute ago."

"It was. It healed to almost nothing."

The hair on Roger's arms stood up. "What the hell caused that?"

"This's all that's left when someone shifts, like I told you before." Jedd pointed at the wall. "See, it's healing as we speak. There's hardly anything left, but I think we can get through if I open it back up."

"What do you mean, 'we'? How do ya know it won't kill ya or shrivel your damn head, just like your finger? Worse yet, your *couilles* could shrivel to Raisinets and drop off, *mon ami*." The words came out rushed and unfiltered. "Besides, I can't see it, so even if it does work, how the hell am I supposed to get through?"

Good question, thought Jedd. *But maybe if I open it, you'll see it, too.* He had to try. If he waited too long, Madelin would be lost.

"We don't have time to test different theories. It's closing, and given another hour or so, it'll be sealed." Jedd tried to discern where the healed scar was. "I can't even see the parts that have permanently sealed. Stand back, Roger," Jedd ordered, summoning his courage.

Roger walked back to the car and watched with skepticism. Jedd reared back with the same hand and thrust the edge of his flattened fingers through the scar like a samurai sword. The front half of his hand disappeared into the wall. A banshee's wail resounded through the alleyway in a voice that was and wasn't Jedd's.

Roger watched as time slowed, leaving Jedd exposed like a snapshot. The scene violated the laws of science. Jedd's hand was somehow half inserted in the brick wall.

Bright light flooded the night around his fingertips, illuminating his anguished face. His lips drew back, teeth clenched, in a cruel, guttural scream. The taint on Jedd's finger flowed up his arm and under his shirt, blackening it entirely in an unstoppable wave. Time returned to normal as the dreadful howl persisted, but with added strength he curled his flattened palm around the bright edge. Then, shifting his weight, he ripped the rift wide open.

Jedd let go and stumbled to his hands and knees, heaving up all he had eaten that day. Deep waves of nausea flowed through his body, but as the minutes passed, the shuddering side effects faded. Roger watched his friend's bowed form, unsure what to do. Each haggard breath came at a cost as Jedd attempted to regain his composure. The gambler's attention was drawn to Jedd's arm, where the sickening infusion was abating.

The infection drained out the way it had come, leaving his arm half healed. A dark stain still covered his hand and wrist. Glancing back at the wall, Roger admired the four-foot rip. It fluttered in place under unusual wind currents. Through it, he saw the wonders of another realm… another world. The edges of the tear glistened in the temporary light that remained.

The Cajun's attention returned to Jedd, and his amazement was overshadowed with concern. He stepped up to the prone man and went down on one knee. "How ya feelin', Jedd?"

Jedd gave a labored reply. "Better… I… think I… can… get up."

Roger placed his hand under Jedd's arm and helped him rise to one knee, then to his feet. He wavered in the shadowed alley. Unable to maintain his balance, he placed his damaged hand on Roger's shoulder for additional support.

Roger's wary eyes glanced at the blackened skin. Seeing this, Jedd's gaze shifted to his hand, and his eyes widened. The headlights of the car illuminated both hands in contrast, like day and night, and the numbness had spread throughout the blackened skin. He poked it, then flexed his fingers and wrist, happy to find them operating as usual. However, there was still an absence of sensation. Jedd looked back at his new companion, who was watching his every move.

"What does it feel like?"

"It still works fine, but it's numb and cold to the touch."

Roger lifted his own hand and touched the affected skin as though it was a contagious disease. It was slick, and the strangeness of its arctic temperature sent a visible chill through his body. He looked from Jedd to the tear hovering against the brick wall, then back again, unable to express his internal conflict. "Ya did it," his voice echoed.

"You can see it?" A smile crept onto Jedd's lips.

"Yeah."

"You believe me now, don't you?" he asked, energized with the discovery.

"Damn straight. I'm not sure how ya did it, but... damn."

"Yep, and we have to go through."

Knowing Jedd was right didn't stop the unnerving feeling from creeping up Roger's spine. "I know," he whispered.

Jedd ran to the car, shut off the engine, and retrieved their bags. He threw Roger's to him and stepped up to the unorthodox window. After a few deep breaths, he stepped through.

Roger searched the depths of his mind for a question or some way to postpone the inevitable, but failed to speak before Jedd disappeared. Roger stood in place, petrified by the idea. Jedd's hazy figure moved like a shadow beyond the blue film. A few seconds later, Jedd's disembodied hand emerged from the portal and waved him forward.

Roger closed his eyes and swallowed his fear. Hoisting his bag over a shoulder, he stepped into the veil-covered portal. A cold shiver ran across his body as he passed from one world to another. It was like stepping into a pool of water, but emerging dry. Once through, a columned courthouse greeted him. His eyes scaled the building to its peak before assessing his new environment. Jedd stood next to the rift, examining it with his blackened hand while his other massaged his chin.

"What is it now, Jedd?"

"We have to close it or people might follow us."

"Well, shit," Roger mumbled. "Can we get back?"

"Yes. We just have to find Madelin. For now, I've gotta close it."

He grasped the rift's edges between a blackened thumb and forefinger. Roger winced in anticipation of another horrible scream, but it didn't come. Jedd grimaced at the subtle pain that stemmed from the touch, and they watched the black circle around his wrist creep higher, but slower than before. When he finished, the split disappeared. Only a shimmering scar hung before them. It looked identical to the one he had opened from the other side. The edges were already beginning to dissolve.

"Where'd it go?" Roger asked.

"I closed it."

"Right," muttered the Cajun, his eyes searching the spot after the rift had vanished from his sight. "So what do we do now?" The Cajun peered around the vacant street. There were no digital displays and far fewer lights than in his world. The distant lamp poles gave off an eerie, yellow glow, and the absence of nightlife was comforting. The only sounds were those of crickets chirping a quiet symphony.

Jedd reached into his bag and pulled out a small flashlight. The bright beam illuminated the rock-filled yard at their feet. Sweeping the light back and forth, he found yet another creature working on this arid night. Black ants swarmed over what appeared to be crimson footprints.

Jedd leaned closer and became certain they were Madelin's. He took off on her trail. "Here, this way." His words echoed over his shoulder.

Roger followed across the vacant street and down the sidewalk. The further they went, the more people they came across, walking in pairs and enjoying the night. Some spoke a similar language to the Spanish Maria used in their world. Ignoring the strangers, they continued their fast-paced search to find Madelin. He caught her backtracked trail as the paths crossed and wasted no time searching further.

They passed countless city blocks before the crimson prints dead-ended at a small shoe store, just as Leodenin's had. The red and white sign in the window read, "Closed." Jedd thought back to their last meeting. *Her hands were bandaged, and she even wore shoes. This must be the place she stopped.* He peered at their surroundings for the first time since leaving the courthouse. The buildings were similar to those in his world, except they were older. *Where'd she go from here? They must've been heading to that apartment.*

Jedd allowed intuition to lead him and continued in the same direction, but at a jog. He scanned the buildings ahead for a match to his dream. By the time it came into view, Roger was breathing hard. They slowed but didn't stop. Jedd scanned the building for its fire escape. The hanging ledge with the broken railing peered back at him in the moonlight, answering his silent question with certainty. Yellow 'Caution' tape roped off the alleyway and sidewalk.

Damn him, thought Jedd, reminded of the fight with Father Leodenin and his unsuccessful attempt to eliminate the man. *I'll kill that bastard if it's the last thing I do.*

He pushed the thoughts aside and turned his attention to Madelin. Time was running out like a cracked hourglass. He sprinted across the street. The skittish desk clerk leapt to his feet as the two men burst in.

"What do you want this time?" squeaked the man, his hands already reaching for the sky.

"Sorry to scare you," Jedd huffed as he sprinted past and up the creaking stairs. Broken shards of a glass crunched under his boots as he approached the apartment door. He tore down the yellow tape barring entrance to room 319. Not stopping to check the room, he folded himself through the apartment window and out onto the fire escape.

Roger followed with a groan. "Damn, I didn't realize I signed up for a marathon."

But Jedd's focus was on Madelin, and he heard nothing beyond the pounding of his feet on the metal stairway. As he neared the top, he stared where the last few flights had been. Someone attached a construction ladder as a temporary replacement, but it shook worse than the stairs as he flew up to the foot-high parapet surrounding the rooftop. The hardened tar coating the flat roof glistened under the cloudless sky. Jedd flipped on his flashlight after leaping the wall and soon found what he was looking for—dozens of military boot prints obscuring the roof's surface. Just as Roger appeared, Jedd discovered two prints that stood out from the rest.

"The deep set must belong to Madelin's large friend," commented Jedd when he heard Roger approach. "But it's hard to see. Tons of other prints trampled his. They must've duked it out."

Seeing the prints and pockmarked tar, the Cajun replied, "Jeez, I hope she's all right."

Jedd's scant memories of the fight came to mind. Madelin had sheltered behind the brick smokestack. He rounded the protrusion, and another rift whispered to him from the starlit shadow.

He glanced back at Roger, who was attempting to decipher the order of events by following in their footsteps. "Hey, Roger. Here we go again."

The gambler looked at him with worried eyes that glinted in the moonlight. "Oh no, not again."

"We've got to. This is where they went. Look at it this way, at least Madelin's learning to use her talents."

"What about the other footprints?" Roger asked in his lilting accent.

"Those were the PASTOR agents and their own trained shifter, Father Leodenin."

"Father?" Roger asked in disgust.

"He isn't what you think," Jedd assured him. "PASTOR adopted the persona so their shifters would get immediate respect from the people they encounter."

Roger chuckled, thinking back to the embarrassing church fiasco that had recently become a hot news topic. "Respect... you gotta be kiddin' me!"

"Yes, respect. Even now, how do people treat a man of the cloth when they first meet him?"

It didn't take long for the answer to percolate into Roger's thoughts. Seeing the usefulness of the ploy and the obvious insult to every faith, he spat, "Now, if anyone deserves to go to hell, that should get you a one-way ticket."

Jedd nodded. "Ready?"

"No, but I know you're gonna do it anyway, so be my guest."

Jedd reared back and thrust his hand through the scar. The effect was the same as before, but Jedd was able to fight off the banshee's control. He bottled the pain inside with gritted teeth, but a guttural moan still escaped his taut lips. Shafts of gleaming light spilled out around his deadened hand, and the pain coursed up his arm to the shoulder, accompanied by the black flood.

Determined to find her, Jedd curled his fingers around the lip and ripped it apart. He stumbled backward again, but Roger caught him before he tripped over the low wall. The gambler steadied him as the sickness forced everything that remained from his stomach. The black taint grew, consuming Jedd's consciousness. Roger lowered him to the ground and shook him awake.

His eyes drifted upward, searching for Roger's face. Through a clouded haze, Jedd mouthed, "Thanks."

Roger watched the venom course back down his arm, entranced by the laws of nature it seemed to break. His brows furrowed as the infection left his forearm black to the elbow. It was like the arm had been dipped in paint and left to dry. He gave Jedd a few minutes to gather himself while propped against Roger's shins.

After a short time, Jedd shook off the anesthesia that infused his body. Propping himself up with a hand, he rose to his feet and met Roger's gaze.

"Thanks again, Roj. You're a lifesaver."

Roger swallowed his fear. "Any time, *mon ami*. Your arm okay?"

Jedd flexed his fingers, but refused to look at the appendage. "Yeah, seems to be."

"You sure?"

"Yep."

The bluntness of his answer told Roger all he needed to know. He nodded, understanding that neither answer would affect the path that lay ahead.

Jedd stepped up to the portal. The edges fluttered in the unusual breeze, revealing a moonlit forest through a crimson haze. He glanced back at the gambler, asking a silent question. Roger nodded.

Chapter Twenty-Two

Thank God for Maria

A cooling sensation engulfed Jedd as he stepped through the frosted veil, but his arm refused to acknowledge the feeling. It reminded him of his sacrifice, voiding his attempt at ignorance. He harrumphed in frustration, but said nothing more, suppressing the endless questions that filtered into his thoughts. His hiking boots sank beneath the tepid water. Cool, night air caressed his face, and the woodsy scent of mildew drifted under his nose. He stepped aside and allowed Roger to follow through the portal. The Cajun's face contorted in disgust as his feet slipped into the shallow water. Ignoring the slight discomfort, Jedd's gaze drifted upward through the canopy of trees to admire the three moons above.

A smattering of clouds marched across the sky, attempting to mask the intentions of each orbiting object, but the prevailing winds thwarted their attempts. The revealed moon he knew so well stood high above, beaming down with a yellow, luminescent glow.

Jedd shifted his attention. Another moon loomed off to the side. It gave off a soft but bloody hue and cast the world around them in a grotesque, post-massacre façade. The orbiting addition to this world was unusual, but wasn't what sought out Jedd's attention.

Another more subtle moon hung low on the horizon. Its muted, turquoise haze coated everything in a silken, blue blanket. The glow called to him like the lulling voice of an infant's mother. The hazy moonbeams interwove, caressing the planet in shifting colors.

In the distance Jedd watched the rays interact with a host of solid, glowing lights. Each one moved through the trees, unaware of his existence. After the first few came into focus, others fought for his attention. Two in particular stood out. They were much closer, but the trees still hid their physical shapes.

One showed brighter than the others, as though it were a rare emerald. Jedd knew without question that this was Madelin. How he knew was a mystery, but he was certain it was her. Next to her was a subtle, gray light. Focusing on the orb caused the memory of the veteran soldier to stand out in his mind. A smile crested his face at the reassurance of Madelin's safety.

Her luminous light moved across his vision in slow motion, followed by a third distinct orb. It was a dark smudge on the horizon. Jedd knew who this lavender light belonged to. Calling out from the blackness... was Father Leodenin.

I just can't get rid of that man... but his days are numbered. This time I'll get him if it's the last thing I do.

Leodenin was definitely pursuing Madelin. Seeing him this close sent a chill down Jedd's spine. They would have to work fast if they were to reach her before the corrupt father and his minions. The memory of the other agents nagged at the back of his mind. He focused on the dark light and saw nothing more around him.

Where are they? He wouldn't leave them behind, would he? It was as though the operatives accompanying him didn't exist. Jedd doubted even a man as pompous as Leodenin would leave his entourage in his wake.

Jedd glanced at Roger. The dull picture of a man looked back, but nothing shone around him. Jedd surmised that the turquoise light must interact in different ways with certain people; something Madelin, Leodenin, and the soldier somehow shared. *There must be more to that scarred soldier than I thought,* Altran surmised.

"So what's goin' on?" asked Roger.

After a moment of contemplation, Jedd turned back to the open portal. "Well, this is an odd place."

Roger shouted in exasperation, "Hell yeah it is! With three moons and not even a dry spot to sit on..."

Jedd gritted his teeth and sealed the last window. His arm throbbed, and the black tide settled inches higher, above his elbow.

"I can see Madelin, her friend, and even that damned priest that tracked her here."

"Where? I don't see 'em."

"A ways off. Sight is kind of different here for me."

Roger stopped searching the woods and turned back to Jedd. "Can you see me?"

"Yeah, and other things off in the woods, but we've gotta work fast. Leodenin's gaining on them. We need to make our way around him and get to Madelin first."

Roger shook his head in agreement, but was still rattled by the new experience. His eyes shifted back and forth, searching for new surprises. There was little he understood about the last twenty-four hours. His brows lingered in furrowed meditation, as though intent on making themselves at home. Hefting his bag, he placed his trust in Jedd and prepared to set off through the muck.

Jedd pointed in the direction they needed to head, one that would steer them around the false father and closer to Madelin. Then they began their trek through the wilderness with large, suctioned steps.

Roger whispered, "So after we find her, are we gonna head home?"

"I'm not sure. It's up to Lady Luck, especially with Leodenin so close. Let's hope the lady's with you today."

Roger peered back at him. Considering his less than stellar track record with the feminine essence, he was disheartened by the response. "So far, she hasn't done a bit of good for me," he replied. "I hope ya aren't dependin' on that."

Well someone's luck's gotta change, and I doubt it'll be mine, thought Jedd. *If not, we might as well walk up to them waving a pair of tighty-whities on a stick. I doubt they'll go for it, but if things don't change, we might be better off just sayin', "Hey, you mind layin' off Maddy for a while? We could really use a break."* The sarcasm in his thoughts vanished the instant Leodenin came to mind, within arm's reach. His anger surged. *Something's gotta change.*

"Luck's never been one of my strong suits, but hope I never seem to run out of," Jedd replied, attempting to mask the defeat in his thoughts. "I just hope we can take care of whatever comes our way. Outside of that, we have to roll with the punches."

His determination and subtle optimism was clear, but Jedd could tell the answer did little to raise Roger's spirits. Fortunately for them both, the colored moonbeams masked some of the Cajun's concern in carnival-like stoicism. Depression could be contagious.

The two men progressed through the marshy landscape at a slow, grueling pace. Jedd scanned the plant life and animals around them as they progressed. Much was different in this world. Most seemed to exist separate from the odd moons above, but one fungus caught his attention. A cluster of mushrooms stood out against the base of a few ominous trees. The edges of the white-capped fungus were rimmed in deep blue and soaked up the turquoise glow around them, much like the orbs of light pulsating around Madelin and the others.

With enough time, I might find a use for these things, thought Jedd. *Who knows what mysteries they hold?*

To appease his curiosity, he gathered a small bundle of glowing mushrooms and stored them in a side pocket of his bag. The whole time, Roger droned on about tragedy and Lady Luck's abandonment. The one-sided conversation died off as lightning flared in the distance, foreshadowing the reverberating crash of thunder that followed. They began to drift further away from Madelin and the others, so they quickened their pace, sloshing through the soggy landscape without concern for who was watching. With each step, Jedd's legs stiffened. He fought the growing weariness, ignored his waterlogged feet's cries of strain and frustration, pushing onward. Jedd let his willpower carry him forward in agonizing silence.

Roger said nothing and loyally followed behind. A glance back spoke volumes for his character. Roger was focused, eyes glued on something ahead. He was alert to some unseen goal and possessed strength of will that proved contagious. It motivated Jedd to keep going.

The storm swarmed over them in unprecedented swiftness. Torrential columns of rain poured down as though the flood gates of heaven had been released. The varied lights were reflected through the forest, casting tributaries of luminescent raindrops. They looked like steps leading up to each planetary object. The colors shimmered through the stands of pines and cascaded off tree limbs as the men continued their journey, undeterred.

Jedd watched the glowing auras surrounding familiar people in the distance, but neither group stopped. Time crawled by as they passed through the endless deluge of water. To his dismay, the distance lessened between Madelin and her threatening pursuer. It soon became apparent that they wouldn't reach her before Leodenin.

Jedd considered their options and came up with a plan. It was risky, but he saw no alternative. He turned to Roger and explained. Exhausted and aching for respite, the Cajun agreed with the last-ditch effort. After a few minutes searching, they found a place of sanctuary under a copse of trees. A mound of earth had built atop a collection of roots, and the two hunkered down for the initial and most crucial step in their plan. Jedd

settled himself on the soft mound for a strenuous attempt to reach
Madelin.

* * * *

It didn't take long to drift off to sleep, but maintaining his focus
proved difficult. His body and mind would rather lapse into unconscious
bliss. Fighting through his exhaustion, he found himself in a short tunnel
ride of twists and turns. Afterwards, Jedd appeared in marshland similar to
what he'd just left. One difference was the figures stumbling through the
swamp ahead of him. Madelin was dragging a limp veteran alongside her.
Jedd rounded on them, and Madelin jumped.

"Jedd?" She stood shaking in the knee-high waters, more scantily clad
than before. Her tattered, white kimono did little more than accentuate
her slender form, and her soaked, cropped hair gave her the look of a
drowned rat.

Seeing her safe and unharmed, however disheveled, was enough to
bring a smile to Jedd's face. "Yes, dear, it's me."

"But how?" she asked. "And how is it I can see you?"

"I followed you. As for the other, I believe it has to do with this
place," he replied, looking around. "But enough of that, Leodenin's gaining
on you. Can you see him?"

"Yes, but I can't run. I owe Daniel everything."

The reminder of loyalty and indebtedness triggered memories of her
parents. His own pledges came to mind. It was enough of an answer. "I
understand. I've got a plan. Can you see me off in the distance?" He looked
in the direction from which he'd come, but he couldn't point himself out—
for obvious reasons. Jedd stopped mid-sentence and reconsidered his
words. "You'll see me when I wake up. Circle around to meet up. If
Leodenin follows on your heels, we can come together before the bastard
catches up. We'll be able to put up a better fight than you and Daniel can
alone."

But if Leodenin tries to cut you off, we may be in some trouble,
thought Jedd. He chose not to voice the concern. There was nothing either
of them could do about it.

Madelin nodded, comprehending the plan. Daniel tilted his head, the
one-sided conversation having woken him from his vertical slumber. "Is
that your friend?" he mumbled through chattering teeth.

"Yes," she replied. "He has a plan I think might work, but we'll have to stay out of the agents' reach."

Daniel gave a fatigued nod and attempted to stand on his own. He stood straight and stared into the wet world, using her shoulder to steady himself.

Jedd's voice spoke up once more before disappearing into the night. "Okay, now get moving. They aren't far behind."

Madelin saw his tan aura pop into existence in the direction he indicated. "Okay, let's go," she ordered, ushering Daniel forward. Her voice and determination clung to the fragile hope that they might make it.

Chapter Twenty-Three

Family Reunited

J edd awoke with renewed vigor but was shocked to find that Roger had drifted off. "Roger!"

His shout woke the gambler with a start. Roger looked down at the deck of cards he had been shuffling and stashed them in a pocket. "So what'd they say?"

"It's a go. We have to move, though. Leodenin's getting closer."

Sensing the urgency in Jedd's voice, Roger leapt to his feet with more energy than Jedd thought possible. He reached into the blue sports bag Maria gave him and pulled out a gleaming .44 Magnum. Jedd gawked as the Cajun opened the cylinder and loaded a round of bullets from a jacket pocket.

He was reminded of an old Dirty Harry film he'd seen years earlier. "Where the hell'd you get that?"

Roger answered with an energized smile, "Well, it's like I said, Maria has somethin' for every occasion. After I told her I was goin' with ya, she handed me this monster and a butt load of ammo. Be prepared's my motto, kind of like those woodsy boys say." With a chuckle, he tucked the loaded gun under his belt and zipped the jacket. "Ya know, prepubescent Boy Scouts. We used to call ourselves We-blows!" He guffawed.

Jedd chortled with comic disbelief before marching into the pouring rain. "I just hope you know how to use that thing, Roj."

"We'll just have to find out, now, won't we?"

The men steered toward where he planned to meet Madelin, hoping to reach her before Leodenin. As they grew closer, Jedd watched the false father adjust to the change in tactics. His heart sank as the shifter moved to intercept the two groups.

"Looks like we've gotta pick up the pace," Jedd muttered in exasperation. The torrential rain pelted his uncovered head and clothes. In the desert, a light jacket would have stopped the fiercest of weather. The unexpected climate change left him miserable, but it seemed nothing would dampen Roger's newfound spirits.

Jedd's legs shouted in pain as he pushed through the murky waters, but his thoughts were on the young girl who once sat astride his lap. Her green eyes glowed with innocence, returning the love he and her parents doted on her. He dwelled on her for hours.

Before he knew it, a drenched but determined warrior strode into view less than thirty yards away, across what would soon become a war-torn battlefield. Jedd scanned the trees to his right and found Leodenin's dark aura gleaming in the moonlight. He stood a stone's throw away.

The false father slipped behind a tree while his adept companions disappeared into the marsh. Jedd pointed him out to Roger as Madelin did the same for Daniel. Just as she did, the ex-mercenary thrust her behind a tree. He ducked as gunfire from the agents' pistols permeated the air. The bullets pelted the trees around them.

Jedd and Roger each selected a thick trunk for cover. They watched Leodenin's position, waiting for a clear shot. A seldom-used .22 caliber pistol appeared in Jedd's hands, and his eyes promised vengeance. His blood boiled at the sight of Leodenin shouting orders and waving in their direction, but the trees still offered him cover.

A vivid image appeared in front of Jedd's eyes: an orphaned girl standing outside her parents' burning home, tears streaming down her ashen face. Jedd saw red—the kind best seen in a 1970s horror video. He stepped around the tree and pointed the small handgun at the false father. Round after round fired at the pull of the trigger until the wretched man took cover. When the hammer fell on a hollow chamber, Jedd flipped back behind the tree to reload.

The Cajun's revolver was steadied on Leodenin's men. The magnum flared in the damp, night air as a thunderous roar echoed through the trees. Surprised by the backlash of the hand cannon, Roger caught it just before it recoiled into his face. The unlucky card player ducked behind the plant life and looked over at Jedd with a malevolent grin. Blue lightning seared the sky, illuminating his distorted face like a gruesome demon. An onslaught of silent killers rained down on them as the agents returned fire, but it didn't diminish the gambler's excitement.

He yelled over the chaos, "I got one!"

Rejuvenated, Jedd smiled and flipped back around the splintered tree trunk to find another victim. Seeing no one, he let his adrenaline take over. He sprinted to a felled tree a few yards closer to the operatives. Roger followed on his heels. Not five yards ahead lay a half-submerged agent clad in black. Blood poured from his vest and infected the swamp. The red water streamed past Jedd's feet.

The magnum must've pierced the armor.

A sinister smile grew at the thought of one less hunter. It was hard to subdue his anticipation, but he waited for another barrage of bullets to wane. Jedd's smile widened as Daniel's guns sprung to life, hammering back at Leodenin's men from the opposite direction.

This couldn't have worked out better.

The firing slowed, and Jedd took advantage. Slipping over the hulking tree, he added his own bloodthirsty bullets to the fray, accompanied by Roger's roaring cannon. Leodenin and his men retreated inch by inch into the night. Jedd and the gambler relished their success.

After losing sight of the operatives, Jedd focused on Leodenin's aura, but it scampered further away, putting as much distance between the two groups as possible. Soon, the booming sounds of battle died away. Periodic bursts of thunder disrupted the silent night's return as the heavens above cried out. The time between clashes grew, and the silence was accompanied by soft rain. Jedd and Roger approached the group's previous position but saw no one, aside from damaged trees and the fallen agent's body. With the coast clear, they set out for Madelin and her friend.

Jedd slid through the shallow marsh, a few feet from where he had seen them earlier. "It's us. I think they left. Is everyone okay?"

Daniel's eyes widened, and he sprang to his feet as though his legs were coiled aluminum. Madelin smiled as they appeared, but her enthusiasm was subdued by the damp night and fatigue.

"Good to see you're all right. Did you manage to wing any of them?" asked the scarred man, but his tone was reserved.

A toothy grin filled Roger's face as though he hadn't noticed. "Yep, I got one of them dirty bastards real good," he replied, hefting his .44.

Daniel glanced at it before looking back at the slender man with newfound respect. "Now where in the Sam Hell'd you come across an ancient thing like that?" The question seemed genuine, as though curiosity had gotten the best of him.

"It was a good friend's, and when she found out I was gonna be sailin' with this guy," he said with a shrug toward Jedd, "she figured it might come in handy."

"I guess you've had some trainin' then?" added Daniel. "Was it with that particular weapon?"

"Nah," he replied, "but it sure does pack a punch—went right through the guy's vest."

"It damn well better have, or else Dirty Harry would've been known as the Patron Harry, donating bullets for the cause, or some shit like that." They each enjoyed a lighthearted laugh, and the awkward strain between strangers lessened. The two ex-servicemen became engrossed in conversation, as though they had known each other for years.

"Where'd you go for your training?"

"The Maritime Academy?" Roger flashed the tattoo on his arm.

"Ah, Death Before Dishonor," commented Daniel.

The night's shadows obscured the wince that crossed Roger's face. "How about you?" he asked, attempting to sidestep a discussion about his less than stellar past.

"A lifetime ago I was a marine, before I joined a private security venture." Daniel's face turned sour as he dredged up the memories. Ignoring the sudden desire for something wet and eighty-proof, he continued in a dry and sober voice, "I learnt to fight, shoot, and be everything a man should be in the marines. Then Black Force Security taught me to ignore those things when the money's right, somethin' I've been tryin' to make up for ever since."

Daniel divulged what had consumed him each night. The past he could never outrun was something another military man would understand. As he finished his somber confession, he was greeted by the natural voices of insects in the night.

Roger nodded, having known men that went down that route. Giving the conversation a necessary lift, he probed into the ex-mercenary's training as a US Marine. The two men fell into a black hole of conversation about various military armaments, techniques, and weapons.

The Cajun sat down on a fallen tree as Daniel checked his bandages and ammunition. His various pockets were still nearly full, but the assault had put a dent in his supplies. The memories of long-dead children turned into afterthoughts, postponing their haunting till later. "Always gotta be prepared," he said with a halfhearted chuckle.

* * * *

Madelin stood stunned at the openness with which Daniel greeted a fellow serviceman. Allowing the two of them to trail off on their own, she gazed at the man who freed her—a man hours before she assumed was dead. Jedd stood tall and lean in his wet jacket, although just inches taller than Madelin herself. His eyes welcomed her, twinkling in the moonlight like a long-lost friend. He was a stranger, but he knew her better than she knew herself. She closed the distance between them and wrapped her arms around him, filling her voided memories with his presence.

In turn, Jedd embraced the little girl he lost so long ago. His thoughts returned to the red-headed child standing in front of her burning home, her world falling apart around her. He squeezed her shivering body and kissed her forehead. "I swear I'll never let you out of my sight again," he whispered. Madelin clutched him tighter, as though he might disappear at any moment.

When they separated, tears merging with raindrops, Jedd watched as salty emeralds danced down Madelin's smiling cheeks. In the glow of the tri-moon light, her chin reminded him of her mother. The memory of Waverly Boatweit flashed through his mind, just as a yellow, fletched dart blossomed at the nape of Madelin's quivering neck.

The smile never left her face. Before he could react, her legs buckled. Her drenched body fell to the shallow marsh below. Jedd ducked to catch her head and shoulders before they submerged, cradling her as her father would have, had he been alive.

In an instant, the air filled with deadly wasp-like bullets, whizzing by and striking the trees around the group with rapid-fire *thuds*. The wasp intended for him embedded itself in a nearby tree, striking right where his head had been. Jedd failed to notice. His concern for Madelin intoxicated him.

He removed the dart from her neck. It was fletched and made of a small, empty vial, the end tipped with an inch-long syringe. Jedd's face contorted with rage, and he crushed the vial in his blackened fist. Turning his attention to their attackers, his eyes threatened vengeance with a murderous fury. The operatives flitted through the shadows, shifting from tree to tree. Leodenin was still in the distance but must have separated from his crew.

* * * *

It took precious seconds for Daniel and Roger to discern what had happened, but they flew into action when they saw Madelin fall. A split second later, the forest erupted in a shower of bullets. Seeing Jedd cradling her body, they leapt up, weapons bared. The ex-mercenary positioned himself between Madelin and the oncoming assault, picking his targets with deliberate attention. He leveled his weapon on the agents' shrouded movements. Their bodies were highlighted in the moonlight but disappeared before he could get a shot off.

"*Cowards!*" he roared.

Roger ducked behind the closest tree and hefted his Magnum. Sliding around the edge, he spotted a black-clad man approaching his position, sidestepping from tree to tree. He aimed at the target and timed the agent's movements, then fired as he left cover. The recoil was growing easier to handle. A bullet tore into his target, and the man yelped in pain.

Daniel spotted the agent and sent a second shot into his shoulder for good measure. A smile played across each of their lips as they reveled in their gruesome success. They scanned the forest for other targets without missing a beat.

"Jedd," shouted Daniel through the rapid gunfire. "Get her up. We're movin'."

Her godfather stifled his desire to slaughter each of the assailants and did as instructed, hefting Madelin over his shoulder with one hand while gripping his .22 in the other. They sped away with the young woman in tow, distancing themselves from Leodenin and his group.

"I'm gonna kill that bastard," Jedd muttered, "but I've gotta get Maddy safe first. Then that jerk's mine."

Roger and Daniel returned fire in sporadic bursts. Reloading and shooting again, they forced the operatives to remain hidden. As they fought, the distance between them widened. Jedd watched the two men work their magic but knew it couldn't last long.

How much ammo do they have left? he worried. To his surprise, each time Daniel finished a clip, another appeared from under his belt or out of a pants pocket. Within seconds, the veteran was back to spewing death from each hand.

While slower to reload, Roger plucked a handful of spares from his jacket and jammed them into the revolving chamber like an expert. He was quite adept at popping the chamber into place with a jerk of his wrist. Before Daniel could finish his own clips, Roger was back to filling the night sky with lead insects that could fell an elephant.

The return fire was sporadic. Each man possessed an iron will and confidence unmatched by the greatest Titans in history. Roger and Daniel paced backward through the marshy terrain with anchored steps. They made their way through the trees and over rotting, wooden corpses.

Jedd searched his surroundings for something that would offer proper defense but found nothing. Ahead, a multitude of glowing orbs were fast approaching, led by one lone individual. The man in the forefront had no aura, but the speed with which they moved was unnerving.

The swift wave of men and women overtook the small group before they knew what was happening. The angry boom of the hand cannon was soon overwhelmed by a mass of shouting voices. Hordes of glowing people were upon them before Jedd could alert his friends to the new arrivals.

Chapter Twenty-Four

Interesting Neighbors

Leodenin watched as this world's tenants poured through the trees at unconscionable speeds. *Perhaps,* he thought, *this world will be more to my liking than those before.* He imagined the onslaught about to befall the mixed group, and his lips knitted themselves into a wicked smile. *If this many people are capable of doing what I do, then the loss of one simple-minded girl is worth the discovery.*

Leodenin's thoughts cemented themselves in reality as the first of the crowd overtook the group. The solitary man barreled past without giving them a thought. Bewildered, it dawned on him where the man was now heading. Panic took root in his stomach. He selected one operative from his huddled group and shoved him forward. "Shoot him down," shouted Leodenin, "or I'll spread your entrails across this world and the next."

As the oncoming tsunami swept over Madelin and her protectors, the man leading them continued to hurtle from tree to tree, bearing down on the group of PASTOR operatives. The PASTOR operative raised his pistol at the speeding target and attempted to follow its zigzag dance through the forest. A shot rang out seconds before the milky-white abomination crashed into them.

"Got him," shouted the black-suited youth, but before the words had left his lips, the color drained from his face.

The shot didn't faze the mysterious man, but it caught his attention. He hurtled toward them with terror-filled eyes and a face entrenched in pain and rage. The impact of the collision threw the agents into the trees and scattered them across the forest floor.

The shock left Leodenin with no time to react before he too suffered the consequences. He didn't see the man's fist, but felt it splinter his ribcage. He flew into the air, landing what felt like minutes later on the waterlogged soil.

After the world stopped spinning, Leodenin took stock of the damage. Every bone in his body flared at the thought of moving, but he forced his arms to work and pushed himself to his knees. The man who had wiped out his well-trained instruments of war was nowhere to be seen, and Leodenin's world became a silent film, aside from the ringing in his ears.

Leodenin grimaced at the ease with which the mystery man had dispatched his men. His agents were scattered. He scanned the shadowed forest and found some in the surrounding area. They were slow to get up. Not far away lay the unlucky operative who had followed his orders. He didn't move, and his head was submerged under the putrid water. Dismissing him, Leodenin turned away, his thoughts wondering back to the pale attacker.

I could use such a man.

His bones protested as he rose to his feet, but the thought of Marlin or the others seeing him prone and injured spurred him onward. His feet were shaky, and he stifled a scream as pain erupted within him. His thoughts went to the pouch at his belt, but with a limited supply of Satia, he rejected the idea.

Within seconds the glowing crowd that had born down on them became a reality. The world exploded as bloodthirsty howls and shrieks pierced his muted world. Leodenin stood, wavering, expecting the worst as they sped by within inches, but not one touched him. The flood of people was short-lived, and their voices soon trailed in the distance. The pale shifter strode back to his group of underlings, hiding the pain that blazed with each step.

* * * *

At a questioning look from Daniel, Jedd shouted through the throng of voices, "They all glow like me and Madelin." There was no need to elaborate. The evidence of their speed was all around.

The leader flew through the group as though they didn't exist, his pale complexion flashing in the moonlight as he leapt from tree to tree. Each step propelled him further through the forest with increasing alacrity. Jedd caught a fleeting glimpse of the man's face as it looked back at the others in pursuit, and their eyes met. His stare was cold, almost lifeless, and his face was etched with something more—fear.

A split second later, he burst through the group of agents and sent them flying like bowling pins before disappearing into the shadows. Then they were set upon by floods of howling people that moved in the same distinct way. Each of the men attempted to target the transitory images as they swept by, but none were visible for long enough. However, as fast as they came, the massive group left. Their vicious howls dwindled in the distance. Each of the three men stood in shock. None had been harmed or even fired a shot, but a glance at Leodenin's men left them in awe.

The group of agents were now scattered over the forest floor. Some of the men lurched to their feet, while another was slumped against a tree. They doubted he was even alive. Leodenin's deep-purple aura stood in the heart of the woods behind his men, and Jedd knew he wouldn't pursue them alone. They now had the upper hand.

Without another thought, Jedd gave the order. "Now! We move now!"

He secured Madelin with his free arm, turned away from the agents, and scrambled through the soaked wetlands.

Each step's that much further away, he reassured himself.

The agents dwindled to nothing as the group sped through the forest. A weight lifted from Jedd's chest the further they travelled. He felt like a football star he saw years ago, running in a game-winning touchdown. The difference was that his end zone was beyond sight and his prize more valuable.

I've got Madelin, he wanted to yell, but didn't dare. *And we all have our lives.*

Jedd forced his feet onward with measured breaths, deeper into the dense marsh. Even the callous wind failed to tear the triumphant grin from his face.

Chapter Twenty-Five

Trapped Memories

As Altran and his crew sped through the soggy night, the terrain changed. Although still saturated, the endless lake gave way to small, island sanctuaries. Jedd glanced at his watch and smiled with the little energy he had left. It had fared well through everything and showed 2:00 a.m. He glanced back at Leodenin. The shifter's aura was a speck on the horizon. They had put a great distance between them and Leodenin's surviving men and slowed to a stop on an eight-foot island.

"This should do," he muttered, breathless. "I saw two of Leodenin's guys on the ground after that last attack… They weren't moving."

Daniel nodded as he approached, exhaustion dragging at his limbs. It was as though even the last few inches were too far to ask a man to walk, especially with his dirty, bandaged wounds. Rather than complain, the stout soldier lifted Madelin's unconscious form from Jedd and laid her on a soggy bed of moss and lichen. "Yeah," he muttered. "That makes five left and that pale devil. We're slowly whittlin' away at them."

Jedd breathed a sigh of relief. "Yes, we are. Soon we'll outnumber them, assuming we last that long."

Giving the area a cursory look, Daniel added, "I think we made it far enough. A fire shouldn't be a problem. Besides, that snivelin' brat in the duster can already see you two."

Jedd smiled back. "That's a good idea, but you know they can see you, too." Spotting the soldier's wounds, he asked, "How are you holding up?"

Distracted by the question, Daniel didn't have time to consider the initial comment. "G-good," he said, stumbling over the word. "It hurts, but I always seem to find the energy to keep goin'. It's kinda weird."

"Still got the bullet inside?"

Daniel nodded. "Pretty sure. Aside from that, it feels a little better, believe it or not. I'm just so tired."

On that note, Jedd wondered aloud, "What'll we use to make the fire? Everything's wet."

"I'll take care of it." Daniel groaned as he began gathering handfuls of moss from the islet edges. Roger scoured the trees for the few limbs that weren't waterlogged. He broke the low-hanging limbs from the trees, and his arms were soon laden with green firewood.

It might light, thought Jedd as he watched. He seated himself next to Madelin's prone form and checked her vitals. When he was satisfied that she was sleeping, he removed a handful of spare clothes from his duffle bag and placed the rolled bundle under her head. Then he tended to his own screaming muscles, massaging his aching legs and lower back.

Within minutes Roger and Daniel had piled enough wood on the small island to last the night. Daniel's knees popped as he fell to the ground in front of the wood. From his pocket, he pulled out a metal lighter that looked as though it could crack coconuts. With a flick of his thumb, a flame sprang to life and cast his chilled fingers in a yellow glow. He smiled at the welcome warmth and bundled the moss together. A teepee of wood sheltered the small, fibrous ball.

Roger pulled out a six-inch Bowie knife and whittled at a limb as Daniel worked. The gambler tossed the shavings onto the small teepee. It took some time for the slivers and lichen to ignite, but soon a larger flame grew in the tented branches.

Within the first half hour the men were seated, smiling through the flames. Their socks and shoes huddled near the dancing flames like a captive audience awaiting an encore. Each man's dire gaze spoke of the exhaustion they all felt. Conversation was limited as each tended to his own aches and pains.

"I'll take the first watch," Jedd mumbled.

The others succumbed to Queen Mab's dreamy calls within minutes, their heads resting on anything available. Jedd chuckled when he noticed Roger's head propped on one of the veteran's wet boots.

The next morning came too early for the group. Jedd was the first to wake as the sun peeked over the eastern tree line, casting its burning arms in far-reaching waves of orange and red. The vibrant pastels swept across the sky, forcing the remnants of clouds to flee. Each of his joints complained like a squeaky wheel as he pushed himself up. Snores greeted him from the others.

His mind began to clear, and he looked around for a possible ambush, but was surprised to find the agent's dark aura locked in the same place as last night. With a glance at his unconscious goddaughter, thirteen years of worry began to disappear. The porcelain-skinned beauty lay motionless, as though awaiting her charming prince. The calmness with which she slept could almost be mistaken for a gentle death, and Jedd's breath caught in his throat at the thought. He looked closer; her tattered shirt lifted with each shallow breath. Relieved, Jedd exhaled the fear that had built up.

He nudged her shoulder, and her breathing altered. She slowly emerged from the poison-induced fog clouding her mind. The worry had plagued his sleep through the night and settled into the creases of his forehead for a prolonged stay. His concern diminished as she drifted to consciousness and her eyes fluttered to life.

Madelin's angelic voice was music to his ears as she tried to focus on the face hovering over her. "Hey," she whispered with a smile, reassured that their short-lived meeting wasn't a figment of her imagination. As the abruptness with which the meeting ended slipped into her thoughts, Madelin's face contorted in confusion.

"Where are we? What happened? Is everyone okay?" Each question stumbled over the heels of the one previous.

Jedd replied with a deep, reassuring murmur, "It's fine... Everything's fine. We took care of things, and now you're safe." The anxiety on her face eased. "Do you remember the attack?"

"Not really," she replied, searching his face for answers.

"Well, they shot you with enough tranquilizer to put down a horse." The flatness of his statement startled her, but as he continued, his hands emphasized what she missed. The tale unfolded under her gaze, and she relived each event for the first time. Even knowing the outcome, she was still caught up in his words.

By the end of the story, the others began to stir from their damp beds. Daniel knelt a foot from the burning embers. He stirred them with a branch until the fire was resurrected. He added a handful of kindling and fed the coals the last of the wood. The flames responded in kind, dancing up the moist bark.

Roger took a seat beside him, massaging his hands over the fire. When the storytelling session ended, he pulled out his playing cards and shuffled the deck. The cards whizzed through his fingers, and he spoke over the smoking fire. "So, Maddy, how ya feelin' this mornin'?"

"Not too bad, just a little woozy. How about you...? What'd you say your name was?"

"Doin' okay," he grumbled. "The name's Roger. I just miss my mornin' cup of Joe."

"Hell, I'd even take a cup of rotgut this mornin'," Daniel added, his words barely tinged with sarcasm.

"Joe?" asked Madelin.

"You know, coffee." The question seemed absurd, but Jedd's earlier explanation came to mind and comprehension dawned in his eyes. "Ah crap, yeah, there ain't much ya remember, is there?" Pity consumed his face as he gazed at her. Any doubt about the validity of Jedd's story was washed away the moment he stepped into this waterlogged world.

Jedd answered for her before she could dwell on the missing events of her life. "Well things didn't go the way we wanted up to now, but I have no doubt we'll fix what they did."

Madelin turned to him, her voice filled with amazement. "How?"

"You remember the dream that troubled you so much the night we met?" Jedd's voice was filled with concern and pity, having relived it with her.

Madelin's eyes probed for answers as he spoke of events known only to her. "Y-yes, but how do you know about it?"

"I wasn't sure it was you, but I saw that you were troubled. So I drifted into the dream with you," he answered with hesitation. The rest of his explanation flowed out in a rush. "It was the first time I'd traveled like that, and I wasn't sure what I was doing, but it happened... I didn't mean to." He watched the words sink in, and her condemning gaze turned from suspicion to intrigue. "The point, though, is that it wasn't a dream. It was a memory. It means that your memories are still there, we just have to unlock them."

"I... I kind of figured that was the case."

His eyes widened. It was more than he'd hoped. "What do you mean?"

"I've had that dream almost every night, and it's more real than anything I've ever dealt with in the hospital. Up until the last couple of days, nothing seemed real except for that dream." Her words were accented with passion and frustration. "Also, I had Deedee."

"Deedee?" Roger asked, the conversation absorbing all three men.

"Yeah. Deedee's my stuffed teddy bear. Helga gave it to me, but in the dream I'm holding it so tight that I know something's missing. It was once a part of my life, a happy life. I know that much..." Despairing over the loss, her words trailed off.

"Well you're right, and I think it's time you learned what really happened," Jedd chimed in.

With a swift glance at Daniel, Roger caught his nod toward a copse of trees standing atop another mossy mound. Understanding the privacy he sought, they rose and prepared to leave.

"How far is that son-of-a-bitch priest?" asked Roger as he stretched his arms in the warm sunlight. The sun's rays helped to refresh him, but they were subdued here, as though filtered through a sieve.

"They still haven't moved," replied Jedd, glancing back the way they came. The only thing that had changed that morning was the distance the sun stretched over the horizon.

Daniel Madelin a knowing wink and said, "Well, I think I'll just step over to those trees and keep watch." He turned to Roger and asked, "You still got that pocket knife?"

Roger's eyebrows flexed in confusion, but he nodded.

"Do me a favor and sterilize it in the fire."

Roger's gaze landed on the seeping bandage at Daniel's side, and his confusion disappeared. He rotated the blade through the fire a few times. Then they swept past Madelin. Daniel shot her an affectionate smile. "We won't be far." As he stepped into the marshy bog, he explained to the gambler what needed to be done.

Once they were alone, Jedd turned his attention to Madelin's longing gaze. "You're right, your life was ripped apart that night. The agency I told you about is called PASTOR. They oversee the capture and memory conditioning of children with abilities like yours. Then they train the children to do and think what the agency wants. In the end, they're just trying to create loyal operatives with the capabilities you possess. If they had their way, you'd be just like Father Leodenin."

"And how do they get these children?" The question weighed on Madelin's mind, and Jedd could see the answer she feared looming in her expression.

"I'm not gonna sugarcoat it. After they find out about a child, through spies or whatever else, they approach the family with a financial offer in exchange for the child and all evidence of its existence. If the family refuses, they take more drastic measures," he replied, pausing for effect.

"The agency doesn't take 'no' for an answer, and they aren't governed by the same laws as you and me."

After a brief moment, Madelin asked the question that had been rattling around in her head. "Is that what happened to my family?"

"Yes," he replied and waited for the answer to sink in.

Tears streamed down her face, forming rivers that conformed to the contours of her blotched skin. "What exactly did they do?" she asked, the inability to remember overcoming her desire to huddle in a nonexistent corner and cry for eternity.

"Do you really want to know the specifics?"

"Yes…" Pausing, she sorted her thoughts and carefully chose her words. "I have to know, especially if they did what I think."

He nodded, understanding the conflict battling within her. "When your parents refused the offer, the suited men left. But it wasn't long… In fact, that very night, the men returned. They burst into your parents' lake house while they were both asleep. Minutes later, they emerged with you wailing for your mother. Then they set the house on fire. I never saw your parents come out. The rest you know from the memory. That was your house, and those agents killed your parents."

Her tears fell like the ominous weather of the previous night. Jedd hadn't intended to hurt her, but she needed to know what lengths PASTOR would go to and what they did.

"I checked the news the next day. The reporter said your entire family died in the fire, including you. According to the media, there was no suspicion of foul play. Your parents never came out, so I assume they knocked them out with the same drug they used on you last night."

"How did you see it?"

"Your father, Lane, was my closest friend. We met in college, and I even introduced him to your mother, Waverly." A smile creased his lips at the memory. "We were so close that he asked me and my wife to be your godparents. After the meeting with the two negotiators, your father called me over." Jedd hesitated before divulging his own shameful contribution to their deaths. Then he summoned the courage to carry on. "I had just left after speaking with your parents about the visit. They asked me to watch over them for the night and take care of you if anything happened." Jedd searched the ground in front of him as the story went on. "I agreed and was pulled off at the side of the road that night, overlooking the house through the trees… It all happened so fast that I couldn't do a thing.

Watching you standing there in your nightgown... the tears streaking down your face... It... it was heartbreaking."

His eyes met her tear-filled stare. "I've always loved you like my own daughter, but I didn't do anything that night. It's unforgivable. I wish I'd done something, but even today I don't know what. I just wish I'd done something... anything. Since then, all I've done is try and find you. Finally I did, and now here we are." By the end of the confession, salty droplets flowed from both their eyes like broken faucets.

"I know it's hard to hear, but I think you know it's the truth," he whispered, caressing her head. He obscured the waterfall flowing over her cheek with a thumb. "The one thing we have now is each other, and I'll always be here for you. Do you want a few minutes to yourself?" She nodded and Jedd slipped away, leaving Madelin to dwell on her broken past by the warmth of the campfire.

Chapter Twenty-Six

One Lucky Patient

Jedd entered the shaded grove the ex-servicemen had ducked into and stumbled onto a sight he expected, but still didn't believe. Roger knelt over Daniel's prone body, a stick clenched between the older man's teeth as he stared at the sky. Roger clutched a bloody pocket knife in a white-knuckled grip. With the other hand, he removed what was left of the bullet from the soldier's midsection.

"Now, how in the heck ya lucked out like this, I just don't know," muttered the Cajun in disbelief. "It's like your stomach lining caught the bullet. There's no serious damage or anything." To emphasize his point, he flipped the Bowie knife around and tapped the end of the handle on Daniel's stomach. A dull thud echoed from the open wound. "See, it's like a rock."

Daniel's gaze turned from the heavens to Roger's curious face. The impact vibrated through his midsection. Irritated, he added through clenched teeth, "Dammi', jus' ge' on wi' it. Qui' payin' aroun'."

Daniel's voice pulled the gambler from his wandering thoughts. Blood flowed from the wound, reminding him of his unfinished task. Roger set the smashed projectile aside and grabbed folded wads of Daniel's wafer-thin shirt. Pressing two of them over the wound, they stemmed the stream of blood but were soon saturated. Roger added a few more, and Daniel held them against the wound. The gambler soaked up the excess blood running down the ex-mercenary's side and then tied a large piece around the veteran's waist to hold the makeshift bandage in place.

Roger exhaled the nervous breath he had held since the surgery began and broke the silence, "Not bad for an old sailor who spent most of his time in the mess hall, if I do say so myself. I'll bet ya five bucks that'll hold her, *mon ami.*" His smile met that of the pained veteran's. "But ya should really have that sewn up."

Daniel spat out the stick and slapped him on the arm. "Hell, boy, you think you could have dug any deeper with that steak knife of yours? I thought we'd have to buy a herd of shirts to stop up the hole you were coring through me."

The debt-ridden surgeon smiled at the lighthearted comment.

The ex-mercenary lifted himself up, accepting Roger's hand of assistance. Both men strode to the edge of the landmass and washed their bloody hands. Upon their return, Daniel greeted Jedd on the outskirts of the copse with more enthusiasm than his washed-out face looked capable of. "Hey there, pops. Get a good look at my innards?"

"Enough to know I don't want that man anywhere near me," Jedd replied in jest.

"Ah, come on. I did fine. There's no reason to be like that. If I'd had some alcohol, I'd have done as good a job as a doc."

"If you had alcohol, I would've drunk it," replied Daniel. His hands twitched with the truth of the statement.

Both men enjoyed a hearty laugh as they walked back to the campsite. Madelin sat in silence, searching her mind for the things she lost.

Their chuckles startled Madelin out of her inner exploration. She glanced at Leodenin's distant glow, uneasy with his lack of movement. Knowing what his agency had done to her family was disturbing, but she felt something stir inside that she never felt before. Thus far she'd just wished to escape, but now she was driven to do more.

Vengeance had a way of taking hold of people, and as Jedd walked up to Madelin, he caught sight of her distant gaze. She was weighing her options, deciding what to do about Leodenin and the PASTOR agency. Her eyes reflected the revenge she sought.

At least she feels it… what I've felt for an eternity. Jedd looked in the direction she gazed and found the pale shifter's dark aura. Madelin's godfather allowed his imagination to take flight, relishing the torture they would force upon Leodenin and his compatriots. *Revenge and her safety are all that matters now,* he surmised.

Daniel and Roger gathered their things and smothered the fire, leaving their reunited friends staring off in the distance. By the time Jedd's gaze broke, the makeshift camp had been scattered and their possessions stowed. Jedd could see no evidence that they had stayed the night. "Wow, y'all work quick."

"I just didn't want to leave those bastards a proper place to sleep," replied Daniel.

Jedd tapped Madelin's shoulder and broke her timeless gaze.

"Sorry, I was thinking." Her voice echoed as though from a deep well.
"I know. What do you want to do?"

She stood for a few minutes, lips pursed in thought, unable to pull her eyes from what Leodenin represented. "I know what he's here to do, and I can't let it happen. I won't go back to that place, not until I'm ready to take them all down. Were there others like me?"

Pictures and faces from files and the hospital flooded Jedd's thoughts. "A lot of children were taken over the years."

"We can't just leave them in that horrible place. We have to take the agency down and free them." Her declaration carried over the waters lapping at their small islet.

Jedd gripped her shoulders and spoke with calm certainty. "You don't understand."

"What…? What don't I understand?" she cried, her voice bolstered into a semblance of hysteria.

"We can't just free them and let them go," he replied with transfixing eyes. The uniqueness of his voice caught her attention, and she floated back to reality. "If we take them now, many will die."

The fear of Jedd's words subdued her passion, and tentative questions rose to her lips. "Why? Surely we can help them. What could the agency do if they don't have them?"

"Sometime, yes, we'll help them, but we're not prepared to now. The reason these people became aware of these children's abilities was because they weren't able to control what they could do. Many vanished the first time they used their ability, never to be seen again. We have to control your talent and take over their training before they hurt themselves. But before that, we have to reverse what's been done to them… or at least find out how. If we don't, what reason do they have to come with us, or even view us different than how you view PASTOR?"

His answers were logical and well thought out, but dashed her hopes of immediate retribution. From downcast eyes, she replied, "I see."

"Don't lose that passion," Jedd whispered, tilting her chin up. "There's no reason to be ashamed. I've been thinking about this, and you, for years. My research has shown me what the agency's done. We'll save them, and we'll take these tyrannical bastards down, but we have to prepare first." He paused. "First thing's first. We need a place to defend ourselves."

Daniel lowered himself onto a log with Roger. He hid a grimace behind veiled eyes, but the anguish he felt was evident. The sight drew Jedd's attention. He nodded at the veteran, who appeared older than his years, and mumbled, "He hides it well, but he's wearing thin and needs a doctor, too."

Madelin followed his gaze, noticing what she had overlooked in her protective friend. "I know."

Madelin turned to the forest and squinted at the horizon. "Take a look over there, far away. What do you see?"

Jedd peered through the morning light, but could make out nothing. "Not a thing. What are you looking at?"

"You don't see the small specks of light just under the skyline?"

"No."

"They're people like us moving around, many of them." After a moment's thought, she voiced the question weighing on her mind. "Should we go to them? They might be able to help."

"They might be the same people we saw last night, too," he cautioned. "They glowed like us, but they were very different. They were incredibly strong and fast, and couldn't be human. If they aren't friendly, we won't stand a chance."

"But we have to try."

"Well, let's see what the others have to say."

The idea was a good one, and she approached the coffee-deprived men with Jedd in her wake, a look of concern creasing his face. Roger had discovered the remains of a few candy bars in his bag, a blessing from Maria, and the two ex-servicemen munched on them greedily. Madelin ignored her own hunger pangs and spoke with confidence, having embraced her future with fervor. "Got a question for you, boys."

Her approach startled them out of murmured conversation. Daniel's eyes considered Jedd before returning to Madelin. She repeated the question with a smile, purposefully leaving out Jedd's assessment of their chances if things went wrong. However, his fears spoke aloud as he stood behind her, hands hidden in his pockets.

Summoning his strength, Daniel strode over to Madelin and jerked her aside. After they had gone a safe distance, his tongue lashed out, "Look here, you silly girl. I've put my life on the line for you time and again, and I'll be damned if I sit here and allow you to manipulate us."

"But I didn't—"

"Don't give me that shit. You know what I'm talkin' about. I don't give a damn where we are. If you try pullin' that shit without telling me everything again, the only thing you'll see is my backside. I'll leave you to those bastards."

Madelin blushed. "Okay... I'm sorry. I am. I just didn't think you'd go along with me if you knew what Jedd thought." She found it hard to meet his eyes.

Daniel left her shamefaced in the ankle-high water and stalked back to the rotting tree trunk. Roger's curious expression was answered with a glance—now wasn't the time. With his adrenaline flowing, Daniel felt as though he'd gained the vitality of a twenty-year-old and the confidence of a drill sergeant. He slapped Roger's knee. "Let's go. We've got a town of fanatics to find." Then Daniel gripped Jedd's shirt collar and dragged him closer. Madelin's godfather attempted to hide a smirk as he looked the veteran in the eyes. The soldier's breath was hot and stale as he rasped, "What the hell's your problem, Jedd? Why didn't you speak up?"

In a voice shrouded with subdued laughter, Jedd whispered, "I know your kind pretty well, Danny boy, and I did speak up, loud enough for you to hear. Sometimes she needs a firm hand after she's made a mistake. We have to remember that she hasn't learned how to act around people. So in a way we'll all have to teach her some life lessons."

Daniel harrumphed, released Jedd's shirt, and hefted one of the bags over his shoulder. Then he and Roger set off in the direction Madelin had indicated, neither glancing back. Jedd waited for his goddaughter to collect herself before following at a distance. He kept the grueling pace Daniel set and shadowed Madelin in silence.

She needs her space, and time to think. She's got to grow up quick, or there won't be anything I can do for her.

Jedd watched Leodenin keep pace in the distance, waiting for the right time to strike. Birds chirped as they passed, as though accustomed to seeing people. The orbs Madelin had mentioned earlier were now visible and growing larger. There were many more than he imagined, but they never moved far from the solitary point ahead. It was as though they lived there.

The fractured group continued as the sun climbed a ladder of clouds into the sky. When it reached its summit, Jedd retrieved a handful of dehydrated turkey from his pack and nibbled as he walked. He lost himself in thoughts of the future and what they needed to do with PASTOR lurking a few miles behind.

Alerted by hunger pangs and the loud crinkling of Jedd's wrapper, Madelin watched him eat until hunger overshadowed her stubborn nature. Giving in, she allowed the few feet separating them to diminish... or tried to. Jedd kept his distance and watched the similar, yet somehow distinct forest surrounding them.

Most of the trees look like those on my world, thought Jedd, well aware of the distance he kept between Madelin and himself. *But there's something different... something... If I could just put my finger on it— maybe that would tell me more about this place and what changed it... why it wound up so different than our own.*

To her disgust, Madelin was forced to turn and wait for him to catch up. Her lips were thin and strained as she watched him approach. He smiled at her stubborn disposition and took another bite, relishing her immature misery as only a father could. She fell in step next to him, and he handed her a stick of spiced meat. She chewed the tough ration and kept pace with Jedd's lengthening steps, unaware of the closing distance between them and the military veterans.

"So, what should we do?" she wondered aloud.

Jedd spoke between mouthfuls. "Well, to teach those young, brainwashed minds, we have to understand what you can do. Plus, I need to figure out what I can do to help. So far the only thing I've had time to think of is finding you."

"So what do I do then, just go and find a book on the subject?" asked Madelin with a hint of sarcasm.

"It won't be as easy as going to the local library," he replied. "We'll have to do it the old-fashioned way, through trial and error." He lifted his blackened arm to emphasize his point. "We'll learn more through our mistakes, but we can't allow them to overwhelm us."

They both peered at the defunct arm.

"Was that a mistake?" asked his goddaughter.

Jedd pondered the question. Nothing seemed to have been harmed other than the skin. He poked the darkened forearm with a finger and was reminded of the lack of feeling. He poked it harder and harder yet, but still felt no pain. *What's it doing to me? Will it spread?* The questions ate at him, finding a home in a cavernous hole of his psyche.

After a moment, he answered, "I'm not sure." His voice quivered with uncertainty. "When I touch one of your portals, this grows, covering more of my arm. At first the pain was unbearable, but each time since then, it's diminished, making it easier to follow you." Jedd looked up into her eyes as he finished the stick of meat. "I wonder if it might've been necessary to help me find you."

"You think it was supposed to happen then?" The question seemed absurd, as though pondering the pragmatic possibility of a buffalo growing wings to reach a distant pasture.

"Maybe," he replied in the same wavering voice.

"So what if I try to do something and fail and wind up dead... or worse?"

"If we're going to be ready, then that's a chance we have to take," Jedd answered with a flat stare. "But I doubt you're destined for that. You already have a ton more experience than any of the naïve children that fall prey to their own abilities."

Jedd could sense her uneasiness with the potential consequences, but her words showed none of it. "I'll try. Since I started shifting, the outline of webs seems to call to me. I can find them wherever they are, like those over there," she said, pointing to a dense clump of trees nearby.

Jedd looked for the vibrant lines he saw when observing the scars, but instead noticed a natural growth of tall pines.

He shook his head in frustration. "I can't see it."

Daniel overheard the conversation as they approached and glanced at the trees she identified. He turned back to her and asked, "You can see that?"

"See what?"

"The weird outline. It's like a building should be right there, but isn't. It's almost like seeing the building's ghost."

Madelin smiled with excitement. "Yes, yes, that's it. How can you see it?"

"That's how I found you," he replied with a smile. The two friends looked at one another with newfound appreciation while Jedd and the gambler stood stunned.

"I knew there had to be something about you, Danny boy," Jedd added with a smile.

Bolstered by the possibilities, Madelin fired questions at the veteran. He answered them one at a time, as best he could.

Aware of his own inability, Jedd asked, "So how is it that you two can see it, yet I can't?"

They all considered the perplexing question as they continued their march through the forest. While engrossed in conversation, Jedd ensured that they were maintaining their distance from PASTOR's blessed son. It only took a look behind to see that they were.

After some thought, Madelin proposed an answer. "What if the ability affects people in different ways?"

"Go on," prompted her godfather.

"What if it just hasn't finished developing?" She paused for effect before continuing, "Daniel, have you tried to do anything with the colored outlines you see?"

"No, I haven't given it much thought. I've been a bit preoccupied with all these people tryin' to kill us." He gave her a mischievous smile.

"Jedd, when did things start to develop for you?" she asked.

After considering the question, he saw her point. "I didn't try anything until I remembered how you and I talked when you were a child. I'd never even realized it, but you told me what you wanted without saying a word. It was because of those memories that I tried to find you with such unusual methods. On those sci-fi shows, I think they call it 'Astral Projection.'" He emphasized the name in jest.

Caught up in the potential of their abilities, Madelin spouted, "When we find a place to bed down, I want to try some things." Her mind whirled with ideas and tests she wanted to attempt. Every effort would be supervised by another person, for safety's sake.

The reminder of their limited time and the distance they needed to cover sent Jedd into a temporary, thoughtful silence. The orbs moved in the shadowed tree line ahead and grew with each step. He gauged that they would arrive tomorrow evening. The sun had begun its journey downward, eager to reach the depths of night. Jedd mentioned as much, and their conversation went on in huddled procession. They would make it as far as they could before nightfall. The following day, they would test the generosity of strangers.

Chapter Twenty-Seven

Haunting Memories

Jedd watched remnants of dwindling light peer through the tree branches overhead. *At least most of the swampland dried up.*

His socks still squished in his boots, and his feet had developed painful blisters. Sitting around the campfire, Jedd relieved himself of his footwear and set them next to the fire to dry. He massaged the pain from his feet while searching the area behind them, his shifting gaze glowing in the rays of the rising moons. It wasn't long before he found Leodenin's aura shining in the ever-present shadows.

Very little grew under the old trees, and as dusk set in, the evil pawn shone like a beacon. He was still a great distance away and appeared to have settled down for the night. Jedd expected him to make a try while they slept. He was sure the gaunt man could see the people they were headed toward. Even though he was young, he was intelligent. But it would take Leodenin and his men most of the night to cover the distance between them.

What's he up to? Jedd wondered. *Why's he staying so far away...? Could he be trying another sneaky attack? Time will tell.*

Madelin plopped down nearby like a child after a long day of terrorizing the neighbors. A smile played across her lips, as it had all day since their decision.

"So, what do you think we should do first?" he asked as his own curiosity piqued.

"Well, I think I should make a portal like I've done before to start out, and you can tell me what you see."

The idea seemed logical, so he waited for Roger to finish gathering wood for their fire. He brought his final load and sat down across from them, yawning with the effort.

"Don't fall asleep on us yet, Roger," said Daniel from nearby, where he'd slumped against a moist tree trunk. "We're gonna try a few things, and I could use your help in case something goes wrong."

Roger gave a weak smile under drowsy eyelids. "Will do, Danny."

Daniel threw some larger pieces of wood onto the fire before moving closer to the group. After they had huddled around the comforting campfire, Madelin briefed them on the test.

Daniel agreed with Madelin's idea for the first trial, but then asked, "Where should we try it?"

They noticed that no trees or walls were nearby. The pleasant clearing they'd discovered now posed an interesting problem unless they wished to move away from the fire and light.

Roger pulled out his deck of cards and shuffled them from hand to hand. Every once in a while, he glanced down to see which card he pulled before returning his attention to his newfound friends. He couldn't understand what they were talking about, but by this point he had given up trying.

"Well what about the webbing of the building by Jedd's shoulder?" inquired Daniel.

Jedd started and glanced over his shoulder. Seeing nothing, he turned in place, searching for what Daniel had mentioned before the answer occurred to him.

Madelin and Daniel stared at the spot in thought. With a shrug, she shuffled to Jedd's other side. They adjusted themselves, and Madelin assessed the gold webbing from various angles.

"We can try. I've never done it on thin air, though," she muttered thoughtfully. Running her hand along either side of the florescent line, she trained her focus. "It's right here."

Daniel nodded without moving his eyes while Jedd tried once more to see the illusory line. His eyes dried out as he struggled to keep them open, afraid he might miss something essential.

All were focused on Madelin's hand as she ran her thumb along the thread. Subtle emotions of the linked plane flowed into her at a touch. Feelings of another rudimentary land sifted through her fingers. Intent on the thread, she summoned the dark rose to her with a silent call. After a few minutes, the air around the string rippled like the subtle disturbance of lake water. The waves flowed outward like a nodding current, dissipating the further they drifted. The edge of one petal materialized from liquid air, followed by another. It was as though the flower were submerged in nothingness.

Each man gasped as it grew forth in front of them. When free of the invisible surface, the petals glistened with ominous intent. Each sharpened edge oozed a familiar liquid. The golden hue of the dark substance made its way down the nearest petal, streaming along the exposed stem before dripping to the mossy ground below. Madelin thumbed the stem, found the glowing lifeline near the surface, and followed it to the linked petal above.

"Okay, now watch this, guys." Her voice was distant, but still held an edge of stifled excitement as she maintained her focus.

She grasped the petal of choice and plucked it from the exposed flower. A small rip appeared along the stem and down through the air below. Lifting the edges apart, all four of them gazed through the golden haze overlaying the open window. Roger leaned forward, absorbed in the spectacle. He teetered over the fire but caught himself at the last second.

A calm lake appeared before them with a deer drinking at its shore. Madelin smiled as both men let out held breaths. Then she motioned as if to close the rip, but Jedd stopped her with a blackened hand. Their eyes met.

"Let me do this. That way you can see what happens each time."

Jedd held up his arm for all to see, and in silent acknowledgement, they both edged away. He stepped up and grasped the edge in his discolored hand. His teeth clenched as pain coursed through his arm and found healthy cells to inflame at his elbow and shoulder.

At least the pain's dulled, he thought. *I'm not sure how much I could take otherwise.*

The icy, black taint spread through his skin and encompassed his elbow. Then he pressed each edge together like modeling clay. A thick scar sealed the rip as the world began repairing itself. Letting go, he exhaled as the pain eased from his limb. He expected the nausea to come, but this time it didn't.

Daniel reached over and lifted Jedd's sleeve. He and Madelin watched as the darkened skin flushed the poison out like the sloshing of a dark, bottled drink. It stopped before traveling far, leaving the entire arm dark as night. His shoulder was all that remained free of the taint. They both slid weary hands over his skin, but Jedd didn't notice. He stood in place, breathing deep after the exertion.

"Can you feel this?" asked Daniel, his hand circling the deadened arm.

Jedd shook his head, unable to speak quite yet.

"How about this?" the old mercenary asked, clenching down. He half expected the arm to collapse in his hands, but it held firm.

After taking in a long breath, Jedd responded, "Maybe. I can tell you're touching it, like if you were pressing on scar tissue, but not much more than that."

"Was the pain as bad as before?" came the gambler's inquiring voice.

"Nope. It hurt, but not like before—wasn't even any nausea."

"Well hell, that's a mite better, *mon ami.* You think maybe this is part of the process? Your arm should have fallen off by now."

"Yeah, maybe. I'm still not sure." Jedd met Roger's gaze, and although his voice didn't hold the concern he felt, his eyes did. It was a comfort for Jedd.

Daniel flipped open a large pocketknife with his free hand. "I'm gonna try something. Just trust me."

Jedd glanced at the knife with an uneasy nod and watched as Daniel slid the razor-sharp blade across his deadened forearm. The skin sank away from the pressure but refused to part. Both men watched the severed hairs fall from his arm, but the skin revealed nothing.

"Did you feel anything?" asked Daniel.

"Just the pressure, but it didn't hurt at all." Jedd watched the skin, expecting a delayed response, but the knife had failed to pierce the top layer.

"Want me to try again?"

Jedd nodded, and Daniel plunged it into his arm, but the skin proved resilient. Daniel put his weight behind the knife, but still Jedd's skin stood solid. Daniel gave up, secured the blade, and slipped it back in his pocket. "That's incredible. That would have skewered any man to the hilt. Can you still move it all right?"

"Yeah, not a problem. I just can't feel the skin."

Morbid curiosity got the best of Madelin, and she exclaimed, "Stick it in the fire!"

Jedd repeated the question in a look to Daniel, then shrugged and reached into the fire. He felt nothing and inched closer, half expecting his fingers to burst into flames. The hair along his arm sizzled in the heat and permeated the air with its smell, but when the flames at the center of the campfire failed to stir his pain center, Jedd retreated. The heat had grown the closer he came to the flames and his shirt was singed, but he was able to move the hairless arm like normal. The skin was still cool to the touch, as though nothing had happened.

Roger sat in awe, his jaw threatening to fall to the floor. The deck of playing cards fell from his grasp. Realizing the peril of his constant companions, Roger gathered the cards and batted the small flames that were attempting to ignite the worn edges. He pooled them together and deposited them in a jacket pocket before returning his gaze to the miracle in front of him. The flurry of movement caught the group's attention, but only for a moment. Daniel patted Jedd on the back with a congratulatory smile.

"That's wonderful!" Madelin commented, masking her uneasiness with feigned excitement.

Daniel sent an envied look Jedd's way; however, he said nothing, just peered back at the scarred opening with longing.

"I wonder how our abilities can differ so much, while the auras are so similar," Jedd thought aloud.

"I'm not sure. Maybe mine'll be like yours," Daniel proposed.

"One way to find out," Madelin chimed in. "Can you see the scar I left?"

"Yeah," replied the soldier, looking back at it again.

"Okay, you need to focus on it."

Daniel followed her instructions and stepped up to the freestanding scar.

"Search for your own doorway."

The directions were vague, but Daniel complied, working his way down the scar and sifting through the underlying luminescent webbing.

"Clear your mind, and focus everything you have on searching for it," she continued.

Daniel attempted to focus, but the instant he did, voices echoed through his thoughts. The muttered pleas of a Middle Eastern woman filtered through his solemn control.

"Help us... Help us please," came her thick, accented prayer. Her words crept up from the depths of his memories.

Daniel tried to shut her out, but no door would keep away the innocent woman's haunting memory. Her sudden scream shocked his system, even as he remembered slamming his rifle butt into her face. The flash of memory sent a shudder to his very core. Soon, her pain-filled cry faded away, to be replaced by those of her children pleading for her life.

"Spare her... Leave us... Go away!" they cried as their tears flowed.

The impassioned voices were tinny with youth as they haunted his thoughts, disrupting any semblance of focus he might have attained.

Daniel's hands faltered and quaked as he strained through the memories. He tried to push his cursed actions aside, but the accusing eyes refused to leave him. They stood framed in small, sun-darkened faces. Remorse consumed him before he could attempt anything more.

Daniel sank to his knees. His body shook with what appeared to be a cross between guttural anger and anguish. Each vocal inhalation sounded as though it were emanating from a gaping cavern. His wind-filled screams alarmed the others, but he couldn't bring himself to stop. Everything he'd bottled up spilled out that very moment: memories, torturous dreams, the haunting eyes of each person he had massacred.

Jedd looked back at Father Leodenin. He was pacing but stopped as the guttural cries echoed through the forest. Birds, sensing the horrific scene, scattered to the winds. As far as they could tell, Daniel hadn't been harmed, but his reaction said different. Jedd and Roger stood staring, unable to do anything, while Madelin wrapped her arms around the grown man, cradling him for support. He pounded the ground with his fists. Time eked by. It was awkward watching the unstoppable soldier, brought down by something they could neither see nor comprehend.

Madelin whispered into his ear as he lay curled in her arms. "Daniel. Hey, Danny. It's okay."

Through his terror-filled visions, he heard her murmured words, but dismissed them outright. "No, it won't," echoed his muffled voice, "not after what I've done."

"You haven't done anything wrong," Madelin prompted.

"Oh... you have no idea." Daniel's voice cracked with a hint of sardonic laughter. An inhuman smile slid onto his face but failed to mask the pain stirring within his soul.

His eyes opened. As Daniel looked upon his friends, he wondered how they could stand the sight of him. "Like I told you before, Maddy, there's a lot you don't know about me—and a heck of a lot that I've got to atone for."

"But you've changed, Daniel. I know it. You wouldn't hurt us."

"Oh, I wouldn't?" he patronized, the smile hiding his sanity. "What if the money was right?"

Roger stood up, unable to remain silent any longer. "Danny, shut the hell up!"

The words shocked the leathered man out of his belittling glare, and he turned his attention to Roger. "Boy, don't you dare say that crap to me if you wanna live." Daniel leapt up and closed the distance between them, stepping on glowing coals without a care. He never broke his gaze. The ex-mercenary tried to fix his fingers around Roger's throat, but the sailor's own training kicked in. Roger knocked his hand away and laced nimble fingers around Daniel's esophagus. Slipping a leg behind him, the Cajun swept Daniel to the ground with a thud and planted his knee on the soldier's chest.

Roger met Daniel's infuriated gaze with clenched teeth and a deadly calm composure. "I know what you've been through and what you've done, but none of these people've done a damn thing other than be your friend, *mon ami*." His accent thickened. "So how about this? Ya get hold of yourself before ya say somethin' we'll both regret—ya guys because ya might drive away the only damn friends ya've got, and me because I'll have to do somethin' about it."

Roger's clenched hand rested on Daniel's jugular, forcing the mask of insanity to clear. The rage passed like shadowed clouds crossing overhead. The gambler lifted himself from Daniel's body, returned to the campfire, and began shuffling his deck as though oblivious to the world.

Daniel got to his feet but winced at the sharp pain in his side. His adrenaline had drowned the feeling seconds before, but he was now reminded of his condition and the lengths Roger had gone to. He took a few breaths and collected himself before walking into a nearby shelter of trees. As he passed Roger, he whispered, "You're lucky I ain't myself."

"I know," answered Roger, but his attention remained on the cards he'd fanned out.

Jedd and Madelin stood staring. Madelin made to follow Daniel, but Roger again spoke up. "I wouldn't." The flames illuminated his face like a demon as his words drifted through the night.

Madelin stopped and turned to the gambler. "But why? What was that about?"

"There're some things about Daniel you don't wanna know," he answered, his gaze never leaving his cards.

Madelin waited for more, but that was all he would say. "Should we be concerned?"

"Nah, he'll find his way. Just give him time."

"Well, what caused it?" she asked in exasperation.

"Somethin' he did put him in touch with his past, *ma chéri*. The memories must've taken the chance to attack. Just remember, there might come a time when I ain't around and ya two'll have to save him from himself."

"Jesus, Roj, I can try, but I'm not sure I could even handle that big brute." Jedd's words were distraught. *We could leave him here,* he contemplated. *We could just make for those lights without him.* But seeing the concern on Madelin's face, he knew it was futile to even consider.

"Then let's hope he gets it under control before that comes to pass. Why don't y'all get some shuteye, and I'll stand watch in case any of those landlubbers decide to try and pull a fast one." The brief excitement had left Roger wide awake. Madelin tried to contradict him, but the effort was in vain. The gambler interrupted. "I don't think he'll come back tonight. Leave him be."

"Okay," replied Jedd, "but wake me up in three or four hours, and I'll take over so you can get some sleep."

Roger nodded. Taking his advice, they both settled down for the night, drifting out of consciousness to the encore of the dancing flames.

Roger sat in thought as he listened to the wildlife's night calls. The breathing of his companions settled into a deep, rhythmic pattern. After the brief cacophony of excitement, Roger's heart found its own measured beat. The cards had collected a coat of dirt and ash. He swept the grime away with his free hand, and his eyes settled on one card. A gallant Jack stood on the plastic-coated paper, his eyes covered in ash. Roger ran his thumb over the mottled spots, but just succeeded in smudging the melted plastic. He wiped it clean, but what remained of the Jack's hollow eyes stared back with the impossible knowledge of fate and eternity. It was as though the Jack itself were staring into his soul, telling him something indecipherable. He dismissed the paranoia with a shake of his head and shuffled the cards back together. His eyes cast out for Daniel, but he was nowhere in sight. Roger silently complimented the man on his ability to vanish.

Chapter Twenty-Eight

Revealing the Past

The time sped by as Roger played out entire games of Texas Hold'em in his head, laying out the hands on the ground. When his watch beeped, alerting him of the hour, the gambler picked up a small stone and tossed it at Jedd. His aim was perfect, and the stone bounced off of the man's forehead. Jedd's eyes shot open to find Roger teetering with laughter.

"Your turn, *mon ami*," the gambler muttered with a grin.

Jedd rose from the spongy ground with a glare. "I figured as much when you smacked me."

"Who, *moi*?" Roger said, feigning ignorance.

Jedd strode over and seated himself next to the solitary man as he laid out another hand. "So, who's winning?"

"Very funny. Always me, ain't it?" Roger replied with modest arrogance.

Switching to a more serious subject, Jedd asked, "So, what happened earlier?"

"Just what I told ya. It wouldn't be right for me to say nothin' more than that. Danny'll tell ya guys when he feels better. Don't worry."

That isn't reassuring, thought Jedd, *considering how close Madelin is to the old brute. But what can I do?* He left the matter for later, respecting his friend's wishes.

"What's next?" asked Roger as he lay down a less than desirable hand.

Jedd took a moment to calculate. "Well, at our current rate, we should reach those odd people this evening."

"And what do we know about them?"

"Not much. I suspect they're the same people we saw before."

"Do we even know if they're friendly?"

"No," Jedd replied, "so be ready."

"Did ya see what that one did to Leodenin's men? And that was just one of them. How the hell am I supposed to be ready for that?"

Jedd smiled and gave him the most sensible answer he could think of. "Pull the trigger quicker."

"Ack," cried the gambler, dismissing him with the wave of a hand. He collected his cards and lay down where Jedd had vacated. "I'm goin' to make use of your nicely weathered spot here."

"Be my guest," Jedd replied, leaning against a rotting tree trunk he rescued from the wood pile.

After settling in for what remained of the night, exhaustion took hold and Roger fell into a restful sleep.

Altran threw a few more branches onto the dwindling fire and crossed his arms for hours of silent observation. To his surprise, Leodenin was again maintaining his distance. The hours passed without incident, and Jedd did his best to stay awake.

As the sun rose, a sturdy man strode through the tender, morning rays. Jedd watched Daniel approach with wary eyes. In one hand, the veteran gripped a dead animal around its elongated neck. It had large ears and bat-like wings. Blood leaked from its exposed inner cavity.

Looks like Daniel already cleaned and gutted it. I doubt it came that way. Jedd contemplated the odd possibility of such a grotesque animal trying to survive, without fur and innards. A small chuckle rose in his throat as the morbid image played through his mind. *The thing looks like the bastard offspring of a damned love affair... like God might have a sense of humor after all.* He came to his senses a second into the absurd dream and muttered, "Jeez, I've gotta get more sleep."

In the other hand, Daniel held a collection of long branches that had also been stripped bare. Without a word, he took a seat across the fire and pulled out a knife. He sharpened one end of two branches. The opposing end of each limb was splayed as though to hold a fishing pole. After each was sharpened to his satisfaction, he whittled the end of a third branch. It stood like a short walking stick.

Wow, how'd he find something so straight? Jedd wondered. *Did he find a hardware store in this miserable place?* Everywhere he looked, the tree limbs were bowed and knobby. *He must've found the one straight stick within ten miles.*

Once the thin branch was sharpened to Daniel's satisfaction, he thrust it through the naked animal. Jedd had never been much for the outdoors, and he winced at the abrupt move, but as Daniel skewered the animal, it became clear what he intended. He plunged the splayed branches into the ground on either side of the campfire and set the threaded animal atop them, held aloft at both ends by the forked limbs. The remaining blood dripped into the fire, sizzling as the flames attacked the exposed skin.

Daniel seated himself across from Jedd and met his gaze. "I brought breakfast."

The simplicity of the statement brought a smile to Jedd's face. "I see that. Did you pick up some coffee while you were at it?"

"Tried, but the damn agents got there first. The clerk said they'd cleaned him out."

"Damn those pesky agents. Foiled our plans again," Jedd replied with a wide grin. The sight was enough to crack Daniel's morose gaze, and they both chuckled.

"Look, Jedd," Daniel began after the laughter died away, "I've got to apologize for what happened last night. I wasn't myself. When I did what Madelin told me to, I lost my hold on things. Memories that I've tried to push aside came to me out of nowhere. I've never been that out of control. I've dealt with demons for years, but it hasn't worked. I've gotta do something different—I know that. I'll figure it out at some point, but I can't let that happen again."

"I understand. Although, I'm not sure what you can do different," Jedd replied. "We just have to cope. I think the best way to deal with the situation is to confront your issues, while maintaining control. After you've done that, you should be able to go about discovering your own abilities any way you wish."

"And how do I do that? You saw what happened last night."

"Maybe it'd help if you told me what happened."

With a deep sigh, Daniel resigned himself to do just that. "I used to be a US Marine. I was good at my job. Later, I got out and took up with Black Force Security. There, I followed orders, right or wrong. Somehow I justified everything I did, indirectly you might say, when the money was right."

Jedd listened as he went on, aspiring to learn more about what had driven the weathered veteran to the brink.

"At Black Force, we went where the money was. Sometimes it was the right thing to do, but other times people wanted things done, no matter the cost. A lot of times the cost wasn't just to someone's pocket book. It was paid with innocent lives to make our employers happy." Daniel's voice cracked with the final statement, and he sat in thought.

Jedd was about to comment when the soldier resumed his narration with a wavering voice. "After a while my crew got greedy. We were in the Middle East at the worst of it. We were told to clear out the fanatics in smaller villages so the citizens could go on with their lives. But sometimes I think we were worse than the radicals that had terrorized them before. They, at least, provided some semblance of authority." His voice filled with hatred as he went on.

He must despise what he and the others did. Little did Jedd realize that it was more for the former than the latter.

Daniel's tale went on as salty pools formed in his eyes, but to his credit, not one drop fell. "We started by fighting the terrorists that held their town, but soon it became hard to see who was who. Often children would throw anything they could get their hands on. We had to keep an eye out for the people we were attacking, but we also had to look out for the people we were trying to protect. It got so bad we just started shooting... and didn't stop. We made sure not to shoot our own, but otherwise it was open season. My friends—" He choked on the last word. "Well... we all took up a new motto: 'If it's brown, gun it down.' It wasn't right, but it's the way things were. Any of them could've been a radical. We looted the homes. We even stole jewelry off the dead."

As he continued, his gaze drifted from Jedd's face, unable to look him in the eyes. "I... I was so pissed and so terrified that... that we even took families... hordes of children, women, grandparents, and locked them in their own houses. I still remember their voices pleading with me as I set fire to their homes. They screamed in pain. Their cries haunt me every night. And the eyes... the eyes see into me. Innocent eyes look back at me through the gaps in the roof and walls. They see me. I can't hide from their eyes. It's my guilt they see. They remind me of what I did." With the final admittance of his crimes, Daniel leaned forward and propped his elbows on his knees.

Jedd watched his newfound friend, feeling for the innocent lives lost. The open-air confessional had changed the atmosphere around them, and a moist breeze drifted by. It was almost as though voices could be heard on the gentle currents. Jedd looked around until the spitted animal interrupted them. Juices sizzled and popped in the flickering flames. Alerted, Jedd leaned over and turned the spit. Minutes passed before either man spoke again, but it would be much longer before Daniel could look into Jedd's eyes with confidence.

Altran broke the grief-stricken silence. "Baring your darkest secrets is hard to do, especially for a man like you."

The veteran nodded, acknowledging the difficulty.

"Daniel..., look at me," Jedd commanded.

Daniel raised his head with the slow speed of a rising crane. The difficulty of meeting his gaze became apparent.

"Look, Daniel, we all have secrets and things we've got to atone for, but the important thing is that we try. You aren't the same person you were back then and neither am I, but all that we have is each other. We need to look out for one another. And if there's something that poses a threat to any of us, we need to know. It's real important if it might come from the people we trust, like the incident last night."

Daniel nodded again with shame-filled eyes before they slid back to the grassy floor. "Well, I'm not sure if there'll be any consequences from this since we aren't even on the same world, but my old comrades and commanders in Black Force didn't like it much when I left. I kinda told some people about what we did, and the repercussion cost them millions in government contracts. That's why I was hidin' out in that rat hole of an apartment when you first found us."

Jedd considered the admission for a moment. "Well, I doubt we'll have any problems with them, but thanks for telling me."

A lot of things are the same from world to world, although not much in this one. But many planes are just like the one I left. Jedd pondered the similarities and differences for a few minutes, and his heart began racing. *What if the same thing that happened to me happened on other worlds? What if me, or Daniel, or any of us is found by people from other worlds? Are there agents from other places out scouring the infinite planes for us? What would happen if we found ourselves?* The questions were piling up again. *I don't think we'll run into those problems here, though*, he concluded after considering the vast differences between this world and his. His heart returned to its normal rhythm, and he breathed easier.

"I think you just need to confront your past. Quit running from it," Jedd commented, his mind returning to the conversation at hand. "Make amends before the rest of your life unravels. If you don't fear the past, it shouldn't be able to haunt you in the present."

"I know you're right, but I'm not sure how to do that."

"Talking about it is the best way to start."

Daniel nodded in agreement.

As their conversation came to an end, the others stirred. The smell of roasting meat permeated the small camp, and Madelin awoke with a gurgling stomach. Lifting herself from the matted grass, she said with a smile, "And who found the food? I'm starving."

"Daniel was kind enough to run to the local corner store," Jedd provided.

Jedd smiled at the Daniel and the veteran returned it. "Just my way of saying sorry."

"Oh… well, thank you. Is everything okay?"

"Just fine," Jedd answered for him, waving Daniel down. Daniel looked back at him with questioning eyes.

"Save it for another time," her godfather whispered.

Daniel reassured her with a few words. "It'll be fine. I'll tell you later."

Madelin peered from one man to the other, but her stomach announced its priority. The fragrant smell lured her toward the animal. "Is it done?" she asked, then added, "And what is it?"

"I'm not sure exactly." Daniel sliced off a strip of roasted flesh and handed it to Madelin.

"Those wings are enormous. Without them, I'd have thought you roasted a Doberman." She took the meat, devouring it in mere seconds. "Thank you," she said between bites.

He then tore off a piece for himself and one for Jedd. They all sat in quiet satisfaction, allowing Roger the last few minutes of sleep before they began the final leg of their journey.

Chapter Twenty-Nine

Blessed Hands

The rest of the day went without incident as the group trekked through the wilderness, munching on the remainder of Jedd's meat. Leodenin maintained his distance.

I'm sure he thinks we'll flee back the way we came if things don't go well, Jedd concluded. *It's a pretty good strategy. He may be right. Although Daniel looks like he could go for miles, I'm sure the wounds have taken their toll. With him eventually out of commission, I don't know how much of a fight we'll be able to put up. But maybe it won't come to that.*

As the sun's light waned and the moons began their journey across the sky, a small town came into view. They steadied their hands on pistols as they approached. Stepping into the bustling town, the group was absorbed by the twilight shadows of monstrous trees.

No one accosted them along the semi-vacant street, but the strangers warranted many stares from the townsfolk. Some were sweeping the paths up to their doorways, while others went about their daily chores. The town's occupants were unaccustomed to visitors.

The small group walked down the dirt road, feeling as though they stepped into the middle ages. No cars or technology of any kind were visible. The houses stood two stories high at most and were made of mud-packed brick, wood, and stone. Small gardens grew outside most houses, and people passing by were dressed in fashions of old.

Outside a nearby home, a woman in a tan dress with pleated shoulders and a cinched waist dumped a bucket into the road and retreated from them with wary eyes. The woman was worn, dirty, and appeared to have been plucked from history.

It's like peasant life in the Victorian Age, thought Jedd, at least according to movies he had seen. *This place hasn't evolved.*

He thought of the worlds they came from as being the same, although Daniel's had differed slightly. However, neither of their homes was as archaic as this one.

None of the people near them possessed auras, but cradled deeper within the confines of the town were those they sought. They continued on under the strange stares of the townspeople. After a short while, Jedd's stomach growled at the smell of roasting meat and vegetables. The scent drifted from a well-populated tavern just ahead. After gnawing on the remainder of his rations hours ago, his stomach was about to climb out of his skin in search of food. The others watched the large building, longing for what was inside.

It was squat and apparent from the wooden backside that the stone structure had been built onto. The wood sign hanging over the doorway swung back and forth in the cool, night breeze. Although battered and faded, they could still make out the chiseled image of a sloshing jug of ale standing next to a fresh loaf of bread. Jedd knew their money would be of no use in this strange place. His stomach gurgled again.

If our money's no good, maybe they'll barter. Turning to the others, he addressed what was on everyone's mind.

"It's worth a try," mouthed Daniel through a yawn. "What do we have to trade?"

They stood clustered in the dirt road, looking from one person to another.

"It'd have to be somethin' of value to them," added Roger. "We need to find out more about these people."

Jedd nodded and led the group into the aged building. They were met by a raucous throng of people huddled around heavy, wooden tables. Most drank house ale while rich tobacco smoke circulated throughout the large common room, mingling with the odor of spiced meat. A few patrons stopped to stare, but most were so focused on conversation and games, they didn't notice the newcomers.

They seated themselves at one of the few vacant tables. The tension in Jedd's muscles eased when he slumped into the wooden chair. Leodenin's aura glowed from outside the town, but had stopped before entering. There were other customers milling about the tavern who were also surrounded by a faint glow. Each was unique in color and tint.

It's astonishing that so many strange people are clustered within this village, thought Jedd. *And they interact with the normal clientele as though no one's the wiser. It's odd... Something seems off.* As he sat pondering the oddity, other concerns came to mind. *Can they see the auras? What does the glow mean for these people? Can they see the auras around us?* At that instant he became well aware of how much his group stood out. His gaze floated from one member to the next.

Roger stood apart from the rest of the group, and Jedd noticed a glint in his eyes as the gambler watched a group of men playing cards nearby. The cards weren't dissimilar from the Cajun's, although the artwork was more rudimentary. Each of the four well-dressed men threw gold coins into the center of the table when his turn came. Their fashions were different than most people they had seen. The men were young, but lace flared at their sleeves and gold stitching weaved across the collars of their shirts. The man seated facing them had long, auburn hair tied in a ponytail. Even the green hair ribbon possessed inlaid stitching to match his shirt. These were men of wealth. They cast their money onto the table with a hearty laugh. It was unlike any Jedd had seen. It was difficult to tell from so far away, but one side appeared to have the imprint of a pouncing tiger, while the other held a wide-limbed tree reaching for the sky. He listened to them talk and was amazed to comprehend their speech. Some syllables were inflected in a different pattern. It was as though the familiar words lilted with the accent of a foreign land, but none he could identify.

After a few minutes passed, Roger leaned into the table his group occupied and spoke in a shouted whisper over the bustle of voices around them. "I think I know how we can eat tonight."

"How?" Jedd asked, eyebrows quirked, showing his skepticism.

"*Mes amis*, I can make the money."

Jedd knew what Roger had in mind and the potential cost if his cursed past continued. "You'd have to have something to wager, Roj. Besides, you don't even know how to play the game. Things are different here. What if you lose?"

Roger was still leaning in, having anticipated the question. "I can't guarantee a win," he whispered, "but it's as good as in the bag. I've been watchin' them, and the game's the same. I'm twice as good as those guys."

A waitress came, but Jedd waved her away as he considered Roger's idea. "And what would you wager?"

Daniel and Madelin watched the conversation play out, intrigued by the plan. Seeing that Jedd was at least entertaining the idea, Roger pressed on. "The way I figure it, most things here are valued for their use to the people. My watch is solar powered, and I figure I can wager it." He lifted his wrist and pointed at the digital display.

Jedd shook his head before speaking. "They won't take it, Roger."

"Why the hell not?" retorted the gambler.

Jedd continued with patience. "First off, they don't have a use for it. If they operate the way most agricultural societies did in the past, it's by the sun. If they need to time something, they use candles. Besides, they'd have to be able to read and I doubt many of them can, let alone in our language."

Roger hated to admit it, but Jedd was right. The gambler looked into his hands, their knitted fingers resting on the table, and searched for what these medieval people might want.

Before he got far, the veteran offered his own idea. "Why don't you try this?" he said, pulling the hard, metal lighter from his pocket. He slid it across the table.

"Now, wait a second," interrupted Jedd. "That's our fire. What're we goin' to do when we get back out there?" His hitchhikers thumb pointed back over his shoulder, the way they had come.

"If Roger thinks he can do it, I believe him," Daniel muttered. "Anyways, if we don't eat, we won't be travelin' far."

His haggard face had gotten worse as the day wore on. Jedd was astounded at the man's resilience, but every man has his limits. Unable to argue with the statement without insulting Daniel, Jedd consented.

Roger snatched the lighter with a confident smile and strutted over to the table. Although foreign and penniless, he struck up a conversation and the men found him a chair. He demonstrated the lighter's capabilities. The metallic casing shone in the lamplight, entrancing them with its ease of use. Their eyes followed its flame as he brandished it aloft, telling a story of how he once used it to save he and his friends from an icy death in mountainous wilderness. Whether they understood the landscape he described was impossible to tell, but the table's occupants watched the extravagant show with hearty chuckles. After a while his lighthearted voice was heard laughing with the men, hands were dealt, and the lighter was placed in the center of the table. A multitude of stamped coins accompanied it.

Roger's assessment proved accurate after the first hand and in subsequent hands. Once he built up a respectable stack of coins, he flagged down a waitress in a low-cut blouse and ordered her to bring his friends at the other table whatever they wanted, in addition to a round of drinks for the men whose money he was paying with. A few of the card players balked at Roger spending his winnings, but he smiled and hefted the silver lighter with the US Marine emblem embossed on its shell. Appeased, the men continued their banter, and the waitress took the group's orders. Soon a meal of fresh cooked vegetables, steaming meatloaf, and ale sat before Madelin and her protectors. They stared at it as though presented with a king's ransom. Daniel sniffed at his cup, longing to drain it.

Today's the first day these hands haven't rattled, thought the veteran. *No sense goin' back to that. I can't save Madelin if I'm twitchin'. It ain't got bad enough to affect my aim yet, but it's only a matter of time.* Although he knew the wound was healing—he'd seen it when he adjusted the bandage earlier—he could still feel his energy ebbing with every hour. He resisted the urge and just took a sip.

While they ate, Jedd watched the variety of men and women occupying themselves within the confines of the tavern. The others joked as the night wore on, but he could feel something crawling up his back—a faint sensation that worked its way into his spine. While the regular clientele took little notice of Jedd and his friends, those surrounded by glowing hues kept a subtle watch, eyeing the newcomers with sidelong glances that had so far gone unnoticed by all but Jedd. This constant surveillance was part, but not the entire cause of the sensation. Something still ate at him. He looked from one glowing individual to another. Then, while watching an elder farmer sitting next to a moderately affluent merchant, he hit upon the difference. The farmer's skin had darkened with age, while every person blessed with an aura was pale and youthful, even those who were graying and past their prime. The class and fashion difference also seemed to separate the magical people from the mundane. These prosperous people also possessed a vigor that was uncharacteristic of so many. They exuded a youthful exuberance that was almost childlike, but their eyes held knowledge far beyond their years.

Chapter Thirty

Strangers

By the end of the night, the group was full and engrossed in conversation about the possibilities that lay ahead. Roger interrupted with a polite cough and introduced a pale gentleman whom he'd been playing cards with as "Alain." The first thing Jedd noticed was the brown hue hovering around the man. The tall gentleman's mannerisms were unique to those of high breeding and education: an erect frame, respectable clothes, and smooth motions that seemed more accustomed to a swan than a human being.

The second thing that became apparent, and the most troubling, was the intensity with which he watched Madelin. Alain's desires were painted on his face for the world to see. Jedd's blood found its boiling point, but he held his contempt under wraps and allowed Roger to continue the introductions.

"Alain lives up the road a ways."

The pale man stood a hand taller than Roger, who was by no means short. His posture emanated self-confidence, and he greeted the group with a nod. His gaze hovered on each of them long enough to commit their images to memory. His hair flowed over his forehead and past his ears in waves that caressed his shoulders. They framed a face chiseled from stone as white as talc and hard as steel.

Alain gave a formal bow, even extending his leg like in the courts of old, but his eyes never left Madelin's. Her flushed cheeks revealed that she had noticed the grace with which his slim, muscular body moved. Each motion was somehow accentuated by his well-tailored pants, frilled yellow shirt, and dark overcoat. His attire was of a style long past its prime, but the flourish with which he ended his preamble was oddly appropriate. Madelin acknowledged the bow without a word.

"Very nice to meet you, *mademoiselle*. I am, as your friend said, Alain Traditor. It seems, in the limited time I have spent with him, that he has somehow obtained both my purse and attention. But it is no surprise when he travels in the company of such beautiful... people."

The men of the group were under no delusions about whom the articulate compliment was intended.

"Roger has brokered a place for you to stay the night in my quaint hovel," Alain continued. "I hope you find the lodgings to your liking. If you would please follow me?" Although voiced as a question, Alain walked out the door without a backward glance, accustomed to his requests being followed without demur.

How small of a house does this egocentric guy live in? Jedd wondered as they got up and trailed behind.

Roger slapped a few coins onto the table before following in the wake of his friends. The waitress eyed him from the bar, and he gave her his best smile before exiting the building. He was jubilant with the night's success and satisfied with a full stomach. His luck had turned.

Once back on the tree-lined road, they kept to Alain's coat tails, consumed with the satisfaction of a full stomach and warm place to stay. They passed a small market closing up for the night and moved further through the town. Their presence was strange enough that the people in view stopped to stare like the peasants from earlier that evening. The smell of caged animals and manure permeated the street. The buildings here were more compact and looked as though people lived in tighter . quarters, their livestock bedding down nearby.

Ahead stood an even larger structure, much like the big colonial home Jedd had visited as a kid, back in the eastern states. The columns were somewhat different, almost Romanesque in their detail. Eyes wide, the group trudged up the long path leading to the entryway.

If this is Alain's "hovel," thought Jedd, *then he won't concern himself with a few coins lost in a game of cards.*

The group crossed the groomed lawn and proceeded up the stone path to the crowned double door. Alain knocked with a confident *ratta-tat-tat-tat,* and a pale man dressed in servant livery answered. His jacket was short and black, but stood on his shoulders, stiff and unruffled. He wore matching dress pants with a deep-purple bow atop his pleated, white shirt. He was an iconic representation of a house servant, although the color of his tie, which Jedd assumed was dictated by the lord of the manor, gave him the odd appearance of a stand-up comic. For Alain to knock on his own door astounded Jedd, but the appearance of the servant thrust the oddity from his mind.

"Welcome home, my lord," greeted the man as he pulled the door open and allowed them to enter. His eyes were downcast, focusing on the worn, hardwood floorboards as must have been proper for his station. Closing the door after them, Alain introduced his servant before directing Farlin to show them to their rooms.

"Please follow me," ordered the servant with a self-assurance bred over many years of service. He then turned and strode up the long flight of steps.

Alain raised his voice in an appeal as they made their way up the stairs, "When you are situated, please join me in the study." The request for their company echoed through the open foyer.

Although Jedd didn't know where the study was, he nodded and thanked their host as he stepped onto the top floor and out of sight. The others followed him without missing a step. Alain had enough rooms that each of them was given separate quarters, although he soon found that the idea of using a communal bathroom hadn't faded from architectural fashion. *At least there's running water,* thought Jedd, *if not plumbing.*

A short while later, feeling refreshed, Jedd made his way down the stairs and into what Farlin indicated as the study. The candle-lit room was unoccupied, and he took a seat, admiring the walls of books surrounding him. *How is it that such a poor world, with no real technology, can produce so many books?*

Giving in to his curiosity, Jedd hopped out of the crushed velvet chair to admire the spines of each shelved book. The script wasn't dissimilar from his own, although the flourishes with which the penman created his personalized calligraphy were quite impressive—much more elaborate than that of a normal printing press. Jedd moved down the wall, perusing the library more for curiosity's sake than true interest, until he came across a book titled *A Labyrinth of Elemental Curiosities: The Development of Rare and Unexplainable Human Traits.* Jedd dislodged the book from the shelf and backed into the seat he had vacated.

He opened the handmade book and used the flickering glow of a nearby candle to read the contents. Within seconds he was engrossed in the author's thoughts on human evolution and spiritual augmentations. Its perspectives were far different from the accepted sciences of his world. He soon found himself drowning in a series of arguments and justifications, founded upon the author's fundamental belief in spiritual energy and alterations due to the necessity for change within the species itself. This allowed him to extrapolate on potential similarities to their own developmental state. He was so focused on the book that he was unaware of Daniel and Roger's arrival.

The two men marveled at the collection that Jedd now ignored, having planted his nose within his book of choice. Madelin soon joined them, followed by Alain. When they had all found a seat in the luxurious room, their host stoked the fire back to life.

He spoke while prodding the fireplace with a black, iron poker. "So how do you like our little town?" Without waiting for an answer, he supplied it for them. "It's a great place to live. I have lived here for dozens of years, and it never gets old."

"What's so exciting about it?" Madelin asked, seeing little of interest to her.

"You can't beat the superb weather here... never too cold or too hot. The large shade trees throughout the town help keep it the perfect temperature, shadowing every inch of our small village. Plus the farmers are able to grow just about anything you could want, and without a doubt, it will be more delicious than anything you have ever tasted. I believe you sampled a small portion this evening."

They nodded in unison, remembering the commonplace meal that had somehow tantalized every taste bud—all but Jedd, who was still engrossed in his book.

Alain took note of the title he chose before moving on. "So far as entertainment goes, we make do and are proud of the traditions that have developed over the years."

"What kind of traditions?" asked Madelin.

"My, my, aren't we the curious one," commented Alain with a chuckle. "Well, there may not be too much you outsiders find of interest. However, the sense of family fostered within our small town is something I relish."

Jedd nodded and set the book on the end table, overhearing their patron's comment and understanding the desire for a safe place to raise a family. However, he couldn't set aside what had bothered him earlier. "Alain, if you don't mind, I'd like to pose a question about your fair town."

Seeing the polite necessity with which Jedd prefaced the question, Alain sat down in a worn but elegant chair and propped his leg upon his knee before answering, "By all means." He glared at Jedd while a smile lit his face, as though provoking Altran.

Jedd could see the certainty and confidence their host possessed and understood the likelihood of this man taking exception to his question. With careful phrasing, he continued, "Alain, I noticed a few small differences between some of the people at the tavern. Any idea what might have caused it?"

"To what difference do you refer?" their host replied.

Out of the corner of his eye, Jedd watched Roger smirk at the pompous tone of Alain's voice. Fortunately, the Cajun caught himself and covered his mouth with a hand.

"Well," Jedd began, attempting to keep their host's attention, "the youthful appearance of more wealthy inhabitants is striking, much like yourself. The farmers you spoke of earlier don't possess those features."

"Oh, I see what troubles you," Alain mumbled, as though reassuring himself that Jedd had no further questions. "That is something we have worked to fashion within our small school. It is the result of our local teacher, Mr. Paria. He has worked to develop the confidence within our young children for many years and, if I do say so myself, Juno has done a great job encouraging them to take hold of life with both hands. Over time, how we approach life has shown itself as we aged."

Jedd listened, but was troubled by the answer. *It just seems too simple.* Looking back at Alain's quaint smile, he became certain it was a lie. *There's more to it, but I doubt Alain's willing to confess. I can't believe a word this man says. He's like a snake hiding in the grass, looking for a weakness and waiting to strike. I'll have to check out his story with Mr. Paria tomorrow.*

"And where might we find Mr. Paria?" he asked with a casualness he didn't feel.

"Tomorrow he'll be at the school house, although he is somewhat disturbed, so you might choose your words with care." After a moment of contemplation, Alain added, "In fact, you should think twice about anything he says, assuming he agrees to speak with you at all."

Jedd was caught off guard by the deterring comments after such a glowing recommendation. "I thought you said he was doing great things for the community."

"Of course he is," Lord Alain explained. "However, even the lowest of people can perform admirable acts."

Although the explanation seemed flimsy, Jedd didn't probe further, instead leaving his remaining questions for the following day.

"We'll find him tomorrow then."

"He should have little left to do after the children leave. Find him at the height of the day, although I wouldn't hold out much hope of learning anything worthwhile," finished Alain before asking, "So what brings you to our small town?"

Jedd considered the question before answering. *It's obvious Alain is trying to discredit the teacher for fear of what he might say. It's probably best not to reveal everything, but some things will become common knowledge soon enough.*

"We've been pursued by a group of men who've murdered people close to us. There's nothing they won't do to capture us."

Lord Alain nodded, but wasn't fazed by his answer. Then he probed deeper. "I'm a trader by profession and have traveled all over. Where is it you come from?"

Jedd was somewhat put off by the lack of reaction and replied with purposeful ambiguity, "Nowhere you know. As I said, we've traveled a great distance and as luck would have it, came upon your prospering town."

Seeing their reluctance, Alain gave up on tact and went for the heart of the matter, "And why are they so adamant about capturing you?"

Jedd saw that his vague answers weren't getting them far. In fact, this man, no matter how much Jedd distrusted him, had opened up his home to them. Giving in, he replied, "Because we took Madelin." He gestured to her with a hand. "They work for a government department and killed her parents, my good friends. They abducted her when she was a child. Then they tortured her so she would follow their orders."

The mention of her loss startled Madelin, and a shudder coursed through her body. No reaction registered on Alain's face. It was as though Jedd hadn't answered the question. However, their host had heard and inquired further, "And why choose this petite flower?" He cast a feigned look of adoration and pity her way with his final words.

"We aren't sure why," Jedd lied. *Information is power. Some things need to stay secret, but I doubt Alain will buy it.*

Also seeing their host's looming disbelief, Madelin elaborated, "I can see things, but they're odd. I see ghostlike buildings that aren't there. I thought for a long time that I was losing my mind, but there has to be a reason for why the department took such drastic measures. Maybe Jedd's right. Maybe it means I'm not so crazy."

Jedd hoped the half-truth would be enough.

"I see," the well-dressed man replied. The stoked fire illuminated his face in faint shadows. "Well, I can assure you that as long as you are under my roof, no harm shall come to you."

Jedd heard the comforting statement of salvation, but the man's eyes were devoid of emotion. A shiver ran down his back as he watched Alain's brown gaze encompass them all.

"Now that the formalities are out of the way, please feel free to peruse my library at your leisure. I see some of you have already found books of interest. I obtained them over many years of travel." He stood up from his comfortable seat. "I must retire, for the morn comes soon and I have much to attend to." He strode from the room, saying, "Sleep well."

Jedd motioned the others to him for a quiet warning. "Don't believe a word that man says. Keep your eyes open and your guard up."

The others nodded, each having come to a similar conclusion, or at least trusting Jedd's instincts. With that, they went their own ways. Roger and Daniel retired to their rooms to rest for the following day, while Jedd and Madelin continued to partake in Alain's elaborate library.

After hours of study, they found their way to separate rooms and Jedd left her with a cautionary word of advice, "Block the door with something... a chair, anything. And if you need me, I'm across the hall."

"Okay," she replied before entering her room. "Thanks."

Chapter Thirty-One

We All Have Secrets

Before long, the day's exertions took their toll and Altran fell fast asleep, but a muffled murmur of "No, no, no," alerted him to the loud silence that followed. He resolved that the words were just in his head, a fleeting dream, when a resounding *thud* vibrated through the wall above his head. A masculine voice pleaded through the paper-thin walls, "No... I can't... No!" Daniel's room was next to Jedd's, and the cries sent him hurtling out the door and into the adjoining room.

The veteran lay sprawled across the bed as though flailing in mid-fall, exposed to the world like a newborn babe. Sweat coursed over every inch of his scarred hide, reflecting the moons' rays back at the window on the opposite side of the room. The veteran's damp sheets had been thrown aside in violent, dream-filled throes. Jedd closed the door and pulled a chair up to his bedside. Daniel's memories truly tormented the weathered man.

Jedd reached over and grasped the man's shoulder. Daniel awoke with a start that left him posed in Roman immortality. His eyelids flared open, but saw nothing. He delved through Jedd and beyond. His eyes were consumed in an endless ocean of tumultuous questions and dark, cresting waves of regret.

"Daniel...?" He gave it an instant to sink in before repeating, "Daniel... it's me, Jedd. Wake up."

His eyes soon came into focus. Daniel spied his late-night visitor and rasped with concern, "Hey, what's wrong? Did something happen?"

"No, no... nothin' like that," Jedd reassured him.

"Then why're you here?" A cool breeze alerted him to his state of indecency, and he threw a sweaty sheet over his torso.

"You were having a hell of a dream, bud."

Shame entered the man's eyes with the very mention of the memory, disturbing the mask of solidity and strength he wore every waking moment.

"Was it the same dream you told me about?" prompted Jedd.

"Yeah," Daniel croaked.

"Look, I think I can help."

"How so?" Daniel asked, his tone giving away his skepticism.

"Well, there's a bit more to what I can do than Madelin and I have let on. You know I can project myself elsewhere in the world while I'm asleep, but something we figured out... really by accident... was that I can enter someone's thoughts and see their dreams. I was even able to talk to Madelin when she was awake, while I was resting in her mind. So, I think I might be able to speak with you while you're dreaming. It might help."

The suggestion was intriguing, but Daniel had never let anyone know about his nightmares until meeting Roger and Jedd. That was a huge step for the well-guarded man. What Jedd was proposing violated every rule he had on privacy, but each night was like reliving a hell of his own making. If Jedd was even half right, this could relieve him of the stressful burden he carried every day. With nothing left to hide, Daniel agreed.

Jedd left the room and reentered his own. Slinking back under his covers, he tried to prepare for a different sleep than he had awoken from minutes before. As he drifted toward unconsciousness, he changed the momentum of his dreamlike fall, pushing himself outward in search of Daniel. The familiar tunnel was shorter this time, allowing him to slip into the reality of his personal bedroom.

Standing at his own bedside and looking at his limp body was unnerving. He watched the uneasiness he felt appear in the expression of his unconscious body. A sarcastic thought came to mind and attempted to break his nervous stare. *This gives new meaning to being beside yourself.*

Jedd chuckled then pried his eyes from the sleeping body and looked up at the wall separating the two rooms. He stepped through, bypassing the limitations of mortal reality, and approached Daniel's bedside. Jedd surveyed his sleeping form. Although he hadn't been asleep long, his eyes twitched, wincing in agitation. The dreams had already begun their relentless attack. With a thought Jedd delved into his mind, transporting himself into a world he had only heard about. He was unprepared for what he found in Daniel's nightmarish truths.

Desert wilderness surrounded him, bordered by a mountainous cliff of escaped boulders and rock. It was as though God had left his footprint in the ground ages ago. After millennia of wind erosion, all that was left was the underlying stone and billions of grains of sand.

In the crook of the footprint stood a small town composed of mud and thatch houses. An archaic well sat in the center of town, the one obvious water source for the denizens of this small community. On any other day it would have been bustling with people carrying out their daily chores and business. On this day, however, the town was a flurry of activity as the Middle Eastern residents ran in terror. Their robes streamed behind them, giving the assaulting soldiers a handle to grasp them by.

Armed corpses littered the desert streets, their faces masked by cloth wraps. The ends of some facial coverings came undone, fluttering to life in the wind. They revealed dust-encrusted eyes and vacant stares cast at the blazing sun overhead. A small contingency of dead Black Force agents were lined at the cliff base, as though awaiting their turn to enter the afterlife. The caustic wind blew, coating the bodies and allowing pockets of sand to build up in every wrinkle and crevice.

Jedd pulled his eyes from the morbid sight and found a familiar face sticking out above desert fatigues. Daniel was much younger and hadn't attained the salty grey peppering his crew-cut hair. He held a flaming torch aloft, willing himself to light the roof of the small thatch hut. After a moment's hesitation, he pulled it away and turned to another camouflaged man.

In the center of the chaos, the older, more confident man barked, "Soldier, you know what they've done. I thought you knew better than to question my orders, boy." The last word was tinged with disappointment and anger. He leapt down from the small rock wall and marched up behind Daniel. He raised his voice, intending for his family in Alabama to hear the tongue lashing he was about to administer. "Did you hear me, boy?"

"Yes, Sir," Daniel shouted, although his hand was still unwilling to cross the distance.

"Then why the hell aren't you doing what you're told?"

Daniel's training told him to follow his orders, but his body was still reluctant. "Sir, I can't," he replied, turning back to the small home as his inner struggle rose to a climax.

Jedd watched Daniel's immobilized gaze delve through the cracks in the white-washed walls. The commander was relentless, but Jedd knew from their earlier conversation that his attention was not on the officer hounding him from behind. It was transfixed on the eyes of the victimized children and elderly inside.

Jedd crossed the distance, invisible to both men. Although somewhat shorter than Daniel, the damage to the home allowed them both to peer into the shadowed room. Sun-darkened faces streaked with tears peered out at them. They were vague, but visible in the crisscross of shadows under the makeshift roof. Some elderly squatted in the corner, eyes locked on the floor, while others stared at nothing. Many of the dozen children pled with Daniel over the cries of their mothers and grandparents.

It was astonishing how many people were huddled within the small home. The house itself could not have covered more than two hundred square feet, yet the Black Force agents had stuffed it full, as though it were a Nazi cattle car awaiting transport of its Holocaust cargo.

But transport to where? The answer came to him as the torch in Daniel's clenched hands flared in the abrasive wind. Sheltered in an insubstantial corner of Daniel's consciousness, Jedd could sense the conflicting emotions flowing through his friend. The ends of the soldier's fingers dug into the warm wood, and rivulets of blood leaked from under his fingernails. Daniel stood entranced, unaware of the splinters embedding themselves deeper. The youthful soldier was caught between morality and ingrained military training. Jedd pitied the young man for the decision he was forced to make, one that would haunt him this day and the next, until his dying breath.

A firm shove from behind broke his gaze and brought him back to the moment. "You have your orders, soldier, or do I have to do it my damn self?" the commander snarled, standing inches behind Daniel.

His restraint subsided as his regret grew. Daniel's hand came down on the dry roof. It ignited as though doused in petrol. Daniel watched the flames engulf the inhabited home. They leapt from his hand to the roof, consuming his soul. The conflagration surged across the dry thatch, roaring as it spread, but the devouring inferno was no match for the sounds of innocent screams growing louder with every passing second.

The voices flooded his consciousness, fighting to overwhelm him. Jedd could sense invisible arms reaching out and grasping Daniel's sleeping body. They attempted to submerge him, miring him in deep waters of unconsciousness. He fought for every breath, flinging the invisible attackers away and striving to reach the surface. This was the frightful brawl Daniel battled each night... tearing at the world around him... ripping away linens and anything within reach as he fought for breath. Consciousness was the salvation he sought.

This isn't working, thought Jedd. *This isn't the way. Daniel's won this battle every night for years, but the war is endless. It'll never end unless he tries something else.*

Jedd spoke to the man standing next to him, thankful of the smooth connection this staticless world provided, "Daniel, listen to me."

Jedd's calm, measured tones were soothing, but Daniel's frantic fight for air allowed just a trickle of the voice to filter through.

"Daniel, listen, it's Jedd."

The familiar name was enough to break his struggle, but then it wavered.

"Daniel, I'm here with you. Don't worry, everything'll be fine. You've been fighting for too long. Stop. I've got another way."

The calm reassurance Jedd offered and the trust they had were enough. Jedd sensed a subconscious change as Daniel stopped struggling. Unseen hands grasped his ankles, pulling him down into the recesses of his nightmare. While the younger memory of Daniel stood watching the flames in mute horror, a single tear betrayed the memory and his decision to give in to their wishes.

"We're our own harshest critics, Daniel. What you feel are the hands of fate. They don't want to destroy you. They want to teach you. Hear what they have to say," Jedd pleaded.

The words came to Jedd unbidden and without thought, yet he knew them to be true. Then a tingle of anticipation grew in his gut as he felt the grip of unseen hands take hold of his feet, too.

The hands held them in the memory, forcing them to watch as the building crumbled and fell inward. Burning masses of brick and roof collapsed upon the waiting victims as their gazes condemned their executioners. One pair of bright eyes and then another were extinguished in the smoke-filled darkness, the haunting whites of their eyes disappearing like candles snuffed out in a stiff breeze. More tears flowed down the young soldier's cheeks as he watched the atrocity, torch in hand.

Chapter Thirty-Two

Twist of Fate

Without warning, the world changed. It was as though Daniel and Jedd were in a slot machine of memories and someone pulled the lever. Hundreds of images spun by at a dizzying pace, racing against time as hands of fate searched for the right one. Jedd caught snippets of some that were familiar—not from a recent time, but from an earlier period in *his* life. Images of his son and wife slid past like a jumbled collection of film strips running along the reel.

Wait... I know these people, thought Jedd as fragments from his past flew by on the wheel. *What the hell? I thought this was Danny's nightmare.*

Daniel glanced over at the man he was just coming to trust, knowing the images flashing before him weren't his own. Jedd was engrossed, his eyes glued to the rapid-flowing filmstrip. The reel began to slow, settling on one likeness of still life.

The memory it depicted was one Jedd regretted every day, but if given the choice again, his decision would remain the same. A youthful Jedd Altran pulled up to a quaint blue and white lake house one star-filled night. Except for the few houses huddled across the lake, the world was devoid of life. Madelin's family home had stood within sight, but was now reduced to rubble, invisible in the picture. As their eyes searched the slide, it loomed closer, growing as time sped up. A sudden shove sent them hurling toward the picture and cast them into the memory itself.

They stood in the freshly mown lawn and watched Jedd's younger self get out of the dark sedan and retreat to the open trunk. Reassured that no one was watching, he pulled a black body bag from the trunk and hefted the six-foot object over his shoulder. He carried it across the lawn and under the wooden sign that welcomed all who entered the Altran household.

Daniel watched in disbelief as the young computer programmer passed the two men. His assumptions were confirmed when he saw a trademark stamped on one end of the bag, 'Anderson Mortuary.' Daniel glanced at the doorway with furrowed brows as Jedd's younger self disappeared.

"Was that what I think it was?" asked Daniel with a curious glance.

"Just watch," Jedd replied. "I'll explain later."

Jedd nodded at the door, and both men entered to find Altran's youthful clone unzipping the body bag on the floor, revealing a lifeless shell of a man lying naked. The body was young, about the same age as Jedd, and possessed the same build. Jedd's younger half then dressed the stiff in pajamas from a small duffle bag at his feet. For a final touch, he lifted the silver family cross from around his neck and placed it on the lifeless body. Altran struggled with the stiff corpse, but eventually positioned him on the couch as though asleep and away from the windows lining the living room.

He then rolled the body bag up and inserted it into the duffle bag. Daniel and Jedd watched the youthful Altran turn on the television, check that the windows and doors were locked, retrieve a few items from a small safe, and then reach behind the stove and sever the gas line. With a last look of sadness, the youthful Altran tossed his keys onto the center table and slipped out the back door with the bag in tow—forever locking himself out of the life he had made.

The two observers slipped out of the sealed house and followed the man as he stealthed from shadow to shadow. Steering clear of the moonlight, he crawled up the steep, forested hill. At the top he stepped onto a back road where a car sat idling in the night. The driver was its sole occupant, a man of Oriental descent. Jedd opened the door, slipped into the back seat, and slouched low. The silent observers walked up to the car and listened next to the open passenger window.

"Did you take care of everything?" asked the driver.

"Yep," whispered Altran from the back seat. "Thanks for helping, Koiyo."

"No problem," the driver replied. "It's the least I can do. You locked everything up and left the keys in the house, right?"

"Yeah," he replied, irritated by his friend's insistence on double-checking every part of the plan. "I grabbed a body with the same blood type and switched the dental records."

"Good," added Koiyo with a sigh of relief. "So now we just wait for them to take the bait."

"Yep. It's just a waiting game now. You sure your intel is right?"

"Of course! They're comin' tonight. They have to make it look like an accident. Did you loosen the gas pipe from the stove?"

"Yeah," came Jedd's reply, but his answer sounded distant and hollow.

"I know it's a little late for this, but are you sure it's what you want to do? You have a wife and kid that need you, you know?"

"I know," Jedd replied, "but if I'm with them, they're all in danger. With me dead, those government agents will have no reason to pursue my family. Remember the last time they tried? They almost killed Faith and Matthew in that elevator fiasco."

"I know, I know… but isn't this kind of extreme?"

"I don't know what else to do, Koiyo. Do you?"

The driver sat in silence. They had been over his options time and again. When you are on the radar of a covert government agency, it's not as though they are governed by the strictures of normal civilian law. And even with proof of their existence, their government-sanctioned activities trump any kind of assistance local law enforcement can provide.

His friend's silence was answer in itself, but before he could dwell on the choice, Koiyo spoke up, his eyes alert and observing the lake house far below. "There's movement. A van just drove halfway up the drive without its lights, and a group of armed agents are approaching through the forest."

"What do they look like?" Jedd asked from his prone position.

Koiyo lifted a small pair of night-vision binoculars. "They're dressed in black and moving pretty stiff. They're wearing some kind of prototype armor. Man… they look like football players from hell."

"That's them," Jedd muttered, his voice somber and detached.

His emotions were reflected from outside the car window, in the older Altran's dejected eyes. Daniel and Koiyo watched the ant-like soldiers surround the house. After peering in the windows, the signal was given and the soldiers took their positions. They poured an accelerant onto the sides of the house and set the charge. The squad finished their job in no time at all and vacated the property. As soon as the charge ignited, flames erupted around the sides of the lake house and in front of the doorways.

The dark van left the driveway as silent as it had come, disappearing around the tree line just as the flames breached the outer walls. The gas-filled house ignited, filling the quiet night with a tremendous explosion.

Assured of their success, Koiyo set the binoculars in the glove compartment, rolled up the window, and put the car into gear.

The two dream watchers caught one last thing as he pulled onto the dirt road. "Well, Jedd, you're now officially dead. Congratulations." Koiyo's attempt at humor was lost before it had begun, and the words fell on deaf ears.

As the car disappeared, the world around the two men again spun out of control. Daniel looked over at the man next to him. Jedd's expression was vacant and confused as he found himself looking at yet another dizzying slot machine of life. The spinning wheel settled once more on another snapshot from Jedd's past. However, this was one he hadn't experienced himself, having been unable to attend.

Before them stood a large group of people on a grassy field littered with tombstones. They were huddled around a grave, its coffin wreathed in flowers. A priest stood next to a picture of Jedd grinning with his wife and newborn son.

"We took the photograph a couple days after returning from the hospital," Jedd muttered.

The picture of the young family cradling their newborn spoke volumes about the world Jedd had left behind. Daniel watched his friend's mumbling form relive the death of his life.

"His name's Matthew," Jedd continued for the benefit of his sanity.

The picture grew closer, and the priest's words came to them as the two men were deposited onto the damp grass. "We do not trust in ourselves, but in God which raiseth the dead: 'Who delivered us from so great a death, and in whom we trust that he will yet deliver our son, Jedd Altran, into his loving arms.'"

At the mention of his name, the priest placed the last nail in the coffin. After twelve years, the reminder of the choice he made tore him apart, but he was unable to look away. He stared at the distraught family he left behind. His wife stood shrouded in a black veil, one hand dabbing at her eyes with a folded handkerchief. The other patted the back of two-year-old Matthew, who clung to the hem of her black dress, his face seeking salvation in her leg. His muffled sobs echoed over the priest's sermon, crying out, "Where's my Daddy? I want my Daddy!"

Daniel watched with sorrow and concern as Jedd lost the last semblance of control he had maintained.

"I'm so sorry," he screamed, but the boy couldn't hear him. He persisted, "Matthew, Faith, I'm sooooo sorry, but I had to. I love you so much, but I had to! I had to!"

His hysterical cries reverberated into the black hole that surrounded them, as though from the depths of a deep, dark well. Daniel waited in nervous anticipation for the darkness to reply, thinking Jedd's heartrending screams might have alerted heaven or hell itself. Jedd fell to the nonexistent floor in despair.

Daniel tried to cross to him, but before he could take a step, the world around them swirled counterclockwise in a multitude of artist's colors. The abstract kaleidoscope merged to form another picturesque night sky, one illuminated by a different lake-house fire. Outside, numerous agents stood gazing at the large conflagration.

A small girl in an ash-covered nightgown stood in the midst of it all. She was entranced by the crumbling home, a grubby teddy bear clutched in her hands. As the image panned around the child, Daniel found the jade eyes he knew so well. They reflected the fire in their glossy surface, but also the family she would never know again.

His trusted friend whimpered from behind in a huddled mass of tears. "No, no, no, not again. Not again!" he shouted. "I've seen enough. The misery's... too... much. It's too much." Grief and sorrow challenged Jedd's sanity and forced him to his feet. He shouted into the flame-lit night, but the darkness ate his words and hungered for more.

The only answer was the murmured pleas of a young girl echoing through the darkness. Her mouth failed to move while she stared at the inferno consuming her childhood, but her voice resonated around them. "Help me, please."

It was as though even this brutal reality couldn't contain the entreaty of such an innocent—a young girl that time forgot, who may still have a place in the future. Daniel saw the necessity of what had to be done. With this realization they were thrust from the darkness and into consciousness.

The scarred soldier woke with a start, but for once he didn't flinch as he looked into the mirror across the room. The charred remains of a child stared back. Eyes that had lurked around every corner now greeted him—not with kindness, nor hatred, but with knowledge. Daniel didn't expect his past to disappear, but he felt he could live with the crimes he committed, now that he knew what to do... what his first step toward atonement would be.

Lurching out of bed, he threw on his cargo pants and flew out the door. He entered the adjoining room with a zest for life that he had forgotten. He found Jedd awake and shuddering as he fought to dislodge the tears from his face. He tore at his cheeks, but the mere action would never be enough to erase the memories. Instead, it left his face red and gleaming. Daniel pulled a chair up to the moonlit bedside and seated himself next to his friend. The sight of Jedd subdued Daniel's enthusiasm and replaced it with concern.

"You okay, bud?"

Jedd chuckled at the thought. "I haven't been okay for a long time. Does it look like I'm okay now?"

The sarcastic response was par for the course as far as Daniel was concerned. "I know it's hard to deal with your demons, but I think we were shown that last memory for a reason."

"What the hell do you mean?" Jedd almost shouted. "I've lived with that memory for years. It's one that haunts me every night, like yours."

"Think about it. It showed us the worst things from our pasts, and then Madelin told us how to find our way to salvation. We can save ourselves if we help Madelin," he said, unable to curb his enthusiasm. "This way, our past doesn't define us."

Jedd composed himself and bottled his emotions before turning cold eyes on his friend. "Are you religious, Daniel?"

"No, but I hope I haven't damned myself already, in case there really is a heaven."

"Neither am I," he replied and continued with mocking sarcasm. "What you're saying will bring about our 'salvation' is what got me into this mess in the first place."

Daniel's tone hardened as he tipped toward the edge of anger. "Dammit, Jedd, then finish what you started."

"I'm going to. Do you think I'd leave my goddaughter to the likes of those PASTOR bastards?" Jedd shouted.

Both men stared at one another, their anger flaring as they sat locked in a battle of wills. Daniel was the first to relax, releasing the tension that had built up in his muscles. With a chuckle, he astounded Jedd by saying, "Look, I know it's hard, but we've made these decisions, and we've got to live with the consequences. Like you said, we have to admit our mistakes, confront our demons, and try to be different people. I'm sure your son's an outstandin' boy. You just saw his first reaction to losing you. He's had twelve years to grow up since then. At this point, we've gotta consider how to make things right."

The logic of Daniel's words calmed Jedd, and the flames behind his eyes dwindled. "I know. It's just hard to deal with it all at once."

"Yeah, talk about turning the tables," Daniel replied with a smile.

Jedd chuckled, masking his unease. "Hell, I thought I was coming to help you."

"You did, my man, you did." Daniel stood up and replaced the chair before walking out of the room, saying, "A few minutes ago, I woke up more rested than I've felt in decades. I think I'll go catch a few more Zs before mornin'."

Jedd knew Daniel was right, but couldn't get the visions out of his head. As the gears within his mind churned, he wondered about the genteel lord whose roof they now slept under. With a small effort, he willed himself to sleep, enough to project himself once more.

I'll have to be careful, he thought. *Who knows what these people can and can't see? I already know they're capable of a hell of a lot more than they let on.*

Jedd slid through another worm hole before landing at his bedside. He stuck his head through the door and peered down the long hallway. No one was out, so he stepped through and began his search.

The large, rectangular building was symmetrical, each hallway mirrored by the opposite end of the building. The kitchen and servants' quarters were set apart in back. There were very few people up at this hour, but a few auras wandered the halls of the manor. He kept them at a distance, avoiding rooms they occupied. However, he searched all empty rooms and even those being used by normal people. He found little of interest until he reached Lord Alain's room.

It was an elegant, yet peculiar domicile, large and spacious with one lone window at the far end and a king-size bed sitting opposite. Four enormous masts lifted the corners three feet off the ground.

With that craftsmanship, the thing could weather a squall out at sea.

It was draped in rich, silk linens that gleamed in the scant moonlight filtering through the window. A multitude of elegant, crimson pillows topped it. They were fringed in gold, adding to the air of royalty.

Wow, for the cost of those, he could feed a small family for a year, Jedd thought. He was never one for extravagance when the money could be better used elsewhere.

The sides of the bed posed an intriguing question, though. They were hinged between the cushions, and low to the floor was an elegant handle covered in worn velvet, having seen repeated use.

Jedd speculated on the possibilities of such a bed, but was unable to find a reasonable answer. *It looks like Alain can pull the sides up over him, closing him in like an enormous... coffin.* He considered the possibility of what people in his world called vampires, but dismissed it. *The whole idea's just a myth, a figment of creative imaginations, not truth. If they really existed, people would know. The extravagance of the bed is just the product of a warped mind and too much money. The man's just got too many fetishes to occupy his spare time.*

He nodded with finality and attempted to ignore the feeling of something crawling up his spine. He pushed the nagging feeling aside and settled his rapid heartbeat. Relieved, Jedd decided to retire for the night and vanished. He returned to his room and body with every intention of discussing the oddity with the others in the morning. He was sure they would come to the same conclusion, but something about the man still had Jedd on edge.

Chapter Thirty-Three

Lacking Modesty

The following morning, Daniel awoke to dim sunlight filtering through the shade tree outside his window. The dreams hadn't pestered him for the remainder of the night. He awoke refreshed and lurched out of bed as though it were the first vacation of his life. Daniel stretched as he walked to the window. His muscles groaned with the effort, and his healing wounds ached, but the subtle warmth of the orange rays filtering through the branches helped to sooth them. He stood with arms outstretched and allowed the breeze to cleanse his skin. Days here were milder than on his world, especially under the shade trees that covered the town. Within the town limits, it was as though the settlement went through constant variations of dawn, dusk, and twilight as the sun roved above then receded each night.

It'll be a nice, cool day, he thought, yawning wide as though he were a bear roused from a long winter's sleep. There was no need to find a bottle to drown in this morning, and the dreamless sleep left his body feeling rejuvenated. His hands didn't shake, and the morning felt like a new beginning. The chirp of birds added to the morning's calm.

Daniel cast around for his pants but failed to find them. He remembered tossing his cargo pants at the base of the bed, but now they were nowhere to be seen. As though on cue, a rap at the door interrupted his late start. He walked over and peered out. Whoever knocked had come and gone, but at his feet was a stack of folded clothes. He brought them in and searched for the rest of his possessions. Nothing remained, except his 9 mm, which still sat on the nightstand. He hadn't turned out his pant pockets, and neither had the thief. Daniel's anger flared at the thought of someone intruding in his quarters while he slept. It didn't matter who owned the building.

With no option left but the new pile of clothes stacked on the bed, Daniel resolved to dress and find the man responsible for the theft. He lifted a folded garment from atop the stack and was stunned to find a shirt reminiscent of early French and English fashion.

"What the hell's this?" he growled, scanning the frilled collar and pleated fabric. The ends of each sleeve were covered in decorative lace, and although they were appropriate for this place, Daniel swore he would never wear such a thing. Throwing it aside, he grasped the next garment, a free-flowing, off-white overshirt. The fabric was thick, but smooth and comfortable. *It'll do,* he thought, pulling it over his bandages.

Daniel sifted through the pile before turning to the mirror. He found himself looking like he just stepped out of a Wild West film. He admired the clothes in the mirror with grudging acceptance. The jacket fit well and was made of thick, gray wool. It had a high collar that arched over his shoulders, guarding his neck from the wind. The boots had also been tailored to fit, although they were less comfortable than his own. The pants were tight, as was the tradition. He had seen many affluent patrons wearing their like in the tavern, but they were obviously not made for comfort or utility. Daniel fell back onto the bed and struggled to dislodge them from his legs.

Minutes later, he again stood in front of the mirror, but this time without the trousers. He needed his cargo pants and boots, but admired the other clothes. The knee-length jacket shadowed most things from his knees up. He grabbed the pistol and stalked into the hallway to introduce the person responsible to his close, metallic friend. He passed through the hall with a determined stride and ignored the astonished stares of the other manor occupants.

Where's Farlin, he wondered. *He'll know what happened.*

It wasn't long before he found the head servant chastising the lead chef of the kitchen. The other cooks were attempting to ignore the elephant in the room and busied themselves preparing other dishes. However, Farlin wasn't quiet, nor was the chef willing to take the abuse of a servant.

"And what the hell do you think you are doing barging into my kitchen?" asked the chef, emphasizing who was in charge.

"Trelaine, don't presume that you have any power over me when I am here at the bequest of the lord."

"And what errand has *Lord Alain* sent you on that concerns me?" Trelaine patronized.

Before Farlin could answer, Daniel's stiff form appeared behind him, snarling, "Farlin. Hey, Farlin!"

Lord Alain's head servant turned at the uncivilized greeting. Seeing one of his lord's guests, he shooed the boisterous cook away and turned to greet the man. Farlin feigned a smile and ignored the veteran's bare legs. "Mr. Robertson, it is a pleasure to see you up and around this morning. I see you found the clothes I left. Were the pants not to your liking?"

The rhetorical question was innocent, yet the mocking undertone chafed on Daniel's nerves. He strode forward, saying, "Listen up, Farlin, and listen good. I want the pants you stole from my room." Daniel didn't stop until he was an inch away from the short man. He stared down at the servant's distended, rat-like face.

"But, Mr. Robertson, I did not steal your clothes. I wished to wash them for you. If you do not mind my saying so, they reeked. I could not in good faith allow you to wear them in their current condition."

The servant didn't bat an eye under Daniels intimidating gaze. Farlin sidestepped the brute and walked into the next room. He returned seconds later with the large man's pants, cleaned and folded, with his boots sitting on top.

"These pants were obviously tailored for someone much larger than you, were they not?"

"What do you mean? They weren't tailored at all."

"That explains it then, sir," replied Farlin. "When I first saw you, I noticed that they hung like your tailor had forgotten what scissors were for. I had them pressed, too, but they did not come out as well as I would have liked. The excess material gave them problems."

The shock at what they had done broke Daniel's stare; however, his concerns weren't alleviated. "Look, Jeeves—" Daniel began.

Not to be put down, the man corrected him, "Farlin, sir."

Daniel began again with the tolerance one might offer a child. "Look, Farlin." He paused for emphasis. "Thanks for the cleaning, but if you haven't noticed, I don't give a rat's ass about fashion. I just want my pants and my ammo."

"Oh, that's already been taken care of, Mr. Robertson," Farlin replied, tapping one of the boots as he handed the bundle to the half-clothed man.

"Wait a second, how'd you find out my name?" asked Daniel.

"Your... I-den-ti-fi-ca-tion... card," Farlin stuttered, again patting the cleaned boots.

Daniel glanced inside and noticed a package wrapped in leather in each boot. They were tied with cord. He discarded the jacket without hesitation, throwing it to Farlin to hold, and slipped into the cargo pants. He then pulled the jacket back on with a contented sigh. The kitchen staff stood staring at the ostentatious sight until the head chef ushered them back to work. Daniel pulled up one of the cook's stools and unwrapped the packages, filling his pockets once again and grunting at their stiffness. *What the hell'd they use for starch?*

"Everything is there, sir, but may I ask a question?" Farlin pressed on without waiting for an answer. "I could not help but notice that you and your friends are not from around here. If you do not mind my asking, where did you come from, and why are you here?"

"You're right, we ain't from around here, but look Jeeves—"

Farlin corrected him again, but Daniel ignored the interruption.

"I do mind. Frankly, it pisses me off that you'd come into my room without my permission. Besides, right now I've got other things I need to take care of. You know of a good doctor… or maybe a medicine man?" After pulling on his boots, Daniel lifted the shirt to reveal the blood-encrusted bandage. "I need to have this checked out and get some new bandages."

The head servant's façade cracked at the sight. "My God, what happened?"

"Don't worry about what happened," he commented. "You know where I can get some clean bandages and see a doc?"

Farlin waved him into the washroom and shut the door. Pointing at a small chair, he busied himself in the cabinets. Daniel seated himself with his 9 mm close at hand.

"I have some linen I can dress the wound with," Farlin said while tearing strips from the older sheets he came across. "But first, you will need to take off your shirt."

Daniel did as he was told. Moments later, Farlin seated himself in front of the veteran with a large bowl of water, clean rags, and a handful of linen strips. He got right to work, unaware of the gun resting on the counter next to Daniel's outstretched hand. The servant dipped the rag in the bowl and cleaned the skin around the wound.

"So what happened, Mr. Robertson?" asked the servant, as though he had just taken a seat in a local barber shop.

Daniel answered through clenched teeth, his free hand gripping the side of the wooden chair in a white-knuckled fist. "Someone shot me… a couple times."

"I will have a look at your other wounds, too," replied Farlin, as though planning out his day. "I couldn't help but notice some of the odd items you had in your pockets."

"Yeah, what of it?" asked Daniel, wincing under the man's touch.

"Your fire starter is unlike anything we can make here. Where are you from?"

Daniel gave in and opted for the truth. "We're from another world."

"Like the legends of Lord Alain and the others," Farlin exclaimed. He was like a child hearing a story for the five-hundredth time.

His reaction caught Daniel off guard. "What do you mean, 'like Lord Alain'? And what others?"

"So you do not know," Farlin muttered. "Lord Alain and others like him are different from the rest of us. They came here long ago, and stories of their arrival have been passed down through the ages, but none of them speak of it now. They prefer that people assume this is how it has always been."

"So, the truth has been passed down in their families, too, or are they trying to forget where they came from?" Daniel asked, confused.

Farlin finished cleaning the wound and answered Daniel's question. "Well, they have had children, and most of them know the truth from their parents, but none will speak with outsiders about it. The elders, the ones who made the trip, will not say why they came. People have wondered for years and stories pop up, but no one really knows."

The scarred veteran sensed Farlin wasn't telling him everything. When he met Daniel's searching gaze, a glint of mischief verified the soldier's suspicions. Over the years, he had become an expert at reading people and detecting lies—a necessary skill in his line of work. However, Daniel let him continue. The knowledge that there were some who were willing to talk was enough for him. As he sifted through the information, it occurred to him that the generations didn't match.

"Farlin, are you sayin' that the original ones, the elders, are still alive? I thought you said the stories were legends. How many years has it been since they got here?"

The question struck Farlin as absurd. "Of course they are still alive," he answered, as though chuckling inward at Daniel's ignorance. "You're the guest of the esteemed Lord Alain Traditor, the most revered elder. He is at least a few hundred years old."

"What?" exclaimed Daniel. "That guy we met last night? He can't be over thirty."

Farlin chortled as he tied a knot in the linen strips. "Think what you will." He propped Daniel's foot upon his knee, rolled up the pant leg, and repeated the process.

The lack of an answers left Daniel wondering. Something about the guy had bugged him and Jedd, enough that he warned them not to trust the man.

Before his thoughts could continue further, Farlin posed another question, "Now that I have answered your questions, try answering mine. Why did you come here?"

Daniel replied without much thought, "We were runnin' from the same people who shot me."

Farlin nodded. "But why here?"

This question gave Daniel a bit more trouble. After some speculation, he said, "I'm not sure. I didn't have a say in where we went. I guess you could say, I was along for the ride."

"The people that shot you, are they the same people camped outside town?"

The question struck Daniel as odd. For a servant, Farlin knew an awful lot about what went on in the town. "Yes," he replied. "How'd you know about them?"

"It is my business to know, Mr. Robertson." He pulled each end of the knotted linen tight. The two sat across from one another, each assessing the other. Finally, the knowledgeable man broke the silence. "I believe you, Mr. Robertson, and I believe you are here for a reason, one that even you do not know. Fate has brought you here, and you will fulfill your destiny."

After last night's dreams, the mention of fate was too much to be coincidence, but before Daniel could say anything more, Farlin continued, "I will help you. There is a man you need to meet. He can do much more for you than I have. I will take you to see him later this evening, after dinner." Farlin stood without waiting for Daniel's answer and tugged his jacket straight, becoming the dutiful servant yet again. "If that will be all, sir, I must tend to the rest of the manor." The head servant strode from the room without so much as a good-bye.

Daniel was bewildered. The man had fulfilled his every request and given him a lot to think about. He considered the possibility that Farlin was

206 | WESTON KINCADE

a spy for Lord Alain, but his swift transition into his accustomed role as dutiful servant made Daniel doubt it. *If what he said about our host is true, then there's more going on than we thought.* Maybe he could learn more from the teacher.

He checked the bandage, and it held tight. Impressed, Daniel slipped on his shirt and jacket. Sliding his hand under his coat tail, he tucked the pistol in his pants and left the way he came. A smile crept onto his face as he passed through the hall. After such a successful night, today was turning out more interesting than he expected. Daniel headed for the library in search of the others, ready for anything.

He entered to find Jedd and Madelin planted in a couple of Lord Alain's arm chairs, while Roger had his cards laid out on a side table. Fruit and cheese sat on the table, carefully arranged on ornate, silver trays, so Daniel took a seat. He was ready for a feast.

"How you feeling this morning?" asked Jedd, although the answer was obvious from Daniel's unusual smile.

"Great, Jedd, how about you?"

"Doing okay."

"Yeah, but they ain't got coffee, and fruit's the only thing laid out," added Roger with a grimace. "It's good, but ain't no substitute for some greasy eggs and sausage. Ya know what I mean, Danny?"

Daniel nodded as his eyes searched the trays of sliced fruit. He spotted a spare plate and filled every inch.

"What happened last night, Daniel?" Madelin asked, his change in attitude obvious to the entire group. Even Roger paused in his game, awaiting the answer.

Daniel looked to Jedd and saw the subtlest shake of his head. He thought he was imagining things, but then Jedd's meaning sank in; some secrets were best kept that way.

Daniel finished his mouthful and replied, "Last night... I finally got over some problems I've been havin', and when I woke up this morning, everything seemed a lot better."

The answer was enough for Madelin, who also smiled, but glancing over at her, he could see the gears turning in her mind. She would leave it be for now. Then he noticed her new attire. An elegant red dress housed her slender form. It was long and trim, but more fitting for a ball than anything they might experience today. However, he wasn't about to diminish the smile perched on her lips. No matter the occasion, she looked stunning.

"You look beautiful," he said under his breath.

If it were possible, her grin grew a few inches wider and the hint of suspicion within her green depths vanished. "Thank you. I love it."

In fact, perusing the group, he noticed that they had all acquired new attire. Each man had a jacket similar to his own, thick and warm, but in different colors. Roger's was brown, while Jedd's was pitch black. They were each dressed according to the fashions of this world, a style reminiscent of ages past. It was what Daniel classified as "early crap." Roger seemed to be pleasantly cheery, at least more than usual. The subtle frills added to the sleeves and collar of his shirt seemed to pull out a diva-like trait that must have remained hidden until this moment. Although subtle, Daniel could swear a smile unconsciously played at the sides of his lips... *And is he sittin' up straighter? Wannabe tramp!* Daniel grinned then glanced at Jedd. His shirt was plain and suited his personality.

Daniel thought back to the ornate, feminine shirt he was given and wondered if he was the only one that had been so misjudged. His stomach growled. With a shrug, he filled his plate a second time. After it was more than filled, Daniel shifted his seat to face the others.

Jedd set aside his book when they were all accounted for. "Okay, listen up."

Roger's head popped up from where he had been envisioning the next game at the tavern, and Daniel noticed that his cards were different than those he brought from home. Somehow, he had acquired a deck from one of the locals. *You can take the gambler out of his world, but you can't keep the world from the gambler,* he thought with a chuckle.

"Last night, I decided to check this place out, and as I'm sure you've seen, we're not the only people staying here. But that's not what concerns me." His voice lowered to a whisper as he said in a disapproving rasp, "I found Lord Alain's bedroom."

Jedd shook his head at the absurdity of what he was about to say. "As you'd expect, everything's extravagant, especially the bed. It was huge, but there was something odd about it. It has sides that can be pulled up over-top. It's like he sleeps entombed in his own bed."

He looked to the others for a reaction and was met with skepticism. "You can't be serious," responded Madelin. "The man we met last night was perfectly sane."

Daniel surprised Jedd by nodding. "I'm not sure what it means, but if Jedd says he saw it, then he did. I found out a few things this mornin' from Farlin, and I think it might explain a lot."

Jedd watched him, intrigued.

"I'm not sure whether to believe the lore of this place," continued Daniel. "Most lore's based on superstition in my experience, but he said legends spoke of people who came from another world hundreds of years ago. He even named Lord Alain as one of their elders."

"Wait a second." Jedd interrupted with the same question Daniel had asked less than an hour earlier.

"I know it seems impossible, but Farlin said he was at least a few hundred years old. These are stories, so the years may be off, but Farlin firmly believes it."

Jedd scoffed at the idea at first, but then considered it further. "There were even windows in the bedroom for God's sake," he muttered.

"What?" Madelin asked.

"N-nothing. I just can't quite wrap my head around it. I saw it and can't believe it, but it's the only thing that makes sense."

"I know he's a little weird, but what you're describing's insane. It can't be possible," Madelin replied. "Lord Alain's been nothing but generous to us."

"Look, Madelin," Jedd said, "I know it's hard to believe, but not everyone is who they seem."

"I know that, but what you're describing just makes no sense."

"I agree, but it's true. Just give it time and keep your eyes open, okay, doll?" added Daniel.

"All right."

Then Daniel added, "There's one more thing."

"What's that?"

"Farlin said he knew of a specialist, or doc of some sort that can help me out."

"Wow!" Jedd exclaimed. "But do you trust him to do what Farlin claims? Do you trust Farlin for that matter?"

"I have to. I can tell somethin's going on with Farlin, but I don't think he works for Lord Alain and his men. We might be in the middle of somethin' bigger... somethin' that's been going on for a long time."

"Well, while you're out today, I'll see what I can find out in the library and from Lord Alain if he's around," offered Madelin

"Sounds like a plan," replied Daniel as he took another bite.

Jedd asked, "Are you sure you're up to this?"

"Yes, I'll be fine. And maybe I can find out more about us," she replied.

"Maybe." Jedd tossed her the book he was reading. "We'll check back with you after our meeting with Pariah."

Roger collected the new set of cards and deposited them in his jacket while Jedd grabbed his own. Daniel finished what remained on his plate. Seconds later, the men set out in search of the school and the man no one seemed to trust.

Daniel's thoughts turned to the previous night's conversation with Lord Alain. *Why put the man in charge of the town's kids?*

Chapter Thirty-Four

Unexpected Company

After the men left, Madelin let out a sigh of relief. She had grown fond of each of them, but their constant supervision was unnerving. Madelin picked up the book she had been reading titled *Finding Yourself* and delved into its pages. It didn't deal with specific people who lost their memories but focused instead on self-discovery. She theorized that with its help she might discover what she lost. The afternoon faded, and Madelin absorbed everything she could before the door to the study announced a tall, confident stranger.

The man stepped through the sitting-room doors without a sound but stopped when he saw Madelin. "Excuse me, ma'am," he cooed in a rich accent resembling Alain's. His eyes took in the elegant dress cascading around her like flames rebelling against Newtonian Physics. "Have you seen Lord Alain?"

Madelin looked up from her book and fought to unhinge her tongue. The man's long, black hair shone in the dim room, and his fashionable clothes accentuated his muscular frame. His sleeves flowed down his arms like waves but flared out at the cuffs. In one hand was a brown, leather satchel. A thick coat hung over the other, much like the ones Lord Alain had gifted to her friends.

His gaze walked past the length of his nose and met hers with calm diligence. On other men his highly perched beak would look unbalanced, but it emphasized his tall form, giving him a slender, professorial appearance. The final intrigue for Madelin was the pulsating, dark-green glow that fluctuated around every inch of his body.

Madelin's tongue loosened enough to reply, "I'm sorry, but I haven't. You're welcome to join me if you'd like, though." Madelin hoped the offer didn't sound like a plea, but she was finding it difficult to catch her breath after his sudden appearance. She had never seen a man look so regal and competent without trying.

He seemed uncomfortable with the proposition, but after a moment's indecision seated himself in an adjacent chair. "Thank you."

"No problem. I'm Madelin." She extended her hand.

He took it and wrapped his fingers around hers. Turning her hand over, he replied, "It is a pleasure to meet you, Madelin. I am Juno Paria." His head lowered, and he kissed the backside of her hand then let her fingers slip through his.

Madelin was dumbstruck. She had never before encountered such a man, and her face flushed at the gracious introduction. The name, however, struck her as familiar.

"And what brings you to our neck of the woods, *mademoiselle?*" Juno asked, his tone confident, yet casual.

"We are guests of Lord Alain."

"Oh," he replied with a knowing look. "By chance, are you with some gentlemen I met a short time ago?"

"Yes, you might have met them earlier."

"I see." Juno shrugged.

"And why'd you come to the manor? Did you take the time to speak with my friends?"

"Well, I came for provisions and could not spare the time. Perhaps later."

Madelin wanted to find out more, to protest at the ease with which he dismissed Jedd and the others, but her curiosity got the better of her. "What kind of provisions?"

"Too many to go into. Let us just say, they are necessary for my work."

His vague explanation was perplexing. "And what kind of work did you need it for, Mr. Paria?"

A frown creased his long face, and he answered with sad eyes. "For my lessons. I am a teacher."

"What did you need for your lessons... books? I don't understand..." Her words trailed off as she caught his grim reaction. "I take it you aren't too happy with your job?"

"Well, I fell into it unintentionally."

Having no experience with careers and society, Madelin was unfamiliar with what might cause such a turn of events. However, disappointment and unhappiness were emotions she'd experienced first hand. "I see. Sorry to hear that."

Juno saw that his unhappiness had proven contagious. He smiled and changed the subject. "So, what is it you are reading?"

Madelin's face remained the same, longing for what was missing in her life as she looked down at the book on her lap. "A book called *Finding Yourself*. I'm hoping it'll help."

"With what?"

"I'm trying to find myself," she replied honestly. She couldn't help the ease she felt with Juno. While formal in appearance, his suave nature either left her speechless or gossiping like a witless teenager.

She noticed the perplexing quirk in his expression, and she elaborated further. "A while back, I lost my memory. I'm not really sure how, but I'd like to get it back."

Juno was intrigued, and his brows furrowed. "What does the book say to do?"

"It doesn't really talk about my situation, but it has some ideas I've never heard of. And others I might be able to try."

"Like what?"

"It mentions some odd things like 'hyp-nosis,'" she added, stumbling over the word. "But it recommends other things, too, like going back to places you knew before to reflect. I can't really do that, and I'm not sure what 'hyp-nosis' is…, but maybe I can figure something out through self-reflection… at least that's what the book calls it. I've kind of been doing that already, though, and still nothing. So far, the book hasn't been a great help, but I'm not done with it yet."

"I see. I can at least tell you what hypnosis is." His words flowed with the smoothness of familiar chocolate, and his offer perked Madelin's interest. "Hypnosis is a trance induced by someone who has been trained. During the trance they can ask questions your subconscious might know about, but your conscious thought might be unable to remember."

The prospect was enticing, but she doubted Jedd or the others knew how to do it. Otherwise, they would have tried before now. Madelin sat in silence, her disappointment obvious.

"I know it is kind of personal, but I can try it on you if you would like."

The proposal was music to Madelin's ears, but his generosity was more than she could have hoped for. It was enough to make her question his motives. She was certain alarm bells would be ringing if she were Jedd. He was very cautious, too cautious in her opinion, but it had helped him to find her. If not for him, she would still be stuck in that hospital bed—more brainwashed than before. *No one is that giving.* Jedd's words echoed through her mind as she considered the offer.

"I might take you up on it later," she replied, "but right now I think I'd like to try a few of the simpler ideas and see if there's anything else the book recommends."

Juno nodded and said, "Suit yourself." Then his eyes landed on another book sitting next to Madelin. "Have you read that one, too?"

"I'm working on it," she replied, lifting it off the end table. "*A Labyrinth of Elemental Curiosities: The Development of Rare and Unexplainable Human Traits*," she read aloud.

"Now that is interesting. Why did you choose that one?"

"It has to do with what I said before," she replied then paused. Overcoming her hesitance once more, Madelin explained, "I'm not sure if it's related to the memory loss, but I can see things that others can't."

"Oh," Juno said in a failed attempt at feigned surprise.

Her eyes lost their adoring gaze when she saw through his ploy. "Mr. Paria, why do I get the feeling you knew as much before you asked?"

Juno stiffened, caught off guard by her directness. After a moment's consideration, he answered, "I did suspect as much, but only because it interested you. Otherwise, why pick it up?"

His explanation was logical, but Madelin's gut told her there was more. "I don't think it's as simple as that. That's one reason why my friends went looking for you this afternoon."

Her sudden change in behavior staggered him. He was beginning to think this enchanted beauty might be a femme fatale in disguise. He wished to leave but was intrigued by this extraordinary woman and the odd sickness that plagued her. Strangers seldom ventured this far south, and few of those were women as intoxicating as this one.

"Let us say you are right," he said, humoring her in his accented English. "What is your point?"

"My point?" Aggravated, her voice intensified. "My point is that something is different about me, and something is different about you. I don't know much about it, but I want to know more. How are you different, and what can you tell me about these things I see?" The words careened off her lips without a second thought, and by the time she finished, she was gasping for breath.

"Well, I see we are through with the preliminary introductions," replied Juno. Irritation flashed in his eyes. "Was the flirtation part of your ploy to speak with me?" His tone hid daggers behind each word.

"No, Juno, I wasn't trying to manipulate you. I really am attract—" She stopped before she said too much and took a deep breath. "I just want some answers."

"To tell you about my past will take far longer than we have this evening. As far as what you see, I am sure you are talking about certain aspects that some people have and others... do not."

Juno explained further as the hellcat's claws retreated and her eyes brightened. "The glow you see means that person is of an evolved nature. They may or may not have discovered this for themselves yet, but each one at least has the capability of becoming more than 'normal.' As they evolve, most attain the ability you yourself have, to see the glow around others. Everyone has the potential of seeing more than truly exists in the world, but some are more inclined to see these visions than others. For instance, many people on every plane report seeing small carryovers from similar worlds. Often they call them ghosts or apparitions because they know no better. Far fewer people exist as genetic mutations. These people are anomalies and capable of more than any normal person can conceive of."

"What kinds of things can they do?" asked Madelin, intrigued.

The conversation lengthened, Juno's exasperation disappeared, and his voice became infused with passion. "Each person's genetic evolution is engineered to do certain things. There are ways you can help them to discover more, but there is no way of knowing what each person is capable of."

"What about the intensity of the aura, the deepness of its color?" Madelin asked, watching the glow around Juno pulsate.

"That can give you an idea of their potential, how powerful they can become, but in what way is still a mystery, even to me," he replied, disheartened.

Madelin was absorbed in his explanation and probed further. "How does this change come about?"

Juno considered how to summarize his answer before responding, "Well, simply put, genetics are not set in stone. They change through mutations and abnormalities in order to adapt to their surroundings. Throughout the ages, changes in the world have forced these developments to occur." Juno sought out some semblance of understanding as he peered at Madelin. She nodded and waited for him to continue. "As I think you know, there are many different versions of the world. Each evolved from the same original plane. However with every influential decision, a new plane is made for each avenue not taken. Because of this, there are an infinite number of planes. "The evolution of man stems from this eternal metamorphosis. Each person born with genetic abnormalities is more closely linked to the basic foundation separating each world, and it is because they are products of the world attempting to adapt. It is the world we live in attempting to create a reality capable of surviving. The results of each decision can have far-reaching consequences.

"And so, how the world has progressed determines how people evolve on that particular plane. Some decisions lead to cataclysmic events which cause certain planes to die out. But since an alternate plane is made for each significant decision, when one ends, many more survive. Through this process, life continues to evolve." Juno watched as the attractive woman hung on every word. He hoped she understood his explanation. Putting things into laymen's terms had never been his forte.

Madelin's mind turned over the new information. "But what determines if it's an important decision?"

"That is nature at its best. It must be a decision with the possibility of worldwide consequences."

"Wow," Madelin said, breathless. "I didn't realize there was so much to it. Jedd mentioned something about the differences between planes having to do with decisions, but I didn't know that's what he meant. The book mentioned the possibilities but didn't explain it with such depth. How do you know this for sure, when so many other people don't?"

Juno leaned back in the chair, a knowing smile tweaking his cheeks. "Experience, *mademoiselle*, experience."

Before Madelin could pose another question, Juno's gaze went to the door. Seconds later, it opened to admit Lord Alain.

"Mr. Paria, what, may I ask, brings you to my humble abode?"

"Only the normal procurement, my lord," replied the school teacher.

Alain turned his attention to Madelin. "*Mademoiselle*, I am sorry this eccentric man was allowed to take up so much of your precious time. I was detained." Turning his unwavering gaze back to Juno, he added, "Please excuse us."

The unmistakable cue ended their conversation with the abruptness of a train wreck. Juno stood and made a leg before Madelin. "*Au revoir, mademoiselle.* Have a pleasant evening." Without another word, he picked up his bag and passed out the door, followed by their host.

"I will return in a moment, *mademoiselle,*" said Lord Alain before shutting the study door.

Madeline watched through a window as the two men went a short ways into the garden. Their discussion began cordial enough, but soon Lord Alain betrayed his consistent calm. He began motioning fiercely with his hands. Unaccompanied by his words, the motions were meaningless, but the powerful gestures displayed the frustration he felt. Before long they separated and Juno stalked across the shaded street.

Alain walked back to the manor and into the study, his calm façade having returned. "I am sorry for that disturbance, Miss Madelin. I hope his presence was not too much of a discomfort to you."

"Not at all," she replied. "Wasn't that the school teacher you spoke of last night?"

Lord Alain took his usual seat and again stoked the fire to life. "Yes it was. Now do you see why I said to consider his notions with care?"

Madelin nodded but said nothing of how similar their philosophies were.

Once the fire had grown to a comfortable level, Alain threw another log on, leaned forward in his seat, and took her hand in his. "Now Madelin...," he whispered, "that is such a pretty name... I am glad to finally speak with you alone."

"Why's that?" she asked with coy naivety.

"I have wished to speak with you for quite some time. Your beauty surpasses all I have seen in my many years. The first sight of you left me breathless. It was then that I knew. I have kept the fabric for that dress for centuries, waiting for just the right person worthy of wearing it. I had my personal tailor make it for you just last night. Do you like it?"

"It's gorgeous!" she exclaimed. Truthfully, it was the first time she had concerned herself with fashion, at least that she could remember, but it was more beautiful than anything she had ever seen. "Thank you."

"It suits you. Have you enjoyed your time here?" he asked with a smile.

"I have, very much."

"Good. Better than where you came from?"

Her mind returned to the hospital, the only home she knew, and she shuddered. "Without question."

"Then there is something I would like you to consider."

"Yes, go on."

"How would you like to live out the rest of your life as a respected member of society? To be able to wear a different dress like this each day of the week?"

The answer was obvious to Madelin, but it seemed "too good to be true," as Jedd would have said. There had to be a catch. Curious where the question was leading, she played along. "Yes I'd like that."

I'd also like to live without fear of an attack and kidnapping attempts, she thought, but said nothing of it.

"I can provide all of that, Madelin. I can provide you with security from whatever you are running from, and I can give you a home. Would you not like that?"

"Yes," she replied, uncertain where he was going with this. "That'd be wonderful, but what could we do for you in return?"

"There is no 'we,' Madelin. It is what you can do for me. You can make me the happiest man alive. Just say, 'yes.' Marry me, and it will all be yours."

At first she thought he was joking, but his crystal-blue gaze solidified his intentions. "But, I don't even know you."

"What is there to know? I know that I want you. That should be enough." Alain's confidence left no room for question or debate. He leaned back, waiting for the answer he knew would come. "Take your time, *mademoiselle*. For you, I will wait."

Madelin sat speculating on what to say and how to go about it. "Mr. Traditor, I appreciate your offer, but that's something I'm not ready for right now." His smile disappeared. "My friends and I have enjoyed your hospitality, and I'm sure that they'd like to repay you in some way, but I can't do that."

Alain's gaze hardened with each word, as though he were turning to stone. His hands clenched into fists, and his lips formed a thin line as his anger flared. He leaned forward and encircled her petite wrists in an iron grip. "How dare you deny me!" He dragged her to her feet as he rose from the chair. "I have opened my home to you, doted on you and your friends, given you clothes made by my personal tailor, and offered you a life of riches and respect. And this is how you repay me!" His voice intensified as his malice took flight, and each accented word hung like daggers. "When I ask for something, you do not tell me 'no'! If I ask for something, it is because I choose to do so as a courtesy. And when I want something, I take it."

Alain's eyes took on a predatory look as he flung her across the room. Madelin slammed into the wall, knocking the pictures down around her. She slid to the floor in pained surprise. Alain crossed the distance with the grace of a hungry lion. His eyes promised murder and much... much more.

Seeing his vicious intentions stirred the pent-up hate inside her, and it began to surge. Madelin's leg shot out and caught him unaware. Alain stumbled backward as the heel of her foot found purchase in his groin. He teetered at the edge of his chair, bent double, and took a few deep breaths. It was enough for Madelin to get up. She turned to the door and tried the knob, but it refused to budge.

"You didn't really think I would let you go, did you?" Alain bellowed like a crazed lunatic.

Madelin turned back to him and braced herself as he stepped closer. When he was within reach, she threw out her fist, but a slight breeze was all she felt. He dodged each punch with inhuman speed, taunting her.

"Come on, little girl, you poor tramp, you can do better than that." His words were sadistic and cruel. An evil grin played across his face as though it were a game.

She threw one punch after another, trying to circle away from his threatening advances. She slipped around chairs, kicked at him, and thrust her knee into his midsection, but each time he knocked her leg aside, his frightening gaze never leaving hers.

Feeling his long, cold fingers wrap around her forearms, Madelin summoned her frustrations into one final blow. She leapt into the chair behind her and propelled herself into Lord Alain. The force of the impact carried them both into the air and onto one of the low center tables. The legs splintered and collapsed under the weight of their bodies, and Alain rolled over Madelin with the skill of a trained fighter. Holding her tight, he used the momentum to his advantage and flipped her. She was no longer in control and slammed into the couch's wooden frame. There was a loud *crack* as her skull thudded against the hardened armrest. Then the world went dark.

Chapter Thirty-Five

The Slip

Hours later, Madelin awoke to four concerned faces hovering above in a candle-lit room. She lay lengthwise across the couch. Every inch of her ravaged body called out in pain, as though she had been run over by a semi. Jedd, Farlin, and the others stood over her with matching expressions. They spoke in muted conversation, but fragments filtered through the pain.

"Oh *mon amie*, look at all those bruises," said Roger. His eyes watered, close to tears.

"Who in the hell did this?" Daniel demanded, but no one knew with certainty.

"Like I said, it might have been Alain," replied Jedd. "I wouldn't put it past him."

Farlin chimed in, "I would not be surprised if it was him, but I have worked here for years. I have seen him do many horrible things, but never something like this."

"Then who the hell did it?" asked Daniel, his fists clenched, longing to wrap their fingers around someone's neck. His knuckles popped with the repeated movement, and his eyes roved around the room, searching for something… someone… anything to vent his rage. His sights landed on the Cajun. "You! It's your damn fault. You just had to play another hand of cards."

"I do not know whose fault it is, but you cannot go blaming each other," Farlin replied, but Jedd interrupted him.

"No, you can't. It isn't Roger's fault. It's mine. I should have gotten us out of here last night." Jedd's eyes fell to the floor and Madelin's prone form.

"Look guys, she's wakin' up." Roger allowed her a minute to recover consciousness then asked in his Creole accent, "Hey, darlin', you okay?"

"Ohhhh, God!" she exclaimed, placing her palms over her eyes. "It hurts."

"What does?" Jedd asked. "Is there something we can do?"

"Who did this to you?" asked Daniel with impassioned hatred.

"What hurts?" came Farlin's voice, adding to the growing pile of questions.

Madelin attempted to answer them, but each time she opened her eyes, the faint lights stabbed them with millions of tiny daggers. The men stood in silent anticipation as her words echoed from under shadowed hands. "Everything does. Lord Alain came after me when I refused his proposal."

"Oh God!" Farlin muttered. "No one turns down Lord Alain."

"What the hell do you mean, no one turns the bastard down?" Daniel mocked.

The servant had his suspicions, but asked anyway, "What kind of a proposal was it, Madelin?"

"Marriage." She hid her face in her arms.

"What the hell?" Jedd exclaimed. It took a moment to organize his thoughts, which turned to the actual attack. He found it difficult to ask, but the state of her dress made it impossible to brush aside. "D-d-did he rape you, honey?"

The question alone lit bonfires in each of the men's eyes. They saw her dress and how he left her, lying sprawled and disrobed.

It looks like our suspicions were right, thought Jedd. *If I'd just found another place to stay, then this wouldn't have happened.*

As her eyes adjusted, Madelin uncovered her face and tried to prop herself up. "Yes, I think," she responded with a calm that was only skin deep.

"I'm gonna kill him!" shouted Daniel. Removing the gun from his waist, he turned and strode toward the door.

"No, you can't!" screamed Madelin. Her arm stretched out to him as though she could stop the large man with a thought.

Daniel did, halting at her command. He turned to her, and they all saw their own pain reflected in his eyes. "Why not?" he asked through the confusion. "After what he did to you, why can't I?"

"Because... I tried to fight back and couldn't do a thing."

"He can feel pain, right?" Daniel asked, scorn flecking his words.

Madelin remembered Alain's reaction to her well-aimed kick and nodded.

"Good, I'm about to bring him loads of it."

Daniel took a step forward, but Farlin barred the door. "She is right. You cannot go up against him."

"Why the hell not?"

"He will kill you with the flick of his wrist," replied the servant and poked Daniel in the stomach. He winced, and a dab of new blood blossomed on the bandage. It had been healing faster than normal, for whatever reason he couldn't discern, but it still took time. "The reason he did not kill her is that he actually feels for her," Farlin explained.

Daniel cocked the pistol and checked the chamber. "Well, he hasn't met someone like me. I've killed more people than I can count, some of them for nothing more than livin'. A scratch ain't gonna stop me. Hell'll freeze over before I let someone like that walk away. There're consequences, and I'm here to introduce him to the judge, jury, and executioner." He released the safety on the weapon and attempted to brush by Farlin. The servant didn't move.

Madelin pleaded, "Daniel, don't. His time will come, I promise you that, but neither of us is in any shape to take on someone like him. I don't know what it is about him, but Juno explained a few things that made a lot of sense."

The mention of her conversation with Juno startled them, including Farlin. "When did you meet him?" asked her godfather.

"Earlier today."

"How the hell did ya get him to talk to ya?" asked Roger.

Madelin smiled as she remembered the flirtatious encounter. "Sometimes being beautiful can work in your favor." Then, as the events of the day came to mind, she added a disturbing afterthought, "Other times, not so much."

The ex-mercenary *harrumphed*, but stayed his hand for the moment.

"So you see, Daniel, I need you with me right now. Anyway, didn't you say something about meeting up with Farlin's specialist this evening?"

He was frustrated, but knew better than to argue with her. Daniel flicked the safety on and tucked the handgun back in his pants. Then Farlin met his gaze. "She is right. He is expecting you. I think he would like to see you, too, Miss Madelin. You are in need of his assistance."

"I'll be right back then," Jedd said as he stepped past Farlin. He took the stairs two at a time, adding, "I sure as hell am not letting Madelin stay here again. Be right back with my bag." Roger followed in pursuit of his own belongings.

Daniel shrugged and looked at Madelin's cloaked form. "I'm always packed." She nodded back and pulled the blanket tighter over her shoulders.

"You sure I can't have a go at him now?" he asked, his vain hopes dancing on a blade's edge. But he knew she was right. While he felt refreshed after last night's sleep, his body still complained. He was in no shape to fight, but that wouldn't stop him if given the chance.

She nodded and whispered, "Please don't."

By the time the two men returned, Madelin's arm was looped across Daniel's broad shoulders. His free arm encircled her waist, supporting her fractured form, while his other hovered dangerously close to his firearm. She tried to sustain her own weight, but giving in, leaned into his supportive embrace.

"Everyone ready?" asked Farlin who had already donned his coat and ivy cap.

They all nodded. "Yes, and Alain is nowhere in the manor," Jedd added. "I can see his aura off in the distance, but I'm not sure what he's up to."

"So long as he's not here, all the better," muttered the head servant.

"I take it, he doesn't know what you're about?" asked Jedd.

"Frequently," Farlin replied. "Let us go."

The small group made their way through the moonlit streets, past the schoolhouse, and toward the outskirts of town. Leodenin and Alain remained elsewhere. There was less evidence of civilization the further they ventured. Solitary houses sprung up after passing acres of farm land. The trees that shrouded the town in eternal shadow became far less abundant along the road, but the tree line shown darkly to their right.

By the time Farlin slowed to a stop at a long, dirt drive, Madelin was asleep in Daniel's arms. Jedd assessed the group's condition and noted by the light of the moons that blood was seeping through the veteran's bandages.

He isn't showing any signs of fatigue, but the strain of carrying Madelin has to be taking its toll. The man would go to the ends of the earth for her, no matter the cost, Jedd thought with admiration. His gaze turned to Roger who walked beside him. His eyes were searching the distant forests for signs of trouble. *Good men are hard to find, but luck has blessed me.* At the thought, a grateful smile crested his lips.

"We're almost there," Farlin added before turning down the overgrown road.

Jedd checked his watch. *Almost 2:00 a.m.,* he thought as a yawn widened his face. It had been barely an hour since they left, but the day had been long.

Alain's head servant took the lead at an accelerated pace, striding deeper into the forest along the side road. Weeds and plant life struggled into the air along most of it, making the walk more difficult. However, Farlin stayed to one side where a narrow path was well worn. They found themselves traveling under enormous trees, far larger than those within the city. Each had dense, spreading foliage that hung high above. Even the light of the three moons found it impossible to reach them under the great branches.

"Now, you might be surprised to meet the man, but please be polite. He is the best at what he does, and you will not find anyone like him. We depend on him, and he is your best hope of finding help." Farlin's murmured words echoed off the ancient trunks as though even the plant life supported his praise of this mystery man. "Also, please keep this meeting and his identity to yourselves."

Before long a small cottage appeared in the distance, hidden in a clearing where only the longest branches of trees stretched far enough to overshadow the house. The home was out of a fairy tale with a yellow thatch roof and quaint, deep-set windows. A diminutive garden of vegetables and fragrant spices took up most of the side yard.

The weary travelers followed Farlin up the stone-paved walkway to the front door. He knuckled a *ratta-ratta-tat-tat-tat* on the door and waited for the specialist to answer. They didn't wait long. As the old, wooden entry pulled open with a *squeak*, Madelin glanced up from her slumber to see a slender face framed in long, black hair. The shadowed entryway hid Jedd's astonishment at seeing a man with a sea-green aura almost as vibrant as Madelin's. It ebbed around him as though waiting for the right moment to illuminate the room. Jedd had seen him once before, outside the schoolhouse earlier that day. The man had brushed them off without a care.

"Juno," Madelin whispered as a petite smile played across her lips.

Juno returned it as their eyes met.

Chapter Thirty-Six

Oddities

S eeing the group's condition, Juno waved them inside. "Hurry, hurry, set her on the couch."

He checked that they weren't followed then shut the door and strode into the dining room. It had been converted into a small study and was littered with books and vials. He put Farlin to work gathering more bandages and washcloths. A bowl of water sat next to the couch.

While the servant gathered the other necessary items, Juno concocted a salve using herbs and other things from sealed jars on his shelves. As he mashed them together with a small mortar and pestle, he interrogated the men. "What happened to her?"

"Your damn friend is what happened," replied Jedd in frustration.

Juno paused. "My friend?"

Jedd couldn't contain his anger anymore. "Yes, your friend—the one you went to visit earlier today. He got angry and went after her!"

"I believe you misunderstand my reasons for dealing with Lord Alain, but we will get to that later. Just know that I have every intention of helping the *mademoiselle* and Mr. Robertson."

"Then why the hell did you avoid us today?" asked Daniel, his frustration growing.

Juno finished the paste and carried it to the couch. He shifted Jedd aside and seated himself on the floor next to Madelin's exhausted form. Juno lifted the blanket from her and scanned the devastation Lord Alain had inflicted. "Because I could not be seen with strangers like yourselves in the midst of dozens of townspeople. Did you ever wonder why Farlin brought you to see me in the dead of night?" As Juno answered the question, he dipped his fingers into the salve and dabbed it on her blotched bruises. After the question sank in, Juno added, "You are lucky you were not followed, or else I fear none of you would have stood a chance against Alain and the others."

All three of the men looked at one another, surprised that it hadn't occurred to them. Their concern over Madelin had taken priority, and none had noticed the head servant's manipulations.

"The others?" asked Roger, who was the first to catch the word.

"Yes, the others. There are many who look to Lord Alain," answered Juno. He worked his way down Madelin's body.

Jedd set a firm hand on the slender man's shoulder before he could reveal her lower extremities and waistline. Her godfather leaned down to Juno's ear and whispered, "Keep your hands clean, boy. No need to put her through more pain and embarrassment. We'll make you regret the day you were born if you violate her privacy again."

"Again?" Juno mouthed. His hand held the edge of the quilted blanket as though time had stopped. Juno fought to maintain his calm, but his words filled with hate. "Alain, your time has come," he muttered.

Juno said no more, instead concentrating his energies on Madelin's ravaged body. He set the quilt down and left Madelin her dignity, instead massaging her legs and arms with the salve. After he finished, he turned to the others. Jedd still stood over him, while Roger and Daniel situated themselves in wooden rocking chairs on the opposite side of the room. Farlin sat in the dining room, peering out the window. Juno rose and placed a hand on Jedd's tense shoulder. "I understand your pain. Have a seat. We have done all we can."

The veteran's eyes were glued to Madelin, but as Juno stepped up to him, their eyes met. It was odd, but looking into Juno's soothing gaze put him at ease.

The tall host in regal garb acted out of character. He didn't possess the same egotistic, self-assuredness of Alain, but he was still confident in his actions. He grabbed a bowl of clean water, more salve, and a washcloth before kneeling in front of the leathered man. "Lift up your shirt. What I have prepared will help the wounds heal faster."

Daniel lifted his shirt and peeled away the bandage. The teacher gazed at the oozing wound and shook his head. "What did this to you?"

As an answer, Daniel lifted his hand from the armrest of the chair. In it was his 9 mm handgun. "Something similar to this. It shoots things so quick that they go through whatever you're pointin' at."

Juno nodded and asked, "Is the bullet still inside?"

Roger answered for him with a loud snore, as though announcing his success at surgery only days before.

Daniel nodded at the Cajun and said, "Nah, he got it out for me, but how'd you know it was a bullet?"

"Like I said, there is a lot you do not know about this town, the people in it, and my relationship with those in charge."

Juno stared at the wound, delving into Daniel's side with a finger. "I see where it went in, but it looks like it bounced around a bit..." A deep-throated sigh announced Juno's intrigue as he probed further into Daniel's belly. "I can't believe you are still standing. This should have killed you, but it does not look like it pierced anything vital. How is that?"

Daniel shrugged. "Always been pretty hardy."

Ignoring Juno's medical assessment, Jedd cleared his throat. "Okay, explain it to us," he interrupted after finding a seat. "Your relationship to those in charge, I mean."

Juno told his story while he cleaned the veteran's wounds and applied the salve. Daniel winced under the pressure of the specialist's fingers, but otherwise listened.

"Believe it or not, Alain and many others in this town are not from this plane. They came here fleeing their own world... a place full of guns and many more people. They were outcasts among their own people. One reason for their exclusion was an ability that no other family had. It was a talent passed on through genetics, and families of that world never intermarried with those of other royal lines. Because of this, very few children were born capable of living beyond the competency tests. However, this was not a problem since each individual lived for hundreds of years."

"But what if something were to cause the people to die en masse?" interposed Jedd. "Wouldn't that decimate the family?"

"Yes, that was a problem. Each person is capable of living much longer than anyone on this world. However, they are still susceptible to harm and even violent deaths. The other families grew tired of the tyrannical rule and cast the Traditor Family out. A bounty was placed on the heads of anyone in the Traditorian line, and the other families soon slaughtered each Traditorian they found. There were far too few left at the end. If the murders continued, there would not be enough to actually escape."

The others nodded.

"The last fourteen members of the royal family banded together and used their power to find a new home, one where they could walk around in the high point of the day without fear of harm from people or the sun."

"So, they came here," Jedd finished for him. "But why? And what did they have to fear from the sun?"

"The Traditor Family is very different from families on this world. They are known as vampires," explained Juno.

"Oh, shit," Daniel sputtered. "You've gotta be kiddin' me."

"I take it you have heard of them."

Jedd explained, "On our world, there are stories of vampires walking the streets at night. They suck people's blood, kill them, and sometimes turn them into vampires. The way to kill them is with a stake through the heart, cutting off their heads, using crosses, or garlic... things like that."

"It sounds like someone has taken a few liberties with the truth, but much of what you say is correct. A stake through the heart would do it, along with just about anything else you pierce their hearts with. While you can cause them pain by harming their bodies, it will not kill them. Also, cutting off their heads works. That is why many of the bounties were filled by bringing in the heads of Traditorian family members." He allowed his words to settle before continuing.

"The sun is very much a problem, although not so extreme as to require them to remain out of daylight all of the time. On their own world they could go out during the day, but too much of it would cause a kind of deficiency that resulted in a long, painful death. However, crosses and garlic are products of fairy tales."

"What about the abilities you described. Do they extend beyond shiftin' from plane to plane?" asked Daniel.

"They are capable of more than the people on this plane, but that is not a result of their abilities. As members of the Traditor Family, they are genetically disposed to exceptional strength, agility, and an extended lifespan. This does get transferred, but their ability does not. They also have a thirst for blood as you described, but it is not required each night. In fact, the family only drinks on rare occasions, about once a month."

Jedd leaned forward in his chair and asked, "How do you know how often they drink?"

"Because there is even a method of selection set up by the local government," he replied.

"Your local government supports them?" Jedd exclaimed with credulity.

"They are our local government," replied Juno as a matter of fact.

"From what you have seen so far, who runs the town?"

The difference in social classes and their apparent magic abilities and auras became clear to Jedd, and both men nodded at the established power structure. *But how is it that Juno possesses such an aura?* wondered Jedd. He stored the question for later. Juno was of no threat at the moment, but that could always change.

Then Daniel asked, "So how do they do it?"

"As unoriginal as it sounds, they call it Selection. Someone within the town is selected at random once a month. The Traditorian Family pursues them. Once they are caught, each family member takes a drink. There is enough blood in one human to feed them all... at least for now, but the victim dies as a result. The family has grown, though, and has begun increasing the selections. The last time I checked, there were well over a hundred members."

Something else occurred to Jedd as he listened to Juno's story unfold. "Wait, you said that was part of being in the Traditor Family. In our world, if you're bitten, you can become a vampire."

"There is no 'can' about it. If you are bitten by a true vampire, one of the royal family, the contagion will take hold and you will turn within a day's time. But if you are attacked by someone who has been turned, the contagion cannot be passed on. The one way for the contagion to live long enough to spread is in a body genetically suited to sustain the disease."

Juno stopped before he could say more then took a moment to compose himself. "I thought adopting the Selection process was brutal and pitiful in the beginning, but necessary for the family to survive. They were managing their thirst and governing the town well, having learned from the mistakes of Alain's tyrannical father and his predecessors. But, over the last hundred years, things have changed."

"Wait," broke in Daniel. "You said a hundred years."

"Yes, Alain and his family have, in fact, been here for four hundred and sixty-seven years."

"But how old are you to know their past?" asked Jedd.

Juno rolled back on his haunches as he considered Daniel's question. "You have nothing to fear from me. However, I am of the Traditorian line. I am nine hundred and thirty-two years old. Lord Alain is my eldest brother and leader of the family."

Daniel tensed in the rocking chair, inches away. "And you aren't worried about passin' that damn contagion on to me?" he asked, horror etched across his face.

He glanced at the wound as though expecting to see a large abnormality growing from where Juno's hands had been. Instead, the salve adhered to the edges of the wound and stimulated the cellular growth of his skin. As he watched, the skin began closing over the bullet hole with unprecedented speed. What would have taken weeks of care and attention, even for him, was healing before his eyes. Daniel stared in amazement.

"It should be good as new by morning," added Juno with a quaint smile.

"B-b-but how?" asked Daniel, struggling for words.

"It's a concoction of my own design. The ingredients can be found in my garden."

"That's impossible," commented Jedd, although his eyes were also glued to Daniel's side.

"When you have hundreds of years to test different combinations, it is only a matter of time before you come across one that works. When Madelin wakes up, she should feel much better, too."

"I hope so," commented Jedd as he peered over at the couch.

When Daniel looked up from the wound, he met the vampire's gaze. Juno looked down at the injured leg hidden beneath the soldier's pants and asked with a mocking smile that this time displayed his enlarged canines, "Would you like me to take a look at your other wounds or leave them to get infected?" His thick accent added a sadistic feel to the question.

Daniel wanted to laugh, but first hid the shudder that ran down his spine. The proof of Juno's ancestral heritage was unnerving. He nodded and gave in.

Juno lifted Daniel's pant leg and administered the salve to both sides of his calf then went to his other wound. "As I was saying, Alain and the rest of the family began abusing the selected people. Instead of respecting their sacrifice and being thankful for their contribution to the family, their perspective on humans changed.

"After the humans began forgetting the origins of the royal family, Alain saw a chance to dominate them. Because of their strength and speed, everyone within the Traditorian line was capable of far more than any normal person. Alain was unstoppable with the added power over the local constabulary. Their sacrifice from the Selection became a sham as a result. Anyone who spoke out against them found themselves selected for the monthly family reunion."

"That's horrible!" interrupted Jedd. "It sounds like he became what they were trying to avoid."

"Yeah, the apple doesn't fall too far from the tree," Daniel contributed.

"Well, it gets worse," Juno replied with disgust. "The family chose one member to catch their selection a day early. They would then bite them so that they became infected. By holding the sacrifice overnight, the transition would be complete. This way the victim had a bit more fight in them, possessing the speed, strength, and other benefits of a vampire. Selection became a source of entertainment for the family, not sustenance. It is the thrill of the chase, you see?"

Juno could tell from the revolted look on their faces that they were listening.

"This extreme exploitation of our family's traditional beliefs was the last straw for me. When we came over, we swore not to disrupt the lives of this world's inhabitants any more than necessary. I could not live a life so corrupted that even the core principals of the family had been perverted. So, they ostracized me. I was given a job that was worthy of no respect, nor power over any adult. I am an outcast due to my beliefs and the changes brought about by the atrocities of my older brother."

After Juno finished, the two men thought over what he had said. They both recalled the fleeting encounter with the ghost-like men in the forest, but Daniel was the first to speak up. "The other day, we saw a bunch of people flyin' past, chasin' one guy. Is that what you're talking about?"

"Yes, that was Falos, Farlin's cousin." Juno looked over at his associate. "I am sorry to say that he did not make it." Farlin looked up at the mention of his relative and friend. Then without a word, he returned to staring out the window. "They found out about Falos' ties to me. Last month his name was chosen *at random* for Selection."

Even if I hadn't heard Juno's explanation, anyone listening to his sarcastic tone would know how random such a selection was, thought Jedd. *To think, if a demi-vampire like Falos could tear through Leodenin's agents like they were gingerbread men, what are the real ones capable of?*

"Falos was very adept. After going through the transition, he hid for the entirety of the month, but someone eventually found him. At that point, there was little we could do. They were all after him, as you saw."

"So, does that mean they won't want to have another sacrifice this month?" asked the veteran.

Juno shook his head, "That is doubtful. It is their only real entertainment. It just whet their thirst. They even selected someone else a few days after Falos escaped."

"When do you think the next one will be?" asked Jedd.

Juno was prepared for this question and gave a solemn reply, "Any day now. Like I said, the Selection has become more common because the family is growing. One sacrifice may not be enough anymore."

"Shit," both men said in unison.

Juno gave a sadistic chuckle. "Yes, indeed, and I am responsible for the deaths of the chosen... at least of late. There are no coincidences when it comes to Alain."

After a few moments, it occurred to Jedd that Juno, while being an outcast, still required the same nourishment for survival. "Juno, how do you live if you don't take part in the Selection?"

It took a few moments for Juno to answer. "I am ashamed to say that at first I went to Lord Alain for blood at the end of each month. Although mortified to have me for a brother, he would not deny my survival. Later I found that the blood of animals was enough to sustain me, but resorting to such low life forms for nourishment is a disgrace. Those that choose my path are called the Dedecorum, the shamed. I was cast out because of my beliefs. I teach children because none of my family can bring themselves to look upon me. I enjoy the children, but even pleasure becomes a struggle when it is all you have."

An image came to Daniel—Juno chasing after squirrels and lifting them to his lips one at a time. Although disgusted, he chuckled at the picture. It was almost comical.

Juno heard the guttural sound and peered at him as though reading his thoughts.

Spotting his intimidating gaze, Daniel muttered through stifled laughter, "Sorry, Juno."

"Not long ago," Mr. Paria continued, "I found a blend of vegetables capable of suppressing my thirst for months at a time, while giving me enough nutrients to survive. However, eventually I will have to resort to the real thing."

The two men looked to one another at the mention of Juno's necessity. Seeing their concern, the teacher interrupted, "I would have a hard time taking a life ever again, but it will happen. I swear to you, though, I will never take the life of a friend. I would give my own first."

Jedd shook his head in agreement. The man's words rang true.

As the night wore on, their discussion persisted until Jedd fell asleep in his chair. The sun was perched on the horizon when the other two submitted to their body's desires and slunk off to bed.

Chapter Thirty-Seven

Inevitability

Late the following morning, Jedd and his friends awoke to the delicious smell of a hearty breakfast. Fresh fruits, vegetables, biscuits, and sausage were cooking in the kitchen. They massaged the stiffness out of their muscles and followed the aroma wafting through the house. Farlin had left earlier that morning and was nowhere to be seen. When they entered the kitchen, they found Madelin picking Juno's brain as he slaved over a pot of sizzling gravy.

Madelin greeted the men from a barstool with a merry, "Hey there, gents."

"Good day, *mon amie*," proffered Roger. "You're lookin' chipper, little lady—much better than last night, if I might add."

"I feel better. I can't believe the bruises already disappeared. It's not even tender."

Jedd and Daniel waved with half-hearted vigor and mumbled as they seated themselves at the corner table. Roger grabbed a barstool next to Madelin and propped his elbows on the kitchen island.

"Guys, if you want, there's coffee," teased Madelin.

The mention of the dark, caffeinated beverage perked Daniel's ears after an awkward night spent in the wooden rocking chair. He felt drained, more so than he should have. *It must be a side effect of the medicine,* he thought. He willed his body into motion and stumbled across the kitchen in a sleep-induced stupor. He filled mugs for the three of them and returned to the table. "Thanks," he mumbled. Seconds later the caffeine was coursing through their veins, infusing them with life.

Daniel gave a contented sigh and struck up a conversation about the most enthusiastic topic of late, their developing abilities. Unbeknown to the others, a deep crease appeared in Jedd's forehead. A familiar, violet orb was moving in the distance. He watched it as the others conversed, tuning out the chatter. Satisfied that Leodenin wasn't making his move, Jedd turned his attention back to the table.

"So, your people require nine family members to shift?" asked Madelin.

"Yes. How many do you require?"

Madelin blushed as her power became clear. She raised her hand in answer to his question, but said nothing.

"Just you?"

She nodded.

"Can you do it right now?"

"You want to leave?" Concern marred her rested face.

"No, but can you?"

"Yes," she replied and glanced at the available webs glimmering at the corners of her vision. *That would be the easiest way,* she thought.

Juno looked over at the groggy ex-mercenary, again noticing the subdued, gray glow around him. "How about you, Daniel?"

Daniel rubbed the scarred skin over his wounds, still unable to believe how well they healed. "I don't know," he muttered after swallowing the last of his coffee.

"What do you mean?"

"Haven't been able to so far, but I can see the webbing like Madelin."

"Webbing?" Juno asked before the meaning dawned on him. "Oh, you mean the croisement, the point where two planes overlap."

Daniel and Madelin both shrugged at the unfamiliar term.

"I still can't see those damn things," commented Jedd, breaking his morning silence.

"Hmmm, that is odd," replied Juno. "My people can see them."

Jedd rolled up the sleeve of his blackened arm. "Do any of them have this?"

Juno glanced up from his pot where the gravy now simmered, and the sight staggered him. He slumped onto a bar stool, staring at the sickly appendage.

"Can you heal this?" Jedd asked.

"How did I not see that before?" he whispered. "Why would you want to do such a thing?"

"It's dead. It spread all the way up my arm, and I'm afraid it might kill me in my sleep if it gets worse."

"It is not anything like that," Juno reassured him. "You've been selected..."

Before he could explain further, the meaning of the term "selected" occurred to Jedd. "Oh crap!" he exclaimed. "How can that be? It started when we were in a different world."

Juno amended his statement. "Okay, not selected. You have been chosen by a higher power. Our ancient religious teachings tell of a guardian that will be summoned when there is need. Sometimes the world pulls people together with similar abilities to help one another. You are to become a guardian."

Jedd let out a sigh of relief, but his brows remained furrowed. "So, it's a kind of a 'survival of the fittest' philosophy. But what am I supposed to be a guardian of?"

"A powerful shifter," Juno answered. His eyes were alight with the discovery. "Many years ago, not long before much of our family was slaughtered, there was one man who was to become a guardian like yourself. His name was Persain, and he was my friend. He almost killed himself many times, but always managed to survive without severe injuries. He was able to rip open a window into another world with just his hand, but as he did, the very essence of the worlds infected his arm, hardening it to everything around him. It was as though it existed outside of reality. My people revered him for it, but a few were jealous of his potential.

"Persain was ambitious, though, and a risk taker. One thing I know was, like you, he was not able to discern between different planes. Instead, he thrust his arm through the fabric of this plane and into that of another, ripping a hole between the two. Where he would end up was anyone's guess. He wasn't afraid of anything and cared nothing for the family reputation, which might be why we became close. The difference between Persain and you, though, is that he did not live long enough to find his charge, the person he was supposed to protect. Someone took care of that. There were many opportunities. As I said, Persain was not adverse to danger." Juno paused so Jedd could make the next logical leap.

"I see, and you think I'm destined to become Madelin's guardian," Jedd finished, thinking back to their unique connection when she was a child.

Juno nodded. "Look at her aura."

Jedd and Daniel appraised her with searching stares. Even Roger tried, but he saw nothing of what Juno described. Those that could see it watched the emerald glow pulsate with a life of its own. Madelin tried not to blush under their scrutiny.

"I wish I could see it," she muttered.

"Unfortunately you cannot. Mirrors only work for the physical, and you would have to see your own true form in its entirety." Madelin gave a subdued nod as Juno continued, "You have seen the auras of most of my family moving through town. As you can see, they are not as deep in color as hers. That is a sign of her potential. I suspect that because of her power, you have been chosen as her guardian."

Jedd nodded. "Makes sense, but how do we know for sure?"

"We cannot. As I said, Persain died before he could become a guardian, but our family archive mentioned their existence on rare occasions. To my knowledge, there were no others during my lifetime."

Madelin's thoughts turned to his earlier comment. "You said a true shifter can see which plane to choose."

"Yes, that is right."

"I can get an idea of what a world's like from a touch, but it's just a feeling. Do shifters choose based on a feeling, or is there more to it?"

"No," he replied. "When we were looking for a place to move, Alain peered into other worlds for hours. He just touched the lip of the croisement, the thread or webbing as you call it. I am sure there is more to it, but..." Unable to explain further, he waved the question away. "I will try to help you figure it out after breakfast... if I can."

Juno lifted the wooden spoon to Madelin's lips, and she declared the meal ready with a smile. He set a stack of plates on the countertop and filled one for Madelin. The others were left to fill their own and did so without moderation.

"Hey, Jun. What's this meat from?" asked Roger. His Cajun accent blended with the thick coffee on his tongue. "I never saw pigs or nothin'."

"Sectaches...," Juno replied, but the others only stared back with incomprehension. "Um... it is a big lizard. I have a pen in the forest."

They nodded and tried the meat in turn. The conversation dwindled to idle commentary and a slew of risqué military jokes over the scrumptious breakfast. They laughed at the Cajun's accented stories, and Madelin toyed with the crumbs of food left on her plate.

When they had their fill, Juno grabbed Madelin's attention, saying to the others, "Gentlemen, I hope you have enjoyed the meal. Please make yourselves at home. I have a few things to show Madelin and questions to answer, but we will return soon."

Jedd thrummed his fingers on the table in thought, but Madelin reassured him, "Guys, it's okay. I need the help if I'm ever going to take on PASTOR."

"I am sorry for the isolation, but please trust me. Madelin needs to focus."

He said no more, and the two of them disappeared out the back door, retreating into the garden. Roger and the others sat in silence. They watched as Juno and Madelin seated themselves on a low rock wall to talk. The two soon became immersed in the topic, with Juno gesturing as he spoke.

"Well, what do you think that's about?" asked Daniel.

"I've a feeling it's something we haven't been able to help her with."

"Like what, her shiftin'?"

"Maybe," Jedd answered, "but I think it's something else."

As the other option set in, Daniel took a sip of his coffee. "Oh… what would you do if you lost everything?"

"A blessing and a curse," Jedd replied. His concerned eyes never left his goddaughter.

"Too true, too true… But she doesn't have a thing to regret. She wasn't given the chance to have a life, to make bad decisions, or to make decisions at all."

Jedd nodded in agreement. The same thoughts had occurred to him.

Daniel saw the problem as an afterthought, and dark clouds descended on him. "That's a true curse," he muttered.

Roger donned his jacket and straightened his high collar before walking out the door with a few trailing words. "Be back later, guys. Gotta pick up some stuff in town." The quick exit was a surprise, but before they could comment the Cajun was striding down the rock-paved walkway toward town. His hand rhythmically thumbed the deck of cards in his coat pocket.

"What the hell was that about?" asked Daniel.

Something itched at the back of Jedd's consciousness, but he was still unable to reach it. "Don't know," he replied, finishing off his cup.

The rest of the morning was uneventful. Daniel lay down on the couch and slept for the better part of the day. His body was in overdrive after the week's ordeals and Juno's medicine.

Jedd picked up the dishes and busied himself with mundane, household tasks before settling down to take stock of their ammunition. He kept their extra shells in his duffle bag, but the bag was getting lighter. *What'll we do when we run out?* he wondered.

He even pulled out his laptop computer in a vain attempt to find some semblance of technology in this archaic world, but nothing reached this far out, if it even existed.

Madelin burst in as he was setting the computer aside, resigned that what he'd relied on in the past was ineffectual in this place. "Jedd, you won't believe it!" she shouted to the heavens. "Were my parents' names Lane and Waverly?"

"Yes they were," answered Jedd, "like I told you before."

"But did they ever take me to the circus?" she added in hysterics.

The sudden onslaught of questions was startling, but the accuracy of this new revelation was a wonderful development. "I'm not sure, but I think they must have."

"What was their last name?" she pleaded. "What's my last name?"

Jedd smiled as he answered her, "Boatweit, your name is Madelin Isabelle Boatweit." She smiled, repeating the name to herself over and over. Juno stood watching from the doorway with a smug smile.

"Congrats, Madelin," said Daniel, astonished at the drastic change.

"What'd you do?" Jedd asked, turning his attention to Juno.

"Just a little science left over from the old world. It is called hypnosis."

Jedd nodded, having heard of the technique. "Some scientists practiced that sort of thing in our world, too. Most people thought it was a load of crap, though."

"It's great," commented Madelin. "There isn't much to remember, but I remember my parents... and you. The rest of my life's just made up of repeated tests that grate on my nerves, but I remember it all now."

As she ran through the highlights, tears streamed down her cheeks unchecked. She gathered herself with a look of grim determination. "Damn those bastards. They stole my life."

"We'll take care of them, Madelin. I promise," Jedd reassured her.

"There is no doubt in my mind that you will do just that," confided Juno as he joined them in the living room.

Madelin looked around the room, a question appearing on her face. "Where's Roger?"

"He disappeared this morning," answered Daniel. "Said he was heading to town for a few things."

"When?" asked Juno.

"Just after breakfast."

"Let's hope he doesn't get in any trouble," commented Jedd, his pessimistic tone obvious to the others.

Just then, the front door opened to admit the smiling Cajun. The setting sun dwindled behind him. "Hey, guys!"

"Where you been," asked Daniel.

"Just off playin' some cards and pickin' up a few things. Did pretty well, too."

"I thought we agreed not to do that anymore. Don't we have more than enough money?" commented Jedd. His tone showed his frustration. "Why'd you go and take a chance like that?"

"Well, yeah, we agreed, but I needed to get somethin', and it was kinda expensive," Roger retorted, his frustration showing. He threw a small book onto the table next to Madelin. "That's for ya, Maddy," he murmured in passing. The back door slammed behind him as he stormed out of the room and sauntered into the darkening garden.

Juno shook his head. "Has he won a lot?"

"Every time he's played there," replied Jedd as he lowered himself into the rocking chair.

"Many in my family play there, and they do not take lightly to losing."

"We told him that, but he has a bit of a problem," added Jedd. The others nodded their agreement.

Madelin picked up the leather-bound book while they spoke. In the front cover was a penned note.

To My Little Lady,
I hope that the best will come to an innocent soul like yours. I realize we've only known each other a short time, but it's meant the world to me. You've become like a daughter. Jedd sees the beauty in your heart that we each know is there, and I'll do all I can to help you bring out the wonderful woman inside. Life is full of secrets, but few are hidden from those that

hold them. We'll discover the truth. I promise you. Until then, let these
pages flourish with the passions of your heart so that no memory will ever
be lost.

Your Loving Family,
Roger Talbut

Her eyes welled with tears as she read his note. By the time she finished, the flood gates opened once more and rivers coursed down her cheeks. To the astonishment of the others, she leapt to her feet and rushed after Roger. She found him pacing in one of the paved walkways, illuminated by a large cluster of florescent mushrooms. She closed the distance between them in two long strides and threw her arms over his shoulders.

The irritation of the group's earlier remarks was replaced by the heartfelt affection he felt for her. Circling her in his arms, he ran a fatherly hand over her wavy, red hair that was still growing out and allowed her to sob into his chest. For once, at least they were tears of joy.

"Thank you so much, Roger," she mumbled through the folds of his jacket. "I love it. And it's just in time."

"How's that?" His accent was almost imperceptible in his whispered tones.

"Juno found a way to break through what they did."

His face lit up. "How'd he do that?"

"Something called... hypnosis," she said, turning her head up to him.

Roger nodded and added, "Then ya can write down your most cherished memories, while they're fresh."

Madelin bobbed her head and stuffed her teary-eyed face back into his collar. "I'll write in it every day." They clung to each other until the chill forced them inside.

Chapter Thirty-Eight

Hemmed In

Most of the group retired before much of the night had passed. Daniel and Madelin remained awake by candle light as Juno taught them to develop their abilities. Madelin practiced delving into worlds without entering them. She was delighted by the progress she made in one evening.

Daniel, on the other hand, was unable to do more than look. He could see the strings bleeding through other worlds and even delve deeper than Madelin, but he was still unable to shift of his own volition. He tried once more with less drastic consequences than before. However, the ability somehow remained dormant. Like a starving man watching through a cafeteria window, disappointment had become a part of his life. He could see what he wanted, but seemed destined never to reach it. He gave up for the night and fell onto the couch. He was unconscious by the time his body settled to the cushions.

Madelin and Juno talked late into the night as the candle burnt down to nothing. Their conversation moved from genetic evolution to personal preferences and lifelong goals. Now that she had a past and a future, she entertained the thought of a life of her own design. Neither of them could cut the evening short, so the following morning Madelin awoke alone on the living-room floor. She was unsure when she had drifted off, but it had been the most exciting day of her life. As promised, she pulled out the journal and wrote her newfound memories into the pages. Then, she devoted a chapter to each day since breaking out of the institution.

The others awoke that morning to another fresh breakfast. Jedd mentioned the dwindling stock of ammunition. To their astonishment, Juno offered a solution. He roped Roger into a physical-defense lesson with Madelin and himself before the plates were cleared. They all took up his offer to learn the basics of sword fighting in the hopes of surviving, if it came to that. The gambler and Madelin followed him out to the garden with a few antique swords in hand, leaving the others to finish their coffee.

As Jedd took the last sips, movement caught his attention from the far edge of his vision. Leodenin was on the move again, but this time toward town.

"Come with me," he whispered, walking back into the living room. His eyes never left Leodenin.

Daniel followed as Jedd positioned himself on the couch, "I need to check on Leodenin. He's on the move again, and I'm sure Alain's up to something. If we don't keep an eye on them, we may find ourselves ambushed. Can you watch things here?"

Daniel nodded. He took a seat in one of the rocking chairs that looked out on the garden.

Before long Jedd was awash in twisting colors, sliding through another dizzying tunnel. They soon disappeared and were replaced by a natural world covered in a continent of shade trees. Two men milled about a small campfire a few yards away. A third stood watch at the base of an ancient tree with a trunk that could hide the length of a station wagon.

Leodenin's violet glow was approaching the town, heading away from Jedd. He flew through the aged forest and toward the false father with a thought. When they came in sight, he found Leodenin accompanied by his two remaining agents and the squad commander. A familiar face was in the lead, Farlin. Jedd slowed to a crawl and kept them at the edge of his vision.

Which side is Farlin playing? I'll have to find out what Juno thinks about this.

He followed, but it occurred to him that he also stood out. It worked both ways. Although he left sufficient distance between them, it wouldn't take long for the false father to discover his attempted surveillance.

The town was ahead, and they were undoubtedly heading to Alain. Jedd propelled himself around the small group and into the confines of Lord Alain's manor. Seeing the man's brown glow at the opposite end of the house, Jedd made his way through the hallways. He came up behind the lord unobserved. Alain was standing just outside the back door, speaking with another of his family. The stranger's aura gave off a muted, yellow hue. Jedd was close enough to hear their conversation through the cracked door their murmured voices echoing in the bare laundry room.

"I took care of it," came the accented voice of the hidden relative.

"Wonderful," replied Lord Alain. "Be sure to let the rest of the family know of the scheduled entertainment."

"Certainly, my lord," added the man. He then bowed and turned to leave.

As Lord Alain stepped inside, his eyes locked onto Jedd. The programmer slunk into the wall behind him, but that failed to stop Lord Alain. He sped around the corner and flung open the linen-closet door, but Jedd had vanished.

The programmer squinted at the scant rays of light slipping into the cozy cottage. It was just as he left it. However, hours had passed by in what seemed like minutes. *I must have fallen asleep after the encounter.*

He sat up to meet Daniel's questioning gaze, but took a minute to compose himself. After reconstructing his disjointed thoughts, he broke the silence. "We're in trouble."

"What happened?" asked Daniel, still seated in the comfortable rocking chair.

"It looks like Leodenin's meeting up with Lord Alain. Farlin's leading him into town."

Daniel *harrumphed* at the unfortunate prospect of an alliance between their two enemies.

"And it looks like Lord Alain has something planned for the family. I'm not sure when, though," Jedd added. "But I think you and I both know what that might be."

Daniel nodded with solemn comprehension.

Jedd glanced at the garden where he last saw Madelin. She and the Cajun were mimicking Juno's moves. Then they set the swords aside and guarded their faces while Juno came at them from different directions. He stopped to correct them at times, reminding them of the proper defensive techniques. Soon they both mastered the maneuver and moved on to another.

Jedd watched as Juno had them spar against one another. Madelin deposited Roger onto the pavement with a swift kick to the knees, and a cacophony of laughter enveloped the house as the Cajun glared at Juno. Rising from the ground, Roger brushed off his pants and readied himself again. Madelin attacked with vigor, but this time Roger swept her aside with a rough clothesline to the neck. As the sparring match continued, Daniel calmed.

"So, what did I miss?" asked Jedd after his own laughter died away.

"Juno taught them some basic techniques using fencing swords."

"Rapiers?" asked Jedd, stunned by the choice.

"Yeah." Daniel nodded. "The best weapon for piercing the hearts of his own kind, outside of a gun, but that requires accuracy and ammo."

"Takes a hard man to turn against his own," assessed Jedd.

"That it does, but I'm still not sure about him."

"Even after what he did for you?"

"I know, but it's like he said, 'The apple don't fall too far from the tree.'"

The programmer raised an eyebrow. "Wasn't it you who said that?"

"Yeah, but he agreed," defended Daniel.

Jedd chuckled to himself as he rose from the couch and entered the garden. "Juno, I need a few minutes."

Motioning for them to continue, Juno followed him into the house. "What is this about, Mr. Altran?"

"I followed Leodenin, the guy who's been chasing us, and found Farlin leading him into town." He let the words sink in and added, "Then, I went to check on Lord Alain. He was meeting in secret with another of your family members. They've planned some family entertainment, and I'm pretty sure it's the Selection."

Juno mulled over the new information. "As far as Farlin is concerned, he is doing Alain's bidding and then reporting back to us. It is good that we know of Leodenin's intentions, though. In regard to my family, I am not surprised. I suspected as much after what happened to Madelin. His pride was hurt, but there is a larger concern. If he did what you said, then he went outside the family, which disgraces us all—or so they believe. He cannot let word of it get out to the others."

Jedd massaged his bearded chin, considering what Juno was implying. "So what do you think he'll do to cover his tracks?"

"Just about anything to keep the others from turning on him. The blood runs deep. To many, that would be enough for them to call for his head. He will probably try and eliminate her," answered Juno. He attempted to stifle his own emotions, but was still visibly disturbed.

"God, no," Jedd pleaded.

"We better be ready."

Jedd rose to meet the man's brown eyes. "You don't want to run?"

"Where can I go?" he replied. "There are very few worlds I can live in easily, and I cannot travel on my own. If we ever became separated I would be at the mercy of strangers, which could be much worse than here... Besides, this has been my home for most of my life. I cannot abandon it and the family that has been led astray by my brother."

"I understand."

"Do we know when they will come?" Juno asked.

"No, they just said soon."

"We probably have a few days then. It will take that long for them to get organized," he replied after consideration. "If you and your friends wish to leave, now would be the time."

While tempted, Jedd couldn't consider it after all Juno had done for them. *Family or not, when it comes to eliminating anyone with knowledge of Alain's impropriety, I don't think their brotherly bond will stop Alain's hand.*

Before he could answer, Roger and Madelin stormed into the room. "The hell we will," Roger spat. "We aren't leavin' you at the hands of them damn vampires. Even if ya do share a bit of the Traditorian genes, it doesn't make ya a jack ass like them. You've proven that, right, Maddy?"

"Well said, Roger," Madelin replied with confidence. "We're not going anywhere."

Daniel stepped into the room and added, "Look, Juno, my boy, I don't rightly like or trust you, but that doesn't mean you should be thrown to the likes of them. Everyone deserves a chance."

Juno looked at each of them with newfound respect. "Then, I guess we better prepare a welcome party. It will not be easy. Farlin and a few others have helped me over the years, infiltrating their ranks and assessing tensions within the family. I am not allowed around them since they cast me out, but servants always hear more than you think. Unfortunately, we haven't seen an ideal opportunity," he added. "But I guess this is the one we've been waiting for."

"Can we count on others to help fight?" asked Daniel.

"No... no, that is something I cannot ask of them," Juno answered. "They have helped me as much as they can, but they will not put their families in danger by outright defying those in power. Besides, I would not allow it. It would be a death sentence."

Madelin and the others bowed their heads in silence. It might very well be a death sentence. Then they devoted the remaining hours of the evening to preparing for the upcoming entertainment.

Chapter Thirty-Nine

Unforeseen Developments

The following morning began with another savory breakfast.

"They will not go easy on you," emphasized Juno. "When they come, we will have to work together. I doubt any of you will stand a chance against even the weakest of them alone. So do *not* get separated."

Daniel nodded in harsh agreement, and Roger chimed in, "Now hold on a sec there, Juno. Don't ya think you're layin' it on a bit thick? I mean, I'm sure me and Danny can take on a skinny or two by ourselves."

"Not bare-handed," the teacher replied. He peered at them over the breakfast table as he continued, "That reminds me. Keep your ammunition within reach. Do not let it run out. You will need it all. And it will not help if you run out in the middle of an attack. They are quick and strong, and will take advantage of any opening they see."

Their heads nodded in unison. Even Roger saw the logic of Juno's advice.

Daniel leaned back in his chair and stretched his arms. He was stuffed after the delicious meal and couldn't recall having felt better. "So what all needs to be done?"

"First, we have to make sure you can take care of yourselves. We also need to make preparations. Farlin is trying to find out what time they plan to attack. Then we will have a better idea of how much time we have to construct our defenses. Just to be safe, I hope to get things done by nightfall. If we are lucky, we will have an extra day."

The group nodded and cleared the table, ready for whatever Juno threw at them. The teacher first enlisted the group in strenuous combat practice. They retreated to the shaded garden to spar. Daniel leaned against a waist-high rock wall that enclosed the nearest plant bed while the others converged on the large patio just outside the house. Juno paired the two ex-servicemen together and Jedd with Madelin. As they fought, the vampire rebel circled the groups, assessing their abilities to see how they had progressed from the previous day.

Each time Madelin attacked, she let her guard down. "Hands up, Madelin," Juno shouted. She did as instructed, but a second later he found her repeating the problem. "Hands up, Madelin," he reiterated.

They had no time for mistakes. Sidestepping her, he stopped the fight and instructed Jedd on a defensive technique to take advantage of Madelin's error then turned to the other sparring session.

Roger was making use of the moves Juno had shown him. They were proving effective, but the battle veteran countered most of the Cajun's attempts. The ex-sailor's training was evident over Madelin's and her godfather's, but improvements were still needed. Seeing Roger's knee balancing his weight, Juno shot a knifed hand into the backside and clipped his tendon. The gambler went down in a heap.

"What the hell?" he screamed.

"That is just what I was thinking," the vampire replied. "Did I not tell you to keep that knee in? Balance your weight. Keep it bent. Do *not* lock it. It slows your reaction time. They will take advantage of it and get the jump on you."

Roger nodded and rose from the ground. "Got it."

Juno returned to the other pair and found Madelin's guard dropping once again. In a flash, he leapt between the two and smacked her forehead, coming to a stop a foot away. Astonished by the blur and impact, she failed to react to Jedd's attack. His fist glanced off her temple and sent her to the ground.

"I'm so sorry, Maddy," Jedd professed. "It all happened so fast."

His goddaughter peered up at them from the stone floor. "I know. How'd you do that, Juno?"

"That is how they will move," he replied. "Do not let your guard down."

"I didn't," she exclaimed like a frustrated child. "You're just too fast."

"I may be fast, but you have to stop me," he answered. "Otherwise, you will not have a hope of surviving."

Her eyes flared as she pushed herself off the ground. With a shake of her head, she returned to the stance Juno had shown her the day before. She steadied her breathing without thought and focused on Jedd. "Okay, let's go."

Jedd came at her, but his moves were hesitant and she shoved them aside with ease.

"No, no, no," Juno chided.

Jedd stopped to look at the man as he stepped closer. When his lips were next to Jedd's ear, he whispered, "I know she is your goddaughter. You do not want to lose her. I get it, but what will happen when they get hold of her because you went easy?"

Jedd's jaw firmed. Juno took a step back. As soon as he was clear, Jedd flew at her. He threw a fist high, feinting. Then he switched and threw a few at her gut.

She slipped by the first and leapt back as the onslaught continued. Her eyes were green fire. Jedd resumed his stance, but a second later he was on the move again. He circled, forcing her back against the low wall. Then he leapt forward and went for her throat.

She was determined not to let down her guard and assessed the threat in a split second. Her body acted of its own accord. She switched stances, lowered herself to the ground, and Jedd's assault went high. She thrust her elbow into his stomach and spun to his back then slid to a stop and sent half a dozen blows into his kidneys. Before he could react, she grabbed his wrist, thrust his arm behind him, and sent the edge of her foot into the back of his knee.

The force of her kick sent him tumbling to the ground, and her tight grip flung his head into a rock wall. Jedd stumbled to his feet, his mind whirling from the maneuver.

Where'd she learn that? he wondered. *Juno didn't teach us anything like that.*

Juno appraised her performance with pride. When Jedd had attacked, the meek woman disappeared and was replaced by a trained warrior, but as quickly as it came, the fighter disappeared. Madelin's glare vanished, and she resumed her casual posture, favoring one leg with her hand propped on a hip. He hadn't seen those moves since his days as a youth.

"Where did you learn that?" asked Juno, intrigued.

"I... I... I'm not sure," she replied. "There was training in the hospital, but I remember it like a dream. I don't know the specifics. I just focused on Jedd, and my body took over. It was like it had a mind of its own."

Juno nodded. "That is muscle memory. Your body remembers things, even if you do not. Once you have trained it to do something, it reacts without thought. It is like a habit."

Madelin glanced back at Jedd in apology. "Are you okay? I didn't realize how hard I was hitting you until after I'd done it."

"Yeah...," Jedd replied, still gathering his breath. "Those were well-placed punches, though. I can barely move."

"Good," Juno spat. "It is a lesson for the both of you. Madelin, you need to focus and stay in that frame of mind when the time comes."

She nodded, still astonished by what had happened.

Juno removed a handful of fencing foils from a bag and threw one to each of them. "Now it is time to arm yourselves. Remember what I told you."

Roger hefted the sword in one hand. Its leather grip fit as though it were made for him. In their earlier training, it proved less difficult to use than he expected. The sword was similar to knife fighting, except for the weapon's balance, but he was growing to like it.

It felt like a toothpick in Daniel's hand, but he readied himself like Juno had shown them. His eyes settled on Roger, but he waited for him to make the first move. The Cajun seemed to like this bit of training and often attacked before him.

Roger leapt forward, blade bared. Daniel parried, and the two circled one another. Their blades met again, and the older of the two spun his clockwise, wrestling Roger for the advantage. If he could disarm the gambler, he would win. Knocking the blade aside, he thrust up into the Cajun's shoulder, but Roger dodged his attack and retreated down one of the paved walkways that meandered through the garden. Daniel followed, annoyance showing in his austere look. The gambler surprised him with a feint then brought his blade down on Daniel's bicep with a loud *thwap*. It stung, but not enough to distract him from the fight. He circled Roger again, but the sailor wouldn't allow himself to be pinned against a wall.

Juno massaged his chin with approval then returned to the others. Madelin prodded Jedd with strike after strike. She was no longer as timid as the day before, at least when confronted in battle, and her focus was unwavering.

Just then a thought occurred to him. He waited for the proper timing and leapt into the fray as Jedd stepped forward with his own attack. Madelin batted Jedd's sword away with a practiced hand and switched her attention to Juno, now seeming more in tune with her body. The blunted tip of her fencing sword stopped at his neck, bending under the pressure of his rapid advance.

Her swiftness stopped Juno in his tracks. The tension in the bent sword threatened to snap the blade. "Very good," he croaked and stepped away. "That is quite good."

After an hour more of practice, the group went into the house to assess their ammunition stores once more and construct defensive measures.

"Got anything explosive?" asked Daniel, spotting the collection of jars.

Juno quirked an eyebrow, and a glint of mischief fluttered in his eyes. "Why, yes I do."

"Good, then we just need something to make them stand out at night." Daniel scanned the yard and paved walkways.

"How about these?" Juno added, pointing at a cluster of mushrooms at the far end of one soil bed. He plucked a midsized specimen and cupped it in his hands. In the darkness, a blue luminescence filtered through his fingers.

"Yeah, that's perfect," replied Daniel with an appreciative smile.

Their host gathered large masses of the fungus, leaving nothing behind, and began harvesting other plants from the garden. "But what is it you are planning?"

"You'll see. Got any scrap metal?"

"Behind the house, next to the animal pens. They are just beyond the tree line."

Juno finished gathering the herbs he needed and went inside to concoct Daniel's explosive powder. The others followed, their curiosity getting the best of them. Juno roasted the fresh herbs in a small bowl and ground the ingredients with an adeptness gained through centuries of experience. Less than an hour later, Daniel appeared pushing a wheelbarrow laden with handcrafted nails and other shards. The two men worked to create Daniel's invention, eventually sealing the jar with wax.

Daniel grinned at Roger and Juno. "Field test?"

"You bet, *mon ami*," Roger replied with a knowing smile.

He lifted the jar from the table and deposited it on the other side of the yard. The sun was beginning its southern journey, and the jar glowed under the shade of the tree line. Daniel leveled his pistol on it from the doorway when Roger had retreated to safety. The roar of his gun echoed through the cottage and was joined by a shattered blast as the bullet tore through the container, spewing metal shrapnel across half the yard.

"Shit, that makeshift mine'll take out anything within twenty feet," Roger commented with admiration.

"It will not take them out at that distance, but if some are close enough, the shards might pierce their hearts—could get a couple with each jar if we time it right. Remember, they are like me. It will take a lot to bring them down."

Roger shrugged, but the dread in his eyes overshadowed his uncaring façade.

"Okay, let us get started then," Juno said, as though rousting the troops. "We have many more to make."

Daniel sprang into action, gathering ingredients for as many as they could construct and directing his friends. The light outside was waning by the time they finished, but there were only enough mushrooms to fill half the jars. Jedd remembered his own discovery and retrieved the mushrooms he had gathered days earlier. They still illuminated the area in a foot radius, although the glow was somewhat muted compared to the day he found them. Juno smiled when he saw the large fungi and scattered them within the remaining jars.

After they added the last of the chemicals from his stocked shelves, they admired their progress. The desk in the converted dining room sat covered in dozens of large jars, each glowing in the dwindling light of the sun. Before the daylight vanished, Daniel and Roger placed many of the jars throughout the yard, within sight of the windows. By nightfall, the motley group was ready and waiting.

Chapter Forty

Unreasonable Propositions

While expected, the knock on the door set everyone's nerves on edge. It was just after midnight. Juno recovered from the shock first, lifted himself from the armchair, and went to the window. The others rose in preparation of what stood beyond it. Juno recognized one of his messengers and waved the group back to their seats. A local boy of seventeen years stood at the door, but anxiously peered over his shoulder.

"Care to come in, Byron?" asked Juno after opening the door.

Byron shook his head. He attempted to meet Juno's gaze, but disappointment weighed it down. Instead, he stared at his feet. "No thank you, sir." He lifted a stiff arm and handed Juno a folded sheet of parchment.

The rebel unsealed the letter. It was addressed and signed by no one, but contained the familiar scrawl of Farlin.

Dear Sir,
The family of which we spoke has chosen to select not one, but two people this month. I believe it would benefit you to know that Roger Talbut and Madelin Boatweit have been chosen for Selection. Due to an undisclosed immediate concern, the family has decided to forgo the one-day transition period and will be in pursuit of those selected this evening. If I may be of further service, please let me know. Good luck!

Your friend in the field.

The choice of selecting two people was unexpected but didn't change their plans.

"Thank you for your assistance," Juno murmured after reading the letter. "You have been a great help. You may go."

The youth bowed then whispered, "Thank you, sir," before retreating into the forest.

Juno gazed at the town in the distance and watched as a host of familiar auras began gathering. *We have a few minutes yet,* he thought. He closed the door and handed the letter to Jedd.

"It looks like you stirred up a tekkle's nest," Juno mentioned with a smile that failed to mask his concern.

"What do you mean?" asked Madelin. "What's a tekkle? And didn't we expect them to choose me?"

Jedd answered her after reading the letter for himself. "I believe a few of them took offense to our friend's good fortune in the tavern."

Roger looked up from his rapier and said in disbelief, "I'm on there, too?"

Jedd nodded.

"Well, aren't I making friends everywhere I go?" Roger added in jest.

The others chuckled at the mild attempt to break the tense silence. Just then howls echoed through the forest, signaling the advance on Juno's small cottage. They looked at one another and attempted to summon the courage to confront the oncoming vampires. The screams grew, and the forest shivered.

Daniel was the first to stand as he sensed the time approaching. He walked over and took his position next to the living-room window. As though on cue, Roger headed for the kitchen while checking the chamber of his revolver for the fifth time. He propped his sword against the wall by the back door, in case it came down to close-quarters fighting. Jedd pulled out his .22 caliber pistol and knelt next to the window in the study. They opened the shutters a sliver to observe the approaching people and attack through when necessary.

Juno walked over to the blazing fireplace. An ornate sword hung over it, the faint firelight flickering on its blade. He removed it with reverence and admired the elegant engravings throughout the pommel and up the hilt. He ran his thumb along the edge and tip of the curved blade. After a moment of reflection, he pulled the scabbard from the mantle and strapping it to his waist.

"I guess it is only right that their blood should be spilt by a Traditorian sword," he muttered to the room. "This grosse messer was passed down to me by my father. As the youngest son, it was the one thing left to me." He slid the sword into the well-oiled scabbard and took his place by the front door, prepared to give his relatives the reception they deserved.

Jedd watched the line of trees surrounding the garden and back of the house. Little movement could be seen. As though sensing the oncoming chaos, the woods adopted a silence that could only be the quiet before the storm. Even the animals fled or hid. The only movements were tree limbs quivering with anticipation.

Was it the wind that caused it, Jedd wondered, *or some innate knowledge of what's to come?*

The nervous anticipation grew as screams and howls disrupted the silence, echoing through the forest. Jedd looked beyond the multitude of faces that appeared, searching for a familiar aura. He found it moving across the shadowed horizon. Leodenin advanced from behind to a vacant area amongst the forest. It soon became clear what their tactician had decided.

Even the subtle movement of the tree limbs stopped as the advancing army halted. A line of vampires stood at the edge of the shrouded yard. An eerie silence fell over the clearing as the pale faces peered at the small group through the darkness. Each person within the house stood in expectation and jumped when a loud knock at the door broke the ominous quiet. Juno held up a hand and stepping up to the door, revealing himself to his brother through a crack. Lord Alain stood tall and forbidding in the cramped stone archway. He'd even donned an ornate cape for the occasion.

"Hello, little brother," came his deep, lilting greeting.

"Hello," Juno replied. "I am shocked to find you out this far, Alain."

"Are you?" A slight smile pulled at the edges of Alain's lips. "Then, do you know why I have come?"

"I assume it has to do with my houseguests. What else would pull you away from your tiresome responsibilities? For the last hundred years you have yet to find your way this far out, at least to visit me."

Alain revealed nothing. Instead, he stared down at his younger brother with scalding eyes.

"As I'm sure you know, I have come for Madelin and Roger. Turn them over, and we will allow you to partake in tonight's entertainment," demanded Alain with a grin.

"You know I cannot do that."

"Juno, why must you be so stubborn? You are shaming the entire family with your pathetic attempts at rebellion. How can you stand against those who have bled with you?"

"It is easy when those same people turn on the traditions of old, disrespecting everything our family has stood for." Juno's words grew heated, tinged with hatred that had stewed inside him for years.

"You know nothing of our traditions or what we stand for," screamed Lord Alain, his cool composure breaking. "If you refuse to abide by the laws that bind us, brother, you are no better than those you protect." Alain took hold of his anger and focused it into a calm furnace.

"If it is between your tyrannical rule and those that defy you, I consider myself honored to stand next to your victims."

"Then so be it," shouted Lord Alain. Turning to those at the forest's edge, he announced, "Lord Juno has chosen to violate the sacred laws of our family. As such, the consequences due to those of the Selected now extend to him and all who stand with him." A smile crept up his lips as he turned back to Juno. "I have waited for many years, but finally the day has come. You have been a thorn in my side for far too long, little brother. It will end tonight." With those hate-laden words, he turned and marched back into the night.

Juno barred the door and confronted the silent room. "I believe it is now official."

Madelin smiled with reassurance. "Don't worry, Juno. We're here for you."

Juno returned her smile, but it failed to reach his eyes as his act of betrayal sank into the depths of his mind. He had little time to consider the consequences of his choice, though. The howls escalated into hunger-induced ravings and murderous screams for blood. Within seconds, a barrage of thunderous blows rained down upon the door. Cracks formed as the Traditorian vampires tore at the thick wood.

Juno stepped back and pulled his sword from its scabbard. The room erupted in booming waves of gunfire. The men aimed at the glowing targets as floods of vampires streamed down the garden walkways and over the rock walls lining the plant beds. Chaos reigned as more bloodthirsty creatures attempted to reach the house. Bullets lodged in the bodies of ravenous vampires, and a few found their victims' hearts. But so dense was the assaulting wave that it didn't seem to slow them down.

Daniel slid his pistol through a slat in the window and fired, hitting a glowing jar on one of the garden walls. It exploded, thrusting metal scraps and nails into everything around. A young man and woman who might have been hundreds of years old were passing by when the jar detonated.

Shrapnel embedded itself in their bodies. Pieces found their way into their hearts and necks. Their faces contorted as their bodies fell writhing to the ground. Others around them screamed in pain but continued their rampage. Within seconds, the two vampires were crushed beneath the feet of the assaulting army.

Gunshots rang out and explosions sounded from other sides of the house. *The battle has begun,* thought Juno. *After so many years of being shamefully thrust aside, I will finally emerge from the shadows to take a stand.* As hands began tearing through the door, the time for thought ended.

Juno swept his father's sword across probing hands and forearms, severing them from their owners. As the wounded retreated, they were replaced by others. Juno cleared the doorway time and again until the attackers burst through. The front door finally disintegrated, sending splintered shards flying into the room. He assumed the defensive position his father taught him and prepared to meet the assault. Most of the assailants fell inward, impaling themselves on the tip of Juno's sword.

"Look out. The door gave way!" shouted the rebel as he fought off the seemingly inexhaustible supply of vampires. Bodies piled up on his doorstep, but still more came. Distant relatives, cousins, and even children swarmed over the pile, but Juno fought on. His sword flew over the chasm of bodies to behead a distant cousin whose fangs glinted in the lamplight.

Blood flowed over the wooden planks that had long been the floor of his home, his sanctuary. Pools of crimson spread out from the mass of dead and dying, enveloping his feet and everywhere he tread. It ate at his heart to watch his hands at work, but he couldn't bring himself to stop.

Madelin watched as Juno held the door. He moved like the wind, flowing in and out of reach so fast that she caught nothing more than a blurred glimpse. His sword swept around him, laying waste to people they had seen walking through town the day before. Old friends and family alike fell at his hands. Blood blossomed in small spots that made his black pants glisten. His crimson essence mixed with the blood of his victims, coating his regal clothes, but he slowed for no one.

More explosions erupted outside, and she caught sight of Roger reloading his gun. While preoccupied with the weapon, a hand with talon-like nails reached through the window and dug into his chest. Roger jumped back with a painful start and flung the chamber closed. He leveled the gun on the vampire's neck and pulled the trigger. The recoil flung his hand back, but the muzzle soon sought out the vampire again. With a final, reflexive pull of the trigger, a large-caliber bullet severed the man's head.

He took aim out the window and fired again and again, hitting another glowing target. The Cajun ended the lives of more ageless entities as explosions rocked the house's foundation. Still, the flow of attackers grew. They swarmed the back door. While Roger struggled to hold it shut, Madelin ran to join him. Sword at the ready, she positioned herself behind the door, as Juno had taught her.

The front door had been made of sterner wood, and the kitchen entrance was shredded in seconds. When the bull strength of the assailants brought down the door, Madelin struck at the nearest exposed chest. Those in back pressed forward in ravenous hunger, and the vampires up front were forced into the room. Madelin's rapier skewered them with swift justice, but others took their place. Madelin fought for life itself, but the vampires, young and old alike, were too much for her limited training.

One deft Traditorian youth swept under her plunging blade and angled for her. She leapt back in time and thrust the rapier into the snarling child. The attacker's momentum plunged the sword through his body, stopping when its hilt thudded against the kid's sternum. There was no time for emotion, but something inside her broke.

After reloading, Roger turned his smoking muzzle on the doorway and unloaded on the oncoming rush of people. "Back off! Get a jar!" he roared over the gunfire.

Madelin came to her senses and leapt back, kicking the youth off her weapon. She pulled a jar from the leather bag at her feet and rolled it toward the nonexistent back door. It found its way through the doorway before someone chanced on it. The explosion cleared the entry and sent shrapnel flying into the opposite wall of the kitchen. Bodies fell in murky, red tides that were soon hidden by others racing up the back steps.

Madelin readied another explosive and hurled it at the approaching mob. Ducking out of sight, she narrowly avoided the jagged pieces of metal flying through the air. More vampires swarmed across the yard.

"Juno, how's it going?" she shouted as she readied a third jar. Gunfire answered from the study.

"They are everywhere," Juno replied over his family's bloodcurdling screams.

"Fall back, everyone," Daniel cried as his hand cannon gave a hollow click. He pulled the trigger once more but got the same effect. Stuffing the gun in his pocket, he grabbed a glowing, iron rod from the fireplace and backed up to Juno. He plunged the steaming iron into the first person to step through the shattered window frame. The woman screamed in horror as the blazing poker cauterized her chest. She clawed at the protruding iron but fell to the floor after Daniel pulled it free.

"To the study," cried Jedd. "We can't keep this up. We'll have to move."

Daniel and Juno sidestepped the bodies littering the doorway and inched into the room where Jedd was flinging their makeshift mines out the window. The garden was peppered with bodies and metal shrapnel.

Their retreat into the depths of the house inspired their attackers. Gleeful smiles lit the attackers' faces, and razor-sharp canines glinted in the moonlight. One hungry adolescent dove through the dining-room window and barely missed a glowing jar as it flew past his head and into the yard. Jedd raised his pistol, but the vampire slapped it away and leapt on him, fangs bared. The man's frilled cuff covered Jedd's ear as a fierce hand jerked his head to the side, revealing the programmer's pale neck. The attack happened in an instant.

Oh God! thought Jedd.

Without further thought, he plunged his deadened hand into the vampire's open mouth, cupping his lower jaw. Elongated fangs dug against his blackened fingers but couldn't break the skin. Jedd thrust his thumb up into the man's chin and lifted him from the ground. Blood coursed down Jedd's arm. The man tore at the programmer's face and anything in reach, but Madelin's godfather failed to notice. His anger now had a target. His teeth ground together. Jedd slammed the flailing man into wall after wall, eventually finding the widow and ejecting him from the house with a shouted, "And stay out, you bloody bastard!"

"Jedd, you okay?" asked Daniel as they fell back to the study. Blood streamed down Jedd's cheek, and his sleeve was shredded where the man's fingers had found purchase. "That sucker's fingers went deep."

"Fine," Jedd answered with a grunt and flicked his blood-coated hand. A spray of crimson coated the wall as though suddenly infected with chicken pox. Spotting another group of fanged men sprinting toward the window, he grabbed a jar from the table and threw it into their faces before ducking behind the speckled wall. A deafening explosion echoed through the room.

With a nod, Daniel turned back to Juno and shouted over the torturous chaos, "Hell, Juno, you sure you don't have more than two hundred relatives out there?"

"The family seems to have grown a bit over the last four hundred years," Juno replied between defensive strikes, a sadistic smile now playing on his face.

Madelin and Roger grabbed the remaining bag of shrapnel grenades and ammunition. Before leaping into Juno's converted study, they flung two jars out the rear entryway and kitchen windows. They ducked as metallic slivers penetrated the kitchen ceiling. The shards stood vibrating in the walls, reflecting the moons' rays into the smoke-filled room.

"Stock up! We're moving," shouted Roger as he leveled the hand cannon at the few vampires struggling through the explosions.

Madelin grabbed an armful of jars from the table and deposited them into the bag. The remaining assailants swept through the kitchen doorway and the .44 sprang back to life, echoing in the confined space like the voice of a god. Bullets flew from its muzzle at the two approaching giants and embedded themselves in one man's chest. The vampire howled in pain and stumbled backwards into the wall. His friend swept past with the nimble agility of a cat while the first recovered. Roger's gun spat round after round as the few feet separating them diminished. Bullets found their hearts, and the two fell to the ground with a resounding thud.

After finishing them off with a thrust of his sword, Roger glanced into the kitchen in time to see a slender woman leap over the shattered windowsill. She was dressed in a high-collared jacket, and her coat tail rippled in the wind before settling around her. A sense of something ominous and foreboding sank onto Roger's shoulders.

Chapter Forty-One

Family

"M y goodness," came the enchanting woman's voice echoing through the demolished kitchen. Her words were laced with the natural accent of the older Traditorian family. "You look simply delicious."

She stood tall, her gaze dark and haunting like Juno's, but as she stared him down, she licked her lips. At any other time, the gambler might have relished the sensual thoughts it brought to mind. Her gaze was immobilizing, and she swept toward him with a seductive stride. He stood in stunned silence, the muzzle of his magnum falling to his side. The air throughout the kitchen had stilled in her presence, but whipped up around him as she darted forward, intent on the kill. The gambler was startled by the move, but more at the words that erupted from behind.

"Wake up, Roger!" shouted Madelin as the dark woman advanced. Flitting in from behind, Madelin interposed herself between the two and thrust her sword at the greedy woman. Roger came to his senses and scanned the room, searching for the glorious vision that had enthralled him, but Madelin was in his way.

The Traditorian woman spun past Madelin's blade and knocked it aside. She then paused to assess her new opponent. The woman ran a bloody tongue over her lips in anticipation of the night's entertainment then shot Madelin a maddening smile. She grasped the hilt of her own sword and pulled it free. The curved tip gleamed as she drifted in and out of the luminescent light filling the room. She shifted from foot to foot like a viper waiting to strike.

"Poor, Juno, to have sided with such pitiful excuses for humans," whispered the slender woman.

Madelin leapt forward and thrust her sword in rapid succession, but the elegant woman sidestepped the attack. Then, lifting her own blade, she began her assault. She struck with a hiss, her sword shimmering as it flew through the air. Madelin parried as Juno had taught her, but the swift attack caught her off guard. She controlled her breathing and drifted into the calm focus she had been trained for. Her blade flew up to meet the woman's in sweeping strokes.

Sweat flew down her back and under her lengthy overcoat as she struggled to maintain her footing. It was all she could do to keep the vampire's darting strikes from reaching her. The woman's blows began landing closer, and Madelin's heart skipped a beat. When she came within arm's reach, the demonic woman grabbed her arm and pulled her close, launching herself at Madelin's neck with bared teeth, but stopped inches away as Jedd's goddaughter plunged her sword through the venomous woman's blouse. A tremor ran up her arm as the rapier's hilt slammed into the woman's breastbone.

Madelin watched her face contort in mortal pain before disintegrating under the smoking muzzle of Roger's gun. The echo of the shot resonated through the room with finality. Remembering what his father used to say when he'd angered the man, the gambler shouted, "And one to grow on!"

Madelin sloughed the woman off her rapier with disgust and watched her slump to the floor.

Roger knelt next to the deformed woman's body as the wave of attacks slowed. He removed the grosse messer from the woman's deathlike grip and unbuckled her belt. Wiping the blade on her thick jacket, he offered the hilt to Madelin. She took it. It was lighter than she expected, having attributed the woman's speed and agility to her genetic disposition.

"Who the hell was that?" she asked, having picked up a few of Daniel's choice words. She fought to catch her breath in the brief reprieve.

"Who?" shouted Juno as he cleaved a slobbering goat of a man in two. He turned and glanced at the sword in her hand. His eyes widened as his gaze slid down to the obliterated woman at Madelin's feet. "That... was my sister," he replied with a sigh.

Juno turned away and readied himself for the next onslaught. Understanding the need for silence, Madelin turned her attention to the oncoming wave speeding through the garden and said no more.

Jedd aimed at one of the remaining jars as more vampires tore through the beds of shredded vegetables and herbs. The jar exploded with his well-aimed shot, scattering the pale-faced survivors and dropping the few unlucky enough to have been near. Others were closing on his position. Jedd heaved another explosive at the mob outside the window and ducked as it struck a man in the face. More vampires fell in the explosion, their murderous screams turning to shrieks of pain. Those that escaped were missing limbs and had metal shards embedded throughout their bodies, yet droves of them continued to stream through the ruined garden.

"So, what do we do now, Jedd?" asked Daniel over the roar. "It ain't like they're stoppin'."

Jedd glanced at the vacant tree line he'd noticed before and gauged the distance from Leodenin's approaching aura. "It'll have to be quick, but we can squeeze out through the forest edge," he replied, nodding beyond the garden.

"Is that the only way?" asked the veteran.

"The only one I see."

Juno looked where Jedd indicated. "Go ahead. I'll catch up."

"Grab your bags," said Jedd, hefting his over his shoulder. "Ready?"

They each prepared themselves while eliminating the stragglers that wandered their way. "Yes," Madelin replied after strapping the sword around her waist.

Jedd tossed a jar through the window and waited for the explosion to clear a path before leaping through. He rolled to his feet, pistol at the ready. Roger grasped the windowsill and leapt out, followed by Madelin. Juno and Daniel covered the entryways that were filling with vampires.

"Will you be okay?" asked the ex-mercenary.

Juno nodded.

Daniel leapt through the window with the others and formed a circle at the entrance to the garden.

Surrounded and alone, his family paused, their lips curled in cruel, hungry grins as though savoring the moment. In the brief suspension of battle, Juno lifted a wilting rose from a vase upon the mantle. He brought it to his lips before tossing it onto his sister's mangled body. "*Au revoir,* my darling Adelaide," he whispered.

With a fleeting glance, he launched himself through the shattered dining-room window, twisting as he fell. He unleashed two rounds onto the cluttered desk. A well-aimed bullet tore into the remaining explosives. Shrapnel launched in all directions. The house flexed as the large blast tore through Juno's possessions, destroying everything he held dear. The vampires that infiltrated the home were ripped to pieces as metal shards tore into their bodies.

Juno landed in the midst of the group and sprung up from the ground. They cast around the yard for opponents, but the explosion and their swift escape delayed the marauding vampires from charging. A graveyard silence settled on the ravaged house after the massive explosion. Acrid smoke flowed out the open windows. For the first time since the knock on the door, all they could hear were their heartbeats.

"Lead the way, Jedd," commanded Juno.

They leapt over the garden wall and made their exit, jumping from one rock ledge to another. Jedd watched pale eyes scan the devastation at the tree line, but none of the remaining vampires seemed to realize who they were at first. Some noticed them at last and began their pursuit.

Juno and the others raced headlong into the trees. A final look at the cottage showed the vampire lord with a small contingent of relatives. When Jedd turned back to the forest, he found Leodenin's aura closing fast, leaving them little time.

Chapter Forty-Two

Finding the Fated

The group sped through the shadowed trees, attempting to outrun Leodenin's aura. The screams of murderous vampires grew louder with each footfall. Pale faces darted in and out of the patchy moonlight. Alain's fiends were gaining on them. Gunfire rippled through the trees as the veterans peppered their followers. They peeled away, one after another, but three appeared for every vampire they felled. Before they knew it, Roger tripped and was swept behind in the arms of their pursuers.

"Stop!" Juno yelled.

The Cajun's cries echoed over the tumult, and the group turned to see his sad eyes disappear into the crowd. Daniel let out a vengeful roar and followed, swinging the searing rod like a baseball bat. Juno rushed after him, and they were soon lost in the onslaught of salivating vampires.

Jedd and Madelin attempted to follow, but found themselves cut off from their friends. Juno's relatives encircled them, forcing Jedd and Madelin apart from the others. They backed up to each other and waited for the assault to come, but it was as though the group was toying with them. Daniel and Juno were only yards away, but might as well have been miles. They could no longer see their friends, but bodies flew into the crowd as they fought on. The screams of others told them of Daniel's success, but as the vampires closed around them, Madelin drew Adelaide's sword and thrust it at Jedd. He swung it back and forth to keep the dogs at bay. Drawing her rapier, Madelin lunged at the closest vampire. He leapt back as the tip drew near. The rapier lashed out as another jumped toward her, scoring the side of his cheek. Others slunk by, fingers aching to rake their human flesh. Jedd and Madelin fended them off, dropping them one at a time. Then a familiar voice carried through the chaos.

"Move away from them. They're mine!" shouted Leodenin, but the vampires were caught up in blood lust and circled like vultures.

"Dammit!" cried the dark shifter. "Get 'em, Marlin, before those things tear 'em apart."

As Marlin gave the order to fire, bullets flew into the crowd and tore at exposed limbs. The closest vampires to the back crumpled under the barrage of bullets, and those remaining turned their attention to the new arrivals. The two groups clashed like waves against shore cliffs, leaving Jedd and Madelin to fend for themselves.

They watched as more vampires streamed past, but Jedd's sweeping gaze stopped when he found Leodenin. Recognition flashed as Leodenin strode to meet him. The false father's eyes blazed, and his duster rippled like a flag.

"Stay there. I'll take care of this guy," ordered Jedd. He shoved Madelin behind a tree, but never took his eyes from the pale shifter.

"Oh look! I see they decided to let their dog off his leash. How cute," Jedd sneered.

The comment did little for the man's humor and stoked his anger like gasoline on a bonfire. "I know you," replied Leodenin as he stepped closer. "You're the bastard that threw me down the stairwell." He stopped a few yards away and spat between them. "That's what I think of your pitiful attempts to save your little girl."

"No, tell me what you really think," Jedd goaded with a laugh.

Leodenin stood tall and commanding. His eyes seemed to radiate blue flames, and his duster whipped around him like a tethered animal. He thrust one arm under its flailing tail and revealed his side to the oncoming wind. Flicking the latch on his belt with his thumb, a malevolent grin split his face. The end of a coarse whip trailed out from under the duster and hit the ground. It fluttered to life in the dark shifter's hands, snapping left and right with a slight jerk of his wrist. Before Altran knew what was happening, the frayed end wound around his good wrist and tightened as Leodenin applied the subtlest of pressure.

His grip on the sword loosened under the pressure. He gritted his teeth and pulled back on the braided leather, but Jedd's strength gave way and Leodenin's smile widened. Jaw clenched, Jedd wrapped his blackened hand in the length of whip and pulled with all his might. Leodenin lurched forward, and his smile vanished as the whip flew from his hand.

"What the hell happened to you?" scoffed Leodenin.

"I have no idea," Jedd replied as he unwound the length of braided leather from his arm. He flexed his arm and swung the blade in a circle, testing his wrist's mobility. "What happened to you?" he retorted.

"I don't know what you mean," replied Leodenin with a hint of egotism.

"It's simple. Why do you work for those dogs?"

"I work for no one," the shifter replied with a hearty laugh. As he spoke, he rounded on Madelin's godfather. "I'm on *my* side, the side with power."

"We'll see how powerful you really are," Jedd threatened and lunged for the man.

Leodenin stopped and positioned himself for Jedd's charge. "Hurling yourself at me twice in one lifetime?" he asked with feigned concern. "That isn't smart."

Jedd flew forward and brought the sword down on Leodenin's head, but before they met, the man vanished. He appeared a hand's breadth away and brought a fist down on the back of Jedd's neck. Jedd crumpled under the impact.

"There seems to be a bit more to this than you've learned." Leodenin stepped over to an abandoned short sword and lifted it from the ground.

Jedd flipped over, only to find the shifter advancing on him, sword in hand. Fear filled the pit of his stomach as the lanky man closed the distance. A nauseous dizziness enveloped Jedd's mind and threatened to overwhelm him, but he drove his grosse messer into the ground and pulled himself up, leaning on its hilt for balance.

As Leodenin drew near, he shoved the short sword at Jedd's forehead, as though selecting him for punishment. He brought the sword up and then back down. Madelin's godfather threw his blackened arm over his head to absorb the blow. He expected pain to infuse his arm as the blade slammed into it, but the sword failed to break the skin. Jedd smiled from beneath his blackened limb. *Daniel was right.* He brought up his own sword and Leodenin leapt back, avoiding his extended reach.

Jedd advanced on the shifter and swung with the hatred of a solitary man who has everything to lose. Leodenin met Jedd's sword, blow for blow. They circled one another, locked in a ritual dance and poised for an end to their feud. However, before either could attack Marlin stepped out from behind a tree with an arm draped over Madelin from behind. A bloodied knife hung centimeters from her throat. His hand was still and unwavering, waiting for the next move.

"Stop right there!" demanded the commander.

Each of them backed away, swords held low, mirroring one another. Madelin stiffened under the knife blade. She was putty in his hands, but as Jedd looked in her eyes, he saw childlike mischief blaze to life.

Leodenin watched, rapt with pleasure as Marlin took hold of the long-sought-after woman, but the smile fell away as Madelin put her thoughts into action. Flipping her rapier with a subtle twist of her wrist, she plunged it behind her. Then she lifted her hands to the bladed arm and forced it aside.

Before Leodenin could warn Marlin, Jedd charged forward and forced him onto the defensive. His sword flew forward. Leodenin parried each blow as he was forced back into a tree. Their swords clashed, and Jedd thrust himself into the man's face, attempting to bring the sword's edge up against the shifter's neck. His teeth clenched with the intensity of the struggle, but with a chuckle and a wave of his hand, Leodenin vanished.

Chapter Forty-Three

Retribution

Marlin was stunned by the ferocity with which this timid flower had changed, and he bellowed as the sword plunged through his side. He spun out of reach, but Madelin hammered at the sword handle with a solid kick. The squad commander grunted and tumbled to the ground. He attempted to roll but was hindered by the sword protruding from his back. He teetered but succeeded in pushing himself up off the ground. Taking a large breath, he grasped the handle and pulled. The final edge of the sword sprung free with a torturous cry. Marlin turned haunting eyes on her and a gaze that promised a gruesome, excruciating death.

He dropped the sword and shouted, "You bitch!" Blood trickled from his mouth. "That's it, you little whore. I ain't playin' no more stupid games with you." He spat a glob of blood onto the forest floor and stared her down.

Moonlight flittered over his face, and familiarity set in. Madelin flashed back to that grisly, fire-lit night. She watched as a much younger version of this man flicked a lighter to life and set her family's house on fire. The accelerant caught within seconds.

"You! You killed my parents," Madelin screamed. Her voice took on a harsh, guttural tone and echoed through the trees like a scent on the wind. "I'm going to send you to hell!"

Enraged and seeing her chance at revenge, Madelin sprang into action. She raced forward and threw herself at the stout man, hands outstretched and fists extended, but he was waiting.

Raising a curled fist the size of a small bowling ball, he sidestepped her flying assault and brought his fist down on her tender midsection. Madelin fell to the ground like a lead balloon, crumpling under the blow.

Marlin stepped up to the prone woman and smiled with relish. The blood coating his glistening lips accentuated his hellish appearance. "Ain't you a sight? You had everything given to you on a silver platter, with nothing to worry about. And now, you've got nothing to look forward to. Boy, am I gonna love what comes next." He gave her a maddening grin.

Marlin encircled her neck with a ham-sized fist and pressed down. The pressure forced her deeper into the spongy soil, and mud bubbled up around her head. Unable to breathe, panic set in. She flailed at her assailant and clawed at his hands and face, but he ignored her probing fingers. Marlin squeezed tighter, his own fingertips sinking deeper into the sides of her neck as she struggled.

"No, no, no," she pleaded. Her words came out strained. "This isn't how it ends, you annoying slab of meat—you stupid asshole!" She tried to scream with all the energy she possessed, but her throat protested under the pressure. The only thing that escaped was a weak croak.

A black veil slipped over her eyes as the bud of a dark rose blossomed from Marlin's shirt pocket. Its petals glistened in the moonlit night. With the last of her strength ebbing away, Madelin reached out to the familiar flower and grasped the nearest petal. Her hand fell to the ground as consciousness left her with a petal clutched between two fingers.

The pressure on her neck disappeared, and the PASTOR commander fell to his knees. The darkness faded, and Madelin opened her eyes, blinking away the bright stars that pierced her mind. The world came into focus slowly, and she stared through yet another rift hovering in the air above her. A starlit sky like this one lingered above, but just one moon shone overhead—the blood red one of this world.

Marlin lay inches away, his face and eyes covered in a glazed expression of shock and horror. The look startled her at first, but didn't change. It was the painted look of death. Madelin rolled out from under the rift and backed up to the tree. From her new vantage, she saw that his body had been sliced in two up to his chest. She struggled to force down the nausea that erupted in her stomach.

"I did that," she whispered through a bruised trachea. "I killed him and Juno's sister, but they would have done worse to me." The reminder was of little consolation, but she hardened herself to the reality, assuring herself of what she would have to do in the future. Madelin gathered her bearings and glanced back at the mutilated body. "He deserved it. One down. Hundreds more to go."

Suddenly Jedd came to mind, and Madelin circled the tree. Leodenin stood behind her godfather, a pistol leveled inches away from Jedd's head while his maniacal laugh echoed through the night.

* * * *

The gun cocked next to his ear with the sound of an iron-worker's hammer on anvil. Jedd reached around his head and encompassed the gun's muzzle in his deadened hand. Leodenin pulled the trigger and the gun exploded, but the bullet vanished in his. With a squeeze of Jedd's fist, the pistol became a crumpled lump of metal. He threw the gun aside and spun to meet the shifter. Leodenin's mouth hung open and gave Jedd the second he needed. Madelin's godfather reared back and pistoned his altered hand into Leodenin's stomach. The false father doubled over and wheezed for air. In one final blow, Jedd slammed his blackened hand into the man's upturned chin. Leodenin's head whipped back with a *crack* as he sailed into the forest fifty feet away.

Jedd looked down at his fist in shock, but Madelin's eyes were still on the dreaded shifter. She waited for his moaning form to rise. Leodenin shook his head, forcing the stars to return to the heavens, but before he could find his feet, two vampires tackled him. Their mouths hung open in eager anticipation. They fought to find exposed skin until their elongated canines sank into his neck and body. The metallic smell of human blood permeated the air, drawing other vampires into the fray. Jedd and Madelin huddled together and took a few slow steps back from the approaching vampires. However, the smell of blood was strong. Seeing easier prey, they rushed in for a taste, leaving Jedd and his goddaughter to watch as the feast began.

Chapter Forty-Four

Saving Talbut

The vampires circled Daniel and Juno, but the two fought with the ferocity of demons. Bloodthirsty howls echoed around them, and Daniel continued to plunge the iron rod deep into his victims. Hungry for flesh, the vampires forced the others forward and Daniel skewered two and three at a time. He lunged at anything that came near. He never looked back. His one concern was Roger and inflicting enough pain to force those between them into submission or death. The fierce glow christening the end of his wrought-iron extension had dimmed, but still it flew, severing limbs from those around him, impaling others, and bashing heads. He followed the screams and gunfire of Roger's .44 Magnum.

Daniel glimpsed his prone body fighting from the ground as oncoming vampires flew past him. A few of Juno's relatives dragged him away by his feet, while others tried to grapple the pistol from his hands.

At least he's still fightin', thought Daniel. *He never really knew when to fold a bad hand and give in.* The muscular veteran smiled and fought on.

Juno took a different tack. He rushed after Roger like a man with a destiny. He flung anyone into the air, clearing the path ahead. Some flew into vampires like clustered bowling pins, while others were impaled on tree limbs.

They will not take one of my friends, Juno shouted as an inferno of adrenaline coursed through his veins. He made a promise and would never break it. Juno forced his way through the waves of vampires, ignoring some altogether as the distance between him and the Cajun doubled. Even with his speed and strength, Roger disappeared into the chaotic blood frenzy.

Frustration set in as the gambler's cries echoed through the milieu. Juno again gave in to the necessity for slaughter and drew his agile sword. The distance between them lessened, and his friend's cries grew closer as he cut swaths through the crowd. Juno caught sight of the gambler once more and his arm swung wide, crisscrossing his shoulders with the fluidity of a martial arts master. Back and forth it flew like a pendulum, dropping any who came near. Roger's shredded form appeared ahead, at the feet of many Traditorian attackers.

Daniel advanced just behind him until they broke through the endless crowd and entered a shadowed clearing. Their close friend lay at its center, his gun aimed up at a confident lord they all knew.

"Alain," spat Roger through the pain. He looked as though he had been run through a meat grinder. "I'll have your ass." He pulled the trigger but was greeted with a subtle and hollow *click*. He pulled it again and again, unable to believe his luck, but each time produced another metallic *click* as the hammer dropped on air. "Damn ya! Ya bastard," he shouted from the ground.

Alain stared down at the gambler. As his two friends appeared at the circle's edge, Alain granted him a cruel smile. He grasped Roger's coat collar in a single fist and lifted him up to eye level, dangling. Alain spat in the gambler's face. Instinct forced Roger's head back in reaction, and Alain's teeth sank into his throat.

Juno and Daniel rushed into the circle, but the imposing guardians grabbed the veteran's arms and thrust them to his sides. Their lips threatened with a kiss, and hot, putrid breath danced along the hairs of his neck. A shiver ran down his spine. *I prepared myself for death long ago, but not a life cursed by the touch of a devil's tongue,* he thought as fear gripped his stomach.

Juno stepped into the circle unhindered as Alain finished tasting Roger's essence. The youthful lord held the semiconscious man at arm's length, before dropping him to the ground. He met his younger brother's gaze with a snarl while Roger's blood coursed down his chin. "Where is the girl?" he asked, licking the man's blood from his lips.

"Elsewhere. You will never have her."

Alain laughed. "I will find her and rid the world of that pest."

"Only because her existence is a reminder. You would punish her for the shame of what you did?" Juno's eyes narrowed. "What kind of a man does that?"

Alain repeated his question. "Where is she?"

"Where you will never find her."

The vampire lord's face contorted in anger. Pulling his sword from its sheath, he stalked up to his younger brother with a snarl. Juno stood rooted to the ground, his body tensed in anticipation. Blood dripped from the tip of his sword and stained the ground in small, crimson pools.

"I will have her, *now!*" screamed Alain.

"You have me to deal with first," rasped Juno, "and you *will* deal with me!"

Alain fell back as Juno approached. He swung his grosse messer in tight circles, flinging the last bloody droplets off the blade.

"Guess what?" the younger of the two asked. "We killed Adelaide tonight."

The words scarred him, but he knew they would infuriate his unbalanced brother. Dozens of their family had died at the hands of this small group. It had taken hundreds of years to grow large enough to rule this small community, and in one solitary night they cut that number in half.

As the words sank in, Alain's eyes blazed. "You would kill your own sister? You are no brother of mine."

"Well, we finally agree on something." Juno's words caressed the lips of his patronizing smile.

Testing the waters, he struck out with the tip of his sword. The elder lord was a second slower, but still knocked the sword aside with ease. Juno seized the lapse in focus and leapt forward with his sword at attention. Alain parried and then reversed. Juno blocked with a swirl of his sword, then struck again and was parried. Each deflected blow rang out as the two danced through the forest.

Their eyes blazed with hatred. The blades flashed in the moonlight as they fought on, teeth bared. Juno leapt to avoid Alain's assault and sped up the trunk of the nearest tree. He propelled himself off and avoided another heavy swing as Alain's blade lashed through the air.

Daniel watched as the fight moved skyward into the trees, each vampire lord passing so fast that the swords' reflections appeared as a modest light show. The vampires around him watched the fight above, enthralled. They paid no more attention to Daniel, so long as he didn't do anything to gain it. He ran to Roger's side and felt his neck. There was a strong pulse—unusual for someone so close to death. "Roger. Roger, can you hear me?" he prompted while trying to avoid the attention of the vampires roosting above to watch the show.

The Cajun mumbled a few incoherent words, and his head shifted from side to side as though reliving a torturous nightmare. The blood no longer seeped from the two puncture wounds in his neck, but Roger seemed unable to focus. His pupils were dilated like he had overdosed on a potent drug, and his body had been mutilated by vampires as they ripped him away from his friends.

Daniel pocketed Roger's gun and lifted the gambler to his shoulder. He headed back the way they came, searching for the others. He would come back for Juno. Logic told him that the rebel was the most capable of the group and the most likely to win this fight.

He swept through the forest's shadows and passed under ancient trees, wary of those that might be watching. Most of those in range of the royal duel had set their sights high above, but the further he went, the more vampires he found scavenging the forest.

Soggy leaves and twigs squished underneath him, but Daniel halted when a branch snapped underfoot. Nearby, a stout, blood-hungry vampire glanced his way. The ex-mercenary lowered his friend to the ground and arose with the iron rod in hand. It was dark, the heated end having quenched itself in blood.

The large vampire drifted closer, smelling blood on the wind. He followed it and stepped into a large shadow in time to hear the wind part behind the arcing rod. The force of the blow bent him over, but he grasped the black rod in a fat fist. Daniel tried to jerk it free, but the man held firm. The vampire stood up and glanced where Daniel had been but found no one at the opposite end of the weapon.

The scent of blood was still in the air and with a subtle sniff, the thirst-driven vampire's attention was drawn to Roger. He knelt next to the gambler's body and groped at the ground. Finding a leg, he dropped the rod and grasped the gambler's calf in both hands.

Daniel grabbed each end of the cast-iron rod as the creature raised Roger's leg to his lips. Before it could taste the Cajun's blood, Daniel draped the rod over the vampire's head and pulled it back across his neck. The large man's head was lowered, and the rod entered his mouth like a horse's bit. The vampire's teeth came down on the iron bar with the disappointment of a starving man, foiled in his last meal. He dropped the leg and straightened up, almost bursting from Daniel's grip, but the veteran held tight. He was lifted into the air, but pulled the rod close, clamping the man's head to his chest. A large hand grasped the veteran's leg from below and jerked downward.

It won't take long for the great lummox to pull me off, thought Daniel, fighting through the pain of his leg. *I've gotta do something.*

He grasped the ends of the iron bar with every ounce of strength he had and jerked the creature's head to the side and down. Daniel anchored the point behind the man's shoulder, and the vampire gave his leg one last inhuman tug. Daniel used it to his advantage, forcing the other end of the rod back until the creature's neck *cracked*. His weight and the vampire's pull ripped the man's head from his torso as though he were leveraging a supplanted rock. Daniel landed with a groan then listened for others. The only sound was that of the vampire's disembodied head and torso thudding to the ground.

Through the shadows, a rift glimmered in the distance. Daniel flexed his leg and hammered the knee into place with his palm, then hefted Roger over his shoulder and limped toward the portal.

Chapter Forty-Five

Camaraderie

Jedd and Madelin finished the solitary vampire that had ambled their way and spotted a hunched man shambling toward them. Daniel appeared under the multicolored rays of the moons with Roger hoisted over his shoulder.

The veteran stumbled over and laid Roger on the mossy forest floor. His eyes widened when he spotted Leodenin lying unconscious against a distant tree, covered with vampires. His surprise grew even more when his gaze landed on the remains of the PASTOR commander.

"Looks like you've been busy. I'm glad to see you aren't hurt," he whispered, perusing the shadowed battlefield and then his friends. "Roger wasn't so fortunate. He's been bitten."

"My God, Roger," Madelin chanted, falling to her knees. His body was in ruins, and he moaned from his dreamlike stupor.

"On his neck," Daniel muttered. He was unable to look at what Lord Alain had done, so stared at the bloody mess scattered around them.

Madelin turned Roger's face aside and scanned the uniform punctures. "Sweet Roger, stay with us," she whispered.

"Maddy…," whispered the gambler before trailing off into his tortured sleep.

Jedd asked, "Where's Juno?"

"He's fightin' Lord Alain."

"Jesus."

Both of them looked into the distant darkness. However, only Jedd saw the dozens of auras clustered in a circle. Taking a deep breath, he turned to face his goddaughter.

Worry creased Madelin's brow as she looked into his eyes, but she unbuckled the sword and handed it to him. "Come back to me. I can't lose you again."

"I know. I will." He buckled the sheath over his belt and wiped the blade on the dead vampire's ruffled shirt, then stowed it for the moment. "Take care of Roger."

He turned to Daniel with downcast eyes, ashamed to leave Madelin behind. After swallowing his fear, he mumbled, "Let's go."

The two sprinted through the forest unmolested before reaching the group of vampires. The two men were forced to crane their necks to see most of Juno's relatives. Dozens sat on large tree branches, circling the two brothers as though watching the entertainment from the nosebleeds of a stadium. Even the crisp, night air stagnated in anticipation of this battle.

Juno and Alain flew at each other, crisscrossing as they made their way from tree to tree, swords held high. The clang of weapons rang out as the two met twenty feet up. A sudden fluttering of blades reflected the falling moonlight just as Juno leapt under his brother's plunging sword tip. The younger Traditor twisted midair, but was unable to avoid the blade. It sank into his side before momentum tore it free.

Simultaneously, Juno's sword arced wide as he trailed by his opponent. The edge of the grosse messer clipped Alain's heel, severing the tendons as momentum carried them apart. Alain lit up the night with a pain-filled scream as he tried to land on the tree trunk. His wounded foot slipped under the pressure, and he instead crashed into the ancient tree then tumbled to the floor below with a *thud*. His body lay contorted amongst the large roots. The elder vampire shifted with a grunt and pushed himself to his feet as blood gushed from his ankle in pulsing waves.

Juno landed on a knee and took a haggard breath. He held his side, where blood seeped around his fingers and coated his shirt. Alain leaned against the tree and glared at his younger brother with pained fury. The other vampires fell to the ground around them, but did nothing more than watch.

"I have denounced you, young Paria," Alain shouted through the pain. "You are an outcast and have no claim to the throne. Leave now, and I will forgive your insolence and allow you to live another day."

"Even now, you presume to give me orders," Juno replied and rose to his feet. "This is the one place we can call home, or what is left of it. Your greed and malcontent has thrown it into chaos, but now I have you." Juno held his blade up for all to see, turning in place as Alain's blood coursed down its edge.

"You can never beat me!" Alain raged, staggering to unsteady feet and launching his sword at Juno's back.

The sword whistled through the air, and Juno spun to face his older brother. Sidestepping the projectile, he grasped the hilt as it flew past, spun, and hurled his own at Lord Alain, using the spin to give it momentum. It spun sideways, end over end, blade over hilt. Shock etched itself in Alain's face before the blade decapitated him and embedded itself in the ancient tree. Alain's body hung for a moment before crumpling to the mossy floor.

Another man stepped forward, dressed in a decadent, white shirt and rust-colored jacket. His chiseled face announced his relation to the two brothers. In a booming voice, he ordered, "Hold now, Juno." The words were of a language reminiscent of French and Latin. All member of the Traditorian family listened intently while Daniel and Jedd stood behind the circle, unsure what was taking place.

"Esteban, why am I not surprised?" asked Juno, switching to the traditional language.

Blood seeped from his wounds, but Juno maintained his composure in front of his family. However, as the adrenaline ebbed, he felt his strength going with it. Still, he fought to stand.

Esteban replied, "Because you always knew I would lead the family."

"Snakes like you are not worthy to lead," Juno hissed.

"More worthy than you. You are a traitor and nothing more. I will lead our family out of shame and back into power." Esteban stood untarnished before Juno, as though he had just stepped out of the shower and donned clean clothes.

"Over my dead body," intoned Juno, but his strength faded and fatigue forced him to his knees.

"That, *monsieur*, is the plan." Drawing his own sword, Esteban advanced on Juno, who knelt defeated before him. Unable to raise his sword in protest, the vampire rebel awaited his doom. Esteban brought his blade above his head. Then with a scream of triumph, he brought its shimmering edge down on Juno's neck.

It came to a jarring stop a hair's width away when Jedd interposed the late Adelaide's decorative blade between them.

"Whoever the hell you are, you're about to get a world of hurt," promised Daniel. He tromped through the crowd clutching the iron rod in a large fist.

A stunned expression infused Esteban's face as the two blades ground together. Jedd thrust all of his might into his weapon and forced the Traditorian elder back.

After a few teetering steps, his eyes focused on them. "It can't be true. Where's Adelaide?"

"On my kitchen floor," Juno whispered. His exhausted gaze climbed the polished man. "Brother, I do not imagine there is much left of her after the explosion."

"How dare you!" cried Esteban as the circling vultures began closing in. Esteban held up a hand, and they stopped. "These are mine."

He struck out at Juno with a sweeping arm, but the scarred veteran braced his weapon with both hands. The sword clanged against Daniel's iron rod, and Esteban burst into a flurry of screaming madness. Juno attempted to stand, but his effort was futile. He fell back to the ground and watched as Jedd and Daniel operated in tandem, parrying Esteban's uncoordinated blows.

The sound of sword glancing off steel and iron echoed through the forest. The force of the impact jolted them. Sweat rolled off both men as they weathered the Traditorian vampire's rain of blows. Although his technique was raw and less skillful than Juno's, his strength and agility were overpowering the pair.

Jedd shuddered under the swing of the Traditorian's sword and fell to one knee. The blade sliced toward him a second time, intent on splitting him in two. Daniel lay out of reach and without the strength to parry it. Throwing his arm up, Jedd grasped the oncoming blade in a blackened hand and was again astounded when the sword stopped. The strength behind the weapon pressed down on him, but he held the blade's edge in hand. Esteban stared in horror.

Jedd plucked the sword from the vampire's hands. "You don't deserve this," he muttered from under a rising gaze.

Esteban flew at Jedd with flailing arms, eyes blazing and teeth bared. Jedd blocked the onslaught with his deadened arm, but even his tremendous ability was unable to cope with the vampire's fury. Seizing the moment, he ducked under the man's hands and swung his blackened fist into Esteban's midsection with all his might. At the same time, a jack-hammering knee caught Jedd in the face. Both men flew into the air and landed sprawled on the ground. Jedd got to his feet and straddled the world revolving beneath him while Daniel helped Juno. Esteban rose on unsteady feet, ill-equipped to continue at the moment.

With a look at the salivating vampires, Jedd muttered in panicked tones, "Guys, we gotta go."

Dozens of gazes lapped at their bloody bodies, but Jedd's last blow gave the vampires pause. Madelin's defenders burst through the wall of creatures with what energy remained and made their way toward Madelin. Vampires trailed them but kept their distance, unsure what to do without Lord Alain. The small group covered half the distance back to Madelin before Esteban took charge.

The new vampire lord let out an unintelligible roar in the Traditorian language. It echoed through the forest, and the remaining family members ran toward the voice as quick as their legs would carry them.

"He's forming them up for another attack," murmured Juno, leaning on Daniel's shoulder.

As the three of them came upon Madelin and Roger, they watched the vampires hovering over Leodenin vanish and retreat toward the call. The false father moaned as blood coursed from all over his body.

"Good to see you back," Madelin replied with relief, but concern entered her eyes when she saw Juno held between them.

"Looks like we switched roles," he commented and smiled back.

"That it does," she answered.

A sudden, eerie silence interrupted their banter as the calls stopped. In the distance, the collection of auras began rushing toward them.

"We've got to get out of here. Is that portal safe?" Jedd asked, nodding at the oblong shape over Marlin's corpse.

"I think so." She sounded less than confident. Glancing over the bloody area, she shouted, "No... No, Leodenin can't get away."

Two of the shifter's agents had grasped him by the arms and were dragging him into a jungle of bushes. Embers of hatred burst into flame when Jedd spotted them. His chance at killing the man was dwindling, but the advancing army reminded him of the immediate threat.

"No time, Maddy. We've got to go now," he sputtered. Jedd grasped the semi-conscious Cajun and dragged him toward the portal. Madelin grabbed his feet as the mob of auras loomed closer. They rushed to the portal and lifted him through with Daniel and Juno following behind.

"I don't even know if I can survive in this other world," slurred Juno as his mind slowed with the loss of blood. "Your friend might not either."

Daniel shouted, "I know, dammit, but we don't have another choice!"

Without another word, the veteran placed an arm around Juno's waist and lifted him from the ground. As he stepped into the crimson world, he turned to see the army of pale vampires converging on their position.

Jedd and Madelin began closing the window, but before it shut, one unfortunate vampire grabbed hold of Jedd's collar. Her manicured hand was sliced off the instant the rip sealed, and the dismembered arm fell twitching to the red dirt at their feet—a memento of their survival.

Chapter Forty-Six

Escape

"Hurry Samson, grab an arm," whispered Frank as he leapt to Leodenin's rescue.

"But why?" asked the other remaining mercenary from the squad PASTOR had sent. "Just let the bastard die."

Hefting Father Leodenin, he replied, "You wanna live out your life here?"

The agent saw his logic and emerged from the shadows to grab the other arm. They pulled him out of sight like robbers attempting to hide their loot and ran from the maelstrom of death that had erupted over the last hour. The two of them covered a couple of miles before they sat down. Their bodies were strained, and they panted for air while nervously peering behind them. Even trained agents such as these had their limits. The agents flopped on the ground when they saw no one in pursuit and tried to regain a semblance of their strength.

Leodenin sat looking back as the rush of auras came to a stop where he had been left for dead. The group milled around for a few minutes before another unintelligible command sent them hurtling through the woods again. This time they were heading straight for him.

"Shit!" Leodenin hissed.

He fumbled at the case on his belt. Removing a syringe, he plunged it through his chest and into his heart. The two operatives watched from their prone positions. Stifling the scream that forced its way to his lips, Leodenin removed the needle and dropped it to the ground. As he lay there, his heart pumped like an overworked steam engine, forcing the liquid Satia through his veins. Within seconds, he sat up, feeling better than before but still somewhat unsteady. As the army of vampires sped toward them, their time dwindled.

"What's wrong?" asked Samson.

"We have to go," Leodenin demanded, pushing himself up unsteadily.

He limped over to a shimmering thread outlining a building in an adjacent plane. Leodenin focused on the line and waited for the star-blessed stallion to appear. The horse materialized, galloping forward till it emerged from the plane. It stood suspended on a sheet of air. Leodenin felt the glistening lines and picked one similar to this plane. Running his magic finger along the thread, the stallion followed the path and left the air rippling behind it. As it finished its journey, it reared and galloped back into nothingness, as though retreating from the vampires that emerged from the distant tree line. Roars of hunger and lust echoed around them, and the multitude of inhuman steps vibrated across the distance and up through his soles. Leodenin lifted the rift's edge and dove through, panic gleaming in his eyes.

Chapter Forty-Seven

A Barren Future

Turning to the rest of the group, Madelin stood panting after such a close escape. A ruined world greeted her in all directions. Her previous view of the sky was limited and hadn't allowed her to see the landscape. Everywhere she looked was devastation. It was as though she had emerged on another planet. Barren red rocks and boulders shone in the crimson moonlight. On the horizon, the remains of a large city stood in stark contrast to the barren landscape. Even at this distance, the spires towering into the sky were skeletons of what they once were.

"My God! Who did this?"

"I have a feeling this is the result of humans," replied Jedd, as though expecting the ghosts of this world to rise up against them.

Daniel scanned the endless ocean of ruins then muttered, "To think, this could be our world."

"I hate to spoil the fun," Juno chimed in, "but it will not be long before the sun is up."

At the mention of their dwindling time, they cast their eyes to the heavens. The moon was settling on the horizon.

"Quick," Jedd spat in a rush, "toward the city. We have to find shelter."

Jedd and Madelin hoisted Roger up while Daniel half carried Juno over the rocky terrain. They hurried across the parched landscape but saw no sign of life. The city was too far away. Even the buzzards of the El Paso they knew were nowhere to be seen. It was as if all life ceased to exist. Struggling through the night, the sun opened its eye on the opposing horizon, thrusting its gaze down on the exhausted party. The group ducked into the shadow of a large boulder.

The Cajun moaned in pain as they slid him to the ground. Madelin knelt beside him and felt his head. "He's burning up."

"It isss normal," slurred Juno as Daniel helped him down next to Roger.

Daniel and Madelin walked over to join Jedd, who had wandered out into a large semicircle of overarching cliffs. The rocky giants stood against the morning rays of the sun, as they had for eons.

"What do we do, Jedd?" Panic infiltrated her voice.

Her godfather shook his head in frustration. "I don't know."

"You heard Juno before. They can't stand this heat for long. It'll kill them."

"I know, but there's nothing better within reach. The city's still miles away." *What do we do…? What do we do?* He racked his brain for answers, but came up empty. It seemed that they'd escaped with their lives only to sacrifice those closest to them.

The two turned pitying gazes on their companions, sweltering in the diminishing shade of the boulder. In a matter of minutes the sun would rise higher and clear the rock, leaving nowhere for them to hide. A tear streaked down Madelin's face and leapt to the ground below, taking her hopes with it like a midnight thief.

* * * *

Daniel perused the imposing cliff face in front of them. The rock was sheared and unnatural as though it had been sanded smooth. *Craters aren't this precise,* he thought, noticing the flat ground beneath him. The rest of the terrain rolled across the horizon pierced by jagged rocks. He slammed a foot down on the ground. The impact amazed them all as it resounded across the large cliff face and echoed deep beneath them like a metallic well.

Jedd and Madelin's conversation came to an abrupt stop. Daniel did it again and was greeted by the same hopeful prospect. With no time to lose, he took off around the cliff face with Jedd and Madelin in hot pursuit.

"What was that?" shouted Madelin.

Daniel answered her as he scanned the area. "I think it might be an old missile silo."

He rounded the side of the rock face and climbed its peak. His eyes landed on a flight of ruined, sandstone stairs that led deep within the mountainous cliff. Turning to Jedd and Madelin, he shouted, "Hurry. Get the others," and disappeared down the steps.

Jedd and Madelin retreated back down the cliff. Jedd grabbed Roger while Madelin helped Juno to his feet. They lumbered across the open field of sand and back up the mountainous crag. Juno grimaced as they left the shadow of the boulder and staggered into the bombarding rays of the sun. The distance felt like a lifetime, but as they disappeared into the cliff's shadow, he felt a cooling sensation come over his sunburnt neck and arms.

At the bottom of the stairway, they found Daniel standing in front of a shattered, metal door. "The hinges were rusted," he explained. "Otherwise, I don't think Juno could've gotten in." The veteran removed one of the frilled shirts that had somehow made it into his bag and wrapped it around the end of his rod. Lighting it, he illuminated the vacant corridor ahead of them. He shuffled past the door, hoisting the flaming rod high above, and entered the dark chamber. Daniel soon found himself in a vast room full of large military computers. They were coated in thick layers of red dust.

Jedd stared in astonishment at the blessing lying before him. *I'll have to look into that later,* he reminded himself.

After taking a few minutes to explore the passages, Daniel declared that the area was clear. He helped Juno down the stairs and led them deeper into the compound, into a small room. It contained two sets of bunk beds, and the mattresses were still intact. They lowered Juno and Roger onto the lower beds. The old vampire sighed as his back sank into the cushioned mattress. Turning, Madelin screamed and leapt back against the wall as her eyes fell on a mound of bones lying in the corner.

"It's okay." Daniel placed a firm hand on her shoulder. "The previous owners hadn't quite made it out of bed yet. I just helped them make room for our two."

She nodded and turned away from the corner. Then she sat her bag down and removed the bandages and supplies Juno had given her. Kneeling down, she tended to Roger's wounds in silence.

Daniel turned to Juno and asked, "You need anything right now?"

Juno shook the leather canteen he retrieved from the bag and smiled as it sloshed. "Not right now, but we will need more water tonight. And all of you will need to stay away from Roger till tomorrow. You cannot be around when the blood thirst sets in. I will take him out and try to find something to satisfy his thirst later tonight, but I am not sure what lives in this blasted place."

Madelin jumped at the announcement, but recovered as the logic of his words became clear. She knew what was happening to Roger, but hadn't given it much thought. Holding out a candle, Daniel lit it with his makeshift torch.

"We'll see if we can find some water," replied Jedd as they left the room.

Madelin set the candle on the metal side table. Then, removing Juno's clothes, she began cleaning the encrusted blood and cloth away from the dozens of wounds littering his body. She uncorked his miracle salve and applied it.

"What will you do now?" he asked as he shut his eyes, enjoying her gentle touch.

"All we can. We haven't learned everything we need to yet. Father Leodenin did some odd things. I might be able to do them, too, if I practice. I need to learn as much as I can before we move against the agency. There are others like myself there, but we can't help them if we don't know how to use my skills. What will you do?"

Juno sighed as the answer came to him. "I would like to go home, but that cannot be."

"Why not?"

"Many reasons, but one stands above the rest. I cannot leave you to the likes of that man." Saying his name was unnecessary. Madelin knew all too well the horrors of dealing with Leodenin and PASTOR. She flushed at his concern.

"I know it may not seem like it, but we can take care of ourselves with your training," she replied as she spread the salve over his skin.

"What I have taught you is basic. What if you encounter more people like my family… or worse?" He shook his head, dismissing the thought. "I cannot allow that to happen."

Madelin finished wrapping the wound at his side and objected to his concerns, but as he placed his hand over hers, her voice dwindled to nothing. "I'm staying. Besides, who else can deal with Roger?"

The mention of the man lying across from him caused Roger to stir. Madelin looked over at the occupied bed, and her eyes welled with pity. "You're right." Turning back, she mumbled, "Will he make it?"

"Yes," Juno replied, caressing her hand with his thumb. "But how will he cope with the change? That is the real question, the true test. I do not know if he will be the same man you knew before. Keep away from this room tonight."

With that answer, his hand stilled and he drifted into a deep sleep. Madelin propped her back against Juno's bunk and pulled out the journal to add yet another day.

"Thank you, Roger," she whispered to the man who had sacrificed so much. A tear streamed down her cheek with each word she wrote.

To be continued in *To Kill an Assassin*, available now through most online book retailers.

TO KILL AN ASSASSIN

BY
WESTON KINCADE

The Priors, Part 2

"This book was Ah-Maz-Ing. I could not put it down."
~Reader Review

Redemption is best served cold... and from another plane of existence.

Mutations run rampant. Worlds devastated by war. The PASTOR agency plans to rule them all.

On the run, Madelin and her evolved friends are intent on stopping the black-ops agency and freeing victims like herself—including those attempting to kill her. She must discover her own abilities and learn to harness them... or else entire worlds will be overrun. Even then... it may be too late.

Weston Kincade's sequel in *The Priors* series is a thrilling step into the unknown, exploring the depths of friendship, self-discovery, and above all—revenge.

Take the leap. Read *To Kill an Assassin* today.

ABOUT THE AUTHOR

Weston Kincade has helped invest in future writers for more than fifteen years while teaching. His short stories have been published in a variety of anthologies, including Kevin J. Kennedy's bestselling seasonal horror collections. Weston is a member of the Bard's Tower authors and of the Horror Writers Association (HWA). Best known for his coming-of-age supernatural mystery trilogy *A Life of Death*, his fantasy, sci-fi series *The Priors* is available now.

Visit Weston at KincadeFiction.com to find out about new projects and releases. If you would like to explore Weston's short stories, sign up for his email list and get a free copy of his co-written short story anthology *Strange Circumstances*.

https://strangecircumstances.gr8.com

Printed in Great Britain
by Amazon